"_____ n you out of
tow_____ might be able
to sa_____

W_____ r pale green eyes,
she j_____ Fine. Then what-
ever _____ ould you please just get it over
with? Please? So you can leave?"

Something moved inside him. It might have been
anger. Might have been wounded pride. Might have
been frustration . . . or all of the above. "Just get it over
with?" he repeated, some of his tension edging into his
voice.

"Yes." She swallowed. "Please."

"So polite. Even when you're that pissed off at me.
Still so polite," he murmured. "Okay, Hope. I'll get it
over with."

Then he closed the two feet between them. He wanted
to touch her . . . fuck it, he wanted it so bad, he hurt

By Shiloh Walker

If You Hear Her

IF YOU
SEE HER

SHILOH WALKER

BALLANTINE BOOKS • NEW YORK

A Ballantine Books Mass Market Original

Published in the United States by Ballantine Books, an imprint of The Random House Publishing Group, a division of Random House, Inc., New York.

BALLANTINE and colophon are trademarks of Random House, Inc.

This book contains an excerpt from the forthcoming book *If You Know Her* by Shiloh Walker. This excerpt has been set for this edition only and may not reflect the final content of the forthcoming edition.

ISBN 978-0-345-51754-8
eBook ISBN 978-0-345-51758-6

Printed in the United States of America

www.ballantinebooks.com

9 8 7 6 5 4 3 2 1

As always . . . to my family. I thank God for you all every day of my life, and it's still not enough. I've made this dedication probably close to sixty times now. Another thing that's still not enough. You're everything to me. Love you all!

IF YOU
SEE HER

CHAPTER
ONE

"SHE'S A DISTURBED WOMAN, I'M AFRAID TO SAY."

Remington Jennings pinched the bridge of his nose and tried not to think about the sad green eyes and silken brown hair of one Hope Carson. "Disturbed, how? Can you help me out any here, Detective Carson?"

On the other end of the line, the man sighed. "Well, I'm reluctant to do that. You see, I wouldn't have a DA on the phone, asking about my wife, if there wasn't trouble. And I don't want to cause her trouble."

"She's your *ex*-wife and she's already got trouble. Do you want her to get the help she needs or not?" Remy asked, his voice taking on a sharp edge. Hell, anybody with half a brain could see that woman wouldn't hurt a fly unless she was just pushed . . .

"You want to help her, is that it, Jennings?" The detective laughed, but it wasn't a happy sound. It was sad and bitter.

"If I didn't, I wouldn't have called. I'm not trying to lock her up and throw away the key here. Help me out, Detective." *Damn it, Carson, gimme a break.*

"Help you out. You mean help you help Hope." Once more, Joseph Carson sighed. He was Hope's ex and a cop from out west. He was also proving to be one hell of a pain in the ass.

Faintly, Remy heard a heavy creak. "Mr. Jennings, pardon my French, but you can't help Hope, because she doesn't fucking *want* help. She's a very troubled young woman. She . . . shit, this is hard, but we hadn't been married very long when she was diagnosed with borderline personality disorder. She's manipulative, a chameleon—she can make a person believe whatever they need to believe. You might *think* you're seeing a woman you can help—if she'll just *let* you. But that's not the case. You're seeing what she *wants* you to see."

Remy clenched his jaw, closed his hand around the pen so tightly it snapped.

Shit—that . . . no. Not right. Everything inside screeched just how *wrong* that was. It couldn't be right—it just couldn't.

But his voice was cool, collected, as he said, "Borderline personality disorder, you said? Does she have a history of violence?"

Long, tense moments of silence passed and finally, Carson said, "Yeah. There's a history of violence. Only against herself . . . and me. I kept it very well hidden. I didn't want people thinking bad things about her, and on my part . . . well, I was ashamed. For her, for myself, for both of us. It wasn't until things got really bad that I couldn't hide it anymore."

"You're telling me she was violent with you?" Remy knew he needed to be making notes, processing this.

But he couldn't—couldn't process, couldn't even wrap his mind around it. That woman lifting her hand against somebody?

No. The picture just wasn't coming together for him.

"Yes." Carson sighed once more.

"So you're telling me she *does* have a history of violence?"

"Shit, didn't I just go through that?" he snarled.

Remy clutched the phone so tight, it was amazing the plastic didn't crack. This was wrong—so fucking wrong, and he knew it, knew it in his bones.

She's manipulative, a chameleon—she can make a person believe whatever they need to believe. You might think you're seeing a woman you can help—if she'll just let *you. But that's not the case. You're seeing what she* wants *you to see.*

Damn it, was he just letting her lead him around, he wondered?

Right then, he wasn't sure.

He took a deep, slow breath, focused on the phone. "Can you give me some examples? Tell me what happened?"

"Examples. Shit." Carson swore and then demanded, "Why should I tell you this? Just answer me that."

"Because if she's got a mental disorder, then she *does* need help and if she needs help, I'd rather her get help then get locked up. You should know her better than anybody. So if you do care about her, help me help her. Come on, Detective. You're a cop. You're sworn to uphold the law, to protect people. If your wife could prove dangerous . . ."

"You fucking lawyers, you always know what to say," Carson muttered. But there was no anger, no malice in his voice. Just exhaustion. "Yeah, you could say she has violent tendencies. You could say she has a history of violence. She's very manipulative and all those violent tendencies get worse when she doesn't get her way. She becomes unstable, unpredictable. There is no telling what she might do to somebody she perceived as being in her way."

Abruptly, his voice lost that calm, detached tone and he snarled, "There. I gave you all the dirt you needed and don't tell me you can't use that. God help me, I hate myself even though I know she needs help. Now tell me what the fuck is going on!"

Remy blew out a slow breath and said, "She's in the hospital at the moment—attempted suicide. Plus, there was an attack on a friend of hers. It looks like she might be responsible."

"Fuck." The word was harsh, heavy with fury and grief. "She's tried to commit suicide before, so as much as I hate to hear it, that's not a big surprise. But the friend . . . you said there was an attack on a friend?"

"Yes." Remy scowled absently at nothing. "Maybe you've heard of him—it seems like the two of them go back quite a while. The name's Law Reilly?"

"Reilly." Carson grunted. "Yeah. I know Law. I wish I could say I was surprised to hear that she'd turned on him, but Hope's always had a way of turning on those who've tried to help her. Those who care about her."

Remy closed his eyes.

Damn it, was there anything this guy could say that would make it a little bit easier for him to figure out how to handle Hope?

Of course if he *wanted* her put away, this guy would be making his whole damn night.

But right now, he could almost hear the cell door swinging shut on her and it was just turning Remy's stomach. "So you think she could have hurt Mr. Reilly?"

"With Hope, I just don't know. The one thing I *do* know? She's capable of just about anything. I also know that I wish I could help her. Hell, I'd like to believe *you* can. But I know I can't, and I can't believe you can either. She doesn't want help, won't admit she needs it. Look, if there's anything I can do to make sure she gets that help, just ask. I don't want her in trouble, but I do want her to get help. Before it's too late."

Remy barely remembered the rest of the conversation.

He was too busy finally processing the fact that he'd more or less gotten the supporting evidence he needed.

Hope Carson's fingerprints had been found all over the weapon used to beat Law Reilly.

She had slit her wrists.

She had a history of violence.

A history of turning on people who cared about her.

According to her ex-husband—who seemed to care about her—she was manipulative, prone to doing whatever it took to get her way.

Fuck and double fuck.

Instead of feeling satisfied with what he needed to do, what he *could* do, he found himself thinking about those sad, sad green eyes . . .

Fuck.

By the time she landed at Blue Grass Airport, Nia Hollister was so damned tired, she could barely see straight, so sick at heart, she ached with it, and she longed to curl up in a dark, quiet room and just . . . sob.

Giving in to tears had never been her way, but this time, the temptation was strong, so overpowering, there were times when she felt the tears swelling in her throat like a knot. And a scream—just beyond the tears, there was a scream begging to break free.

She kept it held inside through sheer will alone.

Now wasn't the time to scream, or to cry.

Somewhere inside her heart, she still wanted to believe they were wrong.

All of them.

Joely wasn't dead. She couldn't be. They were like sisters—almost closer than sisters.

They rarely fought. They were best friends, in their hearts, their souls. Even when Nia was on the other side of the country for half the year—or *out* of the country . . .

They could be wrong. All of them—Bryson, Joely's fiancé, who wouldn't even go with her to identify the body, the cops who insisted it was Joely . . . everybody. They could all be wrong.

It might not be Joely.

But if it wasn't her cousin lying dead in a morgue in Ash, Kentucky, then where was she?

Her fiancé hadn't seen her in more than a month.

She wasn't answering her cell phone or e-mail.

It was like she'd dropped off the face of the earth.

No . . . she hasn't dropped off the face of the earth. She's been lying dead in the deep freeze in the morgue, you selfish bitch, while you're off on assignment.

Abandoned—because law enforcement always turned to family, although Bryson might have been able to do it if he'd pushed, especially since Nia hadn't been reachable. Out of contact—*fuck.*

She hadn't been around, while her cousin was kidnapped, hadn't been around while she was killed, hadn't been around at all and because of that, Joely was treated like some worthless piece of garbage.

Nia hadn't been around. Oh, *God* . . . Tears pricked her eyes. She'd been out of contact for almost three weeks. Joely could have reached her, but would she have shared that information with her fiancé? Probably not.

With weariness and grief dragging at her steps, she lugged her carry-on through the airport. Years of living out of a suitcase had taught her to pack light and the bag was all she carried. The rest of her stuff was being shipped back to her house in Williamsburg.

Soon, she'd have to find a Laundromat and wash her clothes, but that was a problem for another day.

Now, she needed to get a rental car. Rental car. Then she needed to . . .

She stopped in front of an ad—it was brightly colored, displaying a chestnut horse racing across a field of green grass. Numb, she just stared at it for a minute and then once more started to walk.

Rental car. Ash, Kentucky. She needed to get there. Needed to . . .

"Miss?"

Nia started, then found herself staring dumbly at one of the airport security guards. Blinking, she glanced around. She wasn't sure where she was, or how she'd gotten there.

He eyed her with a strange mix of concern and caution. "Are you okay?"

Nia swallowed. That knot in her throat swelled to epic proportions and she realized those tears were even closer than she'd thought. "I . . . rough few days."

"It looks like it." He gestured with his head off to the side. "You've been standing in the middle of the hall for the past five minutes. Can I help you find where you're going?"

Nia pressed the heel of her hand against her temple. Shit.

The ache in her chest spread.

Ash—she needed to get to Ash, wherever in the hell that was.

But if she was standing around like a zombie in the middle of an airport, the last thing she needed to do was get behind the wheel of a car. Reality breathed its icy cold breath down her spine and she sighed. "I guess I'm heading outside to catch a cab to a hotel," she finally said.

Getting to Ash would have to wait until morning.

She loathed the idea, but her pragmatic side was strong, even in grief. As exhausted as she was, it would be suicide to get behind the wheel of a car and she knew it. As desperate as she was to get to Ash, she had some damn strong inner demons.

Besides, maybe she'd luck out . . . she'd go to sleep and wake up, realize this was nothing but one awful, horrid nightmare.

The conversation with Detective Joseph Carson was still ringing through Remy's mind hours later as he tossed and turned on his bed, trying to sleep.

Settling down wasn't happening, though. It was past midnight when he finally slept.

There were nights when he hit the mattress and sleep fell on him like a stone. As one of the two district attorneys in the small county of Carrington, Kentucky, he had helped put away meth dealers, a couple of child molesters and rapists, more than a few drunk drivers, and several wife beaters, and he routinely dealt with petty theft.

Even in his small, mostly rural county, crime wasn't nonexistent.

He enjoyed what he did.

But tonight, sleep didn't come easy. Hell, screw *easy*—it didn't want to come at *all*.

Every time he closed his eyes, he thought of a green-eyed brunette and he thought about what he had to do in the morning.

It wasn't a job he wanted to do.

It was a job he'd give just about anything to *not* do.

But he hadn't taken this job just so he could walk away from the hard ones.

All the facts pointed to one thing: Hope Carson was a violent, disturbed woman.

His gut screamed *Screw the facts*. But he couldn't ignore what he saw, couldn't ignore the evidence, couldn't ignore what he'd been told and what he'd learned.

His job was clear.

And his job, sometimes, sucked.

It was well past midnight when he finally fell into a restless sleep, and into even more restless dreams.

Nightmares.

Dreams where he saw her as he'd seen her that night in the emergency room. Covered in blood.

Pale.

A disembodied voice whispering, *You did this . . .*

"*No, I didn't. No, I didn't,*" Hope said, her voice shaking, but sure.

Remy stood there, horrified. All he wanted to do was pull her into his arms, take her away from this, away from all of it. But then Nielson, the sheriff, was there, pushing a pair of handcuffs into his hand.

"*You want us to arrest her? Fine. You do it.*"

But that wasn't Remy's job—he wasn't a fucking cop. He didn't arrest people. He got warrants. He prosecuted.

"*Yeah, you make us get our hands dirty. But you want her arrested, you do it yourself.*"

And that was what he did. Remy put cuffs on wrists that seemed too slender, too fragile for such a burden.

Remy was the one who led her to a cell.

And when he opened the door, she walked silently inside. But he saw it in her eyes.

I didn't do this.

As he turned away, the screams started. Endless, agonized screams. But he didn't know if they were hers . . . or his own.

That was how he came awake.

With the sound of screams echoing in his ears.

"*Shit,*" he muttered, jerking upright in bed, fighting the sheets and blankets that had become ropes around his waist.

With his breath sawing raggedly in and out of his lungs, he sat on the edge of the bed and stared off into nothingness. His gut was a raw, ragged pit and his head throbbed like it hadn't since his college days. Back then, he had thought he could get by on naps and caffeine.

In a few hours, he was supposed to meet the sheriff at the hospital.

Hope Carson was being arrested today, and there wasn't a damn thing Remy could do about it. That woman had the ability to turn him into knots just by looking at him. No other woman had ever done that to him. Not a one. Shit. This was a mess.

Not that she knew.

Nobody knew, thank God.

At least he'd managed to keep that much hidden.

But shit, he had to get it together.

Had to get his head together, his act together, had to do . . . something.

Shoving to his feet, Remy shambled naked toward the bathroom. Maybe if he blasted himself with enough hot water, and then flooded his body with enough caffeine . . . maybe.

Maybe, maybe . . .

He turned on the lights, but they hit his tired eyes with the force of a sledgehammer and, groaning, he turned them off again.

No light. Not yet.

Shower. Caffeine.

Then light.

Maybe.

Not that he really needed light anyway. Not like he needed light to shower . . . or even to get dressed. If he didn't have any light on, he wouldn't have to worry about seeing his reflection, right?

And the last thing he wanted to do just then was look himself square in the eye.

No matter what the evidence said, no matter what the logic pointed to, it just didn't feel right.

It just didn't feel right . . . at all.

* * *

There were days when Hope Carson wished she'd just driven right through Ash. Instead of stopping in the small Kentucky town to see her friend, like she'd promised, she should have just kept on driving.

No matter how much she loved Law, no matter how much she'd missed him, missed having a friend, there were days when she wished she had broken that promise and never stopped.

Maybe she should have driven straight to the ocean.

Hope had never seen the ocean.

She'd wanted to go to the ocean for her honeymoon, but Joey . . . her not-so-beloved ex-husband hadn't liked the idea.

Everybody goes to the beach. Let's do something different.

They'd gone to the mountains.

Skiing in Aspen.

But Hope hadn't been very good at skiing. And she hated the cold . . . it was like it cut right through her bones. She'd fallen down so many times, and had so many bruises.

"Should have just kept on driving," she muttered as she listened to the voices just outside her door.

Would have been wiser, that much was sure.

Desolate, she stared out the window and wondered if she'd have a room wherever they were taking her next.

Would it be another hospital?

A jail?

She just didn't know.

Another hospital, probably. One with real *security.*

Dark, ugly dots swirled in on her vision.

Fear locked a fist around her throat. *Locked . . . trapped . . .*

She barely managed to keep the moan behind her teeth.

When the door opened, she managed to stifle her wince.

Barely.

It was just one of the nursing assistants—this time.

But soon . . . soon, it would be uniformed deputies. She knew it.

Hearing the quiet, muffled sound of shoes on the linoleum, she stared out the window and tried not to think about what was coming.

No matter what, she had to be grateful for one thing.

No matter what, she wasn't trapped back in that house in Oklahoma with her husband, and she wasn't trapped in that hospital where he had complete, total control over her.

She'd almost willingly be held for a crime she didn't commit rather than go back to that particular hell.

At least she wasn't anywhere close to Joey.

At least she wasn't under his control, in any way, shape, or form.

That counted, for a hell of a lot.

But it wasn't enough, and the longer she stared at the plain, white walls of the small hospital room, the more they resembled a cell. So instead, she stared out the window—a reinforced window, one she couldn't open. Not that she'd tried.

But the nurse had been a little too free with that information, right after she'd come in to check her blood pressure and *offer* her the medications—just an offer this time.

Nobody had tried to force it on her again.

Not since Remy . . .

She swallowed and tried not to think about that. It really, really wouldn't do her any good to think about that, about him. As humiliating as it had been, for anybody to see her like that, it had been nothing short of a miracle in the end. Whether he'd said something to one of the doctors after he'd left or just scared the hell out of the nurses . . . well, nobody had tried to force any more drugs on her.

No antipsychotics, no tranquilizers, nothing. That fancy law degree of his, Hope imagined. She didn't know, and honestly, didn't care.

As long as nobody was forcing drugs on her she didn't need.

Her head was completely clear. She should be grateful.

And she would try to be.

But her gut told her she hadn't seen the last of Remy Jennings, and the next time she saw him, it wasn't going to be over the drugs the hospital staff had been forcing on her.

No, the next time it would be over the night she'd been found unconscious, just a few days ago, her wrists slashed open, her prints on the bat that had been used to beat a man damn near to death.

Her best friend—the people here thought she was capable of that.

They wanted her in jail for it.

Closing her eyes, she rested her head against her pillow and sighed. It wouldn't be long now, either. She'd seen it in the doctor's eyes when he'd been in to see her yesterday.

Sympathy, knowledge . . . and a grim acceptance. She was no longer in need of the medical services a hospital could provide. And they weren't about to let her traipse away where they couldn't keep her *secured*.

In their eyes, she'd done something awful, and it was time she paid for it.

But I didn't do anything.

The sad, forlorn whine wanted to work its way free, but she swallowed it, shoved it down inside. She sure as hell wasn't going to go meekly along with whatever they had in mind, but she was done with wringing her hands and moaning, too.

She just needed to figure out what she *was* going to do . . .

CHAPTER

TWO

BORDERLINE PERSONALITY DISORDER.
Suicidal.
History of violent behavior.
Manipulative.
"She can make a person believe whatever they need to believe."

Shit, there had to be some truth to that because some part of Remy was dead set on believing that she wasn't what the facts were showing him.

"She's a very troubled young woman."

Troubled.

Yes, Hope Carson would have to be a very troubled woman, he imagined.

She'd slit her damn wrists, and apparently this wasn't the first time she'd tried to take her life.

"She's tried to commit suicide before . . ."

". . . she doesn't want help, won't admit she needs it."

She'd tried to kill herself before. That knowledge left him both sick and furious.

Damn it, quit thinking about this and just do your job.

Those words echoed through Remington Jennings's mind as he walked down the long hallway. His shoes rang hollowly in the brightly lit hallway, echoing around him.

It was a terribly lonely sound, he thought.

Sheriff Dwight Nielson and Sergeant Keith Jennings were with him, as well as two more deputies. But for reasons that Remy couldn't quite explain, he felt ridiculously alone in that moment.

What in the hell was he doing?

In front of him, the sheriff moved with brisk, economic motion. The man didn't waste any movement, and he didn't waste any words.

Not even now.

Why should he?

Remy already knew every damn word that was going through the man's mind.

It was nearly word for word that same spiel Law Reilly had given him over the phone twenty-four hours earlier.

Both men felt the same way—Hope Carson didn't belong behind bars for the attack on Law, and the facts didn't point to her killing Earl Prather, so they couldn't put her away for that.

His gut instinct agreed—none of it fit.

It was just too fucking bad he couldn't go with what his gut said.

He had to go with what the facts said . . . facts that painted a very, very disturbing picture of Hope's past, painted an image of a very, very disturbing woman.

Those facts had her prints on the weapon that had been used to beat Reilly damn near to death, and then she'd tried to kill herself.

Again.

No . . . she didn't belong behind bars, but she needed help.

"She has violent tendencies. She's very manipulative. When she doesn't get her way, she becomes unstable,

unpredictable. There is no telling what she might do to somebody she perceived as being in her way."

Remy thought of how Prather had died.

It had been ugly.

Messy.

Painful.

Had Prather gotten in her way?

He thought back to that day on the square. Some kid had bumped into her, she'd tripped—stumbled. Knocked against a plant stand and sent the half-dead ficus to the ground, then Prather had bumped into her. She'd freaked out—definitely had a problem with people in uniform, there was no denying that.

Timing-wise, he had Lena Riddle's statement and receipts from their shopping trip. It didn't play out. According to her, Hope had been with Lena most of the day, but still . . . something wasn't right here, and he had to figure out what it was.

Curious, he glanced at the back of Nielson's head and asked, "How does she act around you?"

"Quiet." Nielson looked over his shoulder. "Doesn't say much of anything. Even with the public defender around, she doesn't want to talk. Only time she really talks much is when Lena shows up—she asks about Law a lot, but nobody other than Lena will talk about him." The sheriff sighed.

Keith, one of Remy's endless cousins, gave him an unhappy look. "She doesn't much like people in uniform, I think. Won't look me in the eye—seems the same with others. She's quiet around King, but I think that's just habit. I don't think she's as nervous around him as she is around me."

"Nervous?" Remy asked, cocking a brow. He already knew she was freaked out about people in uniform—namely the boys in blue. Or tan, like the county boys. But he wanted the opinions from Nielson and Keith.

"Hell, Remy. You know damn well what I mean."
Keith shrugged. "I'm sure you've already noticed how
nervous she is around people in uniform. It's not like I'm
telling you something you don't know."

Remy glanced down the hall. Twenty feet or so down
that way, he could see the uniformed officer standing
outside Hope's room.

Hope. Hell. He couldn't even think of her as anything
other than Hope.

Not suspect.

Not Ms. Carson.

Just Hope . . . with sea-green eyes. Long, silken brown
hair.

Hope.

Shit.

Shit.

Shit.

He couldn't keep thinking of her as *Hope*. She was a
suspect in a very brutal assault and she had a history of
being mentally unbalanced. And he couldn't think of her
as a suspect.

Plus, even though the timing didn't add up, he couldn't
entirely write off the possibility that she'd killed Earl
Prather, either, or was involved in it, somehow.

She was dangerous, and he had to remember that.

Maybe *he* was the one who was unbalanced.

If he'd been alone, he might have taken a few minutes
to rip himself a new asshole and remind himself of that,
again. Remind himself, *again,* that he couldn't think
about Hope Carson, that long, silken hair, or her big,
sad eyes, or how much he'd like to pull her up against
him and promise her . . . everything. Anything . . .

Suspect, he reminded himself.

Bad timing, his dick interjected—and something else . . .
some part of him that he couldn't examine too closely.

She wasn't in town when Prather died, remember? She's got an alibi.

It wasn't the most solid alibi, true, but it was definitely enough to shed some doubt.

And do you really think she would have hurt Reilly? She looks at him like he's some kind of god.

Common sense, the lawyer in him, and other assorted and sundry control-freak-related issues pointed out, *So the fuck what? Even if she didn't kill Prather, it's all too likely she* did *attack Reilly. She looks at him like a god, so what happens when she realizes he isn't a god—when he screws up? She's going to be pissed.*

Get over it, man. You can't go getting a hard-on for a woman who is messed up in the head.

Damn it.

Common sense was being a serious pain in the ass here.

Remy was a big believer in common sense. He liked it. He listened to it. If more people listened to common sense versus things like lust, greed, stupidity . . . well, he might not be as busy as he was. That was his lot in life. Lawyers had jobs because people didn't always listen to their common sense.

His told him he needed to forget that Hope Carson was a pretty woman with sad, green eyes. He needed to remember only that she'd been found in a building with a dead man and one who'd been hovering near death.

And it wouldn't hurt to remember that she had a lot of weird shit in her past, too—that kind of stuff he really didn't need to mess with. Big green eyes and that long brown hair, a sad smile, being pretty as hell, none of that was worth the trouble she would come with.

The fact that something about her made him just want to pull her close and protect her and fuck her all at the same time . . . no, he needed to forget that and listen to reason.

Yeah. That's what he needed to do.

For some weird reason, though, his common sense and his gut had decided to veer off into different directions here. Common sense was doing what it should, insisting Remy take the safe road, be the lawyer. Hope was a suspect, after all.

But his gut . . .

It was his gut that had him studying the other two men more closely—particularly Nielson. Although he hadn't said anything, Nielson's disgust at the entire situation was almost palpable.

"Why do you think she's innocent?" he asked softly.

Nielson lifted a brow. "Who said I thought she was innocent?"

"Maybe I'm just a bright kid."

A smirk twisted the sheriff's mouth, and although the man didn't say a damn thing, the message came through loud and clear. *You're the one making us arrest her* . . .

Fuck. What choice did he have?

She might not have killed Prather, but he couldn't ignore the evidence pointing to her involvement in the attack on Reilly.

She had a history of mental imbalance going back for years, and as much as he'd like to think those sad green eyes of hers were the real deal, he knew people with mental imbalances could be pretty damn persuasive. He wasn't going to be played.

"Jennings."

Remy glanced over his shoulder, not quite recognizing the low, rough raspy voice.

Then he blinked. Slowly, he turned, watched as Law Reilly took one slow step, then another off the elevator. The doors closed at his back.

The man was whiter than death—hell, he was lucky to be alive. Less than seventy-two hours ago, he'd been in a coma and the doctors weren't sure he'd ever wake up.

He shouldn't be standing, and that was made pretty damn clear by the fact that he almost collapsed before one hand managed to grasp the railing on the wall, gripping it as though he knew he'd hit the ground hard and fast if he didn't have something to hold on to.

Hazel eyes glittered too brightly in his face, and his skin had that ugly, pasty gray tinge.

But his mouth was grim and determined, and Remy suspected if Law actually made it down the hallway to him, the man just might try to deck him.

Blowing out a heavy breath, Remy said, "Damn it, Reilly, you're supposed to be flat on your back in bed."

"If you'd returned a couple of fucking phone calls, I would be," Law bit off, his face tight, his mouth pinched.

"We spoke yesterday."

"Yeah, and then I get the call that you were heading down here today." Law sneered at him. "And gee, what in the hell are you here for?"

"You don't need to be worrying about this mess right now. You need to rest up. Heal. I was going to speak with you tomorrow," Remy said. *After* he'd done what he needed to do.

Shit, the guy had only been awake for two days. He didn't need to be worrying about this right now. He needed to be concentrating on getting better.

"Tomorrow." Law's lip curled. "Tomorrow. *After* you'd arrested my best friend. For beating the shit out of me. Which she did *not* do. Which strikes me as kind of pointless. Maybe even a waste of taxpayer money."

Remy absently tapped his finger against his briefcase. This was not how he'd wanted to start off his day. He wanted this over. Done.

Wanted to get to the point where he didn't need to think about Hope, all the problems she had behind

her . . . or ahead of her. About her history with Law.
Hell, he'd be happier just to forget about her.

"Look, Reilly, I realize you've got yourself worked
up, you're ready to be pissed off . . . but I've got a job to
do. There's evidence—"

"You don't have *shit* as evidence," Law snarled. "Not
shit. I was *looking* at her, damn it. Do you hear me?
Looking at her when somebody hit me from behind. I
saw Prather lying dead ten feet behind *her* and right
after I saw his *dead* body, somebody hit me from behind. She's a smart woman and I've always known she
was special, Jennings, but she can't be in two places at
once."

His hand closed into a fist, a brutal, tight fist, and he
glared at Remy like he wanted nothing more than to
pound that fist into Remy's face. If he hadn't been about
to collapse, Remy suspected he might have tried to do
just that.

What Law had told him was strange and yeah, it definitely had him wondering a few things, but Law Reilly
would do damn near anything to keep Hope safe, Remy
suspected. Anything.

Sighing, he said, "Look, Law. I know you're fond of
Ms. Carson and I know you just want to protect her, but
the facts are the facts, and all the facts point to her . . ."

His phone rang. Absently, he pulled it out, ready to
put it on silent, but the number caught his eye.

It was the lab.

Frowning, he held up a hand and answered it.

She heard their voices, faint and indistinct, but she
recognized them all the same.

Remy's and Nielson's, they were pretty easy to place.

A shiver ran down her spine. Hope drew her knees to
her chest and reminded herself—*don't cry, don't cry,
don't cry . . .*

The door to her room swung open and she couldn't keep from flinching at the sound, even as she braced herself. She'd known this was coming. Had known—

The sheriff.

It would be the sheriff.

There to arrest her, even though she had the weirdest feeling he believed her.

But it wasn't him.

It was somebody else—a very unsteady somebody else, with unkempt hair, a heavy growth of whiskers on his face, and eyes that looked far too old. The lower half of his right arm was wrapped in a cast, one that would keep his arm immobilized—and Hope had no doubt that he'd be pissed off about that once he wasn't hurting so bad. *If* he wasn't already pissed off about it.

His arm wasn't the worst part, though.

It was his face, his battered, bruised face. That familiar face . . .

"Oh, God," she whispered, lifting a hand to her mouth.

Law.

She started to scramble out of the bed, but the cuff at her ankle stopped her. Swearing, she just stared at him. "Law," she whispered.

He gave her a shaky smile and made his way over to her bed, collapsing on it. "Hey, sweetie," he said, out of breath.

She reached for him and as his uninjured left arm came around her, she started to sob. Shit. She'd been so scared. So scared.

The sobs came harder and harder, until they almost choked her.

"Shhh . . ." He cradled the back of her head and murmured to her, his voice soft and low. "It's okay, sweetheart. It's all going to be okay."

She didn't entirely believe that, but at least now she could believe that *he* was okay.

For now, for her, that was enough.

"Are you sure?"

Dotti Coltrane peered up at him over the half lenses of her glasses, a mildly irritated look in her eyes. "Handsome, would *I* have called you if I wasn't sure?" She sighed—a patented sigh that clearly said, *I'm surrounded by idiots,* and then she pushed the lab work toward him.

Tapping it with a fingernail painted an unreal shade of neon green, she said, "Type AB. That's Hope Carson's blood. That's the majority of what we found in the blood samples. *But* not all. There was also Type O. That wasn't all that easy to find, and it's not like we're the FBI or anything. If it wasn't for how weird this mess was, I don't know that we would have even looked. Everything seems pretty clear-cut—she slits her wrists, falls down, hits her head. Seems pretty normal that she'd get blood in her hair. But it wasn't just blood we found." She produced a slide. "There was body tissue. I just don't see how she could have hit her head and managed to get somebody else's body tissue matted in her hair, Remy. I'm not buying it. Not unless she somehow managed to hit herself in the back of the head with the same bat she used to beat on her friend with—just doesn't add up."

Remy rubbed the back of his neck.

No, he couldn't buy it, either. "And I don't need to ask you if you're sure it's not *her* body tissue?"

She gave him a baleful look.

"Okay." Blowing out a breath, he crossed his arms over his chest and stared off into the distance, building possible scenarios, discarding them. "So the question is, what's going on?"

Dotti watched him over the rims of her glasses, owl-eyed, excitement in her gaze. "I think what we might have here is a setup, Remy. Really."

"Really." He shot her a narrow look and studied the report again. Even as the lawyer in him started to swear and sulk and pace—figuratively—the knot in his gut was unraveling.

This made more sense in his mind.

This didn't leave him feeling like he was trying to force a square, rough peg in a neat, round hole.

This didn't leave him feeling like he was about to go brutalize an innocent woman.

She hadn't done it.

Inside his head, a hundred silent screams eased and he glanced at Dotti, gave her a smile. "Thanks, Dotti," he murmured, plucking the report up. "Mine?"

"Yep." She pushed her glasses back up her nose and focused on the monitor in front of her. "You know, I like Reilly. He's a weird guy—keeps to himself and all, but I like him. He seems to know people pretty well. He's not going to go hooking up with a nutcase, Rem. He's just not."

Remy didn't respond.

Whether Hope Carson had attacked Reilly or not, she still had some unusual blights on her past. It eased the ache in his heart to think that he wouldn't have to build a case against her, and he had enough now to think that maybe he wouldn't have to, but the ache wasn't completely gone.

Just looking at her made him think about things he had forgotten he wanted, but they weren't things he needed to have in mind when he was looking at her.

Blowing out a sigh, he tucked the file in his briefcase.

He needed to talk to the sheriff.

Get some paperwork done.

And let Hope Carson know she was free to go.

Maybe she'd decide to leave town.

That would be best, he thought.

For all around.

Yeah.

Leave town, Hope . . . just leave town.

Even though the thought of never looking into those sad green eyes left him with a bad, bad ache in his heart.

CHAPTER
THREE

THAT WOMAN DIDN'T BELONG HERE.

He watched as she drove into town in a simple, utilitarian sedan. Even without the tag on the back, it had *rental* written all over it. Either that, or cop car.

She wasn't a cop, though. He could peg a cop from a mile away and she wasn't a cop.

The car was basic, navy blue and simple, the sort of car that said, *forget you ever saw me*. It didn't suit the woman who climbed out from behind the steering wheel. *She* wasn't basic and she wasn't the sort of woman that people forgot.

She was . . . rather lovely, he thought. Long and lean, her skin the color of coffee and cream, her hair cut shorter than he preferred, but it suited her. A little broad through her shoulders and hips, but like her hair, it suited her. She looked . . . strong. But still very, very female. Legs that went on forever, full, lush breasts, and what seemed to be a very delectable ass.

He wondered what her name was, what brought her here.

She didn't carry a purse, something he thought was kind of strange—most women did. There was an air of strength about her and that intrigued him. But as she started toward the police department, that air of strength wavered and he watched as she slowed to a stop, paused. Lifted her hands to her face. Those strong shoulders bowed, like she carried some awful burden. Then, less than fifteen seconds later, she lifted her head and squared her shoulders, stared at the building before her.

Who are you? he wondered.

He really, really wanted to know her name.

Then she started to walk, slowly, and with purpose. One foot in front of the other.

One foot in front of the other, Nia, she told herself.

That was how a person handled the tough shit. By just getting through it—one step at a time.

There was an empty, hollow feeling in the pit of her belly, and her eyes were strangely dry.

She knew what they were going to tell her.

She'd woken that morning in a nondescript, bland hotel room with the certain knowledge that her cousin was dead.

Joely was dead.

She'd been dead for close to two weeks, and although the sheriff hadn't gone into detail, Nia knew Joely hadn't gone easy.

In a matter of minutes, Nia was going to know those details. Soon, Nia would see her cousin again and somehow, she knew it was going to leave a scar on her, on her heart, on her soul.

Just keep walking, Nia. One foot after the other . . .

She reached the doors a lot sooner than she wanted and went inside. A blast of cool air washed over her and she shivered, unreasonably cold. Logically, she knew it was hotter than hell outside—the weather in Kentucky could suck, something she had experienced before. Pushing up over ninety and the humidity was worse. But she was freezing. Cold. And now, she was freezing cold with sweat drying on her skin and the air-conditioning blasting down on her.

One foot after the other . . . one foot.

Up ahead, she saw a short, older woman with a helmet of gray hair, wickedly bright eyes.

She caught sight of Nia and instinctively, Nia dodged into the nearest open door.

As she came to a stop in the open doorway, she happened to notice the words *Sheriff Dwight Nielson* on the frosted glass door.

My lucky day, she thought dismally.

Nia swallowed around the knot in her throat and said, "Sheriff Nielson?"

Shock could be a lovely thing, Nia thought, somewhat disconnected.

She closed her eyes and the tears burning there slid free and rolled down her cheeks. She didn't want to be here, standing by Joely's side, staring down at what had been done to her.

Beaten—so badly beaten, Nia couldn't even recognize her.

Her hair, that pretty, reddish-brown hair, was all wrong—cut too short. *Why did you cut it, baby?* Nia wondered, inanely, reaching up to touch Joely's hair with a shaking hand.

So wrong. All of this was wrong. Joely's battered face, the short hair.

Nia barely recognized her.

Swallowing, she looked up and whispered, "I think it's her. But . . . can . . ." She paused and took a deep breath. "I need to see her shoulder. The back of her right one."

The sheriff and the medical examiner shared a look and then together, they rolled the body over.

The sight of that brightly colored tattoo against Joely's

pale flesh—it hit Nia like a dagger, straight in her heart. She wanted to scream. Wanted to hit something—break something. She wanted to sob . . . knew she would shatter if she let herself.

Breathing shallowly, she looked away.

Joely. It was Joely . . . she might not be able to recognize that battered, bruised face, and the hair might not seem right. But she knew that butterfly tattoo.

Nia had an identical one. Joely's was on her right shoulder, Nia's was on her left. They'd gotten them on spring break, their senior year in high school . . . and they'd been grounded for two weeks after, because they hadn't gotten permission.

With a shaking hand, she reached down and touched the butterfly.

The feel of Joely's cold flesh under her fingertips was a brutal, almost painful assault to her senses.

Human flesh shouldn't feel like that.

Ever.

Joely . . .

She bit down on the inside of her cheek before the sob could break free, bit until she tasted blood.

Then she turned and met the waiting gaze of the sheriff and coroner. "It's my cousin. Jolene Hollister. Joely."

The sheriff reached up, resting a supporting hand on her shoulder. "I'm terribly sorry, Ms. Hollister."

Nia nodded. Pressing her lips together, she reached up, touched her neck absently. "She . . . ah, she wore a necklace. Always. Never took it off—it was her mom's. A gold chain, with a heart on it?"

"There wasn't a necklace. Her engagement ring was still on. We have that locked away—we'll get that taken care of before you leave."

"Okay." Her voice came out in a thready whisper and she cleared her throat, tried to find some remnant of strength buried. *Joely . . .*

Tears burned her eyes and she blinked them back, focusing on the wall until she knew she could speak without crying. The screams, they wanted, needed to break free, but she couldn't give in to them—not yet. Not here.

Just under the grief, there was a hot, fiery ball of rage. And *there* she found the strength she needed. She reached for it, wrapped herself around it.

Rage—so much easier than grief, so much easier to handle, so much easier to control.

"Who in the fuck did this to her?"

"Must have been rough."

Nielson looked at him and Keith grimaced at the look in the sheriff's eyes. "Rough?" Nielson echoed. "No. Telling a man his prize hunting dog was accidentally run over on the highway, that's rough. This was past brutal."

They watched as Nia Hollister climbed into her rented car.

"She barely cried," Nielson said as she drove away. "Hardly even a tear."

Jennings blew out a breath. "Can't decide if that's good or bad. Hate it when they cry, but it's not good for somebody to *not* cry either."

"Kept waiting for her to break. She never did." Nielson rubbed his naked scalp and shook his head. "That had to be one of the hardest things I ever did."

Nielson would have been prepared to see it through if she broke down, would have done the best he could to help. But all he could do was watch as she pushed that anguish somewhere deep inside and let the anger take the lead. Not good. Sometimes anger could get a person through sheer hell, but there was something about that glint in her eyes that bothered him.

She could cause trouble, he suspected. A lot of it.

And he had enough trouble on his hands already, thanks.

She was leaving, though. She had a cousin to bury and Nia Hollister would need every bit of strength just to get through that.

She started the car without looking at him and he watched as she backed up, merged with the traffic moving around the small town square. A hard day for that woman. Very hard. And it wouldn't get any easier any time soon, he knew.

He had nothing he could tell her.

No news.

No clues.

No suspects.

And that was the first thing he needed to do for Nia Hollister—find justice for her cousin. "Come on, Jennings. We've got a case to solve."

They headed toward his office—there, the small team he had assembled waited for him. He wished he had the manpower for a real task force, but the county of Carrington didn't often see murders. He could happily go the rest of his life without having anything like this happen again, truth be told.

As he and Jennings walked into his office, the three deputies fell silent.

"We'll keep this as short as we can," he said, glancing at each of them. Settling behind his desk, he reached into a file and pulled out a picture of Jolene Hollister, laid it flat on his desk.

It was nearly seven o'clock and he was tired as hell. He wanted to be home, with a cold beer, a sandwich, and something other than a pretty dead girl on his mind.

But the pretty dead girl was dominating his thoughts.

Staring down at her face, he sighed and looked up, studied each of his men. None of them were really equipped to handle this. Hell, *he* wasn't equipped to handle this. He'd had his share of homicides come his way, but nothing like this. He had dealt with drunk driving, hit-and-runs, jealous spouses, pissed-off employees, and shit like that.

Staring down at the glossy picture on his desk, he kept seeing the superimposed image of what she had looked like in death.

This here . . . what had been done to her . . . that was evil.

And more than likely, it was somebody in his town doing it.

It fucking *pissed him off*.

"She looks so young."

Nielson looked up, met the deputy's eyes. It was Ethan Sheffield, one of his youngest deputies, and one of his greenest. He had a sharp mind, though. Nielson just hoped his instincts were right about this one. "The man who killed her didn't care that she's young," Nielson said softly. "He didn't care that she had her whole life ahead of her, didn't care about anything but the fact that he wanted her."

"Why?"

Nielson shifted his focus to Keith and lifted a brow. "Why?"

"Yes. Why did he want her?" Keith leaned forward and plucked the picture off the desk. "We don't have the slick equipment, the profilers, the brains the State boys are going to have, or the Feds. Which means we just have our own instincts, what we know. We need to figure out why he wanted her."

Nielson smiled and leaned back in his seat. "Yes. We need to figure that out." He stroked a hand down his jaw and murmured, "We might not have the slick equipment, the profilers, or the high dollar brains, but we don't need high dollar degrees to use the brains we have.

Not a one of you is stupid. That's why you're in here.
We need to figure out just *why* he wanted her."

Then he leaned forward and stared at the woman's
face.

There was something about her face that bothered
him—something that had been bothering him ever since
he'd seen the driver's license photo. A few days earlier,
he'd gotten a much better photo, though, a more recent
one, a casual one—one that had sent cold chills down
his spine.

Her eyes were hazel and in the picture, she wore a
pair of wire-rimmed glasses, but the face itself . . .

Blowing out a sigh, he riffled through the files on his
desk until he found the right one. Inside, there was another photograph. The woman in it was a few years
older, though it didn't really show.

They both had the same clear, pale skin, similar bone
structure. Even the hair color was similar and it was an
unusual shade. In the picture, the woman's hair appeared to be longer, pulled back and up. It had been
much shorter when they had found her, but that didn't
mean much.

He tugged on his lip as he scanned a report until he
found the rest of the information he needed.

Height was almost dead-on. Weight, just a few
pounds' difference.

Taking the second picture, he turned it around and
placed it next to the picture he'd recently received of
Jolene Hollister's. Then he looked at his men.

"What do you see?"

A little piece of gold shouldn't weigh that much.

Sighing, Ezra King sat on the edge of the bed and
stared at the gold cross. He'd found it half-buried in the
mud a couple of weeks ago, a dozen yards or so away

from his house. His house had been going up in flames at the time.

"You going to tell me what's got you all broody and down?" A soft, strong hand stroked up his back and he glanced over his shoulder just in time to see Lena's naked torso right before she pressed up against him, nuzzling his cheek.

Her arms came around him and he smiled. "Hey, I wake up in bed next to a beautiful woman. What do I have to be down about?"

"Ezra." She pressed her cheek against his and just waited.

It was almost eerie, how well she knew him. Already. They'd only been together a few weeks. A couple months ago, he hadn't even known her. A little over a year ago, he'd still been working with the state police in Lexington.

For the past few days, ever since the night his house had burned to a charred husk, he'd been living with her and honestly, he had a hard time imagining a life without Lena Riddle.

He was already thinking crazy shit like engagement rings. Weddings. Waking up next to her every day for the rest of his life. He loved her—was shit-faced, stupid in love with her and couldn't imagine his life without her.

He had fallen for her so hard. So fast. And with each day that passed, he fell for her just a little more.

And because he knew she'd want to know, because he knew he'd want her to share whatever burdens she had, he knew he couldn't hide this. It just weighed too heavy on his heart.

Sighing, he reached up and laid a hand on her arm, squeezed gently. "Brody Jennings."

"What about him?" She pressed her lips to his cheek. "He's just a sad, messed-up kid, Slick."

Ezra grimaced. A sad, messed-up kid. Yeah, that described Brody Jennings, all right. Except the sad, messed-up kid's behavior was kind of escalating. All over the place. Looking down at the gold cross, he studied it. There was no doubt in his mind it was the same one.

"I saw him in town, the day Law got back to town," he said softly. "When you and Hope were walking around the square. Remy was there with him—wanted to talk to me. Said he'd make sure Brody came out when I was ready, help me repair some of the damage the kid had done out at my place."

He scrubbed a hand over his face and muttered, "Shit. The damage. A few trashed flower beds are the least of the problems, now, huh? Unless the kid's got a contractor's license, he's not going to be much use out there."

The house he'd inherited from his grandmother was trashed, thanks to the fire, and he hadn't been able to salvage much of anything. What hadn't been destroyed by the flames had been destroyed by smoke or water.

Lena tightened her arms. "Ezra, what's your point here? I'm not following."

"He had a necklace on. A gold cross." Rubbing his finger across the delicately etched surface, he stared off into the distance.

"It was his mother's." Lena rubbed her cheek against his shoulder. "I remember Remy mentioning it. It's like the one thing he still . . . how did he put it . . . I dunno, but when Remy sees him wearing it, it's like he still has hope. Still thinks the kid isn't too far gone."

Early morning light shone through the window, danced off the small bit of gold. So small.

How in the hell could it weigh so much? Be such a burden?

"The kid might be gone farther than he thinks, beautiful," Ezra said, his voice gruff. "I found that cross. It was out by my house the night it caught on fire."

Lena trailed her hand down his arm.

When her fingers touched the cross, a soft, sad sigh escaped her. She rested her head on his shoulder. But she didn't say anything.

His dad had already left.

Brody waited, just to be certain, before he slipped out. He had to air up his tires before he could go anywhere— thanks to Uncle Remy, Dad had taken his four-wheeler away and Brody wasn't about to walk.

Too far away.

Setting off across the fields, he focused on anything and everything but what he'd done.

Or at least he tried.

It was really, really hard to think about anything else.

He needed to tell somebody . . . his dad was out of the question. Maybe Uncle Remy. Maybe the sheriff . . . shit, screw that. But . . . hell. Who could he tell? He hadn't *meant* to do it.

Wasn't like anybody had gotten hurt.

King had sure as hell landed on his feet—shacking up with Lena Riddle, of all people. The woman had legs that went for miles. Brody didn't know why in the hell his uncle had broken things off with her. If *he* had a girl like that . . . ?

Easier to think about her, wonder about what it might be like to make it with her than to think about the fire.

The flames.

So hot, so fucking hot.

If he'd stopped, for five damn seconds, to think . . . and shit, how was he supposed to know the place would burn like that?

The place had been old.

That's what the word around town was. Old places like that? They burned fast.

But how in the hell was Brody to know that?

Nobody had gotten hurt. Nobody had even been there.

And as long as he hadn't lost his mom's necklace there, nobody had to know it was him, either.

He just had to find that necklace.

Tears stung his eyes, but he blinked them away. Wasn't going to cry over it. It would turn up. Always did. The chain was old. He kept meaning to get a new one, but they weren't cheap and he hated asking his dad for anything.

It was the necklace, though, that had him tearing up. Even though he wouldn't cry about it, it was the necklace.

It couldn't be anything else—it wasn't like he needed to cry about that bastard King's place, or the fire, or the trouble he could be in.

Nobody knew.

And he hadn't meant for it to happen . . .

Swallowing the tears that clogged his throat, he wished he could go and talk to Uncle Remy.

Or even his dad, although Dad barely even realized he was alive anymore.

Most of all, Brody wished he could talk to his mom. Wished she was there. Wished she was there to wrap her arms around him, tell him everything would be okay.

Even though he knew nothing would ever be okay again.

Not for him.

Nothing had been right for him since she died, and he didn't see that changing any time soon.

CHAPTER
FOUR

"RUN THAT BY ME AGAIN, MR. JENNINGS?"

"I'm just looking for more information on your ex-wife's past," Remy said, keeping his voice level.

Although honestly, he didn't know how much more information he needed, or even what he was looking for—or why. Even if Hope *had* been involved, he wouldn't have to go this far. He just couldn't help himself.

Officially, Hope Carson was no longer his concern.

He just, hell, he couldn't leave it alone. He didn't even know why, but he couldn't leave it alone. Couldn't leave *her* alone.

"Just how much more do you want me to share?" Carson said, sadly, softly. "I've already shared far more than I feel comfortable with. What else do you want from me?"

Remy sighed and spun around in his chair, staring out the window. "I just need to know everything I can. The more I know, the more I can help her."

"Oh, bullshit." Carson laughed, but even over the phone, there was no mistaking the complete lack of humor in the sound. "Don't hand me that. It's not *help* you want from me. You just want me to give you the nails to close her coffin. I won't do that. Not to my wife."

The phone went dead.

Remy softly murmured, "Ex-wife."

Then, as a knock sounded on his office door, he hung up.

"Come in," he called out.

The last person he expected to see was Brody.

The subdued kid came into his office looking like somebody had kicked a puppy—and he was the puppy.

Remy eyed his nephew, wondering where that brash, borderline mean attitude had gone. "You okay, Brody?"

"Yeah." He gave a jerky shrug and roamed the office, absently jiggling the change in his pocket, the same way Remy did when he was nervous or distracted.

Remy no longer carried change in his pockets for that very reason. Little things like that tripped up a man in court. Showing any nerves, tension—not wise.

Brody stopped in front of the desk, scuffing his feet on the carpet. "You haven't seen Mom's necklace, have you? I can't find it. That stupid chain went and broke."

Ah . . . Suddenly understanding the woebegone look in the kid's eyes, Remy leaned back in his chair. "No. I can't say I have, at least not that I can recall. How long has it been since you saw it?"

"A few days." Despondent, Brody flung his long, skinny body down in one of the leather chairs and stared off into nothingness.

"Remember when you saw it last?"

Brody huffed out a breath. "Shit. How the hell do I know? After I showered one morning, I guess. Then it wasn't there." His gaze met Remy's, then bounced away, never resting any place for longer than a few seconds.

"You talked to your dad?"

"No."

And just like that, Brody shut down. Crossing his

arms over his skinny chest, he shot up out of the chair. "I guess I better get. You've got lawyer shit to do around here."

"Brody . . ."

The kid paused at the door.

Remy sighed. "Hell. I'll keep an eye out, ask around." It wouldn't do any good, but he felt like there was something he should do. Say. "Maybe it will turn up."

Brody nodded and then pushed through the door, his head bent, narrow shoulders slumped.

Poor kid.

Remy wished he could do more for the boy, say more. But his nephew shut everybody out these days, and the kind of heart-to-heart they needed to have would have to wait until Remy had a few more minutes available. He had to get to Nielson's office.

Now that they no longer had Hope Carson as a suspect, he needed an update.

Maybe later, he'd go by Reilly's, see how she was doing . . .

But even as that thought tried to work its way into his mind, he shut it down. Had to shut it down, because he could *not* be thinking about her like that.

Whether she was responsible for what had happened to Reilly or not, the woman was unbalanced.

That right there was a complication he did not want or need in his life.

"The victim's next of kin claimed the body today," Dwight said.

"Finally." Remy scowled, counting the days in his mind. A little over two weeks had passed since the woman's lifeless body had been found on Reilly's property. Far too long. "What took her so long?"

"Delays," Nielson grimaced. "And give her a break, kid. She was out of the country and it took forever for me to get her name from the fiancé. I get the feeling he didn't know the cousin very well. I was going through all the red tape on my end, but he ended up getting in contact with her before I did and she called me just a few days ago. Took her a few days to make it back to the country."

"She's the only family?"

"Yeah." Nielson sighed. "There's the boyfriend, but . . . well, he seems like a nice enough guy, but he's not handling this too well."

"How well would you handle it if your fiancé disappeared, then was murdered only weeks before your wedding?" Remy asked absently.

Nielson shrugged. "Lousy."

"Anything new other than locating the next of kin?"

"Not a damn thing," Nielson said, shaking his head. He looked utterly disgusted.

"So basically, we're back where we started," Remy muttered, skimming the report.

Then he tossed it onto the sheriff's desk and studied Nielson's face. It was a lean, intelligent face, one that might look more suited to a scholar, perhaps a minister. Quite a few had underestimated the sheriff, and Remy had more than once stood aside and watched as more than one learned the error of their ways.

He was a sharp man, and a fair one.

And right now, he was probably about as frustrated and pissed off as Remy was feeling.

"We have no idea who killed Prather, no idea who attacked Reilly—basically, we know jackshit. That's where we stand," Remy said.

"That's exactly where we stand." Dwight shrugged and said, "I can't say I'm terribly disappointed we had to let go of Ms. Carson. I never did like the girl for this attack on Lawson, and it still left too many questions unanswered. She couldn't have done Prather, and my mind just wasn't taking in the idea of separate perps—two different people, one who beat the shit out of Reilly, and one who killed my deputy, and in the same house?"

"Hell, I didn't like the idea, either." Remy brooded, staring out the window at the stingy square of scenery Dwight commanded. He could see a small slice of the square, carefully tended with flowers, the sidewalk. This time of day, it was crowded with people going to lunch or just finishing. Ash was a small town, but a busy one.

The past few weeks had cast one hell of a pall on the quiet little town, though.

A dead woman, her body found on Reilly's property.

Then a cop gets killed by person or persons unknown . . . in Reilly's *home*.

And Reilly gets assaulted.

Reilly.

It all circled back to him. This bloody mess going on all circled back to Reilly. If and when Remy ever had anybody to prosecute, they needed to figure out how Reilly was connected to this.

"We need to talk to Reilly more. Figure out how he's connected to this. I want to know everything you already have on him and everything you can find out on him. What he does for a living, where he went to college, how he knows Hop . . . Ms. Carson, all of it." He pulled out his phone and went to make a few notes and realized that Dwight was staring at him.

Lifting a brow, he said, "Yes?"

The sheriff puffed out his cheeks. "I already know some of that."

Remy leaned back in the chair. "Well, that makes sense. It stands to reason you did some background work on him, although I thought he had a pretty solid alibi."

Dwight jerked a shoulder in a shrug. "Actually, this is stuff I knew before that and yes, he had a damn solid alibi. He had nothing to do with that girl dying, Remy. I'd almost lay my badge on it."

He bent over, rummaging inside his desk. When he straightened, he had a battered paperback in hand and he tossed it at Remy.

Catching it, Remy studied the cover. Then he looked back at the sheriff. "What's this?"

"Law's handiwork. You wanted to know what he did for a living. There you go. Goes by the pen name Ed O'Reilly."

Remy blinked. He looked at the cover of the book and then back up at the sheriff. Then back at the book. "You're shitting me."

"No. I've known for a few years—was curious. Seeing as how he never seems to leave the house for any kind of job, but he damn sure has a regular income." He grimaced. "I've got a nice, quiet town here and I like it that way. I like knowing what's going on in my town and I decided to figure out just who he was. The day that girl died, he was out of town attending the funeral of a colleague."

Still studying the cover of the book, Remy scowled. He was pretty sure he'd read one or two of these books. At least. Absently, he tapped it against his thigh. "Maybe this is where we need to focus. Could be an overzealous fan—"

"Not likely." Dwight shook his head. "Guy's too private. Hardly anybody other than some colleagues even knows who he is. Yeah, it can be found out if somebody really wants to look, but I suspect somebody who's *this* far gone would have stirred up the waters some and Reilly . . . well, he's a sharp guy. He would have noticed something, seen something. And he hasn't."

"Okay. Still, it's an avenue we'll keep open." He tossed the book back to Dwight and went back to his phone, made his note. "Shit. Reilly's a writer. Trying to decide if that surprises me or not."

Dwight snorted. "Doesn't surprise me a bit."

Remy eyed Dwight's face. "I don't think much of anything surprises you. Okay, so we need to figure out where Reilly plays into this—but he has to play into it. It all comes back to him."

"No. Not all." The sheriff plucked a file off his desk, handing it to Remy. "The fire at Ezra King's place. Some weird occurrences at Lena Riddle's. Something's going on out in that part of the county for certain, but I don't think it's just Reilly involved. Shit, maybe he's just a bystander."

"A bystander." Remy shook his head as he flipped through the file. "No, he's a little too involved to just be a bystander."

He studied the brief report about the fire. No doubt that it was arson, there. "When did you get this?"

"Just today." Dwight's face showed little expression, but there was a look in his eyes, one that Remy recognized.

Frustration. Fury.

Remy could sympathize with both. Somebody was fucking with their nice, quiet little town and it was pissing him off.

Handing the report back to Dwight, he said, "There may not be much of a connection, though. Arson? For all we know, it could be connected to something in King's past. He was a state cop—he's bound to have some enemies."

"True. Not something we can discount there." Dwight laid the file down, continued to stare at Remy.

"Shit. What is it?"

Dwight just smiled. "I just don't see his past waiting this long to catch up with him. Besides, if that's what it

was, I think he would have suspected something . . . and
he would have already been here to talk to us."

Then he handed Remy another file. "There's something else you should be aware of. I received this today.
It's . . . this is Jolene Hollister—or was."

The name hit Remy like a sucker punch. He knew
that name—he'd carry it to his grave. He'd never met
her, and he never would meet her—but he owed her. All
of them did. She'd been found dead in their town. Dead,
brutalized.

No. He wouldn't forget her name.

Dread dragged at him and if he had had the option, he
would have tossed the file back down, never looked at
it. But he didn't have that option, so he flipped it open.
The sight of the woman there . . . it was a brutal, breath-
stealing shock.

"What the fuck . . . ?" he muttered.

Jerking his gaze up, he stared at the sheriff. "Is this
some kind of sick joke?"

"No. Relax. It's not who you think it is. Look closer."
He nodded toward the picture and said softly, "That's
Jolene Hollister. I know it's almost spooky, but look
again. The shape of her chin is just a little softer. Her
eyes are a different color. The hair, too. The color is similar, but the cut, the style is all wrong."

He was right, Remy realized.

But still . . . the similarity, it was eerie.

"Has King seen this yet?" Remy asked, forcing the
words out. His throat was tight, tight and dry and raw.

"No. But I suspect we need to tell him." Then Nielson
paused. "Shouldn't we?"

Remy nodded. Then he frowned, as the odd note in
the sheriff's voice penetrated the fog of shock. "Yes, we
should. Why wouldn't we?"

"You have to admit, the similarity is eerie. And none
of this trouble started until he showed up. Now . . . well,

we have a dead woman on our hands, and the dead woman looks an awful lot like the woman he's now living with. A lot like your former lover."

Remy closed his eyes and reached up, rubbing the bridge of his nose. Shit, shit, and double fuck. "It's not King, and you know it. Your gut's already telling you that."

"Can we afford to be wrong?" Nielson murmured.

"No. We can't." Remy slid the picture back in the file and tossed it on the sheriff's desk and then looked at him. "That's why we need to tell him, because if we *don't* . . . what if this guy is out trolling for women who fit the profile? If we don't tell him, how can he protect her?"

Nielson nodded.

"It's not him." Remy shook his head, remembering with no small amount of envy the way King had looked at Lena. The way Lena's face had softened when she heard the other guy's voice.

She hadn't ever once looked at him that way.

He hadn't ever once managed to put that soft glow on her face.

He wasn't jealous of King being with Lena, exactly. He had liked her a lot, had wanted her like hell, but he hadn't been in love with her. Still, he was jealous of the way he saw them looking at each other—envious of what it looked like they had going.

King was a decent guy—Lena, her instincts about people were solid. And that dog of hers, hell, even if Lena's instincts about people weren't dead-on, that dog could tell a bastard from a mile off.

"It's not him," he murmured again.

"Okay. So we tell him." Then Nielson grimaced. "That was my gut instinct, too. I just want somebody else who can help me shoulder the guilt if I'm wrong."

Remy smirked. "Thanks."

The phone chose that particular moment to ring.

Dwight reached down and pushed a button. "Yes?"

The brisk, efficient voice of his assistant, Ms. Tuttle, came through the speakerphone. "Ezra King is here to speak with you. He doesn't have an appointment."

Speak of the devil, Remy thought as he listened to Ms. Tuttle. The disapproval in her voice came through loud and clear and he grinned, watched as Dwight fought not to do the same. If he so much as twitched an amused eyelash, the woman would know and he wouldn't have any peace. The sheriff's schedule was her domain, and she ruled it with an iron fist—hell and damnation would rain down on any who interfered.

Including the sheriff.

"It's okay, Ms. Tuttle. He's probably here to see if there's any news about the fire at his place."

Remy could almost hear her teeth clenching, gritting together. "He could have called. It's common courtesy."

"Yes . . ."

Remy grabbed a pad of paper and scrawled something down, held it up.

Dwight saw it and grinned, winked.

Then, without missing a beat, he continued. "But he's had a rough week, a rough year, really. It's our Christian duty to be understanding, especially in this trying time."

"Humph." Ms. Tuttle didn't sound terribly impressed. "You're right, of course."

"Send him on back. I'll speak with him, and afterward, I'll do my best to make sure he understands the importance of calling. We can't have him messing up the schedule." At that, Dwight rolled his eyes. As he put the phone down, he muttered, "You'd think she was handling the president's daily affairs, sometimes."

In under a minute, there was a brisk knock at the door and Ms. Tuttle stood there, a petite woman with steel-gray hair and snapping green eyes. She stepped aside to let Ezra enter and then, with a dismissive sniff, she closed the door behind her.

They waited until the familiar plodding tread of her thick-soled shoes had faded before Ezra looked at Dwight, a golden-brown brow cocked.

"Our Christian duty?" Ezra asked.

Dwight grinned. "Did she have her speakerphone on?"

"Nah, just turned up loud. Guess she's hard of hearing—I heard every damn word." Then he glanced at Remy, gave him a short nod. "Jennings."

If Remy wasn't trained to notice things about people, he wouldn't have seen it. Ezra was good. Damn good. There wasn't really that much that gave him away. Just a faint tightening around his eyes. No change in his voice, nothing in the way he moved. Just that thing around the eyes.

Knowing what he knew about cops, Remy suspected King had been in touch with Nielson about the fire . . . and other things, like the weird stuff that had happened at Lena's place.

Had the guy suspected something was off?

Was that why he was here?

Regardless, Nielson would probably tell him about the Hollister woman, and it was going to be one hell of a shock when he saw that picture, when he realized who the woman was.

And it was something Remy didn't need to be here for, he decided.

Although he still needed to discuss things with the sheriff, he reached for his briefcase and went to stand up. "Dwight, I'll catch up with you later."

"No." Ezra stopped, hooked his thumbs in the pockets of his worn-out jeans. "Actually, I'd planned to look you up later . . . you might as well hear it now."

Remy paused, then slowly settled back into the chair,

hooking one ankle over his knee. "Exactly what do I need to hear?"

Instead of saying anything, Ezra slid a hand inside his pocket. Tugged something out. Whatever it was, it was small, small enough to hide inside the palm of his hand, and he kept it tucked there, where Remy couldn't see it, where the sheriff couldn't see it.

"I can't give any good reason why I picked this up," Ezra said, his voice distracted. "I was staring at the house, watching it go up in flames, thinking about how proud Grandma always was of that house, how much she loved it. I was so fucking pissed. Still am. I looked down, and there it was."

"There what was, Ezra?" Dwight asked.

Remy's gut went hot, tight.

Clenching his jaw, he stood up.

Ezra's green eyes cut to him.

They should have been hard, cold as ice, or hot with fury.

But what Remy saw was pity.

And he knew. Somehow, he just knew.

Even before Ezra uncurled his hand and let that gold cross swing from his hand. Remy closed his eyes, looked away. But he could still see that cross, swinging there.

Brody's cross.

Dwight stood up, leaning across his desk.

"What is that?" he murmured, more to himself than anybody else.

It's Brody's. The words sprang to his lips, but Remy bit them back. He couldn't say it—shit. Couldn't say it out loud. Wasn't going to admit what that was, not in front of two fucking cops—

Shit. *Shit.* He hurled his briefcase down and started to pace the small office, scrubbing his hands over his face. He couldn't breathe. Damn it, he couldn't breathe.

Reaching down, he tugged at the knot of his tie, but it didn't help.

What if that stupid kid had gotten hurt?

What if somebody had been in the house?

"Remy?"

Turning around, he met Dwight's gaze, clenching his jaw to keep from saying anything. He wanted to yell, curse—wanted to hit something. Wanted to go track down his brother and pound him senseless, make him wake up and see just how screwed up the kid had gotten.

Something had to be done, damn it.

"What's going on, Remy?" Dwight asked.

Remy shook his head. He couldn't say anything.

"It's Brody's necklace," Ezra said, his voice quiet. "I remember seeing him wear it in town, maybe two weeks ago."

He caught the charm in his hand, studied it. "It just didn't seem like the kind of thing a teenaged boy would wear, you know? Unless a girlfriend gave it to him." Ezra looked at Remy as he added, "Or maybe a mother who passed away."

Silence fell.

Dwight settled back in his chair, the wood creaking under him. He blew out a long, heavy sigh and leaned his head against the padded headrest. "Well, shit."

"Nothing puts him there," Remy said, his voice rough and harsh. "That necklace doesn't mean jack shit."

"No." Ezra laid it on the edge of Dwight's desk and pushed his hands into the back of his pockets. "And the necklace, officially, wasn't found there. I picked it up, and for all you know, I found it on the side of the road and I'm standing here lying through my teeth."

"Shit." Remy reached up and rubbed the back of his neck.

Abruptly, he hauled off, slamming his fist into the solid oak of a filing cabinet. Pain flared, his skin split, and dumbly, he stared at his knuckles, watching as blood started to flow. Then he reached inside his pocket, drew out a handkerchief, wrapped it around his hand.

Looking at Dwight, he said, "What are you going to do?"

"I'm not sure what you're asking." He shot Ezra a dirty look. "You like fucking things up for me, boy?"

Ezra curled his lip. "Yeah, it just makes my day, Sheriff. I wake up every damn day, thinking about what all I can do to screw with your cozy little town. Get my girlfriend terrorized. Get my house burned down by some teenaged headcase."

"He's not a fucking headcase," Remy snarled.

"Oh, the hell he isn't." Ezra slashed a hand through the air and whirled around, glaring at him. "I feel bad for the kid. You think I want to see him slapped with a crime like this? What is he . . . fourteen? Fifteen? He's just a fucking kid and he's got his whole life ahead of him. All he needs to do is figure that out."

Then he sighed and shoved a hand through his hair. "He isn't going to do that until he gets his act together. No one was hurt . . . *this* time. But you can't make this go away. You want to give him a smack on the hand, have him come out and sweep up some of the ashes of my house? You think that's going to convince him he needs to straighten up? He needs help, Jennings. And I think you know that."

Gut churning, Remy looked away from Ezra and stared at the gold cross on Dwight's desk, thought about the way his nephew had looked just that morning. Fuck. Why hadn't the kid come to him? Trusted him?

Eyes burning and throat tight, he looked at Ezra. "What do you want me to say? What in the holy fuck do you want me to do?"

"Get him help. For the love of God, you're a lawyer— figure it out, work it out. Get him help—he isn't going to find what he needs in jail, but he can't just walk away from this either."

Remy shifted his gaze to the sheriff.

Dwight closed his eyes. Then he reached over and grabbed the necklace. "I wasn't in here, Remy. Wasn't in here. I left to get me a soda. You two idiots stay in here for the next ten minutes, or so help me God, I'll beat you both bloody." With that, he tossed the necklace at Remy.

On his way out the door, he shot them both a dark look. "If this comes back and bites me on the ass, I'm going to make the two of you very, very sorry."

"Stupid kid."

Keith Jennings, flipping through a book, looked up as Nielson came storming into the breakroom. He looked pissed, Keith decided. Very, very pissed. Leaning back in his seat, he studied his boss for a minute, torn between finishing the book and asking.

Curiosity got the best of him. "Which one?"

Nielson shot him a look. "Nobody."

Huh. Well, he'd hear about it sooner or later, he figured. That's the way it worked in this town. Turning down the page he'd been reading, he tossed the book aside and watched as Nielson plugged some quarters into the Coke machine. "Is anybody telling King about the similarities between the victim and Ms. Riddle?"

Nielson grunted an answer.

Keith thought it might be a yes. He wasn't sure. Damn. Something really, really had the boss in a mood today. He didn't bother asking what it was, though. He kind of liked his head where it was.

CHAPTER
FIVE

SOME PEOPLE MIGHT SAY THAT A WISE MAN WOULDN'T be here.

But he couldn't think of another place to be just then. Watching Hope seemed to be just the thing to do.

Just the thing.

Even though there were all kinds of trouble going on in Ash right now. If anybody saw a strange, shadowy figure skulking about in the woods, well, he might find his ass plugged with buckshot, and yet, here he was.

He couldn't not watch her.

She had been in the hospital and according to the gossip grapevine, just a few hours away from getting arrested. The words he'd heard had been *criminally insane*.

Just thinking about it was enough to make him chuckle.

Her . . . insane.

He laughed.

She looked like she would scream at a loud noise.

She looked like she would run if somebody jumped out from behind a tree.

And they had been ready to arrest her for assault, maybe even for murder?

It was amusing.

But now she was out . . . and he imagined she would run soon.

That was what she did.

And all he had to do was watch.

Once she ran . . .

"I shouldn't be here," Hope muttered.

The sun beat down on her back as she paced the porch, but she was still cold.

Law slumped on the swing at one end, his eyes closed. He wasn't sleeping, though. He cracked one lid open, peered at her with that shrewd, intense gaze, and then closed his eye again.

"You aren't leaving, Hope."

Shooting him a narrow look, she continued to pace.

"Not really up to you, is it?" she shot at him.

He smiled a little, but didn't say anything.

No. She wasn't leaving. Not right now.

Three days. She'd been back at this house for three days, and each day was like a waking nightmare. Her skin crawled, just being inside that place. Memory flashes of the night haunted her, all the damn time. They were vague, so damn vague, nothing but blips, really, but even those were too much.

Neither she nor Law had terribly clear recollections—not too surprising with Law, considering how badly he'd been battered. The hit she'd taken to her head could easily be blamed for her vague memories, but she wondered how much of her hazy recollections were because she was just too big of a coward to remember.

She kept seeing Prather . . . oh, shit. She covered her eyes with her hands, as though that would block out what few memories she had of that night. The clearest one she had of him was his face—lifeless, but his expression had been one of abject, terrified pain—like he'd died all but begging for mercy.

He hadn't deserved that.

She suspected he'd been a chauvinistic jerk, but nobody deserved to die like that.

She couldn't be here without remembering . . .

Law was going to have his office gutted, completely redesigned, but it would be awhile. Even when it was done, she knew she'd still see it as it had looked that night. With the red stain of blood spreading across the floor.

Hell, even now she could see where blood and other things had left their mark.

The sheriff had given them the okay to go ahead and use the room, said they'd gotten everything they'd need, but there was no way Hope would ever step foot in there, not until Law was done doing whatever.

Maybe not even then.

Being in the kitchen wasn't as hard, but she barely remembered any of what had happened in the seconds before she'd been hit. The clearest memories all happened before she'd come in here.

Part of her wished the sheriff had told them they wouldn't be able to come back here yet. And how selfish was that? This was her best friend's home—he loved this place.

Loved it, and just being here gave her nightmares.

The phone rang. "I'll get it," she said, shooting him a dark look.

"I *am* capable of standing up, Hope." He grimaced.

"I'm already standing." Then she flushed, realized how short, how sharp her tone sounded. Turning her back on him, she reached inside the house and grabbed the cordless from the counter. Then she made a face, almost wished she'd let Law get it after all.

She knew that number. The display only showed *Carrington County* before it ran out of room, but she knew the number.

She cleared her throat before she answered.

Still, her voice creaked a little as she said, "Hello?"

When Remy Jennings spoke, the sound of that slow, lazy drawl hit her low in the belly. "Hello, Ho . . . Ms. Carson. May I speak to Law, please?"

Without saying anything else, she delivered the phone to Law, tried not to think about the man on the other end of the phone. Tried not to think of how that deep, easy voice made her feel.

It was amazing, really, that she even recognized *that* feeling. It had been years since a man had made her feel that way . . . and her ex-husband hadn't ever managed to do that just by *talking*.

No man had. Other than Remy Jennings.

But she really, really needed to quit thinking of him as a man. Really.

Don't think of him as a man. Think of him as a lawyer . . . hello, he wanted you arrested! That right there should have made it very, very clear that he wasn't a guy she needed to think about.

Hell, she didn't think about guys period.

She didn't trust them.

She didn't need them.

Other than Law, and he wasn't really a guy in her opinion. He was Law. He was her friend . . . and he was safe.

He was it, though.

The other males of the species, they could go to hell in a handbasket and that would suit her just fine. She'd survived just fine the past few years without a guy, no reason to change that. And it wasn't like she ever wanted another guy in her life again anyway. Not after Joey.

A small, quiet voice deep inside her heart murmured, *Remy is nothing like Joey.*

Against her will, she closed her eyes, remembered the first time she'd seen the man.

Barely three weeks ago.

That day on the square.

She'd crashed into Earl Prather, had reacted—badly—
the deputy had gone to steady her, keep her from falling.
Hadn't done anything wrong, really, but it had freaked
her out, and when she saw his uniform, it had made it
worse. She'd panicked, and that set his cop's instincts
off.

And then, just like that, Remy was there. She'd looked
into those dusk-blue eyes, heard that soft lazy drawl of
his . . . felt like she was falling.

Get a grip, she told herself.

Shaking her head, she leaned back against the railing
and looked up just as Law was lowering the phone.
"Gee, did he change his mind? Is he coming to haul me
away?"

"Shut up," Law muttered, grimacing. "No. He was
supposed to come out, needed to talk a few things over
with me, but something came up. He's rescheduled."

He reached up, rested a hand on her shoulder. "Hope,
you're not getting arrested. You can relax."

"Relax." She pressed a hand to her quivering, jump-
ing belly.

How could she relax, when it felt like somebody was
watching her every step?

Weighing her every move?

Just waiting . . .

Shivering, she pushed that thought aside and focused
on Law's battered face. "Are you hungry? You didn't eat
much this morning."

"Nice, subtle subject change there, darlin'." Law
rolled his eyes.

Giving him a sharp-edged smile, she said, "Fine. Law,
darlin', I don't want to talk about this, so let's don't.
Now do you want something to eat or not?"

To her surprise, a wide grin lit his face. Then he

winced, pressed a hand to his mouth as the flesh of the healing cut on his lower lip split. "Shit, Hope. Don't make me smile like that."

When he lowered his hand, there was a smear of blood on it. He sighed and grabbed a tissue from the counter, pressed it to his mouth.

"You know, you're acting awful bossy. You've been acting like this ever since the two of us left the hospital. Here I was, half-expecting you to take off running like a jackrabbit, but what you did was go and find an attitude. What's the deal?"

She just shrugged.

She couldn't begin to explain it. Something about being forced into that hospital—into *any* hospital.

Something about having people trying to force those drugs on her . . .

Something about these damned bandages on her wrists . . .

Looking down, she touched one of them, touched the wounds the bandages hid.

Then she looked up and met Law's eyes.

There was a familiar look there, compassionate and understanding. He reached out and caught her hands, drawing her fingers away from the scars. "It's going to be okay. You got out of that place before. Whatever this is, whatever put you back there, you'll get out again. I'm right here and I'll help you."

Narrowing her eyes, she jerked her hands away.

The compassion she saw in his eyes, it pissed her off. Fury bubbled inside, hot and potent and deadly. It wanted *out*.

Something dark and frightening pushed at the edge of her memory. She couldn't quite remember *what* had happened that night . . . she wasn't entirely sure she wanted to. Seeing Prather, vague flickers of Law . . . he'd been in trouble—she knew that.

But she hadn't done this. She knew that as sure as she knew her own name, as sure as she knew the color of her eyes, the color of her hair.

And she was so damned *tired* of having people think she'd done this.

Even Law . . . who had always trusted her, believed in her. Helped her.

Even Law.

He believed she was so damned weak that she'd slit her own wrists while he was lying there, hurting and helpless. Turning away, she started down the steps, uncertain of where she was going to go—she sure as hell wasn't about to wander around, but she didn't want to go inside the house, either.

The helpless anger, her frustration and rage bubbled inside her and then, before she realized it, she hit boiling point. Abruptly, she spun around and glared at Law.

"I didn't *do* this."

For long, long seconds, he stared at her . . . like he couldn't quite comprehend what she was saying.

Then, his voice slow and rough, he said, "What do you mean you didn't do this?"

"Just that." Storming up the stairs, all but shaking as unfamiliar fury swamped her. She knew *fear*. She knew *hesitation*. She knew *doubt*. She knew *anger*.

But this kind of fury? She didn't know it, barely understood it, and she could hardly control it as it came bubbling out.

Her hands trembled as she fumbled with the bandages, tearing them away and letting them fall to the ground. The black sutures looked like an ugly stain against her pale flesh, the thin red scars vivid and raw.

Holding out her wrists, she lifted her eyes and stared at Law.

"*This,*" she snarled. "I didn't do it. Damn it to hell, I didn't do it."

"Hope . . ."

"Don't talk to me in that placating, *Oh, it will be all right* tone, Law. Would you just fucking *think*? You were lying there—hurt, bleeding—you're the one person who matters to me, you really think I could just merrily slit my wrists?" Tears—angry tears, hurt tears, scared tears—blinded her, rolled out of her eyes. Furious, she swiped them away and glared at him. "Just *think*, Law."

For long, long seconds, he stared at her . . . and then comprehension dawned, and abruptly he snarled, "*Son of a bitch*."

He spun around and planted his left fist into the wall so hard, the plaster split.

Staring at the second hand of the clock, Brody tried not to let it show that he felt like he was coming out of his skin.

So his uncle had called his dad. Told the old man he needed to talk to the two of them.

So the fuck what?

Glancing at his dad, he tried to get an idea if the old man had any idea what was going on, but his dad couldn't have looked less interested. His eyes, blue like Brody's, blue like Remy's, had that vague, spaced look as he stared at the screen of his computer—answering e-mail, no doubt. Although how many fucking e-mails could the mayor of a small town have on a daily basis?

Dad spent more time being the *mayor* than he spent being *Dad*. After all, he had the whole town of Ash, Kentucky, population 8,312, depending on him . . . Mayor Henry "Hank" Jennings didn't want to let those people down . . . he just forgot about his son.

He let his son down every fucking day.

It had been like that since Mom died.

Brody no longer existed.

Not for anybody . . .

Feeling the sting of tears in the back of his eyes, he shoved back from the table.

His dad looked up.

Storming over to the refrigerator, Brody said, "Did Uncle Remy say how long he'd be? How long this would take? I got shit to do, ya know."

"No, he didn't say. And stop swearing, Brody." The corners of Hank's mouth went tight and he glanced at the clock. "If he isn't here soon, I'm calling him. I've got work of my own to get done and . . ."

They both heard the roar of an engine.

Turning their heads, they watched as a beat-up, busted-up truck turned off the highway and headed toward their house.

His dad was frowning. "Who is that?" He sighed and muttered, "I don't have time for this."

Brody barely heard him. He stared at that truck, blood roaring in his ears. Remy didn't own a truck . . . but Ezra King did. His gut went to water. Locking his knees, he tried not to let his legs tremble. Told himself to keep his cool.

Pasting a bored expression on his face, he reached into the fridge and grabbed a Coke. King could suspect whatever in the hell he wanted. And maybe he didn't suspect anything. Maybe he didn't know anything. He took a deep gulp of the fizzy, cold drink and managed to ease some of the nerves pitching in his gut.

But then the truck stopped, and Ezra King wasn't the only one who climbed out.

When Brody saw Uncle Remy, his heart almost stopped. Fuck. Yeah. Remy was coming, with King. This wasn't good.

For some reason, he found himself thinking about all those dumb cop shows his dad liked to watch. Found himself remembering how he always wondered why in the hell people tried to run. They'd get caught. They almost always did.

Right then, Brody wanted to run.

More than anything, he wanted to run.

Tightening his hand around the drink, he squeezed and didn't even realize it until the cold liquid bubbled up onto his hand.

"He's going to rabbit," Ezra muttered, glimpsing Brody through the window as he parked his truck alongside the house. Grimacing, he rubbed his thigh and wondered if he was up to chasing down a scared, desperate kid.

"He might." Remy's face could have been carved from stone and his blue eyes looked glacial.

"Think he'd do anything stupid?"

"Shit." Remy shot Ezra a dark look. The charming, surfer-boy looks had been tarnished by stress and grief. He looked tired. Tired and grieving. "He fucking burned a house down. Yeah. I think he could do something stupid."

Feeling bad for him, Ezra shook his head. "That's not what I meant. Houses, hell . . . they burn, yeah, but nobody was hurt. *He* wasn't hurt. Are we going to regret not bringing Nielson out here?"

"Hope not," Remy said. Then he climbed out of the truck.

Yeah, Remy could see Brody rabbiting already, just like Ezra said.

The boy's blue eyes were darker than normal, the pupils huge. His face was pale and sweating.

Shit, just how fucking distracted could Hank be? Remy's older brother had always been the type to focus on the end goal, but Remy would have thought his family would be included in that end goal.

Obviously not, because Hank didn't seem to have a *clue* just how screwed up Brody was right now.

Then again, Hank had been like that for a while.

Ever since Sheryl had died.

As he let Remy and Ezra into the kitchen, Hank said, "I hope you make this quick, Remy. I've got an awful lot of work waiting for me and it doesn't help that you didn't make it here until thirty minutes after you said you would."

"Sit down, Hank," he said quietly. "This is important."

Hank gave him a narrow look. "I've got hours of work left back at my office, phone calls I've got to answer, a meeting coming up tonight, and all sorts of other stuff that's important."

"And all of that should pale in comparison to this," Remy said. *Should. Should . . .* but would it? He just didn't know. Moving to the table, he sat down, careful not to look at Ezra, careful not to look at Brody, although he kept the kid in the corner of his vision.

Ezra watched the boy, too, without really appearing to.

All cop, Remy thought. All cop . . . even in the jeans and T-shirt, moving into the kitchen with just the slightest limp, taking care with that bad leg of his.

"This is Ezra King," Remy said, introducing Ezra to his older brother.

"June King's grandson," Hank said, nodding. "I heard about her old place. Terribly sorry to hear about it. If there's anything I can do . . ."

"Actually, that's why we're here," Remy said. Now he looked at Brody.

Brody tensed.

Under the thin cloth of the black T-shirt he wore, his skinny shoulders were board-straight, so stiff, he looked like he'd shatter.

"Brody," Remy said quietly.

Brody stared at the table. A muscle worked in his jaw.

"Look at me, kid," Remy said. He could remember when this kid had been a baby—a squalling, helpless newborn. Remembered holding him, remembered watching him learn to walk . . . remembered holding him again as he fell and cried. Remembered how the boy had cried when his mother Sheryl died . . . and holding him then.

"Brody."

Slowly, Brody looked up.

But then Hank said, "What in the hell is going on here, Remy?"

At the sound of his dad's voice, Brody flinched and then, he withdrew. Just like that.

Mentally. Remy watched as the boy shut down, his face tight, his eyes going flat and hard.

Sighing, Remy flipped open his briefcase and drew out the gold cross.

That was all it took for the boy's thin veneer of bravado to break. Fear danced across his face, fear, knowledge . . . and then abruptly, there was relief.

"I think maybe we should talk, kid," Remy said.

Hank stared at the cross and looked at Brody, then Remy. "What in the hell is going on?" he asked, his voice cold.

For the first time since Remy had arrived, he really looked at his son.

Hell, it might have been the first time he'd really looked at his son in *years*.

Swearing, Hank turned and grabbed the gold pendant from Remy, staring at it. Then he hurled it down onto the table and started toward his son.

"What in the holy fuck did you do, Brody?"

If they could have kept the dad quiet . . .

* * *

Ezra watched it go from almost okay to outright disastrous in seconds.

The boy had been about ready to open up for his uncle—Ezra had seen the relief in his eyes, glinting just under the tears.

But then the dad had to go and open his mouth.

Still, the kid manned up. Ezra had to admit, he was impressed.

"It was an accident. Well, mostly." He looked from his dad to Ezra, met his gaze and said, his voice catching in the middle, "I'm sorry, Mr. King. I was just so fucking pissed off, and it wasn't even at you. It was just . . . well, everything. But then Uncle Remy was on me about the flowers and shit, and I know that was my fault, too, but I wasn't thinking and . . . and . . . and . . . and . . . well. I'm sorry."

Ezra nodded and looked at Remy. Remy reached inside the briefcase, but before he could say anything, Hank hauled the boy out of the seat, hands cruelly gripping the boy's thin arms. Ezra could see the way the kid's skin went bloodless under that vicious grip.

Bruises would form—he could already tell.

"Sorry? Sorry for what? You tell me exactly what you went and did, damn it. I did not raise some sorry-ass punk."

"Damn it, Hank, that's enough." Remy's voice was cool and level, a hard contrast to the anger in his brother's voice.

Hank looked at his brother and snarled, "You stay the fuck out of this. This isn't any of your concern."

"The hell it isn't. I'm family, remember? And in case it slipped your tiny brain, *arson* is a felony—lawyer here."

Hank looked back at his son. "Arson. You really did

it. Damn it, boy. Admit it. Damn it, be a man and admit to me what you did to that man's house. Admit it."

Brody blinked back the tears as he met his father's gaze. "I burned it down, Dad."

"You little punk. Your mother would be so fucking ashamed. I'm just relieved she's not here to see this," Hank said, his voice harsh and angry. "If she was here now, this just might kill her."

"I'm sorry." The kid's face broke, tears building in his eyes.

The look on that boy's face would linger with Ezra for a good long time. Shoving off the counter, he said quietly, "That's enough."

But the man wasn't in any mood to listen.

"Sorry." Hank shook his head. "You think *sorry* is good enough? After everything I've done to make sure you have a good life, you do this and you think *sorry* is going to cut it?"

Abruptly, Brody laughed, an ugly, broken sound. "A good life?" Tears spilled out of his eyes, and his voice cracked as he stared at his dad. "You call this a good life? You never look at me. You don't even want to know me. You probably wish I'd been the one to die instead of Mom."

"At least then I wouldn't have to clean up the fucking mess you made," Hank bellowed, his face red, his hand coming up.

Ezra saw it coming before anybody else and he moved, barely in time, his leg trying to give out under him. He ignored it, gritting his teeth. Catching Hank's upraised hand, he shoved and twisted, using the man's momentum and weight against him as he slammed the man's upper body down into the table.

From the corner of his eye, he saw the boy take off through the back door, but that was the least of his concerns.

As Hank struggled against him, Ezra said, "Now that, Mr. Mayor, was one very dumb-ass move."

"Get the fuck off of me," Hank snarled.

"Sure. Once you calm down. But if you think I'm going to let you belt that kid, you got another think coming. I think life's knocked him around enough . . . and you haven't helped, it doesn't look like."

He looked up at Remy and saw that the man was staring at his brother like he was a stranger.

CHAPTER
SIX

Hope...

He could see her, just up there, pacing back and forth on the porch.

Why didn't she come down?

Come closer?

A breeze kicked up, and long, gleaming brown hair blew back from her face.

He closed his eyes, imagined wrapping those long, long strands around his wrists, seeing her on her knees.

Lust, hunger, rage mingled and mixed inside him. Saliva pooled in his mouth and he rested a hand against a tree trunk, had to fight to keep from moving closer.

Now wasn't the time—

Not now.

He really wishes I was dead.

Swiping the back of his hand under his nose, Brody shoved past the bushes, past the low-hanging branches.

Tears burned in his eyes, blinded him, but he didn't stop walking.

He'd run forever, until the burning in his lungs made him quit, and now he just walked.

He wasn't very sure where he was, either. Somewhere

in the woods near the Ohlman property, he thought. Maybe close to Lena's. Too close to home, that was sure.

He wanted to just keep running, too.

Pushing a hand into his pocket, he checked again, half hoping somehow something miraculous would have happened. Maybe the seventeen lousy dollars he had would turn into more money and he could just disappear. He really, really wanted to just disappear.

Wasn't like his dad would miss him.

Remy might have, but after what he'd done, Remy probably hated him.

A sob tore free and Brody stumbled, fell against a tree. "I didn't mean to do it," he whispered. "I didn't mean to . . ."

But it was too late to think about that, now. He'd done it. He'd fucked it up, royally, and now, not only did his dad despise him, Uncle Remy probably did, too. Up until now, at least Remy had still loved him, but now he didn't even have that.

Shoving away from the tree, once more, he started to walk.

He'd just keep walking for now.

Sooner or later, he'd figure out what he should do.

He didn't want to go home, and Dad definitely didn't want him around.

Hours passed and he found himself standing off in the distance, too far away to clearly see the King house, but close enough to see the ruin of it. He'd done that.

Man, Mom *would* be ashamed. Tears burned his eyes, but he blinked them away. He'd done enough crying now. He needed to figure out what he should do.

A shudder wracked him as he thought about the way his dad had looked at him. Go home . . . ? Could he do that?

Maybe what he should do was just go to Remy's place.

"What would you want, Mom?" he whispered.

He'd done something really, really wrong . . . and she always told him when he made a mistake, he had to own up to it. That's what decent people did—that was what she would want from him.

Swallowing, he turned away.

He needed to go to Remy. That was what he needed to do. His gut clenched, knotted. He'd gotten in enough trouble lately to know it wasn't going to be pretty, but . . .

"Don't think about it," he told himself.

"Just don't think about it. Do it, get it over with, but don't think about it."

Just as he was turning into Lena's driveway, his phone rang. Ezra grabbed it, hoped it was good news, even though he already knew it wasn't.

"Any sign of him?"

"Shit, no," Remy said.

Ezra rubbed his eyes and wished he had a beer. And a chair. Definitely a chair. His leg was killing him.

They'd spent the past three hours trying to find Brody Jennings, with no luck. Night was coming on, too. It left a bad, bad feeling in his gut to think of that kid out there in the dark right now, especially with the crazy-ass shit they had going on around here right now.

If they didn't find the kid soon . . .

Shit. What could they do?

"Has your brother cooled down any?"

"Yes." There was a strange tension in Remy's voice and Ezra decided the two brothers had some issues they needed to work out—badly. Hank Jennings needed to get *over* his issues, whatever in the hell they were. He'd lost his wife, and Ezra felt bad for him, but it looked like he'd been neglecting his kid and the bastard needed to wake the hell up.

That kid needed to be his priority.

"Does he have any idea where Brody might have gone?"

"No." Remy paused and then added, "They don't talk much. I can tell you that Brody doesn't have many friends—he's too quiet, too withdrawn lately. If he'd taken his four-wheeler, I'd have a better idea where to look, but he's on foot."

"We keep looking, then." Parking the truck, he turned it off and climbed out.

"Maybe we should just let him come home when he's ready."

"No." Ezra wasn't about to ignore that bad itchy feeling in his gut. It was the sort of feeling that had him wishing he had his gun—except it had been locked up in his house and while it could probably be repaired, it sure as hell wasn't usable right now. "Look, I'm picking up Lena, running her over to Law's place, then I'll head back out. I'll keep looking for him."

"You don't need to, King. You're already—"

"I'll keep looking," Ezra interrupted. "And you need to do the same. Too much weird shit going on around here for that kid to be out there by himself. Night's moving in, Jennings. We want him found—*tonight*. Call in favors if you need to, see if Nielson can send some of his guys out."

There was another moment of silence and then Remy started to curse, long and low. The phone abruptly went dead and Ezra shoved it into his pocket as he headed for the house.

He'd take care of Lena, first . . . then worry about the kid some more.

He'd forgotten how dark it got in the woods.

Stumbling along, Brody shoved his hands inside his

pockets and focused on the faint flicker of lights ahead. He wasn't sure whose house it was, but he didn't care.

It wasn't *his* house and that was all that mattered.

Whoever it was, he'd ask to use the phone and he'd call Uncle Remy.

A chill raced through him as he thought what might come after that, but he had to do it. Wasn't like . . .

Somebody moved out from behind a tree.

Brody's brain shut down.

In the dim, pre-dusk light, with his aching head and heavy heart, he could almost think he'd fallen into a nightmare.

The man wore camo, from head to toe, and not just his body, but everywhere. Even the guy's face was covered, his eyes shielded behind some sort of goggles that made him look alien.

Brody might have been cool with that.

Except the man held a gun in his hand. And as he stared at Brody, he cocked his head to the side, staring at him like he was some sort of lab specimen. Staring at him . . . like he had already ceased to exist for this freak.

Brody could hear his own breath wheezing out of him, felt the cold trickle of sweat roll down his spine. Blood roared in his ears. Terror gripped him hard and tight, and suddenly, the anger he felt at his dad evaporated—he wanted his dad.

Desperately.

Swallowing, too scared to move, but knowing he needed to, he stared at the man.

With a stillness and silence that barely seemed human, the man tilted his head . . . and slowly lifted that gun.

Brody darted behind one of the trees and took off running. Branches grabbed at him. Roots seemed to snake up out of the ground and grab at his feet. He stumbled, tripped, and each time, he shoved upright and kept on running.

* * *

Stupid little fuck . . .

Irritated, he melted back into the woods.

He'd had some interesting plans for the night, but now, he'd have to rethink things.

He had wanted to go and watch her a little more.

Watch her *closer* even . . . perhaps let her know he was there.

He supposed he could have dealt with the boy, but that wasn't in the plans.

He had to keep to his plan. When you veered from the plan, things got fucked up.

Shooting one look over his shoulder toward the house, he began the long walk through the trees.

It wasn't a problem to wait.

He was, after all, a patient man.

"Have you tried calling her?"

Roz nibbled on her thumbnail and debated whether or not to answer him. Finally she sighed and looked at her husband. "No. She doesn't want to talk to me."

"Well, you had a fight. You two won't ever get over it if you don't try to talk it through," Carter said softly. He sank down on the narrow little couch that graced her office and wrapped an arm around her, cuddling her close.

She leaned against him, pressing her face to his chest. "I know. I just . . ." Groaning, she pulled away and stood up, pacing the office. "She doesn't talk. She comes in, she does her job, and she leaves. Geez, even *Puck* is giving me the cold shoulder."

Carter chuckled. "I noticed. He doesn't want to have anything to do with either of us."

"That's my fault, too, I guess. The dog always knows when she's mad and he gets upset. He won't relax until she does." Roz leaned against her desk and crossed her arms, staring at him. "I miss her, baby."

Those blue eyes of hers were just miserable, he thought, studying her. "I know. So that means you need to decide what to do. You can't expect this to go away if you don't ever talk to her."

"I know." She shifted her gaze to the floor. Absently, she pulled her phone out. "Maybe . . . maybe Ezra could bring her over for dinner. I could talk to her then . . . ?"

"You'll work it out." He stood up and crossed the floor, pressed his lips to her forehead. "I need to get to work. Some slave driver mean lady in Kentucky is demanding I get some more pots for the inn she runs."

Roz smiled at him, but it wasn't much of a smile. "Slave driver, huh? I'd like some more of those rose-colored ones if you can. You still make that glaze, right?"

"A bit, yeah. I'll see what I can do." Hopefully she'd call Lena while he was working. But he wasn't counting on it. She'd sit in here and brood and worry. Stroking a thumb over her cheek, he asked, "Why don't you come to the shop with me? Maybe toss a pot on the wheel or something . . . relax a bit?"

She just made a face. "No, thanks."

Carter sighed. "Don't brood over this too long, sweetheart."

"How is Hope handling this?" Lena asked.

"I don't know. Hell, it *seems* like she's handling it better than I am, but I keep waiting for her to . . ."

"Break?"

"Yeah." Law hated himself for saying it, for thinking it.

"I don't think you're giving her enough credit, man." Lena sighed and drew her feet up, tucking them up next to her on the couch and resting her chin on an upraised fist. "She . . . well, I know she seems pretty damn fragile and I know she's been through hell, but sometimes, that's what a person has to do to figure out what they are made of. I get the feeling Hope's hit her stopping point—she's done. As in fed-up *done*."

Law wanted to think so, but after the shit she'd lived through, he would have thought she would have hit that point awhile ago. If anybody could have made her hit that point, it would have been Joey, but it hadn't happened. Instead, the bastard had all but broken her.

"I don't know, Lena. She *has* been through hell—if she was going to hit some line, you'd think it would have already happened."

She shrugged. "Maybe he, and I'm going to assume there was a he, was pushing the wrong buttons. This time, it wasn't just *her* getting screwed with. It was her, it was you." A vicious smile curled her lips and she shook her head. "You don't know what she was like while you were still out, Law. She was almost another person."

"Shit." He snorted. "She's been like another person ever since we got out of the hospital—it's almost like . . . well, back in high school, she was always quieter, but she had a mouth on her. You wouldn't think it, unless you knew her well. But she had an attitude. Had . . . something, you know? Then . . . hell, I can't go into that—it's her life, but that part of her, I thought it died. The past few days, I think I'm seeing it again, but I don't know. I don't want to think she's going to be okay, and then miss something I need to see because I'm not watching."

Lena laughed for a moment. Her laughter faded and she slid her shaded lenses off, laid them on the couch. She slid off the couch and slowly made her way over to the chair where he was sitting. When she lifted a hand, he caught it. As she eased her weight down on the arm of the chair, he slid an arm around her waist, tried not to think about how fucking close she was—how good she felt, how warm she was.

Not mine, he reminded himself. She was completely gone over the damn cop, crazy about King, all because he'd waited too long.

Lena pressed a kiss to his brow. Then softly, she said, "Law . . . honey . . . don't take this the wrong way, but I don't think it's humanly possible for you to miss something important. You don't ever miss the small things. If there's something going on with her, you're going to see it. But man, you need to ease up . . . and trust her. Let her find her feet, let her try to stand on her own. If her life has been that much hell, and she's just now trying to find her feet again, then what she needs more than anything is to do just that . . . on her own."

He sighed. Told himself she was probably right.

But when the door to the porch opened, he couldn't stop himself from getting to his feet.

Behind him, Lena snickered.

"Way to let her stand, Law."

She could hear Law talking to Lena, and as she slipped into the kitchen, she heard Lena laughing.

Hope slipped out the back door, winced as it creaked behind her. Man, she hoped Law hadn't heard that—

But he didn't immediately appear. He was yakking it up with Lena, probably talking about her, too.

Ezra had driven up, spoken briefly with Law and then left. Lena hadn't told Hope anything. Neither had Law, and now the two of them were inside, whispering and murmuring and Hope felt like she was about to scream.

She felt like her skin was going to split, she was so edgy, but she wasn't going to take off, either.

She was tired of running away from shit, because the

shit she had to run from was all trapped inside her. She couldn't get away from that.

She was tired of having Law look at her like she was going to break . . . even though she knew it was probably justified.

She *had* broken before.

Her stomach twisted in hot, slippery knots as she covered her face with her hands.

Just because she'd broken before didn't mean she was going to do it again. Didn't mean she needed him hovering around her and worrying about her like she was made of glass, too fragile, too delicate.

Hearing the door open behind her, she glanced over her shoulder. "Damn it, Law, I'm just sitting on the porch—I'm *fine*. And I want to be *alone*."

"I was just wondering if you wanted a jacket. Some coffee . . ."

Swallowing a groan, she stood up and turned around, staring at him. "No, you're wanting to check up on me. Make sure I'm not out here panicking, or freaking, or falling apart, or getting ready to run away again or whatever you worry I might do. I'm fine, Law. And I need to be alone."

His mouth tightened and part of her wanted to take it back—she knew he was worried, knew he worried because he cared . . .

"Damn it, Hope, I don't know what in the hell you want me to do—not worry?" he snarled. He caught one of her hands, gently, careful of the wound, and lifted it up, exposing it to the light. "Somebody did that to you—somebody tried to kill you and I'm not supposed to worry?"

Narrowing her eyes, she reached up and deliberately poked him in the swollen area just below his left eye.

He yelped and let go of her wrist. "What the hell was that for?"

"You don't exactly look like *Little Mary Sunshine*, buddy. The same person who did this to me did *that* to you. You want to worry about me, fine. I'm worried about you, too, but you don't see me hovering at your shoulder twenty-four-seven."

He folded his arms across his chest. "It's not the same."

"Of course not," she said quietly. She looked back at her wrists and then sighed. "It's not the same because I'm me . . . and I'm always afraid of everything—I'm too weak to fight back. But damn it, how in the hell am I supposed to get any better when you're constantly try-ing to prop me up?"

"Hope, I'm not . . ." Then he sighed, his voice trailing off. He shoved a hand through his hair. "I'm just, hell, I don't know how to handle this. I wanted you here so you could feel safer, start to heal. And look what hap-pens to you."

"This isn't your fault." Hope looked away. "We didn't see this coming—how could we? But, Law, damn it, you've got to quit hovering. You're making me claustro-phobic. I'm *okay*, I swear. But I need some space, or I'm going to freak out."

Hating the sad, miserable look in his eyes, hating that she couldn't . . . or *wouldn't* do anything to make it go away, she turned her back on him and refused to look back.

Eventually, she heard him slip back inside.

Still, she didn't look back.

She stared off into the distance, into the coming night. All she wanted to do was sit on the back porch. Surely she could do that.

Looking down at her wrists, she tried to resign herself to what she was going to have to do in the morning.

The damned sheriff's office. File a report. Even though it was probably going to be a waste of time, because nobody was going to believe her. They all either thought she was crazy and determined to kill herself, or they thought she was crazy and wanted to hurt Law.

At least it was Nielson, the sheriff they'd be talking to. Law had agreed to that, at least. She could almost handle talking to him.

Something rustled in the woods off to the side. A branch cracked. Jerking her head up, Hope caught her breath. She climbed to her feet and almost darted inside the house—okay, maybe she *couldn't* handle sitting outside alone.

Then a boy tumbled out of the trees.

A boy . . . a crying boy who was as tall as she was.

But still, it was just a kid. And one who looked vaguely familiar.

Instead of backing into the house, she hopped down the two steps and jogged across the grass to him. "Hey, are you okay?"

Behind her, the door banged open.

But Hope barely noticed.

As the boy's eyes locked on her face, all she could think was, *He's so scared* . . .

His hands came up, gripped her upper arms. His throat worked, like he was having a hard time speaking without sobbing.

"There . . . there was somebody in the woods," he said, his voice cracking, the way a boy's does when he's caught in that place between childhood and manhood. His hands squeezed, not to hurt, but with desperate terror, as though he needed to make sure she was really there.

His eyes, huge and blue, dominated a thin face that was terribly familiar.

"Somebody . . . in the woods," he whispered, his voice low and quiet. He shot a terrified glance over his shoulder and then he looked back at her. Abruptly, some of that clouded fear cleared from his eyes, he released her arms and reached for her hand. "He had a gun and he was right over there. It's not safe. We should get inside—call the sheriff or something."

As he started to pull her toward the house, Hope caught sight of Law standing on the porch, his familiar scowl drawing his face tight.

"Brody, damn it, your uncle is looking all over for you—you've got him worried sick," Law snapped.

"Law," she said.

As though she hadn't said anything, Law pointed toward the house. "You need to get inside—call him, now."

"Damn it, Law, ease up. The kid's terrified," Hope said. She gently disentangled her hand from the boy's grasp—he might be rail-thin, but he was stronger than hell. "He says he saw somebody out in the woods."

Law's eyes narrowed, focused on Brody's face. "Is that right?"

Brody wiped a hand over the back of his mouth. "He . . . a gun. Had a gun."

"A gun." Lena appeared in the doorway. "What?"

A scowl darkened Law's battered face and he jerked his head toward the house. "Get inside, Brody. Call Remy. He's scouring the entire county looking for you. Call him, then you tell me about this guy you think you saw."

As the boy headed inside, Hope's brain abruptly ceased functioning. "Remy?" she said quietly, hoping none of the emotion she felt inside showed.

Apparently, it didn't. Law was staring off into the trees, a frown on his face. "Yeah. That's Brody Jennings. Remy is his uncle. Come on . . . we should all get aside."

As the door banged closed behind them, she realized that Remy Jennings would be here. In a matter of minutes.

The kid's uncle.

Hope swallowed.

Her heart started to pound.

Idly, she wondered if she could lock herself inside her room and not come out until this . . . whatever was over with.

Then she closed her eyes and reminded herself. *No. You stopped running; remember?*

But part of her still wanted to go lock herself away in her room. She'd stopped running from her past, and she wanted to stop running from the things that terrified her—

Remy did a lot more than just scare her, so she wasn't sure he really qualified.

As they turned down the long drive that led toward Law Reilly's house, Hank's eyes opened and he said, "Reilly did say he was okay, right?"

"Yes. He's fine. Just scared—something spooked him in the woods."

Hank gave a jerky nod. A sad, shamed look showed on his face and he sighed. "You know I could kick my own ass for what I said to him—I love my son, Remy. You know that. But the past couple years . . . they've been hard."

"You think they haven't been hard on him? He's just a kid, and he lost his mother, and to him, it probably feels like he lost his dad. You shut him out completely—hell, anybody with eyes can see it. Now he feels like his dad doesn't love him and wants him dead," Remy said. He hurt for his brother, but he hurt for the kid more.

He was so damned pissed off at Hank—man, he could just shake the stupid bastard. Shake him, hit him, anything to make him wake up and see what he was doing to his son.

Brody was so messed up, so unhappy and scared.

Remy never thought the day would come when he'd be ashamed of his brother, but . . . now? Yeah. He was ashamed of Hank. He knew grief did bad, bad things to the mind, but he couldn't believe what he'd heard coming out of Hank's mouth, what Hank might have done if Ezra hadn't been so quick to react.

"That boy deserved better, Hank," he said, shaking his head. "A hell of a lot better."

"I know he did, and I've got a lot of work ahead of me if I want to fix things with my boy." Then Hank sighed. "But, well, and this is my fault, completely, but you know that Brody's got problems. I wouldn't be surprised if he's making up this story about a guy with a gun, trying to deflect the trouble he knows is coming."

The thought had occurred to Remy—briefly.

But he figured Brody had had enough crap dumped on him already. Remy wasn't going to make any unfair judgments. Yet.

"He deserved better the past few years," Remy repeated quietly. "And he deserves to at least have us listen to him without judging him. Maybe you can't give him that, but I sure as hell can—and I will."

A pair of lights appeared in his rearview mirror. A few minutes later, as he parked in front of Law's house, he recognized Ezra's truck in the darkness. Grimacing, he eyed the cop as he climbed out of the truck.

"Seeing you way too much today, King," he said.

"Not exactly how I'd planned to spend the day, either." Ezra jerked his head toward the house. "But if your nephew's here, then I can get Lena and go home. It's been one long-ass day."

He shifted his gaze to Hank. "Mayor."

Hank inclined his head. "Detective King. I . . . well, I hope you can understand, it's been a rough day all around. I wasn't in the clearest frame of mind earlier."

"I imagine not. Your kid hasn't exactly had the clearest frame of mind for a while, though. Something you might want to keep in mind," Ezra said pointedly as he started for the house.

Hank's mouth tightened. "Trust me, I'm well aware of that."

Remy reached up and rubbed the back of his neck. This day, it just wasn't going to get any better before it ended, was it?

Then he knocked on the door and it took yet another crazy turn on him.

He should have been prepared to see her.

Really.

But when the door opened and Hope Carson stood there, framed in a wedge of light, those dreamy, green eyes so sad and quiet, her mouth solemn and unsmiling, Remy thought his heart just might stop.

There just wasn't any way he *could* prepare himself for seeing her. There wasn't any way he could prepare himself for what seeing her *did* to him, mentally, physically, emotionally.

Shit.

Oh, shit, he did *not* need this.

Lust reached up and grabbed him around the throat, squeezing and choking the air from his lungs even as it heated the blood in his veins.

This was the absolute last woman on earth he should want—she was trouble, in so many ways. She was *troubled*, and that was just one of the reasons he didn't need this.

This was the absolute last woman on earth he *wanted* to want—she just plain and simple *was* trouble—he could feel that in his bones.

And yet, as he stared into those big, green eyes, he did want.

Hell, did he want.

But *wanting* was only part of it, he suspected.

It was so much deeper than that, so much more.

The world fell away and he forgot about his brother, he forgot about the cop standing just a few feet away, forgot about his nephew. Forgot about anything and everything except her.

Behind him, Ezra cleared his throat.

Hank lost his already shoddy grip on control and shoved past Remy, pushing his way impatiently inside the house. As he did, he brushed close to Hope.

Too close, judging by the look in her eyes.

Something danced across her face and she pulled away, sidestepping him and averting her face . . . hiding that fear.

Abruptly, the hot fury of lust bled into anger—that fear. What had caused it? *Who* had caused it?

Why in the hell was she always so afraid?

His hands itched. He wanted to reach up, touch her face, brush that dark, silken hair back from her face and promise her she didn't need to be afraid.

Shit.

As her eyes shifted to his and then away, Remy reminded himself he really, really needed to stay the hell away from this woman.

As the three men pushed inside Law's house, Hope reminded herself . . . *You're not running. You're not running.*

Ezra paused at her side and reached out, rested a hand on her shoulder. A month ago, she would have flinched, but she was able to give him a shaky smile as he asked, "How are you feeling?"

"Okay."

His eyes, a sharp, intelligent green, lingered on hers, and her smile wobbled, faded. "Maybe not so okay, but I'm still here."

He nodded, squeezed her shoulder. He pushed the

door shut and then, in a friendly, easy gesture that she couldn't easily evade without feeling silly, he slung an arm over her shoulder. "You taking care of Law or is he taking care of you?"

From the corner of her eye, she saw Remy, was acutely aware of him watching her. Feeling the rush of blood creeping up her cheeks, she tried to focus on Ezra, on anything but how nervous the other man made her feel. "Ah, maybe both. He's still not feeling too great. Tired, and sore, but he won't take the pain medicine so that's to be expected."

"And you?"

He didn't look at her wrists, but he didn't have to. She knew what he was asking. Tension crept up her spine and she eased away from him, suddenly unable to have him touching her, even though a moment ago, it had felt . . . well, almost easy. Friendly. Almost the way it felt when Law gave her one of his easy, friendly hugs.

She didn't feel so easy and friendly right now—she was pissed *off*.

"I'm just peachy," she said, her voice sharp. Stalking past Remy and Ezra, past the silent third man, she moved into the kitchen and joined Law, Lena, and Brody at the table. Meeting Law's gaze, she said, "We've got company, Law. Lena, Ezra's here."

A red brow arched. Dark lenses hid Lena's sightless eyes. "Ahhh . . . what did he do?"

Ezra came into the kitchen and said, "I don't think I did anything."

"He didn't do anything," Hope agreed, keeping her voice flat. She wasn't going into this, wasn't talking about it.

Not with the kid here.

The kid. Focus on the kid.

Brody . . . his name was Brody.

He sat at the table, his head bent, his shoulders slumped.

And as the third man came into the kitchen, those thin shoulders stiffened even more.

A heavy, uncomfortable silence fell, like a cold, wet blanket.

Remy moved up to the table and settled down in one of the seats. "Hey, kid," he said softly.

Brody shot him a quick look and then focused on the table again.

It was so damned quiet, Hope could actually hear the seconds ticking away on the clock.

It was broken, finally, when the third man moved forward. He gave her a genial, practiced smile . . . a politician's smile, she thought. "Hello. I'm Hank Jennings, Brody's dad. I'm sorry if he's bothered you."

He went as though to hold a hand out and she pushed hers into her back pockets, careful not to rub the stitches against her jeans. Frowning, she said, "He's scared to death—that's hardly a bother, Mr. Jennings."

"Actually, it's Mayor Jennings," Lena said from behind Hope.

Mayor. Hope smirked inwardly. Now why wasn't she surprised? "Mayor Jennings, then. But he hasn't been a bother."

He inclined his head and then shifted his gaze to his son. "Come on, Brody. We should get home. We've got things to discuss."

Hope opened her mouth to say something else, anything else. But then she closed it, looking over at the boy. He looked sad, scared . . . alone. She didn't know what was going on with him, but she knew what it felt like to feel sad, scared . . . alone. To be so totally isolated from anybody and everybody, with nobody around who could help, who would listen.

Behind her, Law said quietly, "Maybe you should hear what happened."

The mayor shook his head. "He can discuss it at home. Privately. We've got issues to discuss and he's taken up enough of your day."

Hope edged away. From the corner of her eye, she could see Law's face, see the way his lip curled as he stared at the mayor. It reassured her—she was glad she wasn't the only one who didn't quite like the way this guy was handling his scared kid.

Of course, Law was more vocal about his dislike. His voice thick with disdain, he drawled, "Yeah, sure. Those private issues are more important than the fact that he ran into somebody in the woods near my place. That the guy had a gun, one he decided to point at your kid. Fine, Mayor, but man, I really question your priorities."

"My son—"

"Hank." Remy stood up, one hand resting protectively on the boy's shoulder.

Hope found herself staring at him, barely hearing whatever he said next. Despite her determination to not look at that man, not think about him, she couldn't not look at him.

He was staring at the other man. Brothers, she realized belatedly. They had to be. They looked too much alike to not be related. But where Remy had warmth, the other one was nothing but ice, it seemed.

Hank shifted his gaze to Law, then to the boy. "Okay, Brody. Why don't you tell me what's going on?"

CHAPTER
SEVEN

Rain and funerals.

What was it about rain and funerals?

Off in the distance, thunder rumbled and lightning flashed. Some of the mourners cast nervous looks at the clouds, but those standing closest to the graveside ignored the weather.

They'd come to say good-bye and a hurricane wouldn't have pulled them away.

Nia stood at the graveside, a white rose in her hand as she stared at the pale pink coffin.

Bryson, Joely's fiancé, stood at her side.

He stank of whiskey, but he was sober, his dark brown eyes ravaged by grief, his face gaunt.

He had loved Joely, Nia knew. Maybe he hadn't been able to be there for one of the last things he could have done for Joely—standing at Nia's side when it came time to claim the body—but Bryson had loved Joely.

As much as all of this hurt, she was happy her cousin had had the guy, even if it was just for a while. Nia suspected it was the first time he'd been sober since he'd learned about Joely's death.

Distantly, she felt kind of sorry for him. But it was distant.

She stared at the coffin, tried to find the good memories, tried to remember the laughter, the fun times.

But all she could see was the last, awful memory . . . the one of Joely lying in a morgue, her face so battered Nia had barely recognized her.

Who did that to you, baby? Who did it?

"What we have here is a clusterfuck."

Remy snorted and almost sprayed his coffee across the room. Setting his mug down, he grabbed a handful of tissues from the box on the sheriff's desk and wiped them across his mouth and then checked his shirt and tie. "A clusterfuck."

"Yep," Nielson murmured. "It's when you just get a whole bunch of shit going wrong all at once."

"I know what a clusterfuck is," he said dryly. And he had to admit—*clusterfuck* described things to a T.

"So the mayor is okay with getting Brody into residential treatment?"

"Shit, no." Remy scowled as he thought about the past night. He hadn't had more than two hours of sleep, and once he was done here, he had even more work to do. Sleep was a luxury that would have to wait. "He's very much *not* okay with it . . . but I think he realizes he doesn't have much choice. King will draw a hard line on it if he has to, and maybe that's not a bad thing. At least he sees that Brody needs help. Hank . . . well, he *knows* it, but I think he wants to try to fix things himself. But Brody needs more than that. Right now, I think Brody will actually feel better away from his dad, as much as that hurts to say."

"How is your mom handling it?"

Remy grimaced. "About the same way you'd expect. It's breaking her heart—Brody's the only grandchild she has."

Nielson was quiet for a moment and then finally, he

said, "I've always wanted to think that a family's love heals everything—but sometimes, when the hurts go that deep, you have to get the poison out first. Brody's got a lot of hurt, a lot of poison trapped inside him. I know Hank loves him—I remember the way they were back before Sheryl died. But maybe this is a way to get that poison out, and then they can both heal."

"Yeah. Maybe." Brooding, Remy stared off into the distance. "Shit. I should have seen how bad it was before now."

Then he sighed and made himself focus on the here and now. "What do you think about the guy he says he saw?"

"Your brother doesn't think he saw anything." Nielson peered up at him over the rim of his glasses. "I've got Mabry out there, though, going through the woods. If there's anything out there to be seen, he'll see it."

Mabry, the deputy sheriff. Yeah, if things could be found, he'd be the one to do it.

"You think he'll find anything?" Remy asked.

"Do you? I can tell you . . . your brother doesn't think we'll find anything, because he doesn't think anything happened."

"Shit." Remy shook his head. "I get that, and I get why, and that's not what I asked."

"I can't discount either possibility." Dwight sighed and smoothed a hand back over his scalp. "Here's the thing, though. That boy? Well, he had a fear in his eyes, don't you think?"

Nielson had ended up out at Law's place that night, after all. Even hours later, when Remy had gone home with Hank and Brody, the kid had been shaken up. Terrified.

Fear in his eyes? That was putting it mildly.

"Yeah," he said softly. "He was afraid, all right."

Remy thought about that fear, thought about how

pale Brody had been. How his blue eyes had looked all but black in his young face. That fear, it hadn't come from his dad. It was new. Different.

There was a knock at the door and Remy looked up as Nielson's dragon doorkeeper opened the door. Law was there . . . and Hope.

Her eyes glanced over him like he wasn't even there. They bounced over to the sheriff, filled with that familiar strain.

"We're a little early," Law said. He had a hand on Hope's shoulder.

The look on her face was closed in, shut down.

Tense.

Frowning, Remy shot the sheriff a look, then looked back at Law and Hope. "What are you doing here, Law?"

"It's a personal matter, Remy," the sheriff said softly.

Hope tugged on the sleeves of the shirt she wore. Under the hem, he could see her narrow wrists, caught a glimpse of one of the long, narrow scars—vivid red, sliced with neat, black sutures.

A vivid, painful reminder of just how badly he did *not* need to be thinking about this woman.

Slowly, he stood. "We can finish our business later, then." Grabbing his briefcase, he started for the door. Law ushered Hope inside.

Remy's heart did a rough, angry jitter inside his chest as she continued to fidget with her sleeves and before he could stop himself, he came to a halt. Right in front of her. Close . . . close enough that he could smell the scent of her hair, the scent of her skin. Close enough that he could see the soft green of her eyes darken as her lashes fluttered.

"You can get help, Hope. You don't need to live with whatever has you so torn up inside."

Help . . .

Hope stared at him, into those dark blue eyes, and to her surprise, she laughed. It wasn't an *amused* laugh— hell, it hurt her ears, her chest—it was like she was vomiting razor blades.

And as quickly as it came on, it faded and she found herself staring at him.

She could meet his eyes, she realized. She could stare into those blue eyes without wanting to hide.

When had that changed?

When had *she* changed?

Being able to look a man she barely knew square in the eye?

Even this man—

No. *Especially* this man.

"Help. Yeah, I imagine if I had the problems you *think* I have, help would be exactly what I should be looking for." Then she turned away from him. Over her shoulder, she said quietly, "You don't *know* me, Mr. Jennings. You might think you do, and I'm sure you gathered your nice, neat little history on me, but you don't know jackshit."

Feeling the weight of his stare, she focused on the sheriff.

It was harder to look at Nielson, harder to meet his eyes. Was it the uniform? Was it because of who he was? Hope didn't know.

Her throat tried to lock down on her and she knew she'd have to force herself to say every last word, just as she had to force herself to look at him as she settled in the straight-backed, wooden chair. It was as miserably uncomfortable as it looked. Perching on the edge, she folded her hands, pressed them together between her knees.

"Let's get this over with," she said, her voice gritty and rough.

She didn't want to be here. Didn't want to be anywhere even close to here.

Still feeling the weight of Remy Jennings's gaze, the
weight of Law's gaze, the sheriff's, Hope wanted to be
anywhere *but* here.

Her knees were knocking, all but slamming together
and she knew if she hadn't been sitting down, she might
have fallen down. She still wasn't feeling completely re-
covered from the blood loss and right now, she felt
slightly nauseated, light-headed, and more than off-
balance. It hadn't helped that she'd been too worried to
eat that morning, but now, she desperately wished she'd
been able to force at least something down her throat.

Panic crowded into her mind and she clenched her
fists. Pain tore through her wrists and she hissed out a
breath, forced herself to relax her hands.

A hand touched her shoulder. Squeezed lightly.
"Hope."

Law's voice cut through the chaos in her mind. She
sucked in a desperate breath of air, forced herself to
think through the impending panic attack. *Not going
there, not going there . . .*

She wasn't trapped in here—she was here because she
wanted to be, needed to be. She could get up and walk
out whenever she wanted.

Law bent down, put his mouth right next to her ear.
In a quiet, soft voice, he said, "Take a deep breath.
Come on, kid. You don't want to fall apart *here*. Not
here, for crying out loud."

No. Not here. It was the best thing he could have said.

Opening her mouth, she gulped in a deep breath.
Then another. Then, finally, she made herself take another, slower breath, and blew it out.

One . . .

Two . . .

Three . . .

The dark swirl of panic started to ease, started to fade.

Four . . .

Five . . .

She opened her eyes, uncurled her fists, and rested her palms on her thighs.

Six . . .

Seven . . .

Lifting her head, she made herself look at the sheriff. He pretended to be absorbed in something else, giving her some modicum of privacy.

Eight

Nine . . .

Behind her, Remy Jennings was still standing there, watching her.

Ten.

Watching her. Watching as she fell apart.

For some reason, that was all it took for her to clear the rest of the panic from her mind.

You don't know me, she thought again. Squaring her shoulders, she took one more steadying breath.

Damn it, you don't *know me.*

Just then, the door behind her quietly closed.

The room suddenly felt larger . . . and colder. Darker.

Man, maybe she *was* crazy.

She should breathe easier with him gone. So why was there suddenly an ache in her chest?

Stop thinking about him. Even if you could handle any sort of relationship, the man thinks you're a nutjob.

Besides, she was here to try to convince the sheriff she wasn't a nutjob—might be easier to do if she didn't keep acting like one.

Pushing Remy out of her head, she looked at the sheriff.

He had stopped pretending to work and waited patiently, with a kind smile on his face . . . the same sort of smile Ezra had, she thought.

And nice eyes. But they were still a cop's eyes.

Swallowing, she made herself hold his gaze. She couldn't keep living in terror—she couldn't.

"Law tells me there's a problem with the story of events we got. Like about what happened with you," he said softly.

Hope nodded jerkily.

"Are you going to tell me about it?"

She licked her lips. Feeling Law standing at her back, she almost looked at him—needed that support, that strength. But damn it, she'd jumped all over him hovering. Now was the time to prove she *could* stand on her own, right?

Now *was* the time. Now . . . or never.

Taking a deep breath, she pushed up the long sleeves of the T-shirt she wore, baring the healing wounds on her wrists. "I . . . I didn't do this, Sheriff," she said, her voice hitching.

"Okay. Do you remember how it happened?"

"No." She did look at Law, then. "We'd just gotten into the house. Weren't there any more than a few minutes. The lights were out. He'd gone down to the basement to reset the breaker. Then he came up . . . after that, things get blurry. I remember seeing Prather—just his face—he was on the floor in Law's office. I only saw the man's face, but I knew something was wrong. He was on the floor and I don't think I *thought* he was dead, but I knew something wasn't right. I was scared. Then I turned around—saw Law."

Her voice hitched, catching in her throat as the memories started to slam into her, fear building. She paused, closed her eyes. She had to get through this—had to. Swallowing, she counted to ten and then whispered, "I saw something behind Law, a shadow. Just a shadow, somebody behind him. I, uh . . . I . . . I think I must have passed out. I was so scared. I . . . um, well, I don't do fear well. And I was *so* scared . . . but I wouldn't have done this.

"Not with him hurt." She found herself staring at Law's battered face. If she'd woken up, seen her best friend—her *only* friend—lying there, hurt and needing help; no. She knew she wasn't very strong, but she knew she wouldn't have decided to go and slit her wrists. "Not if Law needed help. No matter how scared I was."

Then she looked at the sheriff, braced, prepared for him to dismiss her, to brush it off.

Instead, he nodded. "Okay. I don't know what more we can do other than take a report, but we will do that."

"You . . ." She swallowed. "You believe me?"

He sighed. "Ms. Carson, I didn't think you had hurt Law, but somebody went to considerable trouble to make it look like you had. This? Well, it's not a surprise that somebody decided to try to take things even further. It's sickening, yes. But not surprising."

You don't know me . . .

Why did those words keep ringing in his head hours later?

Scowling, Remy tried to focus on the screen, but he was having a damn hard time. He needed to be ready for a case in the morning, and the last thing he needed to be doing was thinking about Hope Carson—who was no longer any of his concern, really.

You don't know me.

No. He didn't, and it would be best if he kept it that way.

Pinching the bridge of his nose, he focused on the computer once more and made himself read.

For the next couple of hours, he had some level of success focusing on his job—he handled several phone calls, talked to a judge, took a call from his mom and had to promise he'd come by for lunch on Sunday.

Her heart was breaking over Brody—she'd seen the trouble with the boy for a while, but neither of them had had any luck getting Hank to see it.

Maybe they could feel guilty together, he brooded.

He also managed to instill the terror needed to get some information he should have already had.

He was on a roll, really.

And then somebody knocked on his door.

Without looking away from the paperwork he was now dealing with, he called out, "Come in."

Nielson came in and Remy said, "If this is anything else about our current mess, it has to wait. I've got other shit I do need to deal with."

"Just wanted to drop this off. You can add it to the current mess." Nielson tossed a report down on Remy's desk and then sauntered out.

Remy told himself to ignore it.

He looked back at his paperwork.

And then he found himself thinking about Hope's appearance in Nielson's office that morning.

The low, determined sound of her voice as she said, "Let's get this over with."

And the complete, utter terror that underlined her words.

"Shit."

He grabbed the report.

Forty-five seconds later, he found himself seeing through a sheen of red.

That cool, logical voice in his head—the lawyer in him—had no trouble being cool and logical.

Troubled woman, remember?

That borderline personality—attention isn't solely focused on her now and this would be one hell of a way to get attention back on her. Sympathetic attention at that.

Throwing crazy shit into the mix and she doesn't need to have a reason.

But his gut said otherwise.

And Remy believed in listening to his instincts. He'd always been one to listen to his instincts. They didn't tend to steer him wrong, and that was a damn good thing.

Carrington County, Kentucky, was so damn small and their resources were stretched pretty damn thin—more often than not, he ended up taking a more active role in checking things out for the cases he'd have to prosecute than he would if he'd worked in Lexington or Louisville.

His instincts had insisted there was a problem with this whole picture, and damn had they been right. From the get-go, something about this hadn't sat right with him.

He'd tried to brush it off, tried to convince himself that she had just snowed him—born manipulators were good at that, he knew.

He tried convincing himself he was just so tied up because he had a personal attraction to her and that was doing bad things to his brain.

But it hadn't felt right.

He should have listened to his gut—one time he hadn't done it, and shit, had he ever been wrong.

Blood roared in his ears. His hands clenched into fists and he had to unclench them before he ripped the report apart. Slowly, carefully, Remy laid it down.

Slowly, carefully, he stood up and started to pace.

Jamming his hands into his pockets, he paced the worn carpet of his office and tried to wrap his mind around what lay on those sheets of paper. Simple, so damn simple—it shouldn't mean so much to *him.*

Personally.

This was just a job, after all.

Right?

According to that report, Hope Carson hadn't been the one to take the knife to her wrists.

Which meant . . . they had yet another victim.

And while that should infuriate him as a civil servant—and it did—while it should bother him on a personal level, just for the sheer wrongness of it—and it did—it shouldn't leave him shaking, feeling shattered, like he somehow had to put himself back together.

Shouldn't leave him fuming and raging . . . or worse, all but thirsting for blood.

But there he was.

He was shaken . . . on a level he couldn't quite understand.

He was shattered . . . because he hadn't seen this.

He was enraged to the point that he wanted to tear something apart.

It wasn't supposed to affect him personally? Screw that.

From the second he'd laid eyes on that woman, she'd affected him on a personal level and he'd be damned if he could completely understand it, but there was no denying it.

His gut knotted. He knew what had happened that night, all too well.

If Ezra and Nielson hadn't decided to go out and check on Law's place, she would have bled to death.

Not because she'd chosen to, either.

Son of a bitch.

CHAPTER
EIGHT

"Can I ask why you want more information about my wife?" Detective Joseph Carson stared out the window.

"Ms. Carson is no longer your wife," Remington Jennings said, his voice easy and relaxed.

He had that slow, laid-back Southern drawl, rich and smooth. Joey didn't really like hearing the man say his wife's name. At all.

"We may be estranged, but I have hopes that Hope and I will eventually work things out."

"The divorce has been final for two years. That's a bit more than an estrangement," Jennings said.

"Our personal affairs don't really concern you. And I'm still trying to understand why a Kentucky lawyer is trying to get even more personal background information on my wife. Her history is private—you have no need to know any more than I've already shared."

"Well, there's been some interesting updates, some light shed on recent events—it turns out there was an attack on Ms. Carson and I'm just looking for anything that may shed light on it."

Joey echoed. "An attack—I thought she'd tried to kill herself."

"As I said—there was some light shed on recent events," Jennings said.

"Hmm. Regardless of whatever light you think you saw, that attack was likely self-inflicted. I've already told you. Hope is troubled. I love her, but she's deeply, deeply troubled."

"I question whether she really is all that troubled," Jennings said in that neutral tone lawyers managed so well.

The one that managed to sound like it was saying *fuck you*, but it said it so smoothly, so politely. He wanted to reach through the phone and strangle the bastard.

"She spent months in a mental institution. She overdosed on liquor, anti-anxiety pills, and antidepressants. She had to have her stomach pumped. She tells terrible, terrible lies and lives in a delusional world of her own making, one where she's happier to paint herself as a victim. She is a chronic liar, a user, and a manipulator. Mr. Jennings, yes, she really is *that* troubled."

There was a brief pause, followed by, "Well, if she has that many flaws, I have to ask myself, why would you want her back?"

"Because she's mine," Joey said simply.

"Yours? I thought the days of owning our wives ended quite some time ago."

Joey gripped the phone, squeezed it until the plastic cracked. But he kept his voice cool and level as he responded, "You misunderstand me, Mr. Jennings. I love her. There is no logic in matters of love. For all her flaws, for all her problems, I love Hope and I want her back. Now, if you'll excuse me, I do have to get back to work."

He hung up the phone and continued to stare outside.

This, he decided, had gone on quite long enough.

Hope Carson really did need to come home.

* * *

Remy hung up the phone.

In the past day, he hadn't had any luck getting solid information on Hope's past.

Not that he'd expected he would.

Patient confidentiality was blocking him, as he'd expected.

And her obnoxious ass of an ex-husband wasn't helping much.

He'd tried tracking down some friends from her hometown, but . . . well, there weren't any. At least not since high school.

No work history that he could find—he suspected she'd been working under the table for the past two years. It was the only way he could figure she'd been supporting herself.

No volunteer work. Throughout her marriage, the only person who had any regular contact with her was her husband. Already that was painting an image that left a bad, bad feeling in Remy's gut.

Coupled with her skittishness around people, particularly men . . .

Anger started to pound and pulse inside him, but he tucked it away, pushed it aside so he could think, function. He couldn't make any decisions based on his assumptions, couldn't go forward based on what he *thought* might have happened . . . and even if he could, right now there wasn't anything he could do, not as far as his job went.

It was late Friday and he had spent much of that day in court. What hadn't been spent in court, he'd spent on the phone, trying to learn more about Hope. Not that he really had to have that information—there was nothing he really *needed* to do about the report Nielson had given him.

Once they had a suspect, yes.

But until then?

Assuming that even happened.

Turn it off. Go home, he told himself.

Yeah, that was what he needed to do. The past few weeks had been hell on wheels in his small county, dumping far more shit on his plate than he normally had to handle. He ought to go home, collapse on the couch, order a pizza, and zone out with a beer and a movie.

That was what he *should* do.

But after he left the office, it wasn't his sparsely furnished, empty apartment he found himself driving to.

No, he was speeding down the winding two-lane highway that led to Law Reilly's.

Law.

Shit.

What was her history with Law?

Was there a history with Law?

There was a connection there. He remembered the way she had looked in the sheriff's office just yesterday. Like she had been about to completely panic, her eyes all but black in her face, her skin pale, her breathing coming too fast, too hard.

She'd been fighting a panic attack—a bad one.

Remy had seen them, more than once. She'd been getting it under control, fighting to get a grip on it. Law had rested a hand on her shoulder, a friendly, easy gesture, and said something to her, and she'd settled, steadied.

What was between them?

And why the hell did it matter to him so much?

Didn't he have enough on his plate right now? A killer running around his town. A wife-beater to prosecute. His nephew . . .

Even thinking about the kid made his heart ache.

Come Monday, Brody was going to a residential treatment center in Lexington, a place where he could get a grip on the anger and the grief that was eating him alive. He'd be home in a few weeks, Remy hoped.

He hated doing it, but Brody needed some serious, serious one-on-one intervention and Hank, shit, his brother just wasn't up to it.

And Hank—that was another problem.

His brother had to get his head out of his ass and wake *up*.

Ever since Sheryl had died, the man was so focused on his grief, so focused on anything and everything but his kid. That was a huge part of why Brody was so messed up right now.

And then there was Mom. She was now miserably unhappy and blaming herself because she hadn't seen what was going on with Brody, even though it wasn't her fault.

With all the shit Remy had cramming his head, did he really need to be so preoccupied with Hope?

No.

And what was he doing?

Turning down the drive to Law's house and wondering, yet again, what the deal between the two of them was, wondering just what her story was, and whether either of them were going to tell him . . . and how he'd be able to cope with it once he had the whole story, because he already suspected he knew.

And if the true story was anything close to his suspicions . . .

Do you see me?

He stood in the trees and watched. Wondered.

He was careful, though. It wouldn't be good for him to be seen. Of course, if he *was* seen, he could easily excuse his presence here. Not that he wanted to do that. He'd rather nobody see him, nobody notice him . . . all he wanted to do was stand there for a while and watch Hope.

Watch her, and wonder.

Wonder why she didn't run, when it was so clear she was afraid.

Watch her, and wonder.

Wonder what she was thinking, what she saw when she stared into the woods.

Watch her . . . and wonder. She puzzled him, really. Puzzled . . . intrigued him. He hadn't ever had a woman like this that he hadn't wanted to simply take. That had been the plan, of course. But he didn't want to harm this woman. Odd, that.

The purr of a loud, powerful motor came drifting closer and he sighed. With one, final lingering glance at Hope, he withdrew back into the trees.

The sound of the engine interrupted her reverie, but Hope didn't get up.

Law was in the house.

Scowling at his computer, probably, but not working.

He hadn't done much work since he'd come home from the hospital. She was there to help him so he could work more, but since he wasn't working . . . well, he could get the door, right?

Shivering, she drew her knees to her chest and stared at the trees.

No, she couldn't see a face.

Couldn't see a masked face.

But there was somebody there.

Somebody who watched her . . .

Why? Why was somebody watching *her*?

Fear. A small, quiet voice in her head whispered, *He wants to see you afraid. And you're giving him exactly what he wants . . .*

She hated that. Hated that the voice was right. Hated

that she didn't feel she could shut that flow of fear off. Hated that she couldn't control it.

And damn it, this had to stop.

Had to stop *now*.

And still, even though she was certain somebody watched her, there was a ghost of a whisper in the back of her mind, one that murmured, *"Maybe there isn't anybody there. Maybe Joey was right. Maybe all of them are right. Maybe you are crazy . . ."*

"I'm not," she whispered, shaking her head. "I'm not."

Remy studied Law's battered face.

"Pretty, ain't I?" Law smirked as he settled in a broken-down armchair.

There was a laptop open on the table next to it and idly, Remy wondered if he'd been working. Although he didn't know how much the guy could do with a broken arm. He sure as hell couldn't type with the cast he was wearing, not unless he only did it one-handed.

"How are you feeling?"

"Like somebody beat the shit out of me," Law said bluntly. "And imagine that, somebody *did* beat the shit out of me. But I don't have any idea who it was, or why, so if that's why you're here, I'm afraid I can't help you. So . . . you can go now."

Hell. "Actually, that's more the sheriff's department than mine. I ask around, do what I can when I can, but the hardcore investigating—that's on them. There are a few things I need to go over, but it's more to finalize things about . . . Hope."

Law's face tightened. "I thought we'd already taken care of that. She did *not* do this," he said, his voice edgy, heavy with the first ripple of anger. "I thought we were clear on that. What in the fuck is there to finalize?"

"Oh, I get that. And yes, we're clear on that." Rubbing his hands over his face, Remy glanced around. Even though he was glad she wasn't in here, there was still a little ache inside—he wanted to see her. Even if it was just for a second. Man, he had it bad. So damned bad. "Where is she?"

"Outside." Law closed his eyes. "She . . . hell. She doesn't feel safe in here. Can't sleep, isn't eating much. I wanted her here so she could . . . well, that's personal, but she should have been safe here. I promised her that, and fuck, did I break my promise, or what?"

"Safe from what?" Remy narrowed his eyes. His blood, already hot, started to race. Safe—Law wanted her safe, and that meant she had something to fear. Fuck.

"Life." Now Law looked at him and there was a strange, bright glitter in his eyes. "You're not an idiot, Jennings, even if I don't think you're as bright as other people seem to. But can't you look at her and tell she's been through hell?"

"Yes." Remy thought about the way he'd felt the very first time he'd seen her. All he'd wanted to do was shelter her, protect her. Fuck her. What kind of bastard did that make him? She'd been through hell, and even from that first second, he wanted her so bad, it made him ache. "Why don't you tell me about that?"

"Why?" Law's lip curled. "Give you more ammo to use against her?"

"Why would I need it? She's not under arrest, she's not going to be." Leaning back in his seat, Remy drummed his fingers on the arm of the chair and said, "She's now a victim, same as you—I saw Nielson's report. She's the victim of an assault, same as you, only *her* assault could have killed her, and it's worse, because everybody assumes she did it to herself. That's one screwed-up deal there, and you know it. Shouldn't we have all the information we need to find out who did it?"

"And as you said earlier . . . isn't that the sheriff's job?" Law asked.

Remy cocked a brow. "So does that mean you've shared that information?"

"Hell, no." But he wasn't any more forthcoming either. Leaning back in the chair, Law looked at him, those shrewd hazel eyes resting on Remy's face. "But I'm still trying to figure out why you want to know this—why you think you need to."

"I've got a job to do. She was attacked." It was the truth. It was also almost a lie, because job or no job, Remy knew he would have been out there. For Hope. Sooner or later.

As though he had read Remy's mind, Law's mouth curled into a one-sided smirk. "So this is just the conscientious DA doing his job?"

Remy stared at his hands for the longest time, unsure of what in the hell to say to that. What in the hell *could* he say? He *couldn't* get involved with Hope, even assuming she might have once been remotely interested. But there was a hell of a lot more than just a professional concern on his part, and he couldn't honestly say otherwise.

Feeling raw, exposed, he looked up at Law and as he met the other guy's eyes, he realized he probably didn't need to say a damn thing.

Law already knew.

Shit.

Coming off the chair, Law shoved a hand through his hair and, in a perfect echo of Remy's thoughts, he muttered, "Shit."

Then he shot Remy a dirty look and muttered, "This would be a hell of a lot easier on me if I could just kick you the hell out of my house, keep you the fuck away from her."

"Could you do that?"

Law snorted. "With Hope? Yeah." He sighed and shot a glance at the door. "She's . . . damaged. You get that? Damaged in ways I don't think you really understand right now. You might think you do, but you don't. And she trusts me. That means if I really wanted to keep you the hell away from her, if I thought you were bad for her—it would be shitty of me to do it, but I could do it."

Then their gazes met. Hazel rested on blue.

Law sighed and said, "I'm not going to do it."

Then he came to his feet. Immediately, he winced and pressed a hand to his ribs.

Just a look at the man was enough to tell he still hurt like hell, Remy thought, watching as Law made his way to the big, arched doorway. He stood there, staring down the hallway.

Watching for Hope, Remy realized. *Damaged.* Fuck. That word was tearing at him. What in the hell did he mean?

"It's her business," Law said quietly. "It's her concern, and it's not my place to tell."

Then he shifted hard hazel eyes to Remy. "But I know what you *think* you know. You think she's crazy—you got the bare information you were able to get, how she'd done time in a mental institution, and you probably talked to that asshole ex of hers. But you don't know shit."

"I'm figuring it out—and before you say another thing, I *don't* think she's crazy," Remy said. It would be so much easier if he could believe she was. Whatever problems she had, whatever was going on with her, it wasn't anything like what her ex had made it out to be. "If I really thought she was crazy, you think I'd be here?"

Law smirked, but the smile faded, replaced by a dark, brooding stare. "After the hell he put her through, it's a fucking miracle she's *not* crazy."

Anger was a living, breathing thing. Right now, it was a wild dragon, chewing a hole in Remy's gut. Unable to keep still, he started to pace, but it wasn't enough. He wanted to hit something—hurt something—no. Not something. *Him*. The man responsible for all the shadows in her eyes.

"He beat her, didn't he?"

"Beating is mild compared to what he did." Law shook his head.

Remy looked away. "He's a cop."

"Yeah. So was his dad. We all grew up together—the town's golden boy." Law grinned and added, "Kind of like you in that respect . . . but he always had this problem with not getting what he wanted. And he almost always got what he wanted, because everybody loved and adored him. Including Hope, for a while.

"They were high-school sweethearts. Hope and I, we were friends even then. Hell, we all were." Law scowled, anger drawing his face tight and hard.

"Then after school, I left town, kind of dropped off the map. Stayed in touch with her, or tried to. Then she stopped e-mailing. Never called me back. I thought she was just . . . Shit. We fell out of touch. Both of us were busy. Life gets in the way, you know? For a while, I thought that was all it was. But she's always called me back when I called. And if I e-mailed, she would always answer. That stopped." He sighed, shook his head. "You ever wonder what it would be like to be a prisoner in your home? Never able to leave? Ever wondered what's it like to beg for help and have nobody listen?"

That dragon in Remy's gut grew bigger, hotter. He closed a hand into a fist and pain flared across his knuckles. Looking down, he saw the brilliant smear of red—

the healing skin across his knuckles had just ripped open.

Maybe Brody wasn't the only one with anger management issues, he thought.

"Is that why she tried to kill herself? To get away?"

Law didn't answer and a few seconds later, Remy knew why. The soft, quiet tread of footsteps had his heart hitching in his chest and then Hope was there, standing in the doorway.

She had a pair of jeans on, jeans that bagged around narrow hips, and a T-shirt that all but swallowed her slender form. Her hair was pulled back from her face and she looked like she could have been about fifteen years old . . . except those eyes of hers, those sad, wise eyes. The knowledge in her eyes wasn't the knowledge any kid should ever have.

Hell, nobody should ever have to live with that kind of knowledge.

There were bruises in her eyes, on her soul, bruises and scars, and it was a sucker punch right to his heart to realize that he had added to them. Had almost added more. He remembered the look in her eyes as the nurse had tried to restrain her, force drugs on her that she hadn't needed.

Once more, fury burned inside him all over again.

Fury, self-disgust, pain.

Shit, this was a mess he didn't need, and the longer he stared at her, the more he realized he was already too fucking close to this. Even though he had tried *not* to let that happen.

It had been inevitable, though.

From the very first time he'd looked at her, looked into those sea-green eyes of hers.

He was already lost. Lost to her, and there wasn't a damn thing he could do about it. Nor did he *want* to do anything about it and it didn't matter that it was a mess.

A big-ass mess, one bigger than he wanted to think about, and not just because he didn't want to get involved with somebody who came with the kind of baggage she came with.

He was a fucking lawyer, and now she was a victim in a crime—a victim, a potential witness, and he couldn't look at her without wanting to touch her, couldn't think about her without wanting her.

He was screwed.

Man, he was *royally* screwed.

Her misty green eyes lingered on his for a minute and then shifted to Law. She lifted a brow.

Words passed between them—unspoken, perhaps, but they were there, nonetheless. Jealousy rippled through Remy. He wanted to push between and have her looking at him again, even if it was with that wary, watchful gaze. And how fucking foolish was that? He knew there was history between them.

History, shit.

That made it seem so mild.

Tearing his gaze away, he reached up and rubbed the back of his neck. He needed to get out of here, away from her.

And that was exactly what he was going to do . . .

She moved so quietly, made next to no noise. But when she moved in his direction, every last part of him knew. Felt it, sensed it. Looking up, he met Hope's gaze.

She tensed and he clenched his hands into fists, the muscles bunching as he tried to keep his rage under control.

Shit, the sight of that fear in her eyes, it gutted him.

He abhorred the way people could hurt those weaker than them, but with this woman, it was worse.

With this woman, he was learning the meaning of *visceral rage*. He understood, now, why some people needed, craved revenge when somebody hurt their loved ones, because he could easily see himself hunting down the bastard who had put that bruised, battered look in her eyes.

Stop it—just stop, Remy told himself.

"Was there something you needed from me?" Hope asked, keeping her voice low and soft.

He could still hear the fear in it, though. Could see the rapid beat of her pulse under the fragile skin in her neck.

"No," he said, forcing the word out through a throat gone tight. Fuck, she was so scared of him and he couldn't blame her. How in the hell could he fix this? "No. I don't need anything, Hope."

Yeah, he did. He needed to see that fear leave her eyes. But how could he make that happen?

"I just needed to talk to Law," he said.

She swallowed and looked back at Law, then at Remy. "Has . . . is there any news about what happened?"

"No."

She nodded.

Fuck, she was killing him, standing there, so quiet, so solemn, so determined not to let him see how much fear there was trapped inside her. When she would have turned away, he reached out and caught her arm. She tensed, and he could have kicked himself.

But he didn't let go.

Fuck, her skin was so soft. Silken soft. He knew he had touched women with skin that soft before—hell, it was just skin, right? Pale, smooth skin . . . stretched over lean, delicate bones . . .

But for some reason, the feel of her skin, it left him dazed. The smell of her, the sight of her. He was a fucking goner.

"You don't need to keep worrying that somebody's going to show up and arrest you or . . . well, anything else," he finished lamely. "There . . . ah, there's no trouble here. You don't need to worry anymore."

"I don't?" she asked.

"No." He had to force himself to let go of her arm, had to uncurl his fingers and once he had his hand at his side, he had to jam his fist into his pocket to keep from giving in to the temptation to touch her again.

"Why is that?" A solemn, sad smile curled her lips and she shook her head. "You can't tell me that you suddenly believe me."

"Hope . . ." Law reached up, rested a hand on her shoulder.

"It's okay." She patted his hand and then eased away, moving to stand by the window, sliding Remy a look from the side of her eye. "I know the lawyer type. He's already got it in his head that I'm guilty, Law. So I'm curious why he isn't interested in arresting me."

Lawyer type? he thought, studying her with narrowed eyes. Some part of him wanted to be offended, feel insulted. But another part of him was just too surprised—he wouldn't have thought she'd have it in her to stand up to him like that. Not to anybody.

But, shit. If he said he didn't plan on having anybody arrest her, then damn it, he *meant* it.

"It was just a couple of days ago when you made it clear that I didn't know you," Remy said, brusquely. "You're right. I don't. But you don't know me, either. You might know *lawyer types*. But I'm not a type. I'm just me. And if I wanted you behind bars, I'd find a way to get you there. If I say you don't need to worry, then I mean it. I don't say things I don't mean."

"Everybody says things they don't mean," Hope said quietly. "That's the way the world works."

"Even you?"

She frowned.

Those soft green eyes of hers, the secrets and the hurts inside them, fuck, she was killing him, and what he wanted to do, more than anything, was the one thing he couldn't do. He wanted to pull that slender, sleek body against his, cuddle her close, promise her that she was safe, that nobody would ever hurt her again. He wanted to make her smile, make her laugh . . . make her trust him. Then he wanted to make love to her, over and over.

And he couldn't do it.

"Not everybody's out to hurt somebody else," he said quietly. "I'm not out to hurt you."

Then he glanced at Law and gave him a short nod.

Cutting a wide berth around the two of them, he started for the door.

He needed to get away from her.

Very far away from her.

And then, he needed to find someplace where he could pound on something.

For a good, long while.

"Why was he here?" Hope asked, watching as Remy Jennings made his way out to his car.

For once, he didn't have that easy, *I-own-it-all* gait. Hope knew that gait. After all, Joey had moved the same way.

You're not being fair, that soft, chiding voice whispered as she turned to look at Law.

He was busy straightening up the magazines and books that littered the desk next to his chair, taking his time with it, too. *Too* much time, even though he only had the one good hand.

Giving her an absent smile, he just shrugged. "Just checking on things, I guess. Who the hell knows?"

"You know . . . for somebody who tells lies for a living, you're not very good at lying." Hope pushed her hands into her pockets and rocked back on her heels as he straightened.

"Lying about what?"

"He was here for a reason." Hope swallowed the knot in her throat. "I can tell. What was it?"

Law's hand curled around the stack of magazines, tightened. Pages crumpled and then abruptly, he hurled them down and spun away. "Shit, Hope." Under the faded shirt he wore, muscles strained as he lifted his hand, rubbed it over his face. "He was here about you, okay?"

A chill raced down her spine.

And for reasons she couldn't even begin to explain, her heart ached.

"So much for him meaning what he says," she muttered, reaching up and wiping the back of her hand over her mouth.

"What?"

She just shook her head.

"What are you so scared about?"

She laughed, and even to her own ears, the sound was hard and brittle. "Oh, come on, Law. He just stood there and told me I don't need to worry about him causing trouble for me, that he means what he says and yet he was here grilling you about me."

"Yes. He was." Law crossed the room and reached down, caught one of her wrists and lifted it, exposing the healing scars. "Mostly because of these, honey."

She curled her hand into a fist, tensed. Staring into his hazel eyes, she whispered, "What about these?"

He held tight, his grasp gentle . . . but firm. He couldn't, *wouldn't*, let her get away. "Hope, somebody tried to kill you. He beat the shit out of me, but he tried to *kill* you. And up until recently, everybody just assumed you'd done it yourself. Remy's a DA. He's got a job to do, and now you're just as much a victim of a crime as I am."

Hope swallowed the knot in her throat—*victim*—damn it, she was so fucking tired of being a *victim*.

Closing her eyes, she reminded herself that she wasn't one now, not unless she let herself *be* one. So what if the law decided to view her as one? That didn't mean she had to *see* herself as one, that she had to let herself *be* one . . . act like one . . .

Taking a deep, steadying breath, she opened her eyes and looked at Law. "So if he was here about *these*, why didn't he talk to me?"

A shutter fell across Law's eyes.

And just like that, she knew. Pain, shame, horror, they sliced into her heart, into her soul. A scream rose in her throat, but she swallowed it down.

He knew.

Remy knew.

For some reason, that knowledge was like a lash across her heart. Raw and unending and painful.

"Oh, shit." Jerking away from him, ignoring the sharp sting it caused in her wrist, she turned away from him. Nausea churned inside her and if she had had any food inside her belly, she would have vomited every last bit of it up on Law's polished, gleaming hardwood floors.

Instead, she made her way over to the windows and opened one, fighting with the screen until she'd freed that, too.

Leaning forward, she sucked in a breath of air. But it lodged in her lungs when she saw Remy.

Doing the exact same thing.

He was leaning over the hood of his car, a sleek, silver sports car, a Jaguar, if she wasn't mistaken, his shoulders bowed, head low.

As though he felt her stare, he lifted his head.

A good forty feet separated them, but she still felt the impact of his gaze and it shook her clear down to her very core. Heat . . . wrapped in fear, and nerves, and need, and . . . surprise.

Because he looked every bit as shaken, as worried, as confused as she felt.

Those blue eyes bored into hers.

Her heart raced and for the first time in her life, Hope understood the concept of what it might be like to actually have the world fall away. In those few seconds, it seemed like nothing, and no one, existed, except for him, and her.

Then, he looked away and the moment shattered.

Without sparing her another glance, he climbed into that sleek, sexy car and drove away.

With her knees shaking and her heart still racing, she rested a hand on the windowsill and sank down to the floor, turning so that her back was to the wall.

Staring into the living room, she found herself looking at Law.

He stared back at her.

"He knows," she whispered. Tears burned her eyes, shame clawed at her throat. "He knows all about me, what happened, what Joey did to me, doesn't he?"

"He knows enough." Law sighed roughly, his shoulders rising and falling. "I didn't tell him, but he's a smart guy and he knows what to look for, where to look. Plus . . ."

He closed his eyes.

When he looked back at her, she saw the apology, the sadness in his eyes. "I think he talked to Joe, honey," he said, his voice gruff.

Hope drew her knees to her chest and tried not to whimper. Tried not to cry. It took every last bit of strength, every last bit of courage she had to keep those wounded, broken sounds trapped inside. But she could hear them, echoing inside her head—an animal, trapped, helpless, wanting to get out.

That was exactly what she had been.

What he had made her into.

"Does Joey know where I am?" Hope whispered.

"It doesn't matter," Law snarled. He stalked across the room and crouched down in front of her, taking her cold hands in his. "Baby, he won't hurt you again. I'd kill him first. I'll take care of you, I swear."

I'll take care of you . . .

"So fierce," she whispered, her voice breaking a little. She stared at him and there was a huge part of her that wanted to let him do just that—take care of her. This was Law, she could trust him to do just that. Take care of her.

She wouldn't, though.

She couldn't.

Staring into his glittering, angry eyes, at his battered face, she knew he would, knew he meant it. Forcing herself to smile, she reached up and touched a hand to one stubbled cheek. "Law, I love you . . . but I have to start taking care of myself."

Then she leaned forward and pressed a light kiss to his lips.

Although her legs felt like water, she stood and made her way out of the room.

At the door, Law called her name.

Turning, she looked at him.

"Tell me you're not going to run away," he said. There was a plea in those hazel eyes.

Giving him a sad smile, she said, "I finally figured it out, Law. I can't keep running. If he comes looking for me, he'll find me. But if he tries to touch me, tries to drag me back—you won't be able to kill him. *I'll* kill him. I won't let him take me back to that."

Absently, she touched her wrist, studied the healing scars.

Hot, burning anger rippled through her and she welcomed it, because it chased away the icy, aching fear. "I'd die before I'd go back to him, you know. And I'd kill him and pay whatever price before I'd let him take me back. But I'd also rather kill him and pay that price before I'd settle for living the rest of my life with this kind of fear. I'd do it, and be happy with it."

Then she walked away, one shaky, unsteady step at a time.

Ezra stalked into the sheriff's office and said, "Look, if you keep calling me in here, you're going to have to get me some sort of free pass to get me through the dragon keeper's gate. That woman out there, I hate to say this, but she almost scares the shit out of me."

"Ms. Tuttle has that effect on people," Nielson said. He smiled, but it was a strained, tired smile, one that didn't reach his eyes.

Ezra wanted to flop into a chair, but the ladder-backed, hard-ass chairs the sheriff's office boasted weren't exactly made for it. So instead, he settled down and stretched his legs out, crossed them at the ankle. The muscles in his right thigh twinged, twitched, and pulled, but he ignored them and focused on the sheriff's face. That grim look in the man's eyes? He didn't like it.

"Where's Lena?"

"It's Thursday—she's working. I dropped her off at the Inn on my way in."

"That your normal routine?"

Ezra shrugged restlessly. "We don't exactly have a *routine* yet," he said. An itch settled between his shoulder blades and he had the weird urge to fidget, but he squashed it. No, he and Lena didn't have a *routine*. They just barely had a *relationship*. Nielson probably knew that. "This is still . . . new."

"You two look right together," Nielson said softly. "You know that?"

"Yeah." A slow, pleased grin curled Ezra's lips. "I know that. I see it. And I feel it. I think she does, too, otherwise she wouldn't have asked me to stay out at her place. Although, I gotta say, I wouldn't have expected the romantic streak, Sheriff."

Nielson snorted. Then he leaned back, skimming a hand over his bald scalp. "I've got to show you something, but it can't go any farther than this room. Technically, I shouldn't be sharing this information, but my gut says I need to, so I'm doing it."

The smile faded from Ezra's face. Drawing his legs in, he braced his elbows on his knees and leaned forward, focusing on the sheriff's face. "What?"

Instead of saying anything, Nielson just placed a picture on the edge of his desk.

Ezra stared.

It looked like Lena.

A *lot* like Lena.

The shape of her face, almost down to the chin. But Lena's chin had that sharp, almost feline angle and this woman's chin had a softer curve. The eyes were hazel, not pale, icy blue. The hair, though, the color was almost identical, even if the woman in the picture wore hers longer than Lena did. The skin, the cheekbones.

This woman was probably a few years younger, but just a few and even with the slight difference in age, the similarity was . . . eerie.

Swallowing, he looked up and stared at the sheriff.

In the pit of his stomach, he already knew who she was.

But he asked anyway.

"Who is she?"

"Her name was Jolene Hollister."

Ezra's stomach sank.

Even before the sheriff continued, Ezra already knew.

"It's the woman we found at Reilly's place."

Closing his eyes, he reached up and rubbed his hands

over his face, tried to battle down the bile rising in his gut. Shit, shit, shit. Fuck.

"They look enough alike to be sisters," Nielson said. "Almost twins."

"I'm not blind," Ezra snarled, opening his eyes. "I can see that."

Nielson nodded. "Yes, I know." Then he put the picture away. "Do you think you've ever seen the woman before?"

"No, I haven't." As much as she looked like Lena, if he'd seen that woman before, he'd know. There was no way in hell he *couldn't* know.

He blew out a breath, tried to reconcile the two images in his mind—the bloody, battered carcass he'd seen in Law's workshop weeks earlier, to the woman in the picture. But he couldn't. The woman, she'd been beaten, brutalized, beyond all recognition.

His heart started to pound, slow, heavy beats as something occurred to him. The screams . . . holy shit, those screams. The screams Lena had heard.

Fuck.

Was it somebody after *her*?

Adrenaline started buzzing through his system. He wanted to crawl out of his skin—find a target, *any* target. Instead, he kept himself focused. That was the only thing that would help right now.

"The screams Lena heard . . . how likely is it that it was Jolene?" he said.

"You know there's no way we can know that," Nielson said, shaking his head.

Ezra curled his lip. "Yeah, well, you're perfectly capable of having a hunch. Of listening to your gut. My gut tells me this . . . it was that girl. The sick fuck who killed that girl was in the woods out by Lena's house chasing her down—just yards away from her."

Abruptly, he surged to his feet and started to pace. Shit.

The room was too damn small.

He felt caged in, trapped—so damned trapped, and helpless. Useless.

Completely useless.

Near the minuscule window, he stopped and rested his hands on the sill, staring out over the town square. Ash, Kentucky—middle of nowhere. Was supposed to be quiet, safe . . . boring. Some place for him to just sit, do nothing, while he figured out how to waste the rest of his sorry life.

He'd spent just a few weeks doing that, too. Then he met Lena. Bye-bye, Boredom. Now he was shit-faced in love with Lena Riddle, and ass-deep in the middle of a mess the likes of which he had never expected.

Stuff like this wasn't supposed to happen in quiet, pretty little small towns. In an ideal world, it wouldn't happen *anywhere*, but definitely not here.

He closed his eyes only to open them back up as the image of the dead woman's face flashed through his mind, haunting him. Taunting him.

So like Lena.

What the hell.

"So why are you telling me this?" he asked softly.

"Because it seemed like what I needed to do."

Ezra glanced over his shoulder and looked at Nielson. "Why?"

Nielson lowered his gaze and Ezra, despite himself, found himself doing the same. Although he couldn't see the picture, he knew the sheriff was staring at it, seeing that woman's pale, pretty face.

How old had she been?

What had she been planning to do with her life?

And what the fuck did it matter? Some bastard had robbed her of that. All of it.

"It could be nothing but a coincidence that she looks so much like Lena," the sheriff said. He closed the file and set it aside before he looked up and met Ezra's gaze. "It could just be one of those things."

"But you don't believe that."

Nielson shrugged. "I don't *not* believe it. But I'm also not going to discount any possible connection . . . and I'm not going to take any chance that she could become a target of his. Especially considering that she *did* hear something. The more aware you are of the situation, the more you're going to watch her."

Ezra scrubbed a hand over his face.

Shit, if he watched her any more closely, he'd have to hide in her back pocket. Not that he'd mind, but it might get a little tedious for her after a while.

Grimacing, he focused on the town square once more, watching the people as they passed by.

"I bet you never imagined anything like this happening here, did you?" he asked absently.

There was a long, heavy moment of silence and then Nielson sighed. "No. No, I didn't. You know, some cops probably dream of shit like this—it's the kind of thing that makes a career."

Ezra nodded. He knew plenty of cops who would be all but salivating to have this kind of potentially fucked up case on their hands.

"Is that how you feel about it?" he asked, staring at the sheriff.

"Hell, no," Nielson said, shaking his head. "I wish to God it wasn't happening—wish more than anything else none of this had ever happened in my town."

It was a bad thing to have a strain on a friendship.

Lena Riddle knew this very well.

She hadn't had so many friends in her life that she could afford to be dismissive of any. But then again, be-

cause she hadn't had all that many good, *solid* friend-
ships, she was still madder than hell that one of her
supposedly *good* friends had dumped on another friend
the way Roz had dumped on Law.

It had been a few weeks since it had happened, but
still, walking into the Inn . . . well, it no longer felt like
a second home.

With her hand gripping Puck's harness, she made her
way into the kitchen, half-hoping Roz would be busy
with a phone call, a meeting. Hell, even upstairs screwing Carter.

But as the door to the kitchen swung open, she caught
the scent of Roz's familiar perfume and managed to bite
back a sigh.

"Hey, Lena!"

The forced gaiety in her friend's voice almost had
Lena gritting her teeth. "Roz."

"I was thinking about going into Lexington on Sunday . . . you wanna come with me?"

"Sorry." Fortunately, she even had an excuse. She had
some vague idea of doing a cookout—she had already
planned on making Law bring Hope. Both of them
needed to get out of the house. "I'm having Law and
Hope over."

"Oh . . . well. Some other time."

The despondent tone in Roz's voice poked at Lena's
conscience as she made her way over to the opposite
side of the kitchen and knelt down, slipping Puck off his
leash. "I'd invite you over, but I imagine you're still not
overly comfortable being around Law."

Take that, conscience.

"Lena, that's not fair," Roz said, her voice soft, hurt.

"Fair?" Lena shook her head. Hell. Her conscience
could get screwed sideways. "No, Roz. What's not fair
is you thinking he could have killed that girl. So don't
bitch to me about fair."

"How long are you going to stay mad at me about this?" Roz asked quietly.

"I don't know. Maybe when you admit you were wrong?"

Roz was quiet.

Lena sighed and pushed a hand through her hair. "You won't do it, will you? You know, I hate it when I screw up just as much as anybody else, but when I *am* wrong? When I'm unfair to somebody, I do try to own up to it. Whether I like it or not. Law's a friend of yours and you were ready to all but throw him to the wolves— you never even gave him the benefit of the doubt, as far as I'm concerned."

"Shit, Lena. You're acting like I was ready to go and lynch him or something."

"You thought he'd killed that woman," she said, her voice low, angry. She had to fight not to yell. Her hands curled into fists and blood roared in her ears. "*He wasn't even in town,* but screw that, it shouldn't have mattered to his friends—it shouldn't have mattered to *you.* I believed in him from the get-go. I can understand some people in town thinking that shit, but you *know* him and—"

She stopped, made herself take a deep breath.

She had to stop this, had to get past this, or she and Roz were going to push this friendship beyond any hope of repair.

She took her time hanging up Puck's leash and went over to the sink, washed her hands. "You know him, Roz. You've known him for years, but you didn't trust him, didn't believe in him. That wasn't fair and I'm having a hard time forgetting that, or forgiving that." She dried her hands off on a towel and then turned around.

"Lena, it's not like I wanted to think he'd do something like that," Roz said, her voice hesitant. "I just . . ."

"It was easier for you to go along with thinking every-

thing the rest of town thought than to think for yourself?" Lena lifted a hand. "And you didn't *want to think*
it? You know, when I don't *want* to think something—I
don't. It's that simple. Then again, I've never been one
for letting people think my thoughts for me. But that's
me. Maybe it's not you. Whatever. For now, I think
maybe you and I will be better if we just . . . take a
break. We have to work together and right now, I'm
sorry, but Law needs me a hell of a lot more than you
do."

"Are you saying . . . what, you don't want to be
friends anymore?"

With tears pricking her eyes, Lena shook her head.
"No. What I'm saying is, right now, Law needs his *real*
friends—those who are going to stand beside him, no
matter what. And I'm not going to be pulled in two. If
you're ever able to be that friend to him, fine. But until
then, until things are more settled around here, we have
to work together, but that's all I want."

Roz said nothing.

A few seconds later, Lena heard the soft *swish* as the
door swung closed.

Then she leaned back against the counter and wrapped
her arms around herself.

One crazy thing she'd discovered about friends—you
never really knew just who they were until everything
went to shit.

She would have sworn that Roz would have stood
beside Law. Solid and sure.

But she would have been wrong.

Considering how very little information he had, it
sure as hell amounted to an awful lot of paperwork,
Remy realized.

It was pushing eight thirty and outside, it was dark,
the cool, brisk breeze heavy with the scent of fall.

He had an early morning meeting with another DA. He'd spent the past few hours coming to the realization that he couldn't handle anything remotely connected to this case. He was too fucking close to it.

If it was just Reilly, he'd be fine.

If it was just the one murder victim, he'd be fine.

But throw Hope Carson into the mix . . . and *fine* went out the window.

And they were connected. Somehow, they were all connected. He knew it in his gut. Of course, if Nielson didn't turn up some sort of evidence soon, this case could very well end up going absolutely nowhere.

With his mind on the case, and on Hope, when the phone rang, he wasn't entirely thinking when he answered. "Jennings here."

"Remington Jennings?"

It was a familiar voice and just the sound of it had Remy's back up.

"That's me," he said. Years of practice let him keep the edge out of his voice, but he found himself squeezing the receiver and realized his other hand had curled into a fist.

"It's Joseph Carson."

Remy waited in silence—it was either be quiet or start snarling like a chained, trapped wolf.

When he said nothing, Carson elaborated. "Detective Joseph Carson . . . we've spoken a few times about my wife?"

"Ex-wife," Remy said. *Ex-wife, you fucking bastard*.

There was a brief pause and then Carson said, "Of course. As I've said, I still have the hopes that we'll reconcile."

Over my dead body. Forcing his muscles to relax, Remy said, "What can I do for you?"

"I was just wondering if everything was okay with Hope. It's been a few days since we talked. I wondered if anything new had been discovered. I've been worried."

Yeah, I just bet you're worried. Remy had no doubts that Carson had been doing the exact same thing as him—investigating, checking up on things—things made so much easier by the Internet. Ash might be smaller than hell, but they did have a little, locally run newspaper, with a website, and plenty of people who'd talk to an out-of-state cop who knew how to ask the right questions.

"Ms. Carson is fine, as far as I know," Remy said, keeping his answer noncommittal and impersonal—the last thing he wanted the bastard knowing was . . . well, much of anything about Hope.

"There haven't been any more incidents?"

"None," Remy said as he fantasized about creating his own incidents, mainly by doing bloody, brutal things to the man on the other end of the phone.

Then, reason started to override the rage, and he began to wonder just what in the hell the guy was expecting to hear. Why the hell was he calling?

Frowning, Remy checked the caller ID. Yeah, it was the same number he'd called when he'd spoken with the man.

"Has there been any progress made on the investigation?"

"No, but it's early yet. Besides, I'm a DA, not a cop."

"Yes, well, that didn't keep you from calling me. Besides, if your small town is anything like my small town, sometimes the DA ends up doing a bit more investigating than the cops would prefer . . . asking all those questions like you kept asking me," Carson said. "You still think she was attacked, though? No changes in that theory?"

"Oh, we're pretty certain she was attacked, all right."

"Seeing as how you've got some crazy stuff going

around . . . well, it would be an easy way for her to manipulate those details. Get you and the local boys into thinking whatever she wants you to think," Carson said softly.

Remy damn near bit his tongue to keep from telling the bastard to shove it up his ass—hell, there was definitely a manipulator afoot, but it wasn't Hope.

Carson mistook his silence and sighed. "You didn't really think I wouldn't check into things a little, did you?"

"Oh, I'm sure you did check into things," Remy said, keeping his voice level, despite the fact that his free hand was now gripping the edge of his desk so hard, the beveled wood was all but cutting into his flesh. "You're a smart guy, after all. You probably talked to people around town, people who know me, that sort of thing. Now, here's a thought. I'm a pretty smart guy, too. I've also talked to people, people who know you, people from your neck of the woods. You're right, you know. I did a bit of my own investigating. And Hope's not quite the . . . troubled woman you wanted me to believe. So why don't we just table that discussion?"

Now it was Carson's turn to be quiet.

Remy smirked. "What's the problem there, Detective? Were you banking on people buying into that deal with her being crazy?"

"Hope spent months inside a mental facility. Her problems are well documented," Carson said.

Remy heard that slight fracture in the guy's voice, though. The slightest rumble of rage leaking through.

"Oh, yeah. I know. I found out all of that information . . . and I suspect her rights were violated six different ways to Sunday. She's not crazy. You know it. Was she getting ready to leave you, Carson? Is that why you had her put away?"

His voice sly and cool, Carson said, "No. She overdosed on a nice little cocktail of whiskey, antidepressants, and anti-anxiety agents. If I hadn't come home from work unexpectedly, she would have died. Does a sane woman do that?"

"Depends on the hell she's trying to escape." Remy paused, then asked, "Tell me, what sort of hell was it, being married to you?"

"What sort of lies has she been telling you? The same sort of lies she tried to spread around home? She tried to ruin me," Carson said, his voice ragged, harsh.

Oh, temper . . . Remy grinned, feeling rather savagely delighted with those not so subtle signs.

"You should watch out," Carson continued. "She'll do the same to you, you know."

"Will she?"

"Yes. You think I can't tell why you suddenly changed your mind? What did she do? Throw herself at you? Try to tell you how she needed help? How afraid she was? She did the same to that Reilly bastard, you know. She's got him so fucking wrapped—he's like her fucking slave, sniffing at her skirts everywhere she goes. I'm surprised he never tried to kill me—all she had to do was ask him and he would have tried. Watch your back around him, because he just might try to stab you in it."

Remy rolled his eyes. Shit. Talk about a quick-change artist. The guy went from suave to sleaze in seconds, from calm to clusterfuck in a heartbeat.

"So what am I supposed to watch for? Hope ruining me? Law killing me because she asked him to? And . . . why, again, for either?"

"You think this is a *joke*?" Carson snarled.

"No, I'm actually starting to think *you* are."

"Fuck *you*." His breathing hitched again. Then, abruptly, it smoothed . . . calmed. "Stay away from my wife, Jennings. She is mine, and I will have her back."

Then the phone went dead.

CHAPTER
NINE

YOU NEVER FORGET YOUR FIRST . . .

Hope sat in bed, wide awake, at three A.M., shuddering and shaking and remembering.

No.

People didn't forget their first.

Their first car.

First job.

First lover.

The first time they were hit.

She could still feel the nasty dregs of the nightmare pulling at her and if she had the strength in her limbs, she would have forced herself out of the bed and into the shower.

Where she could stand under the hot, scalding water and scrub away the memory, scrub away the lingering ache of bruises long faded.

All because of a fucking haircut.

One that had never happened.

It's insane the things that can bring on a bad dream.

Earlier that night, she'd trimmed Law's hair.

And now she was shaking and all but sick over a nightmare.

The first time Joey had hit her had been because she'd

mentioned getting her hair cut. He hadn't ever liked it when she did more than trim it, and sometimes, if she had more than half an inch removed, he'd go days without talking to her.

She'd almost always had long hair, but she'd been getting tired of it, tired of the weight, tired of the hassle of dealing with it. One time, just once, she'd mentioned trying a shorter style.

That was the first time he'd hit her.

Oh, he'd been sorry after.

They always were.

A harsh, muffled sob escaped her and she reached up, clapped a hand over her mouth.

But when she did, she caught a hank of her hair, and for some reason, just the *feel* of her hair at that moment was enough to make her feel almost violently ill. Shaking, she slid out of the bed and made her way to the dresser. No, she was too weak, too shaky to go to the shower, but her hair . . .

Hell, if she had scissors, she might have chopped it all off just then.

But for now . . . she found a ponytail holder and wove it into a tight, heavy cable, tucked it back behind her shoulder.

A cable—a chain.

Fuck.

Even her own body parts, her own hair felt like chains.

Felt like restraints.

"You sure you're up to this?" Law said as he turned his keys over to Hope.

"Yes," she said as she took the keys. Her car was on its last legs, but she didn't have the money for repairs. She had to get out of here, had to. Before she screamed, or worse. Before she went after her hair with a butcher knife—and as shaky as she was, she might cut herself and nobody would believe she hadn't done it on purpose.

"Okay. Lena's going stir-crazy, too, so . . ."

"Look, I'm the one who called her, asked if she wanted to go to town." She gave him a tight smile. Tried not to let him see the strain she was feeling. "I'm okay, just need to . . . get out. And I promise, Daddy, I'll be home before dark. Earlier, even, since Lena has to work this afternoon."

"Smart-ass."

She smiled at him, but didn't linger. In another five minutes, she was out the door. Her hands were sweating as she gripped the steering wheel, and her heart raced.

She didn't think—couldn't think. If she thought, she was screwed.

She was doing something today that felt . . . drastic.

He took a week.

It was hell, but Remy took a week.

He should probably have taken more than that—and hell, if he had any sense of self-preservation, he should just steer clear of the woman, but he couldn't do it anymore.

Now that he was no longer officially connected to any case she might be connected to, screw it.

But he did make himself take that week. If he was half as smart as he was supposed to be, he should have taken longer, but Remy couldn't quite make himself do that.

It was hard enough just taking those seven days, even though he had plenty of things to keep his mind occupied. He needed to catch up on his work, he needed to check up on Brody . . . and his mom. He wanted to help his brother, although Hank didn't want help, wouldn't admit he might need it, and until the man opened up, there wasn't a damn thing Remy could do.

But one week to the day from the time he'd seen Hope

last, Remy found himself back on the road that led to Law Reilly's place.

This time, damn it, he was going to find out at least *one* thing.

Whether or not there was something between Hope and Law.

Now if Law had feelings for Hope, well, fuck that. He didn't have a problem with Reilly, but he wasn't turning away from that woman, either. May the best man win and all that.

If Hope had feelings for Law, that would make it harder.

But . . . he had to know.

Had to. If he was lying awake at night thinking about a woman he wouldn't ever have, then he needed to know so he could figure out what in the hell to do about it, and how in the hell he could get over it. Although he didn't have the slightest damn clue—even when everything had pointed at her being completely *not* the type of woman he should be interested in, he hadn't been able to quit thinking about her.

Turning down the long, winding drive, Remy parked in front of the house, but instead of getting out, he found himself sitting there, staring up at the front door.

His heart was racing and his hands were sweating.

Shit, he hadn't been this nervous since his first date.

Oh, shit.

The door opened and his heart stuttered in his chest, almost stopped.

But then Law's face appeared and Remy started to laugh at himself.

Aw, hell. What was he doing?

His pretty little mouse was in town . . .

He watched as Hope climbed out of the car. The wind kicked up, tugging playfully at the strands of her ponytail. He imagined tugging the band out of it, smoothing that hair free.

He wanted to talk to her. Just talk. Even as part of him wondered about taking her, he knew she wasn't meant for that. And he'd never taken anybody from around here. Not smart. He wouldn't be that foolish.

But he'd like to talk to her, for a while. She wasn't alone, though. As the long, slender redhead climbed out of the car, he sighed.

Damn it.

But he'd wait. He could definitely wait.

He'd been waiting awhile anyway.

"I want to cut it off," Hope said abruptly, stopping in front of the beauty salon, staring up at the plate glass window, her mouth dry and her palms damp, sweaty.

The heavy cable of her hair was plaited into a braid.

Memory after memory slammed into her head.

Times when she'd had it trimmed and he'd given her the silent treatment for days after. Finally, it got to the point to where she had one quarter of an inch taken off, never any more.

Then once, a couple of years after they were married, she offhandedly mentioned that she'd like to try getting her hair cut short.

One absent, offhanded comment . . . and he'd hit her so hard, it had knocked her into a wall.

The bruising had kept her from leaving the house for weeks.

It had been the first time he'd hit her. He'd apologized later, said he'd had a bad day, and wasn't thinking . . . but he loved her hair . . .

"Cut what off?" Lena asked, her voice vaguely mystified.

"My hair." Hope swallowed and then looked at Lena. "My hair—I want to cut it off. All of it."

"Are we talking a Sinead O'Connor thing, Britney Spears thing, a summer 'do, or what? Not that it's going to make much difference to me, but I don't want to hear you complaining about it, either. And I couldn't *see* it, but that Britney thing sounded scary."

Hope didn't say anything, just looked back at the salon.

The other woman reached over, caught Hope's hand and linked their fingers. "Okay, then. Let's get to it, Britney," Lena said, smiling. "Just keep in mind . . . I'm going to *suck* when it comes to telling you if it looks cute, lousy, or whatever. Forward, Puck."

Three minutes later, Hope found herself sitting in a beautician's chair. Her heart still racing away in her chest, she had no idea how to answer when the lady asked her, "So, what are we doing?"

"Hope, do you just want her to figure out what will work for you?"

Terrified, Hope nodded, not even thinking about the fact that Lena couldn't see it.

"She wants it all off," Lena said. "But please, let's not do the Britney Spears thing—I couldn't even see it and I was scared."

The beautician laughed.

Hope closed her eyes. As she heard the first snip of the scissors, she flinched.

The woman stopped. "You okay, honey?"

Lena murmured to Puck, "Lie down, boy." Then she moved forward and caught Hope's hand. "Hold my hand, why don't you? Go ahead, Beth. Cut, and I don't think you should pay any attention to Hope—I think she needs to do this."

Thank you, Lena, Hope thought.

Then, as the scissors started once more, she squeezed Lena's hand again. Tighter, and tighter.

"I was thinking about trying something short for once, Joey . . ."

A hard, brutal fist, cutting through the air. The pain—the shock.

"I'm so sorry, baby. I . . . I just had a bad day . . . and you know how much I love your hair. It won't happen again, I swear."

But it did.

Over.

And over.

"Damn it, Hope, I'm sorry. But you know I expect dinner on the table when I get home. I didn't mean for this to happen, but you know how tired I am when I get home."

Snip.

Snip.

Snip.

"What do you mean, you want a divorce? You think anybody else is ever going to put up with you?"

Snip.

Snip.

"I think what you need is some medication for depression, baby. Nobody really believes all this crap you're saying—you're just bored . . ."

Snip . . .

Snip . . .

Tears were running down her face by the time it was done, and a thousand ugly memories flashed through her head.

And somehow, when it was done, she felt a hundred pounds lighter . . . no.

A thousand.

Law sat on a fat, overstuffed chair, a beer in hand, but every few minutes, Remy saw his eyes flicking to the laptop sitting on the table by the chair.

Remy held a beer of his own, rolled it back and forth between his hands, and tried to figure out just how to ask the questions he wanted to ask—and whether he should wait until Hope was there or not.

Law finally solved the problem for him by reaching out and closing the laptop and pinning him with a level, direct stare. "So, did you come out here to mooch a beer, grill me about Hope some more, or what?"

"Well." Remy took a quick drink of the beer and then lowered it. "Actually . . ." Then, still trying to figure what was the best way to ask the questions he wanted to ask, he took another drink.

Shit. He felt tongue-tied. He made a living arguing with people—he knew how to talk, damn it, and all of a sudden he couldn't do it.

Law grinned and stretched his legs out. That grin of his took on a sly, knowing slant as he studied Remy. Then and there, Remy realized the other guy saw a hell of a lot more than he let on.

A *lot* more.

"Maybe I can help you out with one thing here. Hope and I aren't involved. Never have been." Law lifted his beer and saluted Remy with it. "If I'd realized that was on your mind so much, I would have cleared that up last week. Or maybe not—depending on my mood. But relax. There's nothing between us. Never has been."

"There's . . . what . . . you're not?" Then he scowled and took another drink of the beer. "Am I that obvious?"

Law just shrugged. "Hell. I just know the signs. I know what a guy looks like when he has a hook in his mouth, so to speak. And you had the signs all over you last time you were out here." He leaned forward and braced his elbows on his knees, letting the beer bottle dangle from his fingertips. The grin on his face faded and he studied Remy with sober eyes. "But you need to know that doesn't mean you'll have an easy time of it. Hope's . . . well. She's pretty battered, still."

"She left him two years ago, right?" Remy asked, before he could stop himself. He hadn't meant to ask that—he'd invaded her privacy enough.

But the question was already out there.

"Yeah. But it's like yesterday for her in some ways." Reilly rested his head against the back of the couch, staring off into thin air. "I tried to get her to come here right after it happened, but she wouldn't go for it. She drifted all over the place—had a little bit of money in the bank from when her parents died, money she hadn't touched when she lived with that sick fuck. I kept trying to get her to come here, stay with me . . . but I don't think she could. She just felt trapped any time she was in one place for too long."

Reilly shook his head and sighed. "Two years, but I don't know if it's been enough time for her. He had more than a decade to fuck with her head. It's not going to be a fast thing, her getting back to any kind of normal." Then he grimaced. "Hell, she might *never* get back to that point."

"Is this your way of telling me to leave her alone?"

Law's mouth quirked up in a smile. The swelling there had finally gone down and the bruising on his face had gone from a black-and-blue rainbow to that nasty, greenish yellow and was finally starting to fade altogether.

"Nah. We've already been over this ground anyway. Hope's been alone for most of her life," Law said quietly. "Even when she was married. She went through that hell alone. Spent the past two years alone, because she thought she'd heal better, and maybe she was right. She had to figure out she *could* be alone, and not break. No. I'm not telling you to leave her alone. I think having some guy who isn't an asshole in her life would be good for her."

Then he looked up, met Remy's eyes and shook his head. "But that doesn't mean she's going to want it. Doesn't mean she's going to be interested in you. You scare the hell out of her, Remy, and you've got to understand, she may not be able to get past that—you don't look a damn thing like him, but you've got a lot in common with that bastard ex of hers. She might not be able to deal with it."

Something sour and hot twisted through Remy's gut.

"I'm nothing like any bastard who'd ever hurt a woman," he said, his hand tightening on his bottle of beer.

"Not like that," Law said, shaking his head. "It's other shit. I told you—the town's golden boy."

Remy grimaced. "I'm no golden boy."

"Yeah, you are." Law shrugged. "It's not an insult. People like you, they like your family—that's gone back for generations, and from everything I've ever heard, you actually come from decent people. It's not like it was back home, where people turned a blind eye to the evil shit he was doing to his wife. You're decent—even your brother with his head up his ass over his son, he's a decent guy. The Jennings are good people. This is a different place, even. Here, the people care.

"Back home . . . well, the Carsons, some of them are okay. But others, like Joe, his dad . . . too many bad apples and some people just didn't care. Those who did, they were too scared, or too used to how things were to do anything."

Law fell silent and then he lifted his bottle, drained half the beer. "Even me."

"What do you mean?"

Shooting a look at Remy from under his lashes, Law said, "I heard rumors. About how Joey had screwed around on Hope back in high school—some of it was the kind of shit that would have made a person think twice—what he'd done to the other girl. Nothing confirmed. But I never said anything to Hope. I should have. If I had . . ."

"High school." Remy sighed and shoved a hand through his hair. "You were kids. Just kids. And rumors—there's nothing to say she would have believed you. Without proof? Would she have believed you?"

"I don't know." Law lowered his gaze. "But now I have the rest of my life to think about what he did to her, and the rest of my life to wonder if maybe I could have stopped it somehow."

"That's the kind of thinking that will tear you up inside, you know." Remy grimaced. Then he looked up as the sound of a motor caught his ears. From where he sat, he could see out the window without moving, but it took all his restraint to continue just *sitting* there as the little black convertible came up the drive.

The top was down.

But he couldn't see that long, gleaming brown hair blowing in the breeze.

It was Hope, though.

No mistaking that . . . he'd recognize her even if she was in a room with five hundred other women, he suspected.

As the car came to a stop, his heart started to race.

Across the room, Law laughed. "Man, you need to take a breath or two before you pass out."

Shit. Breathe? Remy didn't know if he remembered how to do it. He tried it, though, and managed to take a breath, then even managed to shoot Law a glare and say, "Fuck off, man."

Taking one more drink of his beer, he set the bottle down and stood.

Then, as Hope climbed out of the car, he almost choked.

Her hair . . .

She'd cut her hair.

Hope felt a strange little jitter in her chest as she eyed the sleek, silver Jag parked in front of the house.

Remy.

Licking her lips, she lifted a hand to fluff and fiddle with her hair only to stop. She didn't know why he was here, but it didn't matter. She still had some work to get done. Books to pack up. Stuff to file. And they needed to figure out what to do about Law's office until they were ready to work in there again.

Until—geez, who was she kidding?

Hope was thinking she *might* be ready to step foot back in there about the dawning of the next ice age.

Maybe.

Taking a deep, steadying breath, she started toward the house.

Whatever Remy was there for, it had nothing to do with her.

Nothing.

She would just peek in and make sure Law didn't need her, and then she'd go work in her room. She already had a box piled with work in the hallway. She could work in her room just fine. With him there, she'd work in her room better.

But as she headed inside, her heart skittered up into the territory somewhere near her throat. Remy wasn't sitting in the living room, calmly and coolly talking to Law, and he wasn't wearing one of those slick lawyer suits, either.

He stood in the arched doorway between the living room and hallway, a bottle of beer in one hand, hanging loose from his fingers, almost like he'd forgotten he held it.

He had a blue polo on, one that made those impossibly blue eyes of his look even bluer. The faded blue jeans he wore were old enough that they looked almost white at the seams and his tennis shoes were almost brand-new.

She felt a little foolish eyeing the shoes, but it was easier to look at his shoes than to look at the jeans—the jeans were dangerous territory because then she couldn't help but notice the way the material outlined some nicely muscled legs—not *too* much muscle—he didn't do that bodybuilder crap like Joey had done. But nice, lean . . .

Stop it, Hope!

And the shoes were definitely safer than looking into his eyes—a lot easier, especially considering he was staring at her. Man, was he staring at her.

Swallowing around the knot in her throat, she tried to figure out just what in the hell to say.

But he beat her to it.

"You cut your hair," he said, his voice soft, quiet. Almost dazed.

Abruptly, the nerves drained out of her and she narrowed her eyes. Reaching up, she pushed her hand through her hair—it felt so weird. And her head felt so light. "Yes. I did. Is that a problem, Mr. Jennings?"

"No." The thick, dark fan of lashes lowered over his eyes and he glanced down, lifted the bottle he held and studied it. Then he took a drink.

"You cut your hair?"

Law appeared in the doorway. His eyes went wide, then he grinned. "Damn, you did."

He came over and tugged on the short strands, heaving out a heavy, false sigh. "Well, hell, Hope. How am I going to pull on it now? There's hardly anything left . . ."

She smacked his hand away. "There's plenty of hair left." The stylist had called it an angled bob, shorter in the back than it was in the front, the edges falling to frame her face. She thought maybe it made her look a little less . . . fragile.

She hoped.

"So why did you do that?" Law asked, lifting her chin and turning her head, peering at her first one way, then the other. "You've always had it long."

"I . . . uh . . ." Her throat went tight. Remnants of the dream grabbed her. Memories she wanted to forget swam up to haunt her. Her voice husky, she said, "I just wanted to cut it, I guess."

Easing away, she cut a wide berth around Law and Remy.

"I'm going to get some work done," she said, heading toward the box she had left in the hallway. She glanced back at Law over her shoulder, taking care not to look at the other man. "I'll be up in my room."

But as she bent over to pick up the box, Remy was there.

"Let me get it for you." He pushed his empty bottle into her hand and grabbed the box.

She straightened up, backed up like she'd been burned. Close . . . too close.

All of a sudden, she'd realized something she hadn't realized before.

He smelled good. Way too good. Good enough that it left her heart racing in the weirdest way and her belly felt all hot and tight.

Blood rushed to her face as she stared at him, watching as he lifted the box, tucking it easily under one arm. The blue polo stretched across his chest and for a few seconds, her mouth went dry.

Self-preservation kicked in and she jerked her eyes away from him, tried to focus on something else, anything else—the box. Yeah, the box . . . that held Law's work.

Oh, *shit*.

Lunging for it, she grabbed at it, juggling the bottle as she tried to wrestle for the box. "I can get it," she said, scowling at him.

"Just tell me where you want it . . ."

"I want you to let go of it." She jerked at it and shot Law a desperate look.

He just stared back at her, looking a little baffled.

Men . . .

Shifting her gaze to Remy, she swallowed and made herself look at him. Close—too close. He was just too close. Standing this close, she could see that his eyes had darker blue striations in them, and the irises were ringed with indigo . . . so damned beautiful. When she breathed in, she was breathing *him* in, and that just made her heart pound harder, her palms sweat, her knees go weak . . .

Distance. That was what she needed. She needed distance.

"It's not that heavy," she said stiltedly. "I'm capable of carrying a box."

"So am I, and I didn't just get out of the hospital not that long ago," he said mildly. "If you want me to put it down, tell me where you want it and I'll put it down."

Shit . . .

Arguing with him would make her look like more of an idiot, plus it would also probably make him curious about why in the hell she didn't want him carrying the damn box. Although she wasn't about to point up to her bedroom.

Even thinking it had her blushing. Damn it, how old was she? Twelve? Thirteen?

"The kitchen!" she said, her voice cracking. She cleared her throat and pointed down the hall, although belatedly, she realized he already knew where the kitchen was.

As he headed down the hallway, she shot Law a narrow look, but he had already headed into the living room. And as she watched, he flopped down in his chair and grabbed his laptop one-handed, that familiar, distracted look on his face. Work—he had work on the brain.

Damn it.

Suppressing a groan, she hurried into the kitchen after Remy, catching up just in time to see him placing the box on the counter. After dumping the beer bottle, she pulled the box toward her, out of his line of sight.

She shot a quick glance down—saw the neat little list of supplies and books. There was another list, but it was tucked under the notepad, so thankfully, he wouldn't have seen that.

Oh, good. *Slow down,* she told her heart. The panic didn't want to subside, but at least she could tell Law that she hadn't inadvertently let his secret slip.

Not that he'd done a damn thing to help—geez, he *knew* what was in the damn box. He'd helped her load it up and, despite her arguments, he'd been the one lugging it out into the hallway . . .

Of course, it was entirely possible—and likely—her panic was related to something else entirely, like Remy himself, but it was so much easier to pretend it was something, *anything*, other than her reluctant attraction to the lawyer.

Focus, she reminded herself.

She had to focus.

Remy was still standing there . . . close. Too close. Standing there. Watching her. Watching her . . . *again.*

She made herself smile at him. "Thank you."

He crooked a grin at her. "Now that's not really what you want to say."

Hope wasn't entirely sure how to respond to that. So she just shrugged. Her mouth was dry again, almost painfully so. Figuring she either had to get something to drink or risk having her tongue glue itself to the roof of her mouth, she moved to the fridge.

There was a pitcher of peach tea in there—hers. Law wouldn't drink any sort of tea with fruit in it. Actually, the only tea *he* liked came in a gallon jug from the grocery store.

Taking the pitcher out, she glanced at Remy. Although she really wanted him to go back out there and finish up whatever business he had with Law, manners dictated she be polite. "Would you like some tea?"

"Sure."

As he slid onto a stool, she turned to the cabinets and bit her lip. Damn it. Now what?

"Ahh, if you need to discuss some things with Law, I can bring it out to you," she offered.

"I'm not here on business."

"Oh?" She shot him a quick, nervous look and then focused back on the glass-fronted cabinets. Relief jolted through her and the tension she hadn't realized she was feeling started to unravel. Taking a deep breath, she set the pitcher down before it fell from her hands. Resting them flat on the counter, she stared at the cabinets and tried to remember what she was doing.

Her dry throat clued her in.

Tea.

Drinks.

For her. For him.

That meant glasses. Two of them.

Even as she thought she could maybe relax, a whole new sort of tension decided to creep in.

Damn it, why was he here if he wasn't talking business?

He and Law weren't exactly friends, were they?

Getting a couple of glasses down, she took her time getting ice from the freezer, tried to pretend her hands weren't just a little unsteady. Friends . . . had Law ever mentioned Remy before—like on the friend-type level? No, Hope was pretty sure he hadn't. But that didn't mean much.

"So you're just . . ."

She turned around and then jumped as she realized he'd gotten up and moved around the table, his feet soundless on the smooth, polished wooden floors.

He stood just a few feet away, leaning against the counter, his thumbs hooked in his pockets, his eyes watchful.

Her heart fluttered.

Spinning back around, she grabbed the pitcher and poured his tea. Anything to avoid looking at him, anything to give herself a chance to settle—not that she *could*. After she poured the tea, she turned around and pushed it at him so fast some of it sloshed out onto her hand, but she didn't care. She needed him *out* of there.

"There you go," she said, forcing a tight smile. "Now, if you don't mind, I really do need to get some stuff done now."

"Is that a polite way of telling me to leave?" Remy said, lifting a golden brow.

Hope swallowed, then bit her lip. "Actually, it wasn't much of an attempt to be polite—I've got things to do and I'm sure you have better things to do than stand around in here with me."

"Actually . . ." He looked down at the glass of tea he held in his hand, stared at it as though he found it fascinating. "Now that you mention it, you're kind of the reason I came out here."

"I am?"

Her heart started racing, but this time it was fear.

Oh, God.

He'd said she wasn't going to be arrested, and for some reason, she *did* believe him. But that didn't mean he wanted somebody like her hanging around his town.

She had already caused all sorts of trouble or at least, it seemed like it had followed her. Despite the fact that she'd only been in town a few weeks, she already knew the kind of influence the Jennings family had around here. Was he here because . . .

"Hope?"

Screw that, she thought, turning away from him once more. She poured her own tea and took a sip, slowly, deliberately. *You haven't done anything wrong. This is Law's home—as long as he says you're welcome, you don't have to go anywhere.*

"Hey, are you in there?"

Shooting Remy a narrow look over her shoulder, she bit off, "I'm standing right here. Where else would I be?"

Turning around, she lifted her glass to her lips, took another drink of the tea. Her throat was still dry, burning tight, and her heart raced. But she was mad, and getting madder. Fed up, she realized.

It had taken her almost fifteen years to find her stopping point, but damn it, she was sick and tired of being pushed around and if this slick lawyer thought he had any right . . .

"Why do you suddenly look so pissed off?" Remy asked.

"Why?" Hope asked slowly. She set the glass down and then folded her arms over her chest, staring at him. "Well, let me see. First I get arrested for something I didn't do. I get attacked. Nobody *believed* me when I said I didn't hurt Law, except Law, of course. Well, Law and a few other people. But that's beside the point. I didn't do a damn thing. And now you're out here harassing me. I didn't do a damn thing wrong and if you think you can make me leave your precious little town, you can shove it."

Remy blinked. Then he passed a hand over his face and muttered something too low for her to hear. Finally, he looked back at her and said, "Okay, exactly what have I done that you consider harassment, Hope? And when in the hell did I say anything about you leaving?"

"Well, why else would you be here?" she demanded defensively. Spine rigid, she shoved off the counter and just barely resisted the urge to back away as he took a step toward her. "It's not like you and Law are best buds or something. Are you?"

"No." He snorted. "Up until the past few weeks, I could hardly stand him, if you want the honest truth."

"Well, then." Hope sniffed. That just proved he was too much of an idiot to waste time on anyway. "See? You're not hanging out here to shoot the breeze with him, so the only other reason you'd be here would be me."

Remy blew out a slow breath. "I'm following *that* part of your logic, but I still fail to see why you automatically assume I'm here because I'm trying to run you out of town."

"What else would it be?" She hunched her shoulders. "Unless you lied about not wanting me arrested. It's the only thing that makes sense."

Remy closed his eyes and tried to figure out if he had ever heard a more convoluted line of thinking.

He was pretty sure he had—after all, he was a lawyer, he'd heard some seriously inventive arguments.

But this . . . Opening his eyes, he studied her heart-shaped face. Without all that hair, she didn't look so fragile, he realized. Not that she really was, he was coming to realize. A fragile woman would have broken after what had been done to her. No matter what people thought, Hope hadn't broken. She had been forced to bend, to take unimaginable shit and heartbreak.

But she hadn't broken.

She had to be one of the strongest women he'd ever met.

Still, just looking at her flooded him with the most insane urges—the need to protect her. The need to touch her. The need to fuck her. The need to see her laugh. To smile . . . at him.

And she thought he was here because he wanted her out of town? *His* town? Like he owned the damned ground it was built on?

Shit.

"I'm not here because I'm trying to run you out of town," he finally said, when he thought he might be able to say it in a somewhat level voice.

With that doubt still glinting in her pale green eyes, she jerked one shoulder in a shrug. "Fine. Then whatever you're doing here, would you please just get it over with? Please? So you can leave?"

Something moved inside him. It might have been anger. Might have been wounded pride. Might have been frustration . . . or all of the above. "Just get it over with?" he repeated, some of his tension edging into his voice.

"Yes." She swallowed. "Please."

"So polite. Even when you're that pissed off at me. Still so polite," he murmured. "Okay, Hope. I'll get it over with."

Then he closed the two feet between them. He wanted to touch her . . . fuck it, he wanted it so bad, he hurt with it, ached with it, would have gone to his knees and begged if he thought it would have done any good.

Instead, he jammed one hand into a pocket, closed it in a fist.

He raised the other hand and used the tip of his finger to lift her chin.

He had just a second to see her eyes flare wide before he dipped his head and brushed his mouth against hers. Just the lightest brush—hardly enough to even get a taste.

Still, that one taste blistered through him, rushed through him, setting his blood to boil.

He heard her gasp, felt it . . . and as her lips parted against his, he wanted desperately to tease that slight opening with his tongue, see if he couldn't coax her mouth into opening for him, just a little more.

Instead, he whispered against her lips, "I've wanted to do that from the first second I laid eyes on you."

Then he turned around, and without looking at her again, he left the kitchen.

He didn't stop to say anything to Law, didn't stop until he was in his car with the seat belt fastened. And even then, he wouldn't let himself look back, wouldn't let himself look and see, if maybe, just maybe, she had come to watch him leave.

She was still standing there, dazed, when Law came into the kitchen about two minutes after the front door closed.

Still standing there, with her hand touching her lips, and her heart racing.

Remy had just kissed her.

And right before he had lifted his head, he'd whispered, *"I've wanted to do that from the first second I laid eyes on you."*

"Hey."

Shaken, she looked up and saw Law standing by the island, staring at her, his face drawn tight in a worried scowl. "You okay there?"

"Um . . . I . . . I'm not sure."

He leaned back against the counter, assuming almost the same pose Remy had stood in just minutes earlier. Hope closed her eyes and then immediately wished she hadn't, because she could see that image in her mind, the way his shirt had stretched across his shoulders, the way the light glinted off his hair.

Then she found herself thinking about how he'd stared into her eyes as he'd lowered his head and kissed her . . .

"Hope?"

Gulping, she opened her eyes and stared at Law.

"Remy kissed me."

If she'd expected Law to be shocked, well . . . she was expecting too much. All he did was lift a brow and fold his arms over his chest. "Okay. So is that a problem for you?"

"A problem?" She shoved a hand through her hair and shook her head. "Damn it, Law. He kissed me! A week ago he was out here grilling you about me and today he thinks it's okay to *kiss* me?"

"Actually, a week ago, he wasn't *grilling* me about anything." Law's mouth softened in a smile. "He just wanted to . . ."

She grimaced. "Find out things he had no right finding out."

Law sighed. "Hope, he already had most of it figured it. He just wanted to make   hell. Look, cut him some slack. The guy was in one shitty place—I get the feeling he was . . ." He scowled, a dull red flush climbing up his cheeks. "Damn it, this is like giving a kid sister dating advice or something. Look, I think he's been attracted to you like from the get-go, but can you figure out where that put him? Whether we *like* it or not, somebody did a damn good job trying to set you up and I hate it like hell, but what kind of man would he be if he turned a blind eye to his job just because he thought the girl involved was cute?"

Hope blushed and looked away. "I'm not . . ." Then she stopped herself. The hell she wasn't mad about it. But she understood what Law was getting at. "I understand he had a job to do—I do. I don't have to *like* it, but I understand it. Still, this is giving me whiplash." Looking down, she stared at the healing scars on her wrists.

Gingerly, she touched one, winced at the lingering pain. She'd carry those scars for life, forever carry that reminder that somebody hadn't just tried to kill her, but they'd tried to do it in a way that had made the past two years of her life a lie. So what if she'd spent them running—she'd left her husband, that bastard who'd tried so hard to destroy her.

She was trying to be strong. These marks were done to make her look like a coward.

"Law, I don't know if I'm up for this. I'm just . . . I'm so confused," she murmured.

Heaving out a sigh, he lifted a hand. She placed hers in it and he tugged her close, tucking her up against his chest. As he rubbed a hand up and down her back, she snuggled close and tried to relax, but she couldn't. Just couldn't.

Her heart was still racing, her mind was whirling . . . and her mouth. It burned.

"There's only one question you really need to focus on right now," Law said pragmatically. "And it's a simple question. You answer that, and after that, you decide where to go from there."

"Okay."

"Are you attracted to him?"

Hope winced. "Damn it, you call that simple?"

"Well, yeah." He reached up and tugged on her shortened hair. "It's a very simple question."

She pulled away from him and crossed her arms over her chest, glaring at him. "It's *not* simple."

Grinning at her, he said, "Sure it is. And here's how you can tell . . . when he kissed you, did you have that *ewww, gross* moment, or did you, well, you know, like it?"

Blood rushed to her cheeks—stained them pink. She didn't even have to see it—she was blushing, painfully, vividly blushing. Covering her face with her hands, she turned away.

Behind her, Law chuckled. "And there's your answer. Hope, you like the guy, and I can tell you this—he's a decent guy."

"Hell, that shows what *you* know—up until recently, he didn't even *like* you."

"That's no surprise." Law shrugged. He shoved overlong hair out of his eyes and said, "He used to date Lena, and well . . ."

Hope frowned and pressed a hand to her belly, a little dismayed when it clenched. "He dated Lena?"

"Yeah. Rubbed me wrong like crazy, and he knew it, too. So . . ." His voice trailed off.

Feeling the weight of his stare, she shot him a glance and then looked away, trying to shrug off the heavy, weighted feeling in her gut. Lena. Of course, Remy had dated Lena. Why wouldn't he?

She was beautiful. And she had *it*—that indefinable something. She wasn't the kind of woman who would ever—

"Hope."

A hand touched her shoulder and she jerked her gaze up, met Law's. He was smiling down at her. "Somehow, I get the feeling you know how it felt when I saw Remy with Lena, huh?"

"What?"

He lifted a brow.

She rubbed her belly again, realized it hurt.

Envy. It curled through her, tightening in hot, almost painful knots. "I don't know what you're talking about," she mumbled, wrapping her arms around her middle and hoping it would help the ache there. But it didn't.

He watched her with knowing eyes and just shrugged. "Okay. If you say so. But anyway . . . Remy knew I had a thing for her. It wasn't like she ever noticed—she's *still* clueless about it. He knew—and guys, well, we're possessive like that. He didn't like me having a thing for her, and since Lena and I were close, it made it rough on him."

"Does he still like her?"

He just stared at her.

Hope just stared at the floor.

"I'm nothing like her," she whispered. "She's . . . amazing. Shit, Law, she's so confident, and easy. It's like it doesn't matter what life hands her, she just deals with it. And me . . . I'm terrified of *everything*. How could he possibly be attracted to *me* if she's the kind of woman he's looking for?"

Law curved a hand around her neck and pressed a kiss to the top of her head. "Honey, you're overthinking this. And he had a thing with her more than a year ago, but it's over. He came here looking for *you* . . . and no, you're nothing like Lena. You're you. And apparently that's something that appeals to him, otherwise he wouldn't have been here."

Still feeling restless, Hope hugged him back and then moved away, pacing the kitchen. "Why was he here?"

"Isn't it obvious? He was here to see you."

Shooting him a look from the corner of her eye, she snorted. "Don't give me that."

"Shit, Hope, when have I ever lied to you?" Law

grabbed her glass from the counter and took a drink, only to screw up his face. "Peach. Ugh."

He got a glass down and poured some tea from the gallon jug in the fridge. "Listen, he came here looking for you. Well, that and he wanted to make sure we didn't have a thing going."

"A thing?" Hope frowned at him and picked up the glass of tea sitting on the counter. It wasn't until she'd taken a sip of it that she realized it wasn't her glass, but the one she'd poured for Remy.

Okay, this was sophomoric but as she lowered the glass, she found herself licking her lips, wondering if it was her imagination that she could taste him.

Deliberately, she set the glass down and looked up at Law. "What, like me working for you?"

Law, in the middle of taking a swig from his glass, choked. As he turned red in the face, he grabbed a towel and wiped the amber liquid from his face. Once he'd blotted himself dry, he looked at her and said, "No, Hope. A *thing* . . . as in you and me. Together. Get it?"

She gaped at him.

"You and me? He was out here asking about you and *me*?"

Law laughed and threw the towel on the counter. "Yeah, Hope. He was out here asking if you and me had a thing going. *That* sort of thing." He shrugged and took another drink from the tea, actually managing to swallow it this time. "You've been staying out here for a few weeks and it's not like I'm known for having a lot of visitors. I guess he wanted to be sure before he did anything."

"Like what?" she asked warily.

"Like kiss you in my kitchen . . . .?" Law laughed at the look on her face. "Relax, Hope. It's not like you have to *do* anything. He's interested. And I can tell you are, but that doesn't mean you have to do anything.

He'll ask you out, probably soon if I know him. You've got time to decide what you want to do."

"But I don't know what I want." Her hands were sweating, she realized.

Sweating. Swiping them down the front of her jeans, she muttered, "This is stupid, and it's probably nothing but crap anyway. That man is *not* interested in me. He's not."

Then she grabbed her tea—*her* tea this time, not Remy's—and settled down in front of the box at the island. "You're paying me to be an assistant—I should probably get to work on that instead of talking about this. So why don't you go kill somebody?"

After he'd left the kitchen, Hope dropped her head into her hands and told herself not to get worked up, not to think about it.

Remy might have kissed her, and maybe he was a little attracted. She wasn't ugly—she might have self-esteem issues, mental stability issues, and a lot of other issues, but she knew she wasn't ugly, and guys did put a lot of stock in looks.

But that didn't mean he was looking to ask her out . . . or anything else.

Law didn't know what he was talking about. Yeah, he usually did.

But not this time.

Not this time.

CHAPTER

TEN

"YOU GOT ANY IDEA HOW BAD A MESS YOU HANDED me, Jennings?"

Remy managed not to wince as Beulah Simmons's voice echoed through his office, but just barely.

Her voice was . . . big—like her personality.

Beulah, by comparison, was tiny. The other district attorney barely stood four foot eleven and she made up for that fact by wearing heels that added a good four inches to her height. She also had the sort of attitude that dwarfed those around her. Her skin was the color of polished mahogany, her hair cut in a close, cropped style that very, very few women could carry.

Once upon a time, Remy had entertained a fantasy about this woman. Briefly. Very briefly. Then he realized that she mostly terrified him too much—and she could run circles around him.

She was fifty-two years old and her current lover was in his thirties.

Today she wore a suit the color of peaches. Her mouth was drawn in a tight, unhappy smile and she had arms folded over her impressive chest. One nail, painted almost the same shade of peach as her suit, tapped impa-

tiently against her arm as she stared at him from the
doorway and waited for an answer.

Remy was still trying to figure *how* to answer.

"Good morning, Beulah," he said, flashing a smile
at her.

Her eyes narrowed. "Don't you *good morning, Beulah* me, Remy. I'm tempted to tan your hide."

"Oh, come on, Beulah. I thought you'd be all but
drooling to get your hands on a case like this," he said,
leaning back from his desk, still smiling.

"*Case?*" She reached up and rubbed her ear. "*Case?*
As in *one?* Sure. If you had just turned over the homicide of Deputy Prather. Or the murdered girl, although
you better be aware, I plan on looking at the homeowner
a hell of a lot closer than you obviously did. But this
isn't a *case*, Remy, and you know it. This is a fucking
mess and you dumped it on me without any warning."
She scowled and heaved out a heavy sigh. "At all."

"Beulah . . ."

She just shook her head and came inside. Her heels,
the same shade of peach as her suit, as her nails, clicked
smartly on the floor. She lingered only long enough to
shut the door behind her and then she settled into a
chair in front of Remy's desk. Her eyes, sharp as a blade,
narrowed on his face. "'Fess up, Remy. What's going
on? Why did you go and dump this on me?"

"I didn't have much choice," he said quietly. He might
have danced around it if it had been anybody other than
Beulah, but she knew him, a little too well.

One slim black brow arched.

"Oh?" That was all she said. But there was an entire
conversation, all of it unsaid, in that dark gaze. She
crossed one leg over the other and propped one elbow
on the arm of her chair and rested her chin in her hand.

Then she waited.

Remy looked away, unable to hold her gaze as he

tried to figure out how to explain this—how did he say he had turned this over because he was too tangled up with one of the victims? A woman who didn't seem to want to even breathe the same air as he did?

Shit, it didn't *matter*, in the end, what she felt, though. He was too tangled up in her and it left him useless.

Hearing the familiar rustle of pages, he glanced up and saw that Beulah had drawn a fat file out of her briefcase. "So," she murmured, pursing her lips. "What is it?"

She lifted a sheet of paper and then leaned forward, laid the report aside on the desk. "It's not him," she said dismissively. "Although I still don't know why you didn't look into him further."

Remy lowered his gaze long enough to see the report on Law. "He was out of town."

"Confirmed?"

"Yes. At a funeral attended by hundreds." He cocked a brow and added, "That's in the report."

"Hmmm. Still, we need to look more at him."

"No. Not *we*. I'm off this case, Beulah. I have to be."

"Yeah, yeah." She curled her lip again, flipped another sheet of paper.

This one was an autopsy—Prather's.

"It's not that one." Sympathy lingered in her face as she looked up at him. "I didn't like the man. He was an old-fashioned bastard, and very often, a mean one. Mean as a snake, if you get my drift. But still, he was bled like a stuck pig—suffered a lot. Died slow, and painfully. He didn't deserve that."

"No," Remy agreed.

"Hmmm." Beulah turned a few more pages and then stopped.

Remy felt the slow crawl of blood rise up his neck. Even before the woman looked at him.

"Well, well." Beulah flicked a glance at him. "I've got to say, Jennings, I'm surprised here."

"About what?" he asked, his voice stiff.

"She's cute. But I didn't think I'd ever see the day when you turned over a case because of a woman," Beulah said, clicking her tongue. "What did she do, flutter those pretty green eyes at you or what?"

Remy snorted. "Shit, I wish," he muttered before he could bite the answer back.

Beulah lifted her brows and then smirked. "Ahhhh. I see. What's the matter, lover boy? You finally find a girl who hasn't fallen under that spell of yours?"

"Shut up, Beulah."

She started to laugh. "Holy shit. That's it. Although, damn it, boy, backing down from a case over a woman?"

Scowling, trying not to squirm, he said, "It's not that." He sighed and looked away, staring out the window.

From where he sat, he could see the municipal building where the sheriff shared offices with the small city police department, as well as a few other city and county government offices.

"It's not that . . . or it's not *just* that. I'm too fucking close to this, Beulah. Way too close, somehow. And not just because she fluttered her lashes, not that she ever has."

"Wait, you mean she's *not* fluttering her lashes at you?" Beulah asked. She started to chuckle. "She's *not* falling for that smile of yours?"

He rubbed his hands up and down his face and sighed. "There was an event at Lena Riddle's home a few weeks, maybe a couple of months ago. That's when unusual stuff started. I used to date Lena. Then this mess with Law, and while I'm not close friends with Law, I can't deny that I'm attracted to the woman who currently lives in his household. It's just a mess right now."

"A mess?" She snorted. "You think a *mess* is descriptive enough? And have you considered talking to a shrink? Are you *sure* this girl isn't involved?"

Remy shot her a withering look. "I'm not an idiot, Beulah."

"No. You're a man, and you're thinking with your dick. What about all the information you got from her ex?"

Remy curled his lip. "All that information was false, deliberately given in such a way to make her look mentally unbalanced—her ex is a cop, and he used to beat her. And that's not something *she* told me. I got that information from another source—a trusted one."

"Oh." Beulah's face softened with sympathy. "Oh, my. Damn, Remy. You sure as hell know how to pick a complicated mess, don't you?"

He snorted.

"But . . ."

He looked at her.

She lifted a finger. "But . . . what if your source isn't entirely wrong, and what if the ex isn't either? After all, an abused woman is going to have a lot of issues. You and me? We both know that. Shit, more than likely she is *going* to have a lot of issues. You really want to risk getting involved with somebody with that sort of history?"

"Nobody said we were getting involved," Remy muttered.

"Kid, I see that hook in your mouth from a hundred feet away." Beulah stood up, smoothing down the impeccable peach suit she wore. "You're involved, even if she isn't. Whether you want to admit it or not, whether you like it or not. And that could get pretty damn ugly, if you ask me. So again . . . are you sure this is what you want?"

He was silent. Then finally, meeting her eyes, he jerked a shoulder in a shrug. "Well, as you said, I'm involved.

Whether I like it or not. It would seem I don't have much choice in the matter, huh?"

Beulah studied him for a long, quiet moment and then she just sighed and shook her head. "You really did land yourself in it this time. And she's not falling for that legendary charm of yours, either, so you've really got your work cut out for you, huh?"

With that, she turned and grabbed her briefcase. Her heels rapped sharply on the wooden floor as she headed to the door. "Good luck, Remy. And I still think you ought to consider getting your head examined. In the worst way."

Then she winked at him over her shoulder. "That's the lawyer speaking. The woman is curious about meeting this lady. Once this mess is over."

After she left, Remy closed his eyes and rubbed his stiff neck. Mess.

This wasn't a *mess*.

It was a fucking nightmare.

Hunger gurgled in her belly as Hope left the post office. She'd mailed off another box full of books and envelopes for Law. She still had to hit the grocery store before heading back to his place, but as she headed for her car, she slowed down by the café.

Something smelled good—really good.

"Hi, Hope."

She glanced over as a slim blonde came out of the café, arm in arm with a man. The woman looked vaguely familiar, but Hope hadn't met the guy with her, she didn't think. "Hi . . . ah, it's Roz, right?"

"Yes." Roz smiled. "We've only met once. And you haven't met my husband . . . this is Carter, Carter Jennings."

Jennings. Hope arched her brows, cocked her head. "Jennings?"

Carter gave her a smile. "Yeah. This town is lousy with them. My dad and Hank and Remy's dad were brothers. There were seven of them, although only four of them stayed in the area."

"Ah." She studied him closer, trying to see something of Remy there. The eyes were blue, but not as blue. He was a little older, too, she thought. Didn't seem as . . . well, warm, as Remy was. "Just how many of you are there?"

"I don't know. I stopped counting." He smiled at her. "How are you feeling? I've heard about your . . . ah . . . ordeal."

"I'm fine." She jammed her hands into her pockets and looked away. The hunger in her belly faded, replaced by a heavy, leaden weight. *Ordeal*—what a polite word. And *which* ordeal had he heard about? The bullshit version or the real one?

She started to turn away, but a laughing group of women came out of the café at that exact moment. They caught sight of her and their laughter died—cutting off so abruptly, it was almost painful.

Most of them looked past her, through her, around her.

But one of them just stared at her.

Her face was familiar—too familiar.

Hope didn't know her name, but she knew that face; she'd been one of the women trying to talk Remy into arresting Law.

Her pale, almost colorless eyes locked on Hope's face and a sly smile curled her lips. "Well, hello . . . Hope, right? How are you, Hope? Recovering well? You've had a traumatic few weeks . . . I tried to tell you that Law Reilly was trouble, but you wouldn't listen to me, would you?"

"I never was very good at listening to malicious old gossips," Hope said, curling her lip.

Next to her, Roz made a strange choking sound, like a smothered laugh. Hope ignored her, too busy staring at the malicious old gossip in question while she opened and closed her mouth like a landed fish.

She finally sputtered a few furious words. "You . . . I . . . why . . ."

Hope snorted and shook her head. "You're pretty vocal when you're talking about others, but when it's directed at you, you get kind of tongue-tied."

"Hello, ladies."

A shudder raced down Hope's spine.

Remy.

Heat flooded her belly and she had to lock her knees to keep them from melting on her.

All from the sound of his voice . . . and the memory of one all-too-innocent kiss.

Her mouth dry, she glanced over as he strolled up to them. He wore one of his slick lawyer suits, a briefcase in one hand. The sight of him should have been enough to chill the rush of heat his voice inspired—*lawyer, trouble, hello*—but it didn't.

Now it was her turn to be at a loss for words as he came to a stop, subtly placing his body between her and the other woman. Without looking at her, he said, "Lovely day, Deb. You and the gardening club working out the details for the town meeting?"

"That's for Wednesdays."

Hope smothered a smile as the woman drew her shoulders back, her face pinching with disapproval. "Today is *Tuesday*, Remington. We discuss *books* on Tuesday."

"Oh, yeah. How silly of me." Then he glanced at his watch. "You always do lunch before you have the club meeting at the bookstore, right?"

Deb sniffed. "Yes. I'd better get going—Morgan Henshaw is always looking to take my place as the discussion leader, too." With her skinny shoulders rigid, she sailed away and her cronies fell in step behind her.

Roz flashed Remy a grin. "You know just what buttons to push."

"Part of the job description." He shrugged. "Hey, Carter."

"Heya, Remy. You out for lunch?"

"Yeah. It's about that time."

Small talk . . . awesome. They were making small talk. Hope measured the distance to her car, decided she could just sort of quietly mosey her way toward it as these three chatted—so far, Remy hadn't so much as given her one look. While that might have crushed any ego she possessed, if she had one, it was going to make it easier to just slip away, too. Trying to cheer herself up, she figured it would also give her a reason to go *I told you so* to Law.

But as she went to take the first step, Remy shifted his body, placing that lean, oh-so-nicely muscled form directly in her path. "Roz, Carter, I hope you two don't mind, but I'm going to be rude and ditch you. I want to talk to Hope for a while."

Mind! Please. Say you mind! Hope shot Roz and Carter a desperate look, but the blond had already tugged on her husband's arm, pulling him along down the sidewalk with a chuckle.

Her heart slammed against her rib cage, then shifted to lodge up in her throat as she stood there on the sidewalk.

"Have you had lunch?"

Lunch—Hope swallowed, then darted a glance at the café. Had she had lunch? "Um. No."

"Me, neither. Why don't you eat with me?"

"I can think of a hundred reasons," she mumbled, looking everywhere but at him.

"Ouch."

Hope shot him one quick glance and then looked away, staring at the window of the café. People were staring at them—some pretended not to, but others weren't that polite.

"So, you can give me a hundred reasons why you shouldn't, but are any of them a no?"

Blowing out a breath, she made herself meet his eyes. She couldn't keep just standing there looking everywhere *but* at him, after all. For one, it was making her feel a little foolish.

But once she met his eyes . . . whoa.

The world just fell away. *Again.*

"Well?"

Hope blinked. "Well, what?"

A smile tugged at the corner of his mouth. "Are you going to have lunch with me or not?"

"Oh. Lunch." She caught her lower lip between her teeth. Lunch—

"Look, I'll make it easy . . . I'm going to go inside and sit down." He gestured to the café. "And you think about those hundred reasons of yours. If one of them has something to do with not being attracted to me, then you just get back to whatever you were doing. But if maybe you are, well . . . the invitation is open. Your choice, all the way. No pressure."

He gave her another one of those slow, easy smiles and then started toward the restaurant.

A fist wrapped around her throat.

My choice.

Hope closed her eyes.

Okay, her choice.

And she didn't even have to think through her hundred reasons.

But no pressure?

Shit.

* * *

Remy focused on the menu. Of course, he knew the damn thing, front and back, including the prices and the daily specials that weren't even listed. But it was either focus on the menu . . . or stare out the window and see what Hope was going to do.

He gripped it so damn hard, his knuckles were going white. And when the bell over the door jangled thirty seconds after he'd sat down, he refused to let himself look up.

If it wasn't her, it was going to gut him, he knew it.

But then the chair across from his scraped against the floor.

Forcing his white-knuckled grip on the menu to relax, he looked up.

He was pretty sure she looked almost as terrified now as she had that first day he'd seen her—that day on the square.

"Hi."

She swallowed, glanced past him to stare at the wall for a few seconds, then looked back at him. "I'm still thinking of those hundred reasons."

"Okay." He laid the menu down and leaned back. "Don't suppose you want to tell me some of them, do you? I'm not a bad guy, you know. Even if I am a lawyer."

She opened her mouth, but before she said anything, Natalie Greer appeared, coffeepot in hand, an easy smile on her face. "Hey, Remy." Then she shifted her gaze to Hope. "Hi . . . you're the lady living with Law, right?"

"Ahhh. I'm staying at his place, yeah." Hope squirmed on the seat uncomfortably, staring pointedly at the table.

"You've had a rough few weeks." Natalie grimaced. "It's usually a lot calmer around here. A pretty nice town for the most part—of course, you don't really have any reason to believe that."

She didn't say anything else, just quickly took their orders and after that, she disappeared. Once more left alone with Hope, Remy focused on her face. "So . . . you going to give me any of the reasons?"

She scraped a fingernail on the worn Formica tabletop. "What does it matter?"

"Well, because I'm wanting to ask you out on a date and if I know some of these reasons, I can figure out the best counterargument when you tell me no," he said.

"That sounds a little too lawyer-like."

"Is me being a lawyer part of the problem?"

She paused and flicked him a glance, then resumed tracing a pattern on the tabletop. "No. Not really."

"Seriously. You're telling me you don't have any sort of issue with it. After what was going on a couple of weeks ago? You want me to believe you don't have any issues with me?"

A sad smile curled her lips and she shrugged. "I won't lie and say it's not weirding me out a little, but I've gotten past worse things than that. If it was that bad, I wouldn't be here."

He waited, but she didn't add anything else. "You know, getting you to say much of anything is a lot like pulling teeth."

"If you were trying to pull teeth, we'd have a much bigger problem. I hate the dentist." The ghost of a smile danced around her lips for a second and she leaned back on the chair, tucked her hands into her lap.

"Something we've got in common then—my mom always had to bribe me to make me go."

"Mine, too." She smiled again.

"Okay, so if the lawyer isn't one of the hundred reasons . . ."

Hope snorted. "You're persistent." Then she sighed and reached up, only to pause, then lower her hand.

Her hair, he decided. A nervous gesture—she toyed

with it when she was nervous and she still wasn't used to it not being there. "Persistence goes with the territory."

"You're a guy."

Remy cocked a brow. "Yes. Born that way. So, are you telling me if I was a woman, you'd be more inclined to go out on a date with me?"

She blushed.

It was the sweetest damn thing to watch, too. It started at the neckline of her shirt, and Remy couldn't help but wonder just *how* low it started. Jerking his thoughts away from that direction, he stared at her face, only her face, watched as her cheeks went pink and her green eyes glinted with a mix of amusement and embarrassment.

"No. That's not what I'm telling you. It's . . . just, um . . ." She looked away and nibbled on her lower lip. "I haven't been on a date since high school, Remy, and then it was just one guy. I married the only guy I ever dated, and that didn't end well."

"Your ex-husband was a bastard," he said, his voice flat and hard.

She looked at him. Softly, she said, "Yes, he was."

Then she braced her elbows on the table, studying him. "Why were you asking Law about me? About my ex?"

Shit.

That was one question he hadn't been prepared for, not from her. With that shy, nervous exterior, he wouldn't have expected such a simple, direct question.

Natalie appeared just then, giving him a few minutes to come up with the right answer, although he was still composing that answer sixty seconds later when they were alone again.

With the food sitting untouched between them, he eyed Hope. "Should I apologize?"

"That depends on whether or not you can offer a sincere one," she said, shrugging. "Although I still want an answer."

"I can sincerely apologize for upsetting you," he said quietly. Then he leaned forward and reached out, closed his fingers loosely around one narrow wrist. Tugging lightly, he drew her left hand toward him. He eyed the pale strip of flesh on her ring finger. "It hasn't been that long since you've taken your ring off, has it?"

"No. Six months."

"Since he was such an ass, why did it take so long?"

"Because he *was* such an ass. It . . . I don't know, it just took a very long time before I *could* take it off." She glanced down at her food. "And if I talk about him much more, I'm not going to be able to eat. I know I need to eat something, too."

She went to tug her hand away. Reluctantly, he let go and picked up his sandwich. "So basically, you're just not up for the dating scene, and it's not me personally."

"Well . . ." She picked up her fork and eyed the plate in front of her. "I wouldn't go that far."

Remy put his sandwich back down. This woman was going to kill his ego. "It *is* personal?"

"Yeah." She was studying her meal, and although Remy knew the café's open-faced sandwiches were pretty impressive, he didn't think they took *that* much concentration. She started to cut into the sandwich and gave him another one of those quick, nervous glances. "You've got this way of looking at me that makes my heart about to stop."

"Is that a good thing or bad thing?"

"I'm still trying to figure it out." She popped a bite into her mouth.

Remy gritted his teeth and had to spend the next thirty seconds that way as he waited for her to chew that bite and swallow. "What do you mean, you're still trying to figure it out?"

She shrugged and reached for her tea. "Just that. I'm still trying to figure it out. But I think if it was an altogether bad thing, I wouldn't have come in here and I wouldn't be sitting here, either." She took a drink from her tea and then, still staring into the glass, she said, "You make me nervous. I'm used to being nervous, but not like this."

Nervous . . . hell. He could understand that. He opened his mouth, then closed it, entirely too uncertain with what he wanted to say, what he needed to say, what he thought she might want to hear and what might scare her to death.

He reached for his sandwich, although he was no longer at all hungry. "Would it make you feel any better if I told you that you make me pretty nervous, too?"

Hope snorted. "I don't want lines, Remy."

"That's good, because I don't waste my breath on them." He took a bite of his sandwich and washed it down before it turned to sawdust in his throat. "I tend to avoid complications and you've got complication written all over you."

"Gee, thanks."

He grinned. "And here I sit, trying to figure out the best way to convince you to go to the drive-in with me this weekend."

"The drive-in?" A wide smile lit her face—one that damned near transformed it. She went from being pretty to . . . breathtaking. She literally stole his breath, sucked it right out of him.

He felt like he'd been sucker punched as she leaned forward, smiling at him. Her eyes, when they didn't have all those sad, somber shadows, almost danced, he thought.

"Man, I haven't been to a drive-in in years. Not since I was a kid. They tore down the one we had back home."

"It's the main form of entertainment we have around

here in the summer," Remy said, forcing the words out. He wanted to kiss that smiling mouth—desperately. So bad he ached. "Double screens, double features every weekend. I'm thinking now might be a good time to ask you for that date."

She rolled her eyes and went back to her sandwich. "If persistence really is necessary in your line of work, then I'd say you definitely picked the right career."

"So, what do you think? You want to hit the drive-in with me?"

When she slipped out of the restaurant, and never once glanced around her, never once took in her surroundings, it made him smile.

The smile didn't last, though.

She looked . . . happy.

Her hair was short, so fucking short. He didn't like it. Not one bit. She knew better than to do that. Little bitch—he'd warned her. There was a lightness to her step, and she had a smile on her face. She looked easy, carefree.

He started to slip from the store, thinking about following her. But then she paused, looked back.

That was when he noticed she wasn't alone.

A man came out of the café. She stared up at the other man, that small, shy smile on her face.

He brushed his fingers across her hair, said something. *Touching* her. Who in the hell was that bastard?

Whoever he was, he made Hope smile. Made her laugh.

Wasn't acceptable.

CHAPTER ELEVEN

HOPE STARED AT THE MIRROR AND TRIED TO FIGURE just *when* she had completely lost her mind.

Yeah, she knew things were sometimes touch and go for her, but she hadn't ever really thought she'd completely fallen off her rocker.

Until now.

Well, three days ago, actually. Tuesday at lunchtime. When Remy had asked her out and she'd said yes.

She had said *yes*.

She could blame it on the strange, happy feeling of nostalgia that had flooded her when he'd mentioned drive-ins. When she was a kid, her parents had taken her and Law to the drive-in almost every weekend during the summer, right up until the year they closed it when she was thirteen.

Sure, she could blame it on that.

She could also pretend she'd done it just to get him to leave her alone, because certainly once Remy had taken her out once, twice at the most, he was going to realize she was pretty damn boring and just how messed up she was—the politely phrased "complicated" he'd used didn't even touch it. Once he figured all of that out, he was going to beat a very fast retreat, she decided.

And there was also the very legit, if somewhat minor, reason she'd had for saying yes—although Joey wouldn't ever know about it, it was a small, personal victory for her. A guy had asked her out, a decent, intelligent, and drop-dead gorgeous guy, the kind of guy who wouldn't ever raise his hand to a woman—all the mental abuse that Joey had heaped on her way before he'd started hitting her, it had left deep, deep scars.

The way Remy looked at her, it somehow soothed some of those still healing wounds.

But in the end, Hope had to be honest with herself— she was done fooling herself, even with the good things.

She'd said yes for one reason alone.

The same reason she'd gone into the café and had lunch with him.

When he looked at her, everything else just seemed to stop existing.

She forgot about the fact that a few weeks ago, he'd been *this* close to having her arrested.

She forgot about the scars on her wrists.

She forgot about the woman who'd been found in Law's workshop.

She forgot about the attack on Law, on herself.

And while that might not seem like the smartest thing, considering how she'd been living and breathing all of those things, she *needed* that escape.

It was unlike anything she'd ever experienced in her life. Even those first few months with Joey, that first rush of young love hadn't been like this.

Remy looked at her and made her feel like she was his focus—the center of everything.

Scowling, she studied her reflection and tried to figure out why.

She was short, too skinny, with next to no boobs and nonexistent hips, and she jumped at her own shadow.

She liked her hair, though. Sighing, she leaned closer

to the mirror and angled her head one way, then the other, studying the haircut—her angled bob. Hope ran her fingers through it and watched as the brown strands drifted back into place. It was easier to wash, and required hardly any attention, plus, her face looked better, she thought. Not quite so lost with all that hair.

She was pretty enough, even if teenage girls had better figures than she did.

But she couldn't see whatever it was that held Remy's attention so thoroughly.

She just saw herself and there wasn't much special there.

She plucked at her shirt, the too-big T-shirt that covered the low-riding jeans. Suddenly, she wished she'd picked up something a little . . . prettier. Something sort of flirty, or dressy at least. Something even remotely *female* would have been nice.

Something other than another oversized T-shirt.

"Hey."

She glanced up, saw Law's reflection join hers. "Hi."

"You ready for your date?"

He had a wide grin on his face and she rolled her eyes, tried to pretend she wasn't nervous. Not that it mattered with him. Nobody knew her the way he did, and he knew she was nervous.

"Yeah, I guess," she muttered, once more plucking at her shirt and giving it a look of acute dislike.

"Don't sound so enthusiastic."

Hope snorted. "I'm just irritated. I don't have much of anything decent to wear, and it's not like it really matters all that much, right? I mean, he didn't care much what I was wearing when he asked me out, so does it matter tonight?"

Law shrugged. "It doesn't matter to him. But it does to you . . . so here."

He tossed something at her. Something green.

She caught it and the silk almost slipped through her fingers. Jerking her eyes up, she stared at Law for a second before lowering her gaze to the halter top.

"Since when are you into women's fashion, Law?" she asked, holding it up.

"I'll have you know I'm a man of many talents," he said, catching her ear and tugging on it. "Will it fit?"

She held it up and looked at the mirror. "I think so, but . . ." She winced. "Law, this is a halter top. It's going to need a certain kind of . . ."

He dropped a bag on her dresser. "No, I haven't gone through your underwear drawer," he said and his cheeks were as red as hers as she peeked inside and saw what was in the bag. "I was in town earlier, saw the shirt in the window at the women's boutique on the square. Went inside to buy it and Molly, the store owner, said you'd need the right kind of bra. You two are about the same size, so there you go. If it doesn't fit, then don't wear it." Then he stroked a hand over her hair and said, "But stop worrying about it so much, honey, because he's not thinking about your clothes."

The bra did fit.

She stared at her reflection in the mirror and tried not to think about the last time she'd worn something pretty. Ever since she'd left Clinton, she'd done her damnedest to *not* wear pretty things—it had been another way to break Joey's hold over her. He'd all but dressed her as his own little doll.

She'd left every damn thing she owned behind when she left, just picking up what she needed here and there, usually from thrift stores. Baggy jeans, worn T-shirts, and the like.

But she was tired of letting that much *fear* control her. If she wanted to wear a pretty blouse, she could, right?

And if she felt a little weird wearing something Law

had bought, she just had to look in the mirror and think about how much better she looked wearing the blouse than she had in her oversized T-shirt. Self-consciously, she glanced at her scarred wrists as she started down the steps, but there wasn't anything she could do about those unless she wanted to wear long sleeves the rest of her life.

She was tired of hiding, so tired of it.

"I guess everything fit."

Law was sitting at the foot of the steps, a bottle of beer in his left hand. His right arm was still in a cast that went almost up to his elbow. The bruises on his face were mostly gone, but Hope knew she'd be seeing them in her memory for a good long time—maybe the rest of her life.

Sinking down on the stair just above him, she nervously smoothed the silk down and said, "Yeah. It fits. How does it look?"

"Shirt looks fine. You look beautiful." He waggled his eyebrows at her. "If I wouldn't feel like a lecher for saying it, I'd say that maybe you and me should really consider trying to get something going between us."

She kicked at his ankle. "Whatever." Wrapping her arms around her legs, she stared at the clock. "I don't have any makeup. I haven't worn any since . . . well. Never mind. But I don't have any. Maybe I should have bought some."

"He doesn't care." Law rolled his eyes. "For crying out loud, Hope. Relax."

"I can't," she snapped. She surged to her feet and hopped over him to the floor to pace. "I haven't been out on a *date* since high school. And then it was always with Joey. Shit, after the first few months, he didn't even ask me out. It was the thing—I'd be ready on Fridays and Saturdays at seven. Fridays were a movie night and Saturdays were dinner at the country club with his parents. When it's like that, is it even *dating*? It's not a date, then. It's just routine."

Law didn't answer right away. Instead, he took a drink from his beer and then he stood up. As she paced by him, he caught her arm, bringing her to a stop. "Hope, I'm going to make a couple of suggestions— one . . . again, *relax*. It's a movie. Nothing more. Nothing less. Just a movie. Treat him as a friend if you're too nervous thinking about anything more. And two? Sweetheart, do *not* keep thinking about everything that went wrong with Joey while you're out tonight. *You* deserve better, and so does Remy. That part of your life is over and done—don't let it ruin something you might have going here."

Blowing out a breath, Hope said, "That's easier said than done."

"I know." He slung an arm around her shoulders and tugged her close, pressing his lips to her brow. "But you need to do it. You kicked him to the curb and I know that was harder than hell. Do the same with his memory. Stop letting it choke you . . . at least for tonight. See where it takes you."

She sighed and rested her head on his shoulder.

"Yeah." She'd kicked him to the curb, and that was what she needed to do with his memory as well.

"Thank you," she said quietly, snaking an arm around his waist to hug him.

"For what?"

She squeezed him and stepped back. "For everything. You've always been there, you know. Always. I know you don't want thanks, but . . ."

Law went red and looked away. "Where else would I be? We're friends. That's what we do."

"Yeah." She might have said something else, but the phone rang. Sighing, she turned away to answer it.

But the second she lifted it to her ear, the line went dead.

He almost brought flowers.

Remy liked romancing a woman.

There was something uniquely pleasurable about it, and each woman was different.

But his gut told him he needed to move slow—as in glacially slow—with Hope.

So no flowers.

But as he stood on the porch and waited for Law to move his lazy ass and open the damn door, Remy wished he'd bought the fricking flowers. Would have given him something to do with his hands. He tucked them into his pockets. Counted to five. Rang the doorbell again. Nobody answered.

Rang it again. Dread curled through him and his mind, usually so logical and calm, started working overtime. His hands curled into fists and he found himself thinking about what had happened here just a few weeks ago—

But just as he'd worked himself up to take the door down, Law opened it.

Blowing out a breath, he scowled at the other man.

"Nice to see you, too, Jennings," Law said, smirking.

"What in the hell were you doing?"

Law cocked a brow. "Trying to talk some sense into Hope—I thought she had better taste than to date a lawyer." Then he shoved the door open wide. "It's not taking, though, since she's all ready for ya."

Hope stood in the arched doorway between the living room and hallway, scowling at Law.

Remy was damned glad she wasn't looking at him because he almost swallowed his tongue when he saw her.

Oh, holy shit, he was screwed.

She was wearing bright, vivid green, and her pale,

silken skin glowed against the silk. His hands itched to touch all that smooth, soft skin and damn, there was a lot of it bared.

The halter top left her shoulders and arms exposed, ended just where her low-rise jeans started. She sighed, her shoulders rising with the movement and he caught a glimpse of her belly. Another glimpse of pale, pale skin . . .

Oh, hell, was he screwed.

"Law, you're a pain in the ass," she said, shaking her head. Her cheeks were pink and her eyes had that glint in them, like she'd been laughing. A lot.

Law tipped his beer toward her. "I love you, too, honey."

Hope rolled her eyes and then looked at Remy. "Hi. I just need to grab a jacket, then I'm ready if you are."

Ready? Yeah, he was ready, but he doubted she was ready for the same thing *he* had in mind. Swallowing, he said, "Uh, yeah. Thought maybe we could grab a bite from Mac's Grill first—you haven't eaten, have you?"

Actually, he'd planned on taking her to the Inn, but that idea was not going to work. Candlelight on that smooth white skin—

Stop thinking about her skin, damn it!

"No, I haven't eaten." She gave him one of those nervous, shy smiles and then glanced at Law. "I'll see you later."

"Don't forget your curfew."

"Ha, ha." Hope gave him a narrow look and then focused her eyes on Remy.

He stared back at her, and he might have just kept on staring at her if she hadn't started to shuffle her feet, and if Law hadn't cleared his throat—very loudly in a very obnoxious manner.

Suave, Jennings . . . real suave. Let's see how well you manage to impress the lady tonight . . .

He gestured to the door, wracked his brain for something to say. He should say something. He knew he should. But what?

He had no clue.

As he opened the door for her, Law caught his gaze.

The other guy lifted a brow.

A thousand unspoken words passed between them and the nerves in Remy's gut increased. A weight settled on his shoulders.

If it had been anybody but Hope, the look on Law's face—that look that warned Remy to be cautious, be careful, it might have pissed him off a little. After all, she was a grown woman, right?

It didn't piss him off, though.

He just gave Law a short, terse nod and then headed outside, joining Hope on the porch.

The woman had been through hell, and she deserved . . . *needed* . . . to be treated with some care, with some caution.

Remy just hoped to hell he didn't fuck it all up.

"Did you like the movie?"

Hope winced as Remy's low, smooth voice broke through the silence of the night.

Shit, she'd hoped he wasn't going to ask that.

Her mind raced as she tried to come up with an answer, but she thought about it too long.

He sighed and said, "I take it that silence is a polite no?"

"No. Um, I mean, no, it's not a no." She shifted on the seat and rubbed her arms. Even with the jacket, she was still chilly. The nights were getting cool. "I . . . well."

Remy laughed. "Hope, it's not a test. Either you liked it or not—easy question."

"It's not an easy question," she muttered, smoothing her hands down her jeans. She glanced out the window as he turned toward Law's house. "I hardly remember any of it."

"You don't remember any of it?"

She shot him a narrow look. "*Hardly* remember any of it. That doesn't mean *all* of it." She reached up to toy with her hair only to lower her hand. It hovered in the air for a second, then fell to her side, curled into a fist.

He came to a stop in front of Law's house and climbed out, walking around to open the door for her. He held out a hand and she glanced down at his hand for a second before accepting it, that shy, nervous smile curling her lips.

"So you don't remember the movie, huh?" he asked.

The silvery light of the moon was bright enough to let him see the blush highlighting her cheeks.

"Umm . . ."

"I don't remember a whole lot of it myself," he murmured. Unable to stop himself, he reached over, brushed his fingers over the edges of her hair.

Her breath caught in her chest.

Shifting his gaze from her hair to her eyes, he murmured, "I get the feeling there's a story behind the change."

"Yeah. You could say that."

"Thought so. Maybe sometime, you'll tell me," he said quietly. The soft, gleaming strands of her hair felt like silk under his hand. Still watching her face, her eyes for some sign of fear, he combed his fingers through the sleek cut, cradled her nape.

She tilted her head back, watching him from under her lashes.

She licked her lips and Remy groaned. "Damn it, Hope."

"What?"

The soft, shaky sound of her voice should have done something to cool the fire burning inside him. Something. But her eyes gleamed with something other than fear. Unable to pull away, he lowered his head and slanted his mouth over hers.

One kiss, he told himself.

Just one easy, quick kiss.

He had plenty of control.

He could control his temper, his hunger, his . . .

Her mouth opened under his and she met his kiss with shy, sweet hesitation.

Remy felt like the very ground had crumbled under his feet.

Oh, hell.

Hope's hands came up, curled into the front of his shirt. He wanted to grab her, haul her closer. Wanted to feel that slender, soft body plastered against his—

Instead, he traced his tongue along the line of her mouth, teased hers. She tasted like butter and salt and under that, he could taste her. It threatened to drive him insane, threatened to level him. His hands itched to roam all over her body, to learn the delicate curves under that green silk.

But he kept his other hand at his side, touching only her neck, keeping it light . . . keeping it easy.

Even when her mouth opened wider and she leaned against him, her hands coming up to rest on his shoulders.

But when she shifted closer, as he felt the soft press of her breasts, he groaned and tore his mouth away, resting his brow against hers.

Her lashes fluttered open and her eyes, misty and green, stared into his.

She looked dazed.

Good. He'd hate to be the only one.

"Damn it, Hope, you're going to kill me here," he muttered.

"What?"

She licked her lips and shifted her gaze to his mouth, pushed up onto her toes.

Off in the distance, a car honked its horn, blasted its way down the road, driving far, far too fast.

Hope jumped.

Reluctantly, Remy let her go, watched as awareness slowly crept back into her gaze. Awareness . . . and embarrassment. A blush crept up her neck, staining her pale, ivory skin a delicate pink.

He brushed the back of his knuckles down her cheek and murmured, "You pack one hell of a punch, you know that?"

"Um . . . whatever." The blush deepened and a self-conscious smile curled her lips.

Grinning, he dipped his head and this time, he kept the kiss quick and easy, pulling back before he could take it any deeper. Hunger gnawed at him, but he shoved it down, locked it up. Slow. He had to take this slow— *glacier slow,* he reminded himself. Against her mouth, he whispered, "So you maybe want to try this again sometime?"

He lifted his head and toyed with her hair as he waited for her to open her eyes and meet his gaze. "Hmmm. Yeah. Yeah, I think maybe I would."

"So?"

Hope closed the door behind her and leaned back against it.

Law was lounging against the arch between the living room and hallway, a smug grin on his face.

Rolling her eyes, she tried to pretend she wasn't blushing.

"Please tell me you weren't watching us through the window."

"Would I do that?" he asked, cocking a brow at her.

"You? Yes. Absolutely you would. You're the nosiest person I've ever met."

Guilelessly, he smiled. "Yes. I am. And yes, I was watching. So. When you two going out again?"

"Who said we were?" Hope scowled at him, crossing her arms over her chest. Her heart was still racing, she thought. Racing and dancing around like it hadn't since . . . well, ever. She hadn't ever felt quite like this. And if Law weren't standing there, she suspected she might have been grinning like a fool. As it was, she had to fight to keep the smile from tugging up the corners of her mouth.

Happy.

Damn.

She felt . . . light, easy . . . happy.

She hadn't felt this at peace, this easy, this *happy* in years.

Still, with Law smugly grinning at her, she felt obligated to glare at him.

He reached up, rubbed his chin. "Are you going out again?

"Yes." Hope rolled her eyes. "We're going out for dinner at the Inn tomorrow night. He mentioned something about Sunday, but we've been going over to Lena's lately, so . . ."

Law shrugged. "Call him and invite him along."

"Umm . . ."

"Lena won't mind."

Hope blushed and looked away, trying to pretend that was her only concern. But Law knew her too well. He sighed and shoved off the wall, came over and settled against the door next to her.

"Honey, he's not still pining after Lena. Trust me. Okay?"

Lifting her eyes to him, she said, "It's silly to even be worried about it, isn't it?"

"No." He slung an arm over her shoulders. "Hope, it's kinda obvious, there's something between you two—I think there's been a vibe there for a while. Sometimes it happens that fast. The shit going on around here has complicated things, but it didn't kill whatever's trying to happen. So while I don't think you need to worry about his past with Lena, I also think it's perfectly normal that you *do* worry about it."

Resting her head against him, she sighed. "Is it hard for you? Seeing her so happy with Ezra?"

Law grunted. "Shit, you had to go ask that, didn't you?" He thunked his head back against the door, staring off into the darkness of the quiet house. "It was . . . at first. Damn hard. But he makes her happy, and after a little while, I finally figured out one vital thing—if she's happy with him, that means one thing. She's not meant to be with me."

"Law . . ."

The phone rang.

Hope jolted. Law scowled.

Shoving off the wall, he went over and grabbed the phone, studied the blank readout on the caller ID and didn't pick it up.

But he did eye the time on the clock. "It's damn near one in the morning. Who in the hell is calling?"

Three rings later, the phone rolled over to voice mail.

Law went to check the message. Hope, a little nosy herself, trailed along.

But there wasn't any message, other than a few seconds of dead air.

"Must be a wrong number," he mused, as he disconnected.

He hung up the phone.

Wrong number.

But for some reason, Hope shivered.

* * *

That was a bad decision, my girl, Joe thought, watching from the darkness of his car, as each of the lights in Law Reilly's house went dim. It was bad enough that she'd come *here*—to Reilly's. It was his damn fault, Joe thought. His fucking fault that she'd left him. She shouldn't have come here and she'd pay for it.

The whore.

But she wasn't just here with Reilly.

She'd gone out with that pussy lawyer. That fucking asshole who'd called all around his town, talking to people. They thought Joe hadn't seen the way they looked at him, but he had. Yeah, he'd fucking seen those looks. It would stop, though. When he brought her back home, they'd see who was in charge.

The betrayal was like acid. She left him, then she came here not just to Law, but now she was out with Jennings. She'd let him put his hands on her.

She'd fucking cut her hair.

Bad, bad decisions all around.

He eyed his phone, considered calling again.

But in the end, decided against it.

Subtle.

He'd be subtle about all of this.

Be slow as he moved in on her.

He didn't want her too freaked out, didn't want to scare her into running.

No. He didn't want her to see him coming until it was too late.

CHAPTER
TWELVE

IT WAS MONDAY MORNING, AND EXACTLY ONE MONTH to the day after she'd buried cousin Joely, Nia Hollister rode back into the small town of Ash, Kentucky.

She knew she'd caught some looks.

Small town in Kentucky, strange biracial woman riding into town on a Harley—yeah, that's going to catch a few looks.

Those looks only increased when she parked in front of the sheriff's department and got off her bike.

She was five foot ten and most of it was leg. The boots she wore added a good two inches to her height, so she stood a good six feet even. Add to that the fact that she knew she wore her anger and grief like an ugly, red scar, and she knew she'd have people looking at her. She knew many of them would probably be whispering about her behind her back and wondering what kind of trouble she was looking to cause.

Well, she *was* here to cause trouble.

For a few specific people.

Starting with Sheriff Dwight Nielson.

She pocketed her keys and started up the concrete sidewalk.

No news.

Oh, the good sheriff was keeping in touch. She had to give him credit for that.

But he didn't have anything new to tell her.

There *was* nothing new.

Actually, there was *nothing*.

And Nia was fucking *tired* of it.

There had to be something.

Something.

And damn it, she wasn't leaving until she knew something.

The one day Ms. Tuttle arranged to take off turned out to be the one day Nielson desperately needed her.

"You can't honestly expect me to *believe* that you think *both* of them are *innocent*," Deb spat.

She said it like the words themselves tasted bad or something, Nielson thought.

He kept his hands folded on his desk, kept his face impassive, kept his voice mild as he responded, "Deb, if I thought they were guilty, I'd look for proof. And even if I didn't think they were guilty, I'd look for proof. And I have. I've had several deputies assigned to this. Detective Jennings has spent hours on this. I've spent hours on it. There *is* no proof. We have no interest in either Law Reilly or Hope Carson for the crimes. And unless you actually have something other than . . . dislike, you need to let this go."

"Let it go?"

She stood up straight as board, pressed a hand to her chest. The look on her face was one of complete, utter moral outrage. Nielson would have laughed, if he hadn't known just how much worse it would have made things.

If only he had known just how bad things were about to get . . .

"Excuse me, Sheriff."

He glanced up.

Nia Hollister cast a long, lean shadow.

She didn't share much in common with her cousin, other than her name.

But he could see how grief weighed down on her, see the anger she carried like a weapon.

It vibrated around her and his office felt ten times smaller—a dangerous combination.

Her eyes zeroed in on Deb Sparks and Nielson found himself remembering the last time Nia had been in his office.

Deb had also been here.

Going on about almost the exact same thing.

Nia's light gold eyes narrowed.

That sharp mind of hers started to whirl.

Staring into Nia's eyes, Nielson said softly, "Deb, if you don't mind, I need to speak to my guest here."

Deb's spine stiffened. Even without looking at her dead-on, he could see her outright indignation. Glancing away from Nia, he dredged up a smile. "She drove a long way—recently suffered a loss. Surely you understand."

If nothing else, he knew how to play this woman.

Deb's mouth pinched tight, but she inclined her head. "Oh, certainly. But we're not done discussing this."

Of course, they weren't.

Just as long as she left *now*, before Nia Hollister got it in her mind to ask the biggest gossip in town—

"So. I'm kind of curious. Just who is it that you keep bitching about?"

Nia folded her arms across her chest and stared at Deb as the older woman started for the door.

Deb came to stop and met Nia's gaze. "Excuse me?"

Lifting a shoulder in a negligent shrug, Nia said, "The last time I was here, you were here, too. Yelling at the man over there about something. Seems to me it's the same sort of something. Just has me curious."

"If you really want to know—"

"Deb." Nielson shoved up from his desk.

She shot him a dour look over one skinny shoulder. "It's my duty as a concerned citizen to warn people, Sheriff. As *you* aren't taking your job seriously."

Then she looked back at Nia. "We've got two cold-blooded killers in this town—a man by the name of Law Reilly, and his mistress, Hope Carson. They are a piece of work—murdering savages, the both of them. They killed a girl, just over a month ago. He even had the brass to leave the woman's body on his own property and then concoct some *insane* story that the sheriff here believes. They also killed a deputy. But nobody is doing a damn thing about it."

"That's enough," Nielson said.

"They even—"

"*Enough*." Nielson came out from behind the desk and stormed over to Deb's side. He tolerated her, because generally, she meant no harm. She was a gossip and although she needed, *craved* attention, as long as she got it, she was fine.

But this wasn't just malicious—it was dangerous. And cruel.

He could see the fury glinting in Nia Hollister's gaze and he had no idea if Deb was even aware of it.

Fury . . . and grief. They were a bad, bad mix.

Staring into Deb's nearly colorless eyes, he said, "I repeat, that is *enough*. Not only are you overstepping, you're coming dangerously close to what could be considered slander."

"Oh, no, it couldn't. I'm entitled to my opinion."

"*Not* if you're stating it as fact, which you *are*. And there's no damned proof. There is actually *evidence* to the contrary," Nielson snapped, shoving between Deb and Nia.

Nia's pale brown gaze drilled into the back of his

neck, but he ignored it, because right now, he needed to get this viper out of his office, before she caused any more problems. What in the hell had Law done to piss her off so bad?

"Now, if you would, can we discuss this later?"

Deb's eyes narrowed at him, glittering with outrage. "Why won't you listen to reason, Sheriff Nielson?"

"Because it's not reason," he snapped. "And I'm done discussing this. You either remove yourself, or I'll remove you, Ms. Sparks. My patience has reached its limit."

Without waiting to see if she would listen, he turned his back to her and listened as her solid, square, sensible shoes thudded dully on the floor. Nia Hollister stood, her pale eyes narrowed, watching him closely.

Her face, a clean, elegant oval, was unreadable.

Although there were circles under her eyes, in that moment, no emotion showed on her face.

She had one hell of a poker face, he decided.

Too good of one.

And that was what warned him. What worried him. She was keeping too much bottled up inside and after what she'd been through, that wasn't good.

"You'll have to excuse her," he said, keeping his voice mild and low. "She gets excited, and very often, she gets excited about things she has no reason getting excited about."

"She was talking about my cousin," Nia said, her voice low and even. She had a lovely drawl, deeper than even those in Ash, slower, softer.

She came from Virginia, he remembered, Williamsburg, he thought.

When he didn't respond, a black brow arched over her expressionless eyes. "Was she or was she not talking about my cousin?"

"She was. However, she has no idea what she's talking about," Nielson said.

He hoped she'd believe him.

But he suspected he was hoping for too much.

This woman had lost too much. And he had nothing to offer her.

Sometimes, when a person had nothing, even speculation and pure bullshit was better.

Nia curled her lip. "She sounded pretty damn certain to me."

"Well, I've also had her in my office, on numerous occasions, and the stories have ranged from her niece kidnapping her dog, to the local kids trying to poison her cat, and about every other month, she reports seeing a serial killer van."

Nia's brows dropped low over her eyes. "A serial killer's van?"

"No." Nielson said, "A serial killer van. That's exactly how she phrases it. According to Deb, *every* white work van is a serial killer van. She once reported the local phone company's van."

"So because she's a routine complainer, you're dismissing her complaints."

"No." Nielson shook his head. "I don't dismiss complaints. But her suppositions don't hold any water. What she was ranting about has been investigated, completely and fully. The man she's accusing has a rock-solid alibi. Trust me, Ms. Hollister, if you really want me to find who took your cousin from you, then don't make me waste my time on Deb Sparks. There's nothing *there*."

"So you're saying you investigated both of them . . . inside and out."

"Yes." Nielson met her gaze and held it.

She looked away before he did, but in his gut, he knew it wasn't because she was ready to concede a damn thing.

She sighed and rubbed the back of her neck, moving to stare out the window.

Nielson wondered what it was about that window that drew the attention of his visitors so much. Almost every single person ended up in just that spot, staring outside.

"Do you have anything?" Nia murmured. "Know anything?"

"No. I'm afraid not," he said quietly. "We're still pursuing all avenues."

He wished he could tell her something.

As hard as it was to do this job, it was even harder to look into those unusual, pale golden eyes and keep saying no.

"All avenues," she murmured. Her voice was soft, sad.

Then she turned around and glared at him. "Shove it up your ass, Sheriff," she bit off. "I don't want to hear the standard line again. I've heard it *enough*. What I want to hear is what you're doing."

"Now, Ms. Hollister. You're a bright woman and I imagine you've probably been doing some research . . . you know I'm not going to go sharing details of this case with you."

She sneered at him. "What case? You don't have jackshit. Fuck it," she muttered, shoving away from the wall. "I'm starting to think you couldn't find your dick in the dark without a flashlight and a road map."

He winced as the door slammed shut behind her.

She'd just take a drive out there.

That was all.

Okay, so she had placed a couple of phone calls to figure out just where this Law Reilly lived, since his phone number and his address were unlisted and she wasn't about to go asking around town.

She wasn't getting too over-the-line obsessive. Besides, what *was* over the line when her cousin was dead, anyway?

If she didn't kill anybody, she figured she was within the lines.

She came to the drive and had to double-check the directions to make sure she was at the right place. It was one *long* drive, too.

A person couldn't even see the house from the road all that well, not until after that first little dip and bend.

Then the land opened up and what a house.

She hated to admit it, but her heart gave a little skip. Then a sigh. Wistful envy burned through her for the briefest moment, quickly chased away by the rush of rage.

She'd been busting her ass for the past few years and still couldn't do much more than an apartment halfway between Chesapeake and Williamsburg. At least not anything that suited her. And some guy who might have something to do with Joely dying had a place like this? Fuck that.

According to that woman in town, this bastard knew something about how she'd died . . . might even have killed her.

Nausea churned in her gut and if she'd had anything for breakfast other than tea, she might have puked.

Oh, fuck.

What if this guy had killed her? What if she was being stupid enough to go out here . . .

Stop it, Nia.

It wasn't like she was unequipped to take care of herself. She sometimes found herself in very dangerous circumstances.

And it wasn't like she hadn't come out here prepared for that possibility.

Pulling up in front of the house, she kicked a leg over

the bike, taking a few minutes to study the endless expanse of brick and sparkling glass.

Shit.

If Joely's killer lived inside there, it just added one more question to the list she had for her Maker.

Psychotic murderers shouldn't be able to live in places like that.

They belonged in shadowy, smelly hellholes.

Period.

CHAPTER
THIRTEEN

LAW HEARD THE ENGINE.

Vaguely.

But he tuned it out.

He was on a roll—the story was coming solid and strong. It hadn't come like this in . . . weeks. Probably longer. Hope was somewhere working on whatever she was doing to make his life easier.

It wasn't Lena, because she'd call first. It wasn't Ezra, because he was with Lena and Lena would make *him* call first.

So, basically, it wasn't anybody important.

That was all the information he needed to tune the world out as the story unfolded before him.

It was tricky, trying to talk the story free, instead of type it.

The damn voice-to-text software was a pain in the ass, even though he knew he needed to get used to it.

Still, today, for once, it was coming easier and he wasn't about to stop. At least not until the low, throaty rumble of a motor drew closer, closer . . . closer.

A chill raced down his spine.

He tried to ignore it.

But as he went to talk out the next passage—it had

just been in his head—the words froze in his throat and he found himself staring out the window.

He couldn't see anything then.

Not a damn thing.

But still . . . he stared, waited, listened as the engine abruptly cut off.

Forty-five seconds later, there was a knock on the door.

Scowling, he saved and finagled the laptop off to the side, scowling at the cast that still immobilized his right forearm from just below the elbow. He shoved up out of the chair and was already halfway to the door when Hope appeared in the hallway.

"I got it," he said.

She arched a brow at him.

"I'm supposed to be doing this sort of thing," she reminded him.

He ignored her.

He needed to answer that door. In his gut, he knew it.

With a feeling that was a weird mix of both dread and jubilation, he turned the doorknob.

The door opened to reveal an Amazon. That was his very first thought.

His second thought was that he didn't know how in the hell she'd ended up on his property, but he wanted to so he could send whoever a thank-you card.

Her eyes . . . Shit. Her eyes.

They were the palest shade of gold he'd ever seen, paler than whiskey, but just as potent, just as strong. Mysterious and beautiful.

They stared into his, revealing nothing.

Her skin was the color of coffee and cream, warm and smooth and delicious.

The leather jacket she wore seemed too damn warm for the weather they were having, but it suited her. Just like the plain black T-shirt suited her, just like the worn and faded jeans suited her.

He imagined black silk would suit her every bit as well. Black silk, pearls, red lipstick on that lush mouth. Or even nothing at all. Lust punched through him with a force that damn near leveled him.

She lifted a black brow at him.

Those lush lips parted and she said, "Are you Reilly? Law Reilly?"

Oh, shit. She was here looking for him.

Maybe fate had decided to smile on him.

He stepped aside and gestured her inside. "I am. And what can I do for you, Ms. . . . ?"

"Nia. Call me Nia." The thick black fringe of her lashes swept down, shielding her eyes. A faint smile curled her lips up as she sauntered inside, her hips swaying from side to side. He turned and admired the view as he shut the door.

"You've got a gorgeous house."

You've got a gorgeous ass, he thought. But he kept those words behind his teeth—barely. Nia. He liked that.

She shot him a look over her shoulder.

There was a strange look in her eyes, a mix of something. It bordered on satisfaction and contempt. With a smug grin curling her lips, she turned around and faced him from in the middle of the hallway.

"So. You're Law Reilly."

Somewhere in the back of his head, a siren started to wail.

He really, really needed to listen to it.

But he was still so caught up in staring at her . . . it wasn't until she had that gun pointed at his head that he fully realized there was a problem.

But then she smirked at him, and that served as a very, very efficient wake-up call.

Aw, hell.

He almost gaped at her, but he had enough self-control—
barely—to keep from staring at the gun in her hand like
some slack-jawed yokel. Instead, he started ticking
through his options and measuring the escape routes.

Hope had retreated to the kitchen and she was enough
of a loner that unless she sensed a problem, she wasn't
coming out here.

Good.

One less victim.

This woman held the gun in a firm grasp, but there
was something about her white-knuckled grip that told
him she wasn't used to handling weapons. Especially
loaded ones. And he'd bet his busted right arm and his
left arm that gun was loaded—she was looking for
blood.

Still, she wasn't comfortable with the weapon—one
thing he had going for him.

He needed every last advantage he could get, considering the fact that his right arm was all but useless and
his best friend was just a few yards away.

Yeah, Hope was a loner, but if she did meander out
here, it would give this woman another target.

"Yeah. I'm Reilly," he said, keeping his voice low and
steady, even though he wanted to yell. "What can I do
for you?"

That lush, pretty mouth of hers curled in a sneer.

"What can you do for me? How's this for starts?
Bring my cousin back—that woman you killed? I want
her *back*."

That woman you killed—

Staring into her pale, grief-stricken golden eyes, something in his heart turned to ash.

Inexplicably, misery rolled through him. He'd been
dealing with this shit for weeks. Yeah, some people be-

lieved he had something to do with raping and killing a woman. Not a lot, but even one person thinking he could do that was too much.

He'd thought he was getting used to it—thought he could handle it.

What in the hell should it matter what this sleek, sexy stranger thought?

It shouldn't. Shouldn't matter, not one damn bit, but it did.

"I didn't kill your cousin," he said quietly. "I've never raised my hand to a woman in my life."

She glared at him again, and even though she was standing there with a gun on him, even though she thought he was a murdering psychotic, he still found himself drawn to her—found himself wanting to cradle her face in his hands and see if he couldn't soften the hard, angry line of her mouth. Then he wanted to pull her close and hold her, ease the grief he saw in her eyes.

"Yeah, like you're going to say anything different." The gun in her hand started to tremble.

People didn't realize the strain it was to hold a firearm steady, especially for more than a few seconds.

"I wasn't in town when she died." He thought he heard a board creaking and he wanted to look, see if it was Hope, but he didn't dare—couldn't risk drawing attention to her. "I was at a funeral for a friend of mine. There was no way I could have killed her."

"Yeah, I heard about that. Also heard about your girlfriend—some sick shit the two of you got going between you. Is that how the two of you get your rocks off?" Her voice broke as she stared at him.

Law could see the desperation in her eyes and it clawed at his heart.

She didn't really think he did it, he realized. She just wanted to—maybe even needed to. Needed some sort of closure. And because she needed that, she needed to believe he had done it.

"Look," he said softly, edging a step closer. He heard something from the hall—a soft, shaky gasp.

Fuck. It was Hope. He saw her from the corner of his eye. She had her back pressed to the wall and she had a phone in her hand.

Holding out a hand, he said, "Just put the gun down and we can talk. I can prove I wasn't here and you can talk to my friend—you decide then if you really think she's the sort of person who'd kill anybody."

"Get the fuck *back*."

Then she glanced past him. Her eyes widened and he swore. She'd just caught sight of Hope's reflection in the mirror behind Law.

She shifted, taking two long strides and placing herself where she could see Law and Hope. "Put the damn phone down," she snarled at Hope.

"When you put the gun down," Hope said. Her voice shook, but she didn't look away.

"Damn it, I said putting the fucking phone *down*—"

Law's gut turned to ice as he saw her finger tighten on the trigger. Fuck it. She was close enough now. He swept up and out with his right leg. The crescent kick knocked the gun out of her hand and sent it flying. All three of them scrambled for it, but Law blocked the woman and Hope got to it first.

The Amazon swung at him and that long, lean body of hers had some serious power in it. He grunted, pain shooting through him as he blocked the first punch with his casted arm.

She swung again, this time with her right hand and he blocked with his left, trapping her arm and shifting so that he had her pinned against him.

Aw, hell . . .

He immediately shifted position because if he stayed

like *that*, there was no way she'd believe he wasn't a perverted killer. He shouldn't have a raging hard-on, not when she'd just pulled a gun on him and his best friend.

Not when his arm was screaming like a bitch.

Not when she was glaring at him like she'd want nothing more than to see him six feet under.

"Let me the fuck go," she snarled.

Her pupils were huge, just the thinnest sliver of gold showing. Her mouth, so soft and lush, trembled. And although her voice and body were all attitude and fight, there was fear inside her.

Fear and grief and rage.

She struggled against him and he had to lean against her harder, muffling a groan as it put more pressure on his arm. "If I do, are you going to attack me again?" he asked.

Her body tensed.

Her eyes stared into his.

He stared at her like he'd really let her go.

He wouldn't. He was toying with her. He had to be.

That was what she wanted to believe, needed to believe.

But staring into his eyes, she wondered . . .

Nia knew people. It was her stock in trade—she knew when they were scum, knew when they were basically decent people. She knew when she was being conned, knew when she was being told the truth. She also knew when she was staring into the eyes of a human monster.

That was what she'd come here hoping—*needing*—to find.

Fuck.

Silencing that inner voice, she told herself not to write him off yet. Hell, sociopaths could fool anybody, right?

Staring into those all-too-nice eyes, she gave a terse nod. "Fine. You let me go and I'll be good . . . for now."

Not that he would let her go.

Except he did.

Those eyes, green-gold and flecked with brown, stared into hers for long seconds and then the hand that had kept her wrists pinned slowly let go. He eased away and just like that, she was free.

Narrowing her eyes, she shoved away from the wall, glanced from him to the little brunette who'd crept into the room.

Slim, shy, and pale, the woman stood holding the gun in hands that trembled.

She was so frightened, the woman looked like she'd jump if you yelled *boo* too loud.

Scowling, Nia looked from Reilly to the woman.

"Who in the hell is she?"

She kept her gaze focused on Reilly, even though she kept the woman in her line of sight—just in case it was an act. Although she knew it wasn't. *Nobody* acted that good.

"That's my friend, Hope," he said, his voice soft and easy, like he was trying to talk to a mad dog.

The words hit her heart with the force of a sledge-hammer to her chest.

Hope.

"Hope Carson?" she said, forcing the words past her tight throat.

Even as she shot one quick glance at the woman, she already knew the answer.

And she started to kick herself, even as shame and grief crawled through her belly.

We've got two cold-blooded killers in this town—a man by the name of Law Reilly, and his mistress, Hope Carson. They are a piece of work—murdering savages, the both of them.

That gossipy, conniving old bitch—

The woman glanced at Reilly and then at Nia. "Yes, I'm Hope Carson."

Nia closed her eyes and tipped her head back, staring up at the ceiling. A harsh, bitter laugh escaped her. The sheriff had warned her. She had to give him credit. He'd tried to warn her.

"That crazy old bitch," she muttered, shaking her head. "That crazy, crazy old bitch."

Tears burned in the back of her throat—choked her. They stung her eyes, threatening to blind her. But she wouldn't give in to them.

Joely deserved more of her than tears. Joely deserved justice. Joely deserved to have her killer caught.

Waiting until she could face these two without breaking, she took one deep, slow breath, then another. And another. Then, she opened her eyes and made herself face Law Reilly.

He was staring at her with a disconcerting mix of sympathy and understanding. Like he knew too many of the thoughts whirling through her mind.

The woman, though, Hope, she was staring at Nia like she was a time bomb about ready to explode.

You have no idea how right you are.

She still held the gun, too, gripped in skinny, pale hands that looked far too small to hold the weight of the unregistered, and very illegal, Browning.

Holding out her hand, Nia quietly said, "Can I have the gun back?"

"Are you *nuts*?"

Her green eyes went wide and her jaw dropped as she gaped at Nia. Then she shot Reilly a quick look—the kind of look that said, *You do something with her.*

Setting her jaw, Nia said, "Look, I'm sorry. I was given some bad information and I reacted . . . well, badly. I apologize. Now can I please have my fucking gun so I can leave?"

She hardened her voice and glared at the smaller woman, fully prepared to intimidate the hell out of her, if she had to. Hope Carson looked like she had a spine made out of Jell-O and while Nia generally didn't get off on intimidation, if she had to use it to get what she needed, then she would. This was the type of woman who would cave under that sort of pressure—Nia would have almost laid money on it.

But she would have been out the cash, because Hope glared at her.

"Um, no, you can't have your fucking gun," Hope said, her eyes narrowing. "You reacted *badly*? You think that's sufficient? That's sort of like calling Hurricane Katrina a thunderstorm, don't you think?"

"Look," Nia growled, advancing another step. "My *cousin*, my *only family*, is dead and I was told you two had something to do with it. What in the hell would *you* do?"

Hope jerked the gun up.

Sneering, Nia said, "You couldn't use that if you had to, Tinkerbell."

"Wanna bet?" Hope snapped.

"That's enough." Law stepped between them, pushing the gun down. He took it away from Hope and Nia watched as he managed to get the safety on, even though he was somewhat compromised, considering he had his right arm in a cast. But if she thought he was going to turn it over, she was dead wrong.

He looked it over, and shot her a quick glance, one brow lifting. "This is illegal."

Nia just stared at him, wondering how he knew to look. Yeah, the serial numbers had been removed but not everybody knew to check for that.

When he tucked it in the back of his pants, she snarled at him. "Give me my damn gun."

"You managed to get your hands on one unregistered

gun, you can get another and I'm not letting you in my house with a loaded weapon."

"How do you know it's loaded?" She lifted her chin.

Angling his head to the side, he asked, "Well, do you want me to check?" Then he shook his head. "You came here gunning for blood and if you'd decided I was responsible, you were perfectly willing to pull that trigger. I saw it in your eyes. You're not leaving here with the gun."

Nia curled her hands into fists. He wasn't wrong. Yes, she'd been willing, and ready—hell, she'd been *dying* to kill. Anything to avenge Joely. Slowly, she blew out a breath. "You're not off-base," she said softly. "You're not. But you didn't do it, I see that, and I'm not so lost in grief that I'm going to kill innocent people."

"Grief does bad things to the head," Reilly said quietly. "Sometimes innocent doesn't look all that innocent."

"Yeah. Grief does bad things to the head. But I'm not blind. You can be a charming bastard, I'd bet my bike on that." She skimmed him over with a quick look from head to toe and then looked at Hope. "But if I'm supposed to believe *this* woman had anything to do with killing somebody . . . hell, no."

There was something about the way she said it that made it seem both insult and fact, Hope decided.

And for some reason, the fact that the woman had decided Hope wasn't capable was this woman's reason for *not* killing them? It didn't do much to soothe the wild fear in Hope's belly just then.

Of course, she was also completely pissed over the dismissive way the woman had looked her over . . . the way she'd sneered at her and called her *Tinkerbell*.

Weak.

The woman looked at her and saw *weakness*, the same way so many other people did.

Blood stained her cheeks red as the woman's eyes bored into hers.

She had it—that indefinable confidence, that strength. The same kind of confidence Lena had. The kind of confidence, the strength Hope would never have.

Even though grief ravaged her face, turning her dusky skin translucent and leaving shadows under her pretty brown eyes, she looked strong. Confident. Ready.

And she stared at Hope the same way so many others did.

That *Tinkerbell* comment had pissed her off, for reasons Hope couldn't even imagine.

"So because I don't look like much, you think we should just give you your gun and let you go on your way?" Hope said, crossing her arms over her chest.

"Look, I'm sorry. I already said that. What else do you want?"

"How about you give me an idea what made you think we were responsible?" Law asked.

Her mouth twisted in a sneer. "Fine. I can tell you that. Her name was Deb Sparks. Now you give me my fucking gun."

"Deb." Law closed his eyes.

Hope could have screamed.

The woman looked between the two of them and her eyes narrowed. "This woman pulled this before?"

"She's just . . . imaginative," Law bit off.

Imaginative, my ass, Hope thought.

"Fine. You got her name. Maybe you can go have Tinkerbell there give her a talking-to. Now can I have my gun?"

"No."

"Give me my damned gun," she snarled, moving as though she might come after Law.

Law shifted, his body braced and ready. Despite his casted arm, he didn't look at all worried, and the woman scowled at him. "You're not getting the gun, angel. Deal with it."

Hope smiled and angled her head to the phone lying on the floor. "You could always call the cops," she offered. "Tell them we stole your gun."

Her belly jumped even thinking about it, but as the woman's gaze cut to hers, she knew there was nothing to worry about. This woman wouldn't be calling the cops.

Her eyes lingered on Hope's for a moment.

Then she looked at Law, the tension dragging on.

Finally, without saying another word, she turned on her heel and stormed out, her booted heels thudding dully on the polished hardwood floors.

Somehow, Hope knew they hadn't seen the last of her.

It was a terrifying thought.

"Should I call the sheriff?" she asked quietly.

Law shook his head and moved to the door, watching the woman.

"No."

"She just pulled a gun on us."

He didn't say anything, just kept staring out the door.

Long after the dust from her bike settled, Law continued to stare after her.

When he finally turned around and met Hope's gaze, she was braced for him to be pissed, or mad. Or something.

What she wasn't prepared for was the pensive, almost thoughtful look on his face.

She knew his expressions—knew them pretty well, especially after living under the same roof as him for the past month.

He looked . . . interested. Very, very interested.

"Law."

He glanced at her, that familiar, distracted look on his face. The bruises had all but faded, leaving just a few discolored areas here and there. He hadn't shaved, but it wasn't a bad look for him. It was a scruffy, sexy look, she guessed, one that a lot of women would find pretty damn attractive.

"That woman just pulled a gun on us."

"Yeah. I know." He frowned and reached around behind his back, pulled the gun from wherever he had jammed it—hell, people really did just shove them in their waistbands? He eyed the Browning, that bemused, befuddled look still on his face.

He didn't look scared, though. Despite the fact that he was holding that gun in his hand.

Hope, on the other hand, felt like she might puke. Pressing a hand to her belly, she said, "Is it loaded?"

He shot her a glance, then grunted. "Hard for me to check one-handed, but yeah. I'm pretty sure it's loaded."

Hope groaned and when her knees buckled, she happily let them, sinking to the floor and pressing her forehead against them. A cold sweat broke out all over her body. "It's loaded. She came out here with an unregistered, loaded gun and now she's gone—we don't know if she's going to come back and try to kill us while we sleep. You don't want me calling the sheriff's office. And you look like you want to eat her for lunch."

He was quiet and she peeked up at him, saw that he was still studying the gun like it held some great mystery of the universe.

Swearing, she surged to her feet and glared at him. "*Law!*"

"Huh?"

"That woman is *insane*. She all but threatened to kill us—had a loaded, unregistered gun—and you just let her traipse away. And you look like you want to hunt her down and get her phone number! And her bra and panty size, too."

A dull red flush settled over his cheekbones. Sighing, he set the gun down on the table under the mirror.

"Hope, she's not going to come back and kill us in our sleep."

"Yeah, and how are you so sure? Did you go and turn into Ms. Cleo overnight or something?" she asked, her voice thick with sarcasm.

Slanting a narrow look at her, he muttered, "Geez, you went and got mouthy over the past few weeks, Tinkerbell."

"Don't call me that." Shoving a hand through her hair, she glanced at the gun and then back at him. "Look, I'm just freaked out. You said it yourself—grief does bad things to a person's head. You know that. Hell, *I* know that."

She'd been reeling over her parents' unexpected deaths just a few weeks after graduation when she married Joey. If she'd taken a little more time, grown up more, maybe even just gone to college and had some time to figure out who in the hell she was, maybe he wouldn't have been able to hurt her the way he had.

"Hope."

Looking up, she met his gaze. He crossed the hall and reached up, curled a hand around the back of her neck, drew her against his chest. Sighing, she rested her head against him, listened to the comforting sound of his heartbeat. Level, steady . . . alive. He was there—he'd always been there. Nothing had happened.

"Damn it, what if she'd shot you?" she whispered, tears thickening in her throat.

"She didn't. And now that's she's cooled down and figured out just what sort of person she'd gotten her story from, she's not going to. That woman isn't any sort of idiot." He rubbed his hand up and down her spine. "It's okay, kid. Everything's fine."

"But what if . . ."

Oh, shit.

The storm inside her broke.

Reaction settled in hard and fast, and before she knew it, she was shaking, shaking so hard she could barely stand. Her teeth rattled, tears burned out of her eyes and she couldn't think, couldn't see, could hardly breathe.

"Hope . . ." Helpless, Law curled his useless right arm around her as best as he could. "Come on, sweetheart. I'm fine. *You're* fine."

But she didn't seem to hear him. Wasn't even aware of him as she trembled like a leaf.

Feeling a pair of eyes boring into his neck, he whipped his head around. Tension spiked—adrenaline rushed.

And then it drained out when he saw Remy standing there.

Although judging by that strange glitter in Remy's eyes . . .

"Come on in," Law said. "Maybe you can calm her down."

"Calm her down?" Remy echoed, as jealousy tore a nasty, ugly hole in his gut.

They were close.

He knew that.

He'd have to deal with it.

But standing there, watching while Hope leaned against Law . . .

Then he realized something.

Hope was shaking.

Trembling, terrified, and although that ivory complexion of hers was always pale, she wasn't ever *that* pale.

"What in the hell is wrong?" he asked.

At the sound of his voice, Hope flinched.

Then she blinked and glassy eyes focused on his face. "Remy?"

"Yeah. Hey, what's wrong?"

She pushed away from Law, her movements clumsy

and stiff, like somebody who'd been asleep. She took one stumbling step toward him and he caught her, steadied her. To his surprise, she cuddled against his chest, rested her brow against him and sighed. It shuddered out of her and as he brought one hand up to rest it on her waist, the tension in her slender body seemed to drain away.

"What's wrong, Hope?" He rubbed his lips against her temple, not entirely sure she'd tell him a damn thing, but he couldn't not ask.

"Hmmm. Crazy day. Just give me a minute," she whispered.

"I can do that." Yeah, he could stand there for quite a while holding her. Especially when she snuggled closer. Then she slid her arms around his waist and pressed in even tighter, like she couldn't get close enough.

The blood in his head began a slow, dangerous descent.

Oh, damn.

But backing away didn't seem to be an option, either, because even though she didn't seem quite so shaken, she was still worked up over something. Every few seconds, an odd little hitching breath would escape her, like she was struggling not to sob.

Her fingers were kneading the flesh at his waist, kind of like a cat.

And there was so much tension in the air, he could cut it with a knife.

From the corner of his eye, he saw Law moving off to the side. Caught him grabbing something off a table in the hall, tucking it behind him. Narrowing his eyes, he angled his head to catch a glance, but no luck.

Hope shifted against his chest and then eased back, her lashes low over her misty green eyes. "Geez, sorry about that," she murmured. She winced and reached up, smoothing her hands down the front of his suit. "I'm getting you wrinkled."

"Screw it." He cupped her chin in his hand, tipping her face up to his. She had tears drying on her face. And although she tried to hide it, there was fear dancing in the depths of her eyes.

He was sick and tired of seeing her afraid—hadn't she had enough fear in her life? What had caused it this time?

He stroked a thumb over her lip as he asked, "So what's going on?"

It had better not be that sick fuck of an ex. Remy just might decide to pay the bastard a social call. He could get to Oklahoma and back fast enough. Nobody had to even know he was gone, he figured.

Law appeared in the doorway and Hope glanced over at him, her face twisting in a grimace. "Law and I had a visitor. Apparently your town gossip is going around spreading tales about how Law and I have this very torrid, and very twisted, relationship—when we're not tearing up the sheets, we're killing women for kicks."

"What?" Remy shot a glance at Law and then looked back at Hope. "Are you serious?"

"Yeah." Hope sighed and leaned her head back against his chest, but didn't seem too inclined to add anything else.

Shifting his gaze to Law, he waited.

"Afraid she's pretty damn serious." Law leaned his shoulder against the door frame. "The woman who was found here . . . apparently her cousin was in town today, talking to the sheriff and Deb was there."

"Oh, hell." Remy scowled. He could only imagine what kind of stories Deb had decided to tell the woman. Although he was confused on one front. Absently, he stroked a hand up Hope's back, curled it over her neck and started to rub the tense muscles there. She made a rough sound deep in her throat and cuddled closer. "She thinks the two of you killed her cousin and she decided to traipse out here to . . . what?"

"Confront us." Law jerked a shoulder in a shrug. "She was pissed, she doesn't lack for guts, and when she had this idea in her head that the sheriff was just ignoring evidence, she decided to see what she could see. But she figured out pretty quick that Deb isn't exactly a reliable fount of information. End of story."

Remy narrowed his eyes. *End of story*?

No. He didn't think so.

Something had Hope an absolute mess and it wasn't just because some strange woman showed up on Law's doorstep and accused them of being a twisted, modern-day version of Bonnie and Clyde. She'd gone through too much hell for something like that to push her to tears.

"And what else did she do?" Remy asked, cocking a brow at Law.

Law jerked a shoulder in a shrug. "Nothing you need to worry about."

Hope stiffened in his arms and lifted her head. Something about the look on her face had Remy's gut twisted into knots. And her eyes . . . they were dark. Angry. Scared.

"Nothing to worry about?" she echoed. She pushed away from Remy and faced her friend, her narrow shoulders rigid, her hands clenched into fists. "Excuse me, but there were two of us here, Law. Two of us, and it wasn't just *you* she had the fucking gun pointed at."

Everything inside Remy went cold and tight.

"Gun?"

"Damn it, Hope," Law snarled, shoving away from the wall.

Remy pushed between them, blocking her from the other man. "What gun?" he asked flatly.

"It's nothing you need to worry about. I handled it, it's done."

"And where's the gun?" Remy demanded.

Law ignored him, shifting around to stare at Hope. "Damn it, don't you think that woman's been through enough? She doesn't need to have some shark on her tail right now."

"She came out here perfectly willing to kill the two of us," Hope shouted.

"I got the damn gun away, didn't I? And she's not going to try to kill us. If I thought she'd ever hurt you, do you really think I'd take that chance?"

Remy wanted to hit something.

Preferably Law.

Instead, he took a deep breath and then, when the two of them paused in between bouts of yelling, he said, "Law, where in the hell is the gun?"

Law stiffened. Then he blinked and a lazy smile curled his lips. "What gun, Counselor?"

"Oh, fuck this. You going to make me try to get a warrant?" he snapped.

Law laughed. "Oh, you won't do that. The only way you *can* is if you have some sort of proof, and right now the only proof would be Hope's word." He slanted a look at Hope. "And while she's pissed off at me, I don't think you really want to put her in that position, and I know she's not going to want to do it, either."

Anger punched through Remy at the look on Hope's face.

She looked . . . crushed. Like Law had just about ripped her heart out, and while Law didn't realize it, Remy could tell that was exactly what the fuck he had just done.

But just when he was about to say something, Hope shook her head and in a quiet voice, asked, "And why are *you* putting me in this position, Law? Your best friend? You don't even know that woman. She threatened us . . . threatened *me*. Hell. You spent two years trying to talk me into putting down roots—two years telling me I could come here, make a home here, be *safe* here. You don't know her, but you're protecting her and you're using our friendship to do it?"

She swallowed and looked away, closed her eyes.

When she looked back at him, she whispered raggedly, "Thanks a lot, Law."

For the first time since he'd known the man, Remy got to see Law Reilly look flummoxed.

"Shit, Hope." He shook his head. "I don't know. But she's not going to come back and try to hurt you. Or me. I just know it."

He reached out a hand to her.

Hope stared at it.

But then, she looked away.

And found herself staring at Remy.

She loved Law—he was her dearest, closest friend, and he'd kept her sane, or as close to it as she was going to come.

But right then, she couldn't be here. What had happened earlier still left her feeling sick, dazed.

And the position Law had just tried to put her in— had been *willing* to put her in—had her so miserably unhappy, it hurt. It felt like somebody had just punched her square in the chest and she couldn't handle it.

Reaching out, she wrapped her hand around Remy's arm. "I don't suppose you feel like taking me for some lunch or something, do you?"

"Actually, that was why I came out." He dipped his head and pressed a kiss to her forehead.

"Thanks." She glanced down at her clothes—an overlarge T-shirt and jeans. It would have to do, but she needed some shoes. "Let me grab some shoes."

She disappeared from the room, well aware of the tension she was leaving behind.

But just then, she didn't care.

"Where's the gun?" Remy demanded as Hope disappeared up the stairs.

Curling his lip, Law repeated, "What gun?"

"Oh, fuck you." Then he shot a look toward the ceiling. "How in the hell could you do that to her?"

"Shit, Remy. You know what Hope means to me—you actually think I'd let anything happen if I thought she'd be in any danger?"

Remy shook his head. "I'm not talking about the gun. Or the woman, directly. Although shit, she must be something if she's actually got you thinking with your dick—I didn't think you'd ever notice anybody besides Lena." Taking a step closer, he dropped his voice and said, "Hope thinks the sun rises and sets on you—you're the closest thing to a brother she has. I can see that. And you just deliberately used that, used *her*, to protect some woman you don't even know. You used *her*, you bastard—you fucking used her. How do you think that made her feel? I swear, I could kick your ass for putting that look in her eyes, you son of a bitch."

Out in the hall, he heard Hope's footsteps.

Without waiting another second, he looked away from Law and started for the hallway.

He needed to figure out what to do. Needed to figure out who this woman was, if she was a threat to Hope. If she was, it wouldn't matter if it ruined their relationship, he'd do what he had to do to get his hands on that fucking gun.

But for now, he was just going to get Hope out of here and see if he couldn't do something to help get that miserable unhappiness out of her pretty green eyes.

* * *

His gut in a knot, Law watched as the door closed behind Hope and Remy.

Part of him wanted to tell the bastard to shove it up his ass.

Part of him wanted to tell Hope to chill the fuck out.

Part of him wanted to find his keys and go find Nia . . . the sheriff would know more about her.

But the biggest part of him felt half sick. What in the hell had he just done?

Groaning, he leaned back against the wall and slammed his head into it. What in the hell?

A gun. A fucking gun. A loaded one, too, because he'd checked right before he'd stashed it, tucking it out of Remy's sight. She'd come here with a loaded gun and he'd seen it in her eyes—she could have used it.

Rubbing the back of one shaking hand over his mouth, he muttered, "She won't, though."

Not now. He was as certain of that as he was of his own name.

But he knew he couldn't explain that to Hope, and even if he could, he couldn't expect her to understand.

How *could* he expect that? He didn't even understand why he'd decided to protect a total stranger, even though he'd hurt his best friend in the process.

What was worse, though . . . he knew he'd do it again. There was something about that woman . . .

"Shit, Hope. I'm sorry."

He'd just used his best friend. And hurt her. She'd been hurt far too much, and more than anybody else, he knew it.

CHAPTER
FOURTEEN

Hope stared at nothing, tried to think about nothing as Remy drove his silver Jaguar away from Law's house.

He didn't head toward town, but just then, she didn't care.

The wind whipped through the short strands of her hair, stinging her eyes.

"You okay?"

"I'm fine," she said automatically.

"No, you're not."

Glancing over at Remy, she grimaced. "Okay, I'm not. But I'm not about to have a panic attack and I'm not going to go on a crying jag, either. I won't start leaking all over you again, promise."

He reached over and rubbed the back of her neck. "Did I say I minded?"

"You're too much a gentleman to say you mind, even if you do," she murmured. Sighing, she leaned her aching head against the headrest. "Can we just do this day over again, from the get-go?"

"Will you and Law be okay?"

"Yeah. At least I don't see why we wouldn't." She

shot him a glance from under her lashes. "But don't ask me to . . . whatever, Remy. I can't. Not with Law."

He sighed. "Yeah. I know. And I won't. But that doesn't mean I'm not going to figure out what in the hell is going on with this woman. Showing up at a person's house with a loaded gun—not exactly a ringing endorsement of her solid mental state."

Hope started to laugh. "Solid mental state?"

A dull red flush stained his cheeks red. "What I mean is—"

"Relax." She reached over and patted his thigh. The muscles tightened under her hand and she yanked her hand back fast. "I know what you mean. She's not crazy, though. She was pissed. And grieving. But not crazy."

"Hope . . ."

She slid him a look. "She's not."

"And you're willing to risk your neck over that?"

"Hell. Law is." Then she rubbed her temple. "And I trust him more than I trust myself sometimes. Besides . . ." Her voice trailed off as her mind wandered back to a time in her life she'd rather forget.

There was a look in a person's eye. A certain look. That woman, she hadn't had it.

"I know what crazy is, Remy. Once you've seen it, dealt with it, lived it . . . you don't forget it. She's not crazy."

Hope was still chilled to the bone, and still pissed off at Law, but in her gut, she suspected he was right. The woman wasn't crazy. Didn't necessarily mean she would sleep easy at night for a while, but . . .

Pushing that thought aside, she shifted in the seat and focused on Remy. "So what brought you out here today?"

"Didn't I already tell you that?" He flashed her a grin. "I wanted to buy you lunch."

"You just bought me lunch. Actually, I think you've

bought me lunch like six times in the past two weeks." She smiled over at him.

"Is there a rule saying I can't do it again today?" He hit his blinker and started to slow down.

Hope glanced over and then winced, shooting her clothes a look. "The Inn? I'm not dressed for this place."

"You look fine."

"No. I don't."

"Does that mean you want to leave?"

She looked at him. He'd do it, she thought.

Turn around if she asked.

He would look completely in place in the Inn. And he wasn't the least bit concerned that she was wearing a T-shirt that had never fit her well, and a plain pair of jeans.

What was he doing with her? What in the world was he doing with her?

As the butterflies in her belly winged around, she forced a smile. "No. This is fine."

What did it matter what she wearing?

Remy wasn't worried if she wasn't impeccably groomed, and it didn't matter so much to her, either.

If neither of them cared, what did it matter?

He watched as the silver Jaguar pulled out of sight.

Then he looked back at the house, the rage a hot, greasy ball in his gut.

She was making a mistake . . . such a mistake.

Idly, Joey reached down, stroked the butt of his gun.

He had been tempted as the lawyer walked Hope to the car.

It wouldn't take much.

Not from here.

Put a bullet in his head, then hers.

Not immediately, for his wife—he'd wait a few minutes, watch as she screamed when her lover fell dead to the ground.

But not yet.

Behind him, he heard a whisper of sound.

Tensing, he eased deeper into the shadows, keeping his back pressed against the trunk of an ancient oak and studying the perimeter for some sign of movement. Something out of place.

Nothing.

Probably just a deer.

But just in case . . .

He scanned the area, made sure he hadn't left any sign of himself, and then he left, moving slowly but surely.

It wouldn't do to get caught, to be seen.

They had to pay for humiliating him like this.

All three of them.

Reilly and the lawyer were going to die.

At first, he'd planned on just taking Hope back to Clinton with him, but now, he didn't know. Lately, he'd been thinking more and more about killing her. He didn't want some whore—the sloppy seconds left behind by Reilly and the lawyer.

Plans.

He needed to make his plans, and stay out of sight while he did it.

Fortunately, he had the perfect place.

He'd come to see her.

But he wasn't the only one watching her. And that man watching Hope wanted to do her harm, he suspected. He realized he didn't like that idea. Not at all.

As the man disappeared into the woods, he remained hidden in the shadows. He'd grown up in these woods and he knew them well. No stranger could hope to find him if he didn't want to be found.

Once the man disappeared, he retreated.

He'd have to look for Hope later.

He had his own work he needed to see to, after all, and he'd wasted too much time playing statue in the woods while that bastard played peeping Tom.

He'd be back to check on Hope later . . . check on her, watch over her.

The poor girl had been through hell lately. Such a fighter. Such a determined little thing. And she'd seemed like such a mouse.

For some reason, he found himself undeniably drawn to her.

After lunch was cleared, Hope leaned back and patted her belly. "Man, that was good," she murmured.

She was surprised she'd been able to eat.

"So what are you doing the rest of the day?"

Glancing across the table at Remy, she shrugged. "I don't know. Avoiding Law, because I don't feel like talking to him. I've got stuff I need to do—errands and crap. Guess I'll do that."

"Is it stuff you need to do today?"

"Well, no." She gave him a faint smile and hoped he wouldn't ask what she did—she still wasn't sure what she was supposed to say if he asked. He wasn't going to buy the semi-truths Law had told her to use, and she wasn't going to lie to him about it.

They'd been going out for two weeks now, and it hadn't come up. She knew it was going to, sooner or later, and she needed an answer.

Just not right now . . .

"If nothing has to be done right away, why don't you spend the day with me?"

Hope cocked a brow. "Ah, don't you have stuff to do? I thought lawyers were generally pretty busy."

He shrugged. Remy was busier than hell. But that look in her eyes? He knew that look. It was dread. She dreaded going back to Law's right now and if he could help distract her until some of that tension melted away, then he would do it.

"I can take an afternoon off every now and then. All my meetings were this morning for once. So I can be lazy." He'd pay for it tomorrow, but it would be worth it. "You interested? We could see a movie. Maybe I could cook dinner for you or something, then take you home later tonight."

Hell, it was worth it just *then*. To see that slow smile spread over her face.

"I think I'd love that."

Shame didn't mix with grief any better than rage did.

As Nia rode back into town, she decided at least the humiliation gave her something else to think about, though. She'd spent nearly two hours driving around not doing much of anything as she tried to convince herself that maybe she'd been wrong.

But she hadn't been wrong.

She wasn't wrong . . . at least not now.

She'd just been wrong earlier.

So very fucking wrong when she stormed into the house of a man she didn't know, a man who'd never done a damn thing to her or her family, and accused him of being a murderer—a rapist. Insulted his girlfriend, mistress, whoever in the hell Hope Carson was.

In other words, Nia had totally humiliated herself.

Under normal circumstances, Nia hated it when she did that sort of thing—hated putting her foot in her mouth, and no, it wasn't going down easy right now, either.

But it was easier to think about *that* than all the other shit in her head.

It was a sad, sad thing when a woman would rather

deal with how much she'd humiliated herself—in front of a hot guy, no less—than face her own problems.

Law Reilly hadn't touched Joely.

Probably didn't even know her.

And the woman with him. Nia sighed as she slowed her bike down near the town square, pulling off to the side. That woman didn't have it in her to hurt somebody, much less torture somebody.

Neither did Reilly. He could kill—she'd seen the look in his eyes when he placed himself between her and Hope. He was the sort of man, she suspected, who could and would kill to protect those who mattered. But that didn't make him a killer.

He definitely had some moves on him, that was sure. Wincing, she lifted a hand off the handlebars and studied her right arm. It was discolored, the bruise spreading along the inside of her wrist, an ugly rainbow of a bruise. She needed to ice it down, take some Motrin.

What you really ought to do is just get the hell out of here. Call your boss. Get an assignment. Let these people do their job.

That was what the calm, logical, rational voice in her head insisted.

But her heart . . . every time she closed her eyes, she saw Joely's battered face.

Joely.

Heaving out a ragged sigh, she pinched the bridge of her nose.

Joely.

She couldn't leave.

Not yet.

And even if she did, she'd just be back.

She went to pull her bike back out into the flow of traffic but the car going by her made her go still.

The cute brunette from Reilly's.

Leaning back in a silver Jaguar, with her eyes closed

and a not very happy look on her pixielike face. The guy with her glanced toward Nia as he slowed for a stop sign, but then looked away.

Absently, she rubbed her arm and thought about following.

She could catch up with them—tell the lady she was sorry.

But she'd already convinced that chick that Nia was missing more than a few marbles. Following her wherever wasn't going to help, was it?

Sighing, she checked the road and pulled out.

A car came speeding up behind her and then slammed on the brakes. And the horn. Nia put her booted foot down and looked behind her, glaring at the driver.

Through the windshield of the plain, light blue sedan, she could see his face, square and ruddy—midthirties, his white-blond hair cut short, and his expression completely pissed off.

Get out of my way. It was written all over his features.

Nia was still feeling more than a little pissed off, more than spoiling for a fight. Tipping her glasses down her nose, she stared at him.

Make me.

Their gazes locked and held.

Finally, he blinked and she turned back around.

"Asshole," she muttered.

Deliberately, she kept her speed about five miles below the speed limit through the square. The lunchtime traffic was heavy enough that he had no chance of cutting around her and she smirked as he rode as close as he dared behind.

Shit, if he thought that was going to bother her, he had absolutely no idea the hell she'd been through lately. As she neared the sheriff's office, she slowed down to a crawl and waited until the last possible second to pull

over. When he blasted by her, she flipped him off and
took note of the license plate and the rental sticker on
the back bumper.

Stupid bitch, Joe thought as he blasted on by the bitch
on the bike.

A dyke, he thought, smirking to himself.

Fucking dyke on a bike—needed to get laid.

But damn it, he'd lost Jennings and Hope.

Where in the hell were they?

After they'd left the Inn, he'd been sure they'd be
going back to Reilly's, but they hadn't and he had no
idea where in the hell they were and it wasn't like he
could drive around looking for them, either.

Not around here. Too small a town, and he'd get noticed.

Already had, really.

The bitch on the bike had noticed him.

She wasn't from around here—at least the tags on the
bike weren't local, but she'd stopped in front of the sheriff's office, and he didn't like that.

Plus, he'd seen the way she lingered, just long enough
to note his tags.

Shit.

Where in the hell were they?

Hope sat at the island, absently spinning a glass of
wine in her hand and watching while Remy stood across
from her, chopping up vegetables. He did it easily, com-
petently, like somebody who was used to cooking a lot,
and not just macaroni and cheese out of a box.

"Like the wine?"

She glanced down at the glass. "Ahh . . ."

Remy grinned at her. "You'll know if you like it when
you actually try it."

She made a face. Joey had spent about two years on a

wine kick and while she had tried some she liked, most of the stuff he'd liked were dry reds—the ones that had descriptions like *oaky* and *bright acidity*. She'd hated them.

Eyeing the pale pink, she lifted it to her lips and took a small sip.

Her eyes widened. Okay, now not too many of the wines Joe—*stop it. Right there. Just stop.* Determined to cut off that line of thinking, she took another sip, savoring the light, almost fruity taste. "What is this?"

"It's a blush wine, from a local winery. I know the owners and buy the stuff by the case." He cocked a brow. "Like it?"

"Yes." She was tempted to drink it all, in about one gulp, but she wasn't too sure what that might do to her head. It had been a long, long time since she'd had much of anything to drink . . .

Abruptly she set the glass down.

A weight dropped down on her and her throat went tight.

Shit—

One moment, she was right there. Smiling at him.

Then she was white as a ghost and her green eyes were dark and heavy and so full of fear. The familiar punch of fury hit him in the gut, but he pushed it aside, set the knife down.

Going around the island, he came up behind her, murmuring her name as he moved.

"Hope?"

She stiffened, turning glassy eyes his way.

"Are you okay?"

"I . . ."

She licked her lips, looked back at the glass. Then she shook her head. "I don't know if I should drink . . ."

He looked at the wineglass then at her. "Why not? Is there a reason you shouldn't?"

Calm. Logical. Just keep her talking.

"Reason?"

He rested a hand on her back, stroked it, but he was ready for her to pull back. She leaned into him, though, and when he moved closer, she curled her body next to his, rested her head on his chest. His heart banged hard against his rib cage and he had to fight not to wrap both arms around her. Instinct told him it wouldn't help her right now. But fuck, all he wanted to do was cradle her close, so close.

"Yeah. Is there a reason you shouldn't drink the wine? Does it make you sick or something?" But it wasn't that. He already knew.

"No. No, it's not that." She shook her head, mumbled against his chest. Then she straightened up, once more staring at the wineglass . . . mesmerized. Then she looked up at him. "You know about my ex, don't you?"

Breathe, Jennings. Breathe. She doesn't need your anger on top of whatever she's dealing with.

So he breathed through the fury and when he reached up to stroke a hand down her cheek, his hand was rock steady. "Yeah. I know."

"The first time I really tried to get away from him, I did it with alcohol and drugs—I tried to kill myself." She looked down at her wrists, staring at the scars. "I wouldn't have done it this way—I can't stand blood. But I wanted away from him so bad, I did try to kill myself. Sleeping pills, antidepressants, all the crap they gave me to explain why I was so unhappy when I should have been delirious with joy . . . I took all of the pills I could and washed them down with this dumb collector's edition of Maker's Mark whiskey that he had. He didn't even like me touching that stupid bottle and I drank as much of it as I could before I passed out."

A harsh noise, caught between a laugh and a sob, escaped her.

She covered her mouth with her hands and pulled away.

Remy caught her shoulders. "Don't," he said softly. "Don't pull away from me."

"Don't you hear what I'm saying?" She half jerked away, half stumbled, fighting to get away.

Realizing he needed to let her, he released her and it hurt, watching her put more and more distance between them. When she spun around to face him, her eyes were wide, dark, and furious. "Don't you *get* it?" she snarled. "I'm a fucking *mess*. I tried to kill myself. Instead of just *leaving* him, I tried to kill myself. Way to make choices, huh? What in the hell is wrong with me? And what's wrong with you? Why do you want to be around me?"

"You were stuck with a manipulative bastard," Remy said, shoving his hands in his pockets and telling himself to stay where he was. She needed space right then—he could see it, but damned if he didn't want to go to her. "He had probably done everything imaginable to convince you that you had nothing and nobody else *but* him, so why the hell would you think you'd have a lot of options? And you still got away from him, didn't you?"

She just stared at him, her eyes still holding that glassy, panicked sheen.

She was shaking.

His heart broke. He crossed the floor and pulled her against him, one arm going around her narrow waist while he cradled the back of her head in his other hand.

"You got away from him, and damn it, there's not one thing wrong with you. The problem is *him*. Not you. It's *him*. Got that?"

Her hands came up between them and he braced himself, ready to let her go. But all she did was curl her hands into his shirt, clutching him close. "If there was nothing wrong with me, I wouldn't have stayed . . ."

"You thought he loved you," he murmured. "You thought he loved you and you loved him."

She shook her head. "Not at that point." She rested her head on his chest and sighed. "He had me so twisted up inside, but I knew he didn't love me. I just couldn't leave. I wasn't brave enough. So I took the easy way out. What in the hell are you doing with me? Why do you want to be with somebody like me?"

"Because I can't stop thinking about you," he murmured. He slid his hand around and cradled her chin, eased her head back. "The very first time I saw you, I wanted to do just this . . . hold you."

Then he rubbed his lips across hers. "Kiss you."

A soft breath shuddered out of her and her lashes fluttered over her eyes.

"There's nothing wrong with you, Hope." He lifted his head and stroked his thumb over her mouth. "Stop thinking there is."

"You sure about that?" She gave him a wobbly smile and then looked over at the counter. "You give me a glass of wine and I take two sips and have a nervous breakdown."

"That wasn't a nervous breakdown."

She sighed. "No. It wasn't. Especially not for me." She eased away from him, and this time, he let her go, watched as she made her way back to the island. She stared at the wine, as though she hoped to find some deeply hidden answers there.

"If it's bothering you, I'll dump it out."

She looked at him. "No. I don't want it to bother me. I'm tired of letting shit cripple me, Remy." She reached for the glass, rolled it nervously between her hands. "But I am still messed up, you know. And you're blind if you can't see it. Or you're just too polite to say it."

"We've all got issues, Hope. But you seem to think I should look at you like you're a grade A basket case." He went back around the island. If she was going to try to pretend things were normal, he'd try, too. He hoped. "You're not. You had a bad marriage, and that's putting it mildly. If you *didn't* have issues from that, I'd be more worried about you."

She lifted the glass to her lips. As she took a small sip, then a second, he watched her from under his lashes.

"So it doesn't bother you that I was hospitalized?" she said, tossing it out like a challenge.

Carefully, Remy laid the knife down. Then, not trusting himself to speak just yet, he reached for his wine, but he didn't go for sipping it. He tossed it back, but it didn't do a damn thing to cool the rage burning inside. He'd be doing better if it was tequila. Or whiskey—straight, burning a path down to his stomach, and maybe burning through the fog of rage in his brain.

Looking at her, he bit off, "Oh, hell, yes, it bothers me. But not for the reasons you think. You didn't belong in there and we both know it. That bastard you were married to somehow managed to manipulate the system to put you in there and *keep* you in there and that pisses me off in more ways than you can imagine. Yeah, it *bothers* me. But not like you think."

"Thank you." She glanced down at her glass and then back up at him.

"Don't thank me." He reached for his knife and went to work on the rest of the vegetables, chopping up red bell peppers with a vengeance. "Don't thank me, okay?"

It seemed kind of weird, but as he stood there, the sleeves of his blue dress shirt rolled up, the silver knife flashing as he cut up the vegetables, Hope felt her heart flutter.

His blond hair tumbled into his eyes and she couldn't

see that blue gaze right then, but there was a strange, burning glitter in them.

It made her belly go tight.

She slid off the stool.

As she walked around the island, he went still. She rested her hands on his waist, pressed her head against his back. "Why not?" she asked.

"Why not what?"

"Why shouldn't I say thank you?" It meant a lot to have him say he didn't think she belonged where Joe had put her. It meant something.

The muscles in his back stiffened. "I don't want your thanks, Hope," he said, his voice hoarse.

Down low, everything went hot. Tight.

"Remy?"

"Yeah?"

"What do you want from me?"

She's trying to kill me.

Remy put the knife back down and eyed the meal that wasn't ever going to get cooked at this rate. Taking a slow breath, he turned around and looked at Hope.

Then he wished he hadn't turned around, because that lazy, lambent look in her eyes was one he didn't need to see . . . not right now.

Vulnerable state of mind, Remy. She's in a vulnerable state of mind . . .

"I don't want anything from you," he said gruffly. Cupping her chin, he bussed her mouth lightly. "Nothing more than you want to give me, at least. But you don't need to thank me for stating the obvious—and I don't want to hear it, okay?"

"Yeah. I got that. But that's not an answer." She still had her hands on his sides. And her fingers were kneading him, like a little cat; it was the most erotic damn thing, driving him crazy. Tipping her head back, she stared at him, her soft green eyes warm, seductively so.

Oh, shit.

Trouble. Major trouble. How much wine had she drunk?

"What *do* you want?"

"I did answer that—whatever you want to give me. When you're ready. But not now."

"What's wrong with now?"

Remy groaned. "First? You've had one bitch of a day. And now you're feeling rough over some bad memories." He dipped his head, skimmed his lips down her neck. She shivered. Despite himself, he smiled. "I want you—you know that. But when we're together, it's going to be because we both want it, both need it for the same reasons. Not because you need a teddy bear. And right now, I think I'd worry you need comfort more than sex."

Hope stared at him and tried to decide if she wanted to laugh or feel insulted.

"Remy, the last thing I think when I look at you is *teddy bear*."

He chuckled, then dipped his head and nipped her lower lip. "Good. But whatever you're thinking . . . we're not doing it. Not now. Not after the day you've had. Now go sit down. We'll eat, I'll take you home. You can get some rest."

"You're really into taking care of people," she murmured.

He stroked a hand down her back. "Not people, Hope. You."

"You ready to go home?"

It was pushing past nine. They'd had dinner. Watched a movie, cuddled on the couch and for a short while, she'd been able to just not think. Not think about that woman who'd pulled a gun on her and Law. Had a short while when she hadn't thought about what Law had done, how he'd used their friendship.

But time was running out, she supposed. It was late and she needed to get out of here. Go back to his place, face Law. Deal with what had happened.

It was dark and a cool breeze was blowing in through the open doors.

Hope stood on the small balcony of Remy's place, staring out over the town square. With a heavy heart, she turned around and smiled at him. "Sure."

"Liar."

The only light came from the kitchen, throwing him into shadow. But as he moved closer, she was able to make out his face, see the gleam in his eyes, the faint grin on his face.

Grimacing, she said, "Okay, so I'm not ready. But I can't drag my feet much longer, can I? At some point, I've got to go back."

"Why tonight?" He joined her on the balcony and slid his arms around her waist, tucking her against him. She snuggled close, resting her head on his chest.

Then it clicked what he had just said. "What?"

"You don't need to go tonight if you don't want to." He brushed his lips across her temple. "You can stay here if you want."

Hope narrowed her eyes and tipped her head back to study him. "Weren't you just telling me a few hours ago that we weren't going to be doing anything while I needed a teddy bear? You decide you want to be a teddy bear?"

"No." He squeezed her tighter. "This isn't about being a teddy bear. Hell, I'll sleep on the couch. But if you aren't ready to go back there, or if you just don't want to, then don't."

"It's running away," she said quietly. "I'm tired of running away."

"It's not running away." He turned her around and cupped her chin, eased her head back until she met his gaze. "It's about you needing some space. Reilly sucker punched you with that mess earlier—he used you, used your friendship, and don't try to act like it didn't hurt you. Don't try to tell me it's not still hurting you. There's not a damn thing wrong with you needing a little more time before you head back there."

"You make it sound so simple."

"It is simple. If you don't feel like going back there tonight . . . don't."

Law blinked, then lowered the phone and stared at it—like that was really going to change what he'd just heard.

Then he put it back to his ear. "What?"

"You heard me. I'm staying over at Remy's. I didn't want you worrying about me," Hope said, her voice cool. "I'll see you in the morning."

"Wait—"

"I'll see you in the morning," she repeated.

Then she hung up. Just like that. Shit. She'd just hung up on him.

And damn it, she was staying the night with *Jennings*?

Fuck it, he'd thought the bastard had more decency than that. He knew Hope wasn't feeling steady right now, not after the shit he'd pulled. Damn it, he'd been kicking his ass all day over that, working out what he would say and how he would say it. He needed to apologize for what he'd done, how he'd used their friendship, and he *almost* had the words, too.

But she was staying the night at Remy's?

"My ass."

His arm was throbbing, his head was aching, and common sense told him what he needed to do was just grab a beer, sit down, and chill out. What he was going to do was get the hell over to Jennings and convince Hope that what she needed wasn't to go get seduced by some bastard who'd take advantage of her. Shit. He'd really thought Remy was better than that.

When the knock came less than a half an hour after Hope had called Law, Remy wasn't surprised. Judging by the resigned look in her eyes, neither was Hope.

They'd been waiting for it. As though they'd had an unspoken agreement, they hadn't bothered turning on the TV, hadn't left the living room . . . they just waited.

Remy skimmed a hand down her back and pressed a kiss to her temple. "I'll handle it."

But she shook her head. "No. He's my friend, and he's here because he's worried about me." Then she grimaced. "Probably has himself convinced you're taking advantage of me. I'm getting a little tired of people thinking I'm incapable of thinking for myself."

She stood up and handed him the Diet Coke she'd been drinking.

He watched as she padded over to the door. Halfway there, Law knocked again and with enough force to rattle the door on its hinges.

Remy set her drink down, along with his. Yeah, she could talk to him. That was just fine. But he'd be damned if the jackass glared and breathed fire all over her. This was Reilly's fucking fault—he'd been the one to put Hope in a bad place earlier. If Reilly didn't like it, he could shove it up his ass.

"I already told you, I'll be home in the morning," Hope said.

Law glanced up as Remy joined her at the door. The look in his eyes was one of acute dislike. *Back at you, pal.* Resting his hand on the back of Hope's neck, Remy said nothing. But he didn't look away from that challenging glare, either.

You fucked up, man.

"Look, I'm sorry," Law snapped. "I was a jerk earlier and I get that. I had no right putting you in that position. That doesn't mean you need to cry all over lover-boy there and let him take advantage of you."

Remy stiffened.

Hope laughed. "I knew you'd think that." She glanced over her shoulder at Remy and smiled. The look in her eyes did the weirdest damn thing to his heart. He thought he just might melt. She reached up and touched her fingers to his lips. He caught her hand and pressed a kiss to her palm.

She twined their fingers, letting their linked hands rest on her shoulder. "You don't get it, Law. You don't have to keep coddling me . . . I know you think you do. And that's my fault. Hell, your mystery girl, what was her name, anyway? It doesn't matter. She spends five minutes around us and that's enough for her to figure out I'm not the strongest woman in the world. But I don't need coddling. I'm *not* staying here because Remy talked me into it, seduced me into it, tricked me into it."

She backed away from Law and her voice hitched a little as she added, "I'm staying because right now, I'm not ready to talk to you, and I'm not ready to come back to your house. I'm just not. Now please go home. I'll see you in the morning."

CHAPTER
FIFTEEN

"Here."

Hope glanced up and met Remy's gaze in the mirror, then looked at the shirt he held out. It was a faded blue button-down and without touching it, she knew it would smell of him.

She'd sleep with the smell of him on her skin. Her heart raced even thinking about it.

He said he'd sleep on the couch. She didn't want him to.

Taking the shirt, she forced a smile. "Thanks. You take good care of your guests."

He grimaced. "Sometimes Brody and a friend or two of his used to crash here. I got used to keeping spare toothbrushes and stuff on hand for them."

"How is he?" she asked quietly.

"Pissed off. Scared. But I think he's doing better than he has in a while." He stared off past her shoulder, but she knew he wasn't looking at his reflection in the mirror. "I should have seen how bad he was getting. Should have made my brother look."

"Hey." She reached up, cupped his cheek. "What's happening with him isn't your fault. It's not his, either."

Remy shook his head. "I should have seen it."

"He's a kid who lost his mom. And all you ever really saw was an unhappy, angry teenage boy. That sounds like a lot of teenage boys. How were you to know it was more than that?" She slid an arm around him. "If I'm not supposed to be beating myself up over things, then maybe you shouldn't either."

"That's sneaky," he muttered. He dipped his head and pressed a kiss to her neck.

"Hmm. Did it work?"

"Dunno." Then he stepped back. "I'm going to get the couch made up."

"Don't."

The blue of his eyes glittered as he looked down at her.

Hope shifted and licked her lips. "Ahh. I mean, unless you just would rather. I'm . . . ah, well, you were right. Earlier. Mostly. Or partly right." Blood rushed to her cheeks, staining them a hot, vivid red, but she wouldn't let herself stop.

Not now. "I do want you. I never felt like this with . . . well, before. But I'd rather not be a basket case when it happens, and I'm not in a good place today. But . . ."

Her voice trailed off. Her throat closed up.

And he was still staring at her, the blue of his eyes—so burning hot.

He took a step closer, brushed a finger down her cheek. "But what?"

"Could we . . . ah . . . just sleep together? Just sleep?" She tipped her head back, staring at him.

"Is that what you want?"

"If I didn't want it, I wouldn't ask," she said softly.

Heaven, Remy realized, could also come with little pockets of hell.

Looking into her wide, nervous eyes, he tried to figure out if he was going to survive this particular pocket of hell. If he didn't, it would be well worth it.

"Okay." He could do this, right? He could sleep—just sleep—all night with Hope Carson and manage not to touch her.

Right? He stifled a groan.

He needed a shower. Cold. First.

Then he could get into that bed with her.

"I need to shower before I go to bed," he said.

"Okay." She was still blushing, and once more, he found himself dying to know—just how low did that blush go?

Tearing his gaze away from her neck, he nodded toward his bedroom. "If you want to change in there, I'll be in soon."

After he'd done something to relieve the already painful ache in his balls—and preferably after he'd frozen himself into some state of semi-inactivity.

It could happen. He hoped.

With enough cold water.

But he might need to move to Antarctica.

The shirt smelled of him.

So did the bed.

Hope slid between soft, smooth sheets the color of jade. Dark, rich green. She stroked a hand down them and lay on her side, wondered what in the hell she was doing.

Besides shivering.

Nervous. Shit. She was nervous.

Why?

It's not like we're going to do anything. We've already decided that.

But this . . . sleeping in the bed with him . . . *just* sleeping, somehow seemed even more intimate than sex.

She heard the water in the bathroom cut off.

Abruptly, her stomach started to pitch.

She groaned and turned her face into the pillow. The pillow that smelled just like Remy.

What was she *doing*?

Two minutes later, she heard the soft whisper as the bathroom door opened, the click as the light was turned off.

"Hope?"

She turned her face toward him and through the dim light, saw him lingering near the bed.

"You okay?"

No, I'm not.

"Yeah."

His teeth flashed white. "Liar."

"Okay. I'm nervous. But so what?" She pulled back the blankets. "You joining me or what?"

Heaven and hell, he thought. Heaven and hell.

She hissed as his arm brushed hers. "Damn it, you're freezing!"

"Ah . . . hot water thing." She scooted over and pressed her body against his, bringing that slice of heaven and hell so much closer. Remy had just spent long, aching minutes in the shower and he'd made judicious use of his own hands. When that hadn't helped, he'd switched off the hot water and gone for cold.

And now it all proved pointless because all Hope did was rest her arm across his belly and he wanted to push her over onto her back, spread her legs, and crawl on top of her.

Instead, he lay there, gritting his teeth as she wiggled and squirmed around. He shifted and moved his arm under her and she sighed, her head cuddled on his shoulder.

Abruptly he smiled. That felt so right, he almost heard a click.

"This feels nice," Hope murmured.

Nice. That didn't quite touch it. He wasn't ever going

to be able to sleep and it didn't matter. This just felt too damn perfect. Who needed sleep? But in under ten minutes, sleep came crashing down on him, a heavy, warm weight.

"Wuh . . ."

Hope jerked upright, staring off into the darkness, disoriented and confused.

A hand touched her arm.

"It's just the phone," Remy murmured.

Her breath hitched in her throat and she turned her head, tried to make out his face in the darkness.

Remy.

Holy shit.

She'd spent the entire damn night in bed with Remy.

"You okay?" he asked gruffly as he sat up.

"Yeah." Her voice came out in a squeak. She cleared her voice and tried again. "Um, yeah. Just a little startled."

"Hmm." He bent over and pressed his lips to her brow.

The phone rang again.

He sighed and reached for it. "This is Jennings."

She peered at his face.

"Hello?"

He grunted and disconnected the phone.

"Wrong number?"

"No telling. They hung up."

Her eyes had adjusted and she could see his face as he squinted at the clock. "Almost five A.M. Bastard."

Hope snickered.

"Yeah. You laugh. You slept through the first three calls."

"What calls?"

He stroked a hand up her back. "Somebody's called three other times. Probably some idiot kid—might even be one of Brody's buddies." He lay back down and tugged her up against him. "Go back to sleep."

"Hmmm." She snuggled up against him, amazed at how easy it felt to do that. "Called three times, huh?"

"Yeah. They call any more, I'll just turn the damn phone off. I've got my iPhone if there's an emer—"

The phone started ringing. He grabbed the phone and snarled into it. "Yeah?"

Hope assumed there wasn't an answer when he slammed the phone down five seconds later.

"Son of a *bitch*," he swore. Followed immediately by, "Sorry."

He sat up and Hope pushed up on her elbow, watching as he climbed out of bed. "Watch your eyes—I'm hitting the lights."

"What are you doing?"

"Turning off the damn phones and grabbing my iPhone," he growled. "This is bullshit."

She peered at him through her lashes, unable to stop from smiling as he stalked out of the room.

He looked . . . out of sorts, she decided.

And adorable.

That familiar thrill of heat shot through her belly. Catching her lip between her teeth, she shot a glance at the clock.

Five A.M. Would either of them really sleep much more before he had to get ready for work? That thrill of heat spread. Slipping out of the bed, she made her way to the bathroom and eased the door closed. She used it quickly and then washed her hands, brushed her teeth. Morning breath would kill things, right?

Think about the little things. Not what you're going to try to do when you're both back in bed . . .

Easier that way. Definitely. Her breathing hitched.

Her heart started to race and she suspected she just

might have a panic attack if she let herself . . . *little things*!

Idiot phone calls in the dead of night. Morning breath.

The fact that she and Remy both used the same kind of toothpaste.

Three minutes after she slipped into the bathroom, she slid out and found Remy coming out of the bedroom. He gave her a tired smile, stroked his hand through her hair.

Just that light, easy touch and she watched as some of the strain faded from his eyes. "You okay?" she asked.

"Yeah." He scowled. "Just irritated. Tired. And pissed. You were supposed to be here so you could sleep. And here's this . . ."

She smiled at him. "Not your fault."

He just snorted. "I'll be back in a minute."

As he disappeared into the bathroom, she went back into the bedroom and wondered if she could do this.

Hope had never seduced a man in her life.

She didn't even know *how*.

Her heart started to race and insanely, she wondered if Lena would absolutely hate her if she called her before dawn.

No, she thought, disgustedly. *You're not calling her. You can figure this out . . .*

She went back into the bedroom and turned off the lights. That first. Definitely that first. Because the most obvious way she figured out to clue Remy in would be to take off the blue shirt he'd loaned her to sleep in, and there was no way she was going to just stretch out naked on the bed with the lights burning.

On her way to the bed, she reached for the buttons, but her fingers were shaking so badly, she couldn't manage to undo even one. Finally, she just jerked it off over her head and left it in a puddle next to the bed. She shimmied out of her panties and slid into the bed, listening for the bathroom door.

The water came on. Holding her breath, she lay there.

Her heart continued to race. What was she doing . . . why was she doing this?

What if he didn't really want her? Oh, fuck, what if she wasn't any good?

She took a deep breath. And immediately, his scent flooded her head. Somehow, that was all it took, and all those questions abruptly ceased.

She heard the water go off, the door opened. Closing her eyes, she whispered, "You can do this." Then she looked toward the door, watching as his shadow appeared.

You can do this.

You can do this, man, he thought, setting his jaw as he started toward the bed.

Half the night, he had slept next to Hope, feeling her small, sleek form pressed against his. He hadn't shattered yet.

He could manage a few more hours.

In another hour or two, he could even wake her up, make her breakfast.

Yeah. He could do this. And in a few more weeks, maybe she'd trust him enough . . .

Maybe. Maybe. Too many fucking maybes and his dick was a constant ache, his balls felt like they were in a knot and if he took any longer to climb into the bed, she was going to ask him what was wrong.

You can do this.

He slid into the bed.

Hope pressed up against him.

And every last brain cell died.

Oh, fucking shit. She was naked.

As she pressed her lips against his jaw, Remy managed to croak out, "Hope, what are you doing?"

"It's not yesterday now."

Her voice was husky with sleep, but calm and steady. Steady—

Which was exactly what Remy *didn't* feel.

His arm curled around her shoulder, his fingers grazing her naked shoulder and despite himself, he found himself stroking that smooth, soft flesh. "Yesterday?" he said dumbly.

"Yeah. It's not yesterday. I haven't had a bad day. I'm not feeling raw or vulnerable . . . I just feel you. And I want to be with you."

"Hope . . ." He fumbled for the words, certain there was something he needed to do or say. He was supposed to be taking his time, moving slow, at her pace . . .

Then Hope shifted closer and he felt her naked breasts, small and firm, pressing against his chest and every last thought of being logical, of being a gentleman and letting her take her time—*all of it*—just drained away.

Groaning, he stroked a hand down her back, reveling in the feel of her silken skin. Pulling her atop him, he kneaded the taut flesh of her butt and muttered, "Kiss me."

"Hmmm." She pressed her mouth against his, tasting of toothpaste and Hope. He traced his tongue along the curve of her mouth, shuddered as hers came out to meet his.

With one fist tangled in her hair, he tugged her head back, scraped his teeth down her neck. "You sure about this?" And even as he asked, some voice in the back of his head was screaming at him—*Are you nuts? She's sure. She's buck-naked, sitting on your lap—she's sure!*

No, he wasn't nuts. He was desperate and if she

changed her mind, Remy wasn't sure he'd be able to walk out of here. He'd probably have to crawl.

"Yes . . . I'm more sure of this than I've been of anything else in a very long time."

Oh, hell. In the dim light that filtered in through the blinds, he could barely make out the shape of her face, the glint in her eyes, and fuck, that wasn't enough. Reaching over, he hit the bedroom light and she flinched, her eyes squinting against the brightness.

He sat up, brought her head against him, shielding her from it. Pressing his lips against her shoulder, he muttered, "I want to see you. Dying to . . ."

He shifted around and stretched her out on the bed, watching her face. Her cheeks were flushed pink, her eyes glittering bright with embarrassment, but Remy wasn't about to turn the light off. "Damn it, you're beautiful."

"No, I'm not."

He dipped his head and pressed his lips to the tip of one tight nipple. "I'm the one looking at you, and I see beautiful." And he also got to see just how far down that blush of hers went . . . it spread down to the tops of her breasts, turning them the same soft pink as her cheeks.

"Beautiful," he whispered again.

When he looked at her, Hope felt beautiful.

She wasn't, not really, and she knew it. She was too skinny and on top of that, she was too self-conscious and now scarred to boot. But he made her feel beautiful.

A knot settled in her throat and she swallowed around it as she smiled at him. Reaching down, she combed a hand through his hair. "When you look at me, I feel beautiful."

He slid a look at her from behind his lashes, that amazing blue burning hot and bright. "You *are* beautiful . . . and right now, you're mine." He laid a hand on her knee, stroked it up over her hip, her waist, her ribs. Then he cupped her breast and plumped it in his hand, pushing it up.

Her breath caught as he took the nipple in his mouth, laving it with his tongue, stroking it and drawing it deep.

She shuddered, curling her arm around his neck and cuddling him close. The heat of his body was like a brand—marking her, warming her. Warming her . . . all the way through. Hope didn't think she'd *ever* felt warmed quite like this.

It wasn't just on the surface. Remy did something to her—he brought something more to it. To everything. Even just a smile.

But this . . .

He skimmed his lips down over her belly and she hissed out a breath, her fingers tightening in his hair.

"Remy . . ."

"Shhhh."

Her eyes widened as he shifted lower and lay between her thighs. Immediately, she tried to close them, but there was no way—not with those wide shoulders settled there. She squirmed and wiggled, pressing her hips against the mattress.

"Remy . . ."

He slid her a look. "Hmmm?"

"I . . ." Embarrassment, humiliation tied her tongue into knots. How in the hell did she tell him that— He lowered his head and nuzzled her. She bucked her hips. He took advantage of that and slid his hands beneath her, cupping her butt in his hands.

"I don't think—"

"Hope, do me a favor," he said gruffly. He pressed a hot, open-mouthed kiss against her hip bone. "Just stop thinking."

And the next kiss was right against her sex, pretty much guaranteeing the fact that Hope stopped thinking. Her breath caught in her throat as he licked her, his tongue rasping over the swollen, tight bud of her clitoris. She reached out, desperate for something to grab onto. Her hands tangled in the sheets beneath her.

As he stroked his tongue over her a second time, a third, Hope groaned.

Then he sucked on her and everything inside her splintered, shattered.

It hit hard, and fast, coming out of nowhere and as she climaxed, she could feel him muttering against her flesh, talking to her. Each time she started to drift back down, he'd touch her again, lick her or rake his teeth lightly over the sensitized flesh and that would just draw it out . . . endlessly.

She was still shaking and gasping for air when her vision cleared sometime later. She had no idea how much time had passed. Dazed, she stared at Remy, her breathing ragged, her heart like a drumbeat in her ears.

Any embarrassment she might have felt died at the look on his face. That look . . . if it was anybody but Remy, it might have terrified her.

He pushed up onto his heels and then pulled her up against him, one hand cradling the nape of her neck, the other splayed wide over her back. His mouth came down on hers and right before he kissed her, he muttered, "Fuck, you're going to drive me insane, I know it."

Then his mouth crushed down onto hers. His taste was different—darker.

Her, she realized. He tasted of her.

She was shaking. All over.

Tearing his mouth away, he cupped her face in his

hands and stroked his thumb over her lower lip. Rushing it . . . pushing too hard—*slow it down* . . .

Staring into lambent green eyes, Remy muttered, "Are you okay?"

In response, she reached up and hooked a hand around the back of his neck, tugged his mouth back to hers, whimpering low in her throat.

At the sound of that low, hungry sound, *he* started to shake.

Damn it, she really was going to drive him insane. He rolled forward, spilling her onto her back. Her mouth ate at his, hungry and desperate, slowly eroding what little bit of control he had.

While he was still able to think, he pulled back, evading her reaching hands. "Gimme a minute," he muttered, catching her wrists in his. Under his thumbs, he felt the faint ridges of her scars and he turned her hands upward, pressed a kiss to one wrist, then the other. "Just a minute. Thirty seconds."

Then he all but ran to the bathroom.

Condoms. Damn it, if he didn't have any condoms, she was going to see him start crying like a baby. He was saved from that indignity, though. He was back in his bedroom in under thirty seconds and found her lying on her side, sleepy-eyed, her lips parted, her face flushed.

Damn, but he'd give almost anything to have that moment captured forever.

"And you think you're not beautiful," he muttered, coming to his knees beside her and tangling a hand in her hair.

He caught her pretty mouth with his, kissed her until he had to stop just to breathe. Then, and only then, did he stop, pressing his brow to hers and panting. "What in the hell have you done to my life, Hope?"

"Hmmm?"

"You're changing everything." He ripped one of the

foil packets off, tore it open, and then he climbed onto the bed, stretching out next to her. "Every damn thing."

She reached up and stroked a finger over his mouth. "You, too."

He caught her finger between his teeth, bit down lightly as he eased her onto her back. Her breathing hitched and he watched as something too close to nerves, too close to fear edged into her eyes. Rubbing his mouth over hers, he whispered, "We can stop. Just say the word."

Stop?

No. Hope didn't think stopping was an option. For one, if she stopped, she just might go insane—*really* insane, this time.

Two, if she stopped now, she didn't know if she'd ever work up the courage to try this again. She was so terrified, even as she was desperate for him. Working up what little remained of her courage, she wrapped her arms around his neck and kissed him, pressing close.

It was the best she could do, because there was no way she could put into words everything she felt. It just wasn't happening.

Remy reached up, cradling her face in one hand. He eased back, pressing a kiss to her chin, her cheeks, her eyes. Then he shifted back, kneeling between her thighs, pushing the close-fitting boxer-styled briefs he wore down.

She kept her eyes locked on his face.

Her breath tried to catch in her throat again. *Breathe, breathe, breathe . . .*

She couldn't damn well make love to him if she ended up having a panic attack, right? Refusing to let herself think about that, she thought about *him*, staring at him. And she had to admit, she was damn glad he had the lights on.

The soft light gleamed from behind a stained-glass

lamp shade on the bedside table and it danced over the hollows and planes of his lean body, and if her body hadn't already been turned into putty by his oh-so-talented hands and mouth, looking at him would have done it.

His gilt-edged hair fell into his eyes as he rolled the condom down over his length and automatically, Hope glanced down and immediately jerked her gaze back up.

Shit.

Oh, shit—

Her breath caught again and this time, she couldn't snap herself out of it.

But Remy came over to her then, catching her face in his hands again, taking her mouth with his, fast, hard . . . almost roughly. "Kiss me," he muttered.

Her breath shuddered out of her and she groaned into his mouth as his tongue pushed into hers. And she breathed.

Her body relaxed under his even as his weight pressed against hers, letting her feel all of him. *All* of him . . .

He lifted his head, staring down at her. "You with me?"

"Yes." She curled a hand over the back of his neck. "I'm here. Right here."

"Good . . . I really like you being right here." He caught one hand in his, twined their fingers as he pressed against her. "Stay with me . . ."

Always . . . Remy wanted to beg her for always.

But for now, he just watched her face as he sank slowly inside. Tight—so fucking tight. He gritted his teeth, fought against the urge. Her eyes, misty-green and forest dark, locked on his, half-blind, and he knew it wasn't just with pleasure, although that was there, too.

Slow . . . just take it slow, for fuck's sake . . . Cupping her chin, he angled her head to the side and nuzzled her neck, trailed his tongue along the sweat-slicked flesh.

"Say my name," he whispered against her ear. "Talk to me, Hope . . ."

"Remy . . ." Her breath caught and hitched in her chest and the feel of those tight, perfect little breasts was enough to drive him even crazier than he already was.

Groaning, he ran one hand up her side, cupped one round, small breast, stroked his thumb over her nipple. Bracing his weight on his other arm, he watched as the nipple puckered. "Pretty," he rasped.

She shivered and that shy, nervous smile tugged at her lips.

He sank a little deeper inside and as he did, she clenched around him. He groaned and swore. "Fuck, you're so damn tight . . ."

Her eyes went glassy. And dimly, he figured something out . . . she liked talk.

Hell. He could do that, especially if it would keep that damn fear from slipping back into her eyes . . .

Threading his fingers through her hair, he tangled one hand in it and tipped her head back. "Tight," he whispered against her mouth. "And hot. Damn it, you're burning me alive . . ."

She shivered and he groaned as he sank deeper, deeper. Then he withdrew, started the slow, teasing process all over again.

By the time he'd buried his aching cock in her heated core, they were both shaking, hot, and Remy was convinced they were both lost in each other. Completely, utterly lost.

"Give me your mouth," he rasped against her lips. "Kiss me, damn it."

"Remy," she whimpered. But the sound was lost as he crushed his mouth to hers, forgetting that he'd told himself he'd be slow. He'd be gentle. He started to ride her and she moved with him, her nails biting into his shoulders, her body straining against his.

She clenched down around him, so fucking tight, as her climax grew near and he had to work just to bury his dick inside her—too tight, too fucking tight, and so damned sweet. "Damn it, Hope," he groaned.

Her eyes were blind, staring into his. She sobbed out his name, rocking against him with fevered desperation.

"Please."

"Shhhh." He pressed a kiss to her lips. She bit his lip and reached down, gripping his hips, clutching him close as she worked herself against him.

"Please, oh, please . . ."

Remy swore and reached between them.

As he rubbed the stiff bud of her clitoris, Hope's eyes went wide, a low, guttural moan escaped her and her body stiffened against his.

Heaven and hell.

She clenched around him, her sheath milking him, gripping him so tight and snug, it was both pain and pleasure. Still trying to cling to some semblance of control, he sank inside her, but she was so damn tight, almost lost . . . and then she was—lost as she cried out his name and broke under him, climaxing and shaking.

Her nails tore into his arms and he groaned, his hips slamming into hers involuntarily.

She cried out.

"Hope . . . ?"

"Please . . . !"

Sinking against her, he caught her mouth with his and took her hard, burying his cock inside her, deep, deep, deep . . . Losing himself.

No. Already lost.

Her heart was still thudding against her ribs, and she was breathing so hard, it was a miracle she hadn't passed out. Every last inch of her felt incredibly alive and Hope shuddered as Remy roused himself and rubbed his cheek against hers.

He murmured her name. She rolled her head over to look at him.

His lashes were low, slumberous over those dark, lovely blue eyes and she couldn't stop the foolish smile from spreading over her lips. "Yeah?" she murmured.

He caught her hand and pressed a kiss to her wrist.

She shivered as his lips grazed the scarred flesh there.

"Nothing," he whispered. "Just making sure you're really here. That I'm really awake."

She giggled. The sound of it surprised her so much, she clapped a hand over her mouth.

Remy smiled at her and reached up, combed a hand through her hair. "You're beautiful." Then he cocked a brow and said, "And don't tell me you're not."

"When you look at me, I feel that way." She blushed and squirmed.

He chuckled. "I'd look at you all the time, then, but that might get weird. I can see me arguing my next case—convincing the judge he needs to put some bastard behind bars, and all the while, I'm staring at you." He kissed her chin and rolled out of bed. He disappeared for a minute and returned, sliding back next to her.

She snuggled against him, that foolish smile still curving her lips.

"We're not going to get much sleep," she whispered.

He wrapped both arms around her and kissed the top of her head.

"I don't give a damn. You?"

"Who needs sleep?"

Little fucking slut.

Joe dropped down from the vacant apartment and stalked away.

It would be dawn soon and the last fucking thing he

needed was for somebody to notice him peering across the square toward the DA's apartment. Fucking moron should have pulled the curtains closed, huh?

"He fucked my wife," Joe muttered. His hand itched. Itched for the gun he wore in his shoulder holster and he was tempted, so damned tempted, to just use it on them both.

But that was too obvious. Too damn obvious. And too easy.

Hope wasn't getting out of this *easy*.

She had to suffer. And the way Joe saw it? He could make Jennings suffer by making damn sure Hope suffered. Maybe he could even show the bastard she was crazy—just like he'd tried to warn Remy.

"You should have stayed the hell away from her," he muttered. "Just stayed the hell away."

As he made his way out of the quiet, sleepy town, he didn't see the shadow separate itself from the alley just next to where he had watched Hope and Remy.

He glanced at the man striding away, then up toward Remy's apartment.

He hadn't been able to see inside, but he had a feeling he knew what was going on up in Remy Jennings's apartment. After all, Hope had disappeared inside the apartment sometime earlier in the afternoon. The word was all over town. And while it was possible she'd left, people had been watching.

Somebody would have seen.

He even had an idea who it was who had been spying on the two all night . . . her ex-husband. And if that was her ex-husband . . . well, somehow he just didn't figure the ex had been using night-vision binoculars to watch Remy sleep.

Damn.

Whoever would have thought that little mouse could

prove to be this entertaining? She wasn't even a mouse, he knew. But he couldn't quit thinking of her that way. It was . . . a pet name, he supposed.

He found her rather endearing. Odd, he supposed. After all, he'd been planning to take her, at first . . . that fear he'd seen coming off of her, it had called to him. But now, he knew he wouldn't be doing that. Not with Hope.

CHAPTER
SIXTEEN

WAKING UP WRAPPED IN A MAN'S ARMS WAS . . . SOME-
thing.

Hope woke up with her back pressed against Remy's
front, his arm snug around her waist, and his erection
prodding her in the rump.

He also had his hand between her thighs.

As he rubbed his finger over her clit, she groaned and
instinctively rocked against him.

"Morning," he whispered against her ear.

She blinked sleepy eyes, staring blearily at the window. Yes . . . it was morning. Then he made another
slow circle with his finger and pushed it inside her. Anything she might have tried to say died before it had a
chance to fully form.

He pushed her left leg forward, leaning over her. Hope
shuddered as he pressed against her from behind, slowly
easing his way inside her. She started to shift, but Remy
pressed a hand to her belly. "Easy . . . just lie there,
angel," he whispered.

She rolled her head on the pillow, staring up at him.
She could have fallen into that gaze of his . . . just fallen.
Fallen into it, lost herself in it.

As he slowly pushed inside, she groaned and arched

her back. But when she started to close her eyes, Remy reached up and feathered his fingers over her brow. "Don't. I want to see you."

There was something unbelievably intimate, she realized, about this. The way their gazes locked, held. The way he moved inside her, so slow and easy as the early morning light fell over them like gold.

Intimate. And heartrending. She could taste tears burning the back of her throat, wrenching in her heart. It ended far too soon and she lay there, her heart racing, while he climbed out of bed. She rolled over and watched him slip out of the bedroom, listened to him moving around in the bathroom. She glanced at the table and saw a condom wrapper. Blushing, she realized what he was doing and then she felt foolish for blushing.

Groaning, she rolled to her belly and pressed her face against the pillow.

You just had sex with him, so he's throwing away a rubber—why blush over that?

The bed gave next to her and she shot him a look. His gilt-golden hair was rumpled, his blue eyes sleepy and sated, smiling. "How long have you been awake?" she asked, trying to pretend she wasn't still beet-red.

"Never really went back to sleep," he said, shrugging absently. "I'm okay, though. Used to getting by on not a lot of sleep. I need to get moving anyway. Have to get to the office—too much work to get done."

She reached over, touched a finger to his mouth. "You're behind from spending the day with me. I'm sorry."

"I'm not." He gave her a decidedly wolfish smile and lifted his head, caught her mouth in a quick, hot kiss. "Was worth every last second I'll have to bust my as . . . ah . . . butt for the next few days."

Hope lifted a brow at him. "You know, you didn't have any problem cussing around me last night."

He snorted and rolled out of bed. "There's a difference between cussing and talking dirty. And my mother would have my hide for cussing around a lady."

"But not talking dirty?"

"Well, I don't see you telling her." Then he shot her a grin over his shoulder. "But she raised me not to swear around ladies, just like she raised me to treat a lady right. And I think you like dirty talk."

Hope blushed painfully red and he chuckled as he slipped out of the bedroom. She buried her face back in the pillow.

"I can't drive your car."

"Why not?"

Hope looked at the keys, looked at Remy, and then stared at the silver Jaguar parked in the garage.

"I just can't."

"Not a good enough reason." Remy reached down and caught her wrist. "Look at it this way—it's doing me a favor. After all, I'm running behind, right? And you are capable of driving it."

"But what if I wreck it?" Her heart banged against her ribs and she could feel the panic trying to work its dark, ugly claws inside her, just thinking about it. "What if I get a ticket or something?"

Remy started to laugh. "I'd be surprised as hell if you even knew how to drive fast enough for a ticket." Then he dipped his head and nuzzled her neck. "And look at it this way . . . it will give you a very good reason to come back into town later. I'll need my car back. And you'll have to bring it back, right?"

She gulped and looked back at the shiny silver car. Drive that? Hell, that thing cost as much as some houses. As that thought circled through her mind, she looked back at him and blurted that very fact out.

Remy skimmed a hand down her back. "I'm not asking you to drive a house. Look, it's insured. You're not going to wreck it. But if you're that afraid . . ."

She narrowed her eyes.

"Fine." Clenching the keys in her hand, she stared at the car. She could drive the damn car, right?

"Besides, just think," he pointed out. "If you don't feel like hanging around, now you've got a legitimate reason to leave. Just tell Law you promised you'd get the car back to me early."

He pressed his hand against her belly. "And maybe you can bring some clothes . . . spend the night again."

"Hmmm." Her knees wanted to melt. But this was going way, way too fast. "That's a good point . . . but maybe not just yet."

"So, are you driving it?"

Turning around in his arms, she met his gaze. "Looks like I am. Since you seem to trust me with it."

He grinned at her.

"When do you think you'll be done at work?"

His grin turned into a grimace. "Beats the hell out of me. I'll probably have to work late, but I can just run you back home. I'll need to stop for a while and get some dinner or I'll end up turning into a mindless, drooling freak around nine."

"Ahh . . . nice image." She smirked.

"You haven't seen me when I'm forced to go without meals. Why don't you just plan on heading back around seven and we can eat, then I'll run you home? Unless you decide you do want to stay the night? If you do, I can always work from home for a while."

She licked her lips. "Um. I . . . I don't . . ."

He smiled. "Too fast?" Cupping her chin, he angled her face up. "It's okay. I'm not going anywhere. We'll just do dinner, and plan for something this weekend after I unbury myself."

"Okay." The nervous knot in her belly slowly loosened. As much as she'd love the idea of staying over with Remy again, Hope was still too nervous about all of this. Way too nervous.

Of course, when he lowered his head and kissed her, she totally forgot about being nervous. She forgot they were standing in the middle of the sidewalk. Granted, it was in the back of his condo, which wasn't completely public, but it wasn't exactly private either.

When he touched her, she forgot everything . . .

"See you tonight," he murmured.

"Tonight."

It wasn't until she was nearly at Law's drive that Hope realized Remy might have had an ulterior motive for lending her his car. He probably knew she wouldn't let him come in and be a buffer—she and Law needed to work this out, just them.

And he probably knew just thinking about it would have her stomach in knots.

But thanks to the fricking expensive car he'd placed in her hands, she was so panicky about it, she barely thought about *anything* on the drive. She was less than two minutes away before she even gave much thought to anything other than . . . *holyshitwhatifIwreckthedamnthing* . . .

It made it a little bit easier, she realized, to park Remy's sleek, silver Jaguar and climb out of the car. Staring up at Law's house, she took a deep breath.

They were best friends. They could get past this, right? After all, friends had fights.

"But we haven't," she whispered to herself. "Not ever."

They hadn't once had a fight. Not really.

Resting a hand on her belly, she swallowed and told herself she was *not* going to bolt for the car and drive back into town. Although she had to admit, for the first time in forever, it felt . . . *amazing* . . . to have someplace else to go.

Law had always been there. Always. And she knew, no matter what happened today, she knew deep inside, they'd get. past this. They were friends, and nothing would change that. Hope didn't have faith in much, but she did have faith in that friendship.

But sometimes, that friendship with Law was about the *only* thing she had. It was hard having that as the *only* thing.

But he wasn't the only thing now. Inexplicably, she realized it wasn't just Remy, either. She suspected she'd be able to count on Remy, and she definitely wanted to.

But she also realized she just might be able to count on herself. For the first time in her life, she could maybe, just maybe, find the strength she needed to do just that.

None of that, though, made it much easier to make the long walk toward the front porch. And none of that made it much easier to dig her keys out and unlock the door.

She knew the minute she slipped inside that he was already awake—that he'd probably been awake, and waiting for a good long while.

The house had that tense, heavy feel to it. Slowly, she lifted her gaze and found him standing at the second floor landing, staring down at her.

His hazel eyes were dark and unhappy.

Some part of her felt terribly petty, but as she studied his haggard face, she couldn't help but feel a little bit of pleasure at thinking he'd had a rough time.

Crossing her arms over her chest, she met his gaze. "Hi."

"Hey."

In nearly thirty years, Hope couldn't remember ever feeling awkward around Law. But she did then.

He cleared his throat. "Are . . . um . . . are you okay?"

"Am I *okay*?" she repeated. She rolled her eyes. "Shit, what do you think happened, Law? Do you have some idea in your head that Remy seduced me? That he took advantage of me? You think I spent the last eight or twelve hours chained to his bed or something?"

A dull red flush settled on his cheekbones and he shifted his gaze away from her.

Hope sighed. "You can't look at me without seeing somebody you have to coddle. Somebody you need to rescue. I guess I can understand that, but damn it, Law, if I decide I want to spend the night with a guy, you know what? I'm a big girl and you have to just let me do that."

"Did I say you couldn't?" He shot her a narrow look.

"Well, what else would you call it, you showing up at his place?" Hope kept her arms crossed over her chest and many of the words she wanted to say locked behind her teeth.

He opened his mouth and then abruptly closed it, sighed. "Look, you're right. I didn't have any right to do that, and I'm sorry."

"Fine. You're sorry. I'm running behind on the stuff you need me to get done, so I'm going to shower and get to work." She shoved away from the wall, wondered why she felt a little hollow inside. She stormed up the stairs and was almost to her room when he said her name.

"Hope."

"What?" She stopped, but didn't look at him. Just then, she couldn't.

"I'm sorry."

"You said that already."

"Yeah, but not for the right thing." He reached up, resting a hand on her shoulder. "I'm sorry."

Shrugging his hand away, she moved away, putting several feet between them before she looked at him. But even then, she couldn't say anything. She'd never had the least bit of trouble talking to him. To everybody else, yes. But not to Law.

Not until now. Guardedly, she stared at him.

"I said I'm sorry," he repeated.

Mildly, she said, "I heard you well enough."

He scowled and shoved a hand through his hair. It stood up in weird tufts and spikes and she had a feeling he'd been doing that a lot lately. "So . . . does that mean you're not still pissed off at me?"

"No, it doesn't mean that. I'm still very pissed off at you." She shrugged restlessly and looked away, staring through the door to the room where she was staying.

It hit her then. The room where she was staying. Not *her* room.

But the room where she stayed. It wasn't hers. She hadn't put her mark on it, because it wasn't hers.

Heaving out a sigh, she looked back at Law. "I'm still very pissed off. But maybe it would help if you could explain to me what in the hell happened."

"Would you believe me if I said I don't know?"

She just stared at him.

"I don't," he said, shaking his head. "But . . . shit, Hope. You know how important you are to me. You're my best friend—you are like a sister to me. Hell, screw that. You *are* my sister. We might not be related by blood, but what in the hell does that mean? I'd cut my arm off before I'd let anybody hurt you. And Nia *wasn't* going to. Not once she calmed down."

"Okay." *Nia*—she thought. The woman's name was Nia. Tilting her head, she asked, "How can you be so sure?"

"I just am." Absently, he rubbed the heel of his hand over his chest. "I knew it in my gut—the same way I knew you were in trouble back when I decided to head to Clinton. I just knew. If she thought we'd hurt her cousin, it would be different, but she doesn't think that now. If anybody needs to be worried, it's Deb for setting her off."

Hope shot him a narrow look. "Is that supposed to make me feel better?"

"Shit, like she's going to go bust some sixty-year-old busybody." He crooked a smile at her.

But she just stared at him.

"Hope . . ."

"You used me," she said quietly. "That woman came in here with an unregistered gun, threatened us. That's so unbelievably *illegal*, it makes my head spin. And you *know* how terrified I am of the police. But we should have fucking *called* them, Law. You just let her walk away. Okay, I can handle that."

Shakily, she rubbed her hands over her face, willed back the tears. She was *not* going to cry over this. Wasn't. Slowly, she lowered her hands and stared at him.

"Remy showed up and instead of answering his questions, you threw our friendship in the way—you *deliberately* used our friendship. You used *me*."

It still hurt, she realized. Almost as much as the first time Joe had hit her. Almost . . . not quite. But almost. She'd never expected that kind of pain from Law. That betrayal . . .

Shaking, she wrapped her arms around herself and unconsciously started to rock. Law started toward her and she whipped her head up, staring at him.

He froze.

"Hope, I didn't mean to hurt you," he said quietly.

"I know that." Miserably, she looked down at her shoes because if she looked at his face, she was going to cave and she didn't want to cave. She was entitled to be angry—she didn't want to hold a grudge, but she had a right to be angry, didn't she?

Her breath hitched in her throat, the tears tried once more to come, but she fought them back. Then she made herself look at him.

The misery she saw in his hazel eyes stabbed at her heart, but she wouldn't, *couldn't* just walk away and she couldn't just let this go, ether.

"You'd never intentionally hurt me, Law, I know that. But you did. I still don't understand why. Now I get that you don't understand why. And I *trust* you, so if you really do think she's not going to hurt us, then I . . ." She took a deep, ragged breath. Her heart ached. "If you think it's safe, like I said, I trust you. But I *don't* understand why you used me. I *can't* understand that." She shook her head.

He looked about as miserable as she felt. "Damn it, Hope, do you think I *planned* on that?"

"No." The tears caught in her throat, and although she hated like hell to do it, if she let it stay inside . . . it would fester. It would fester, and scar. "But you know what? I really don't think Joey ever planned on hitting me that first time. Cruelty isn't planned, Law. It just happens. And for some reason that I can't fathom, you decided it was better to be cruel to *me* than just give Remy the plain and simple truth. And I *get* that you're *sorry*. I get that. But right now, it's just not what I need to hear."

She stared at him, saw the savage glitter of fury, disgust, and grief that swirled in his eyes. "Damn it, Hope."

"I'm tired," she said quietly. "And unless you can say something to me besides *I'm sorry* . . ."

She just shook her head and looked away.

"I'm tired and I'm done talking about this. I've got work to do and I'm going to get it done—after that, I have to take Remy's car back to him."

Then she turned away from him.

Her heart ached and when she closed the door behind

her, she stopped fighting the tears and let them fall. As they ran unchecked down her cheeks, she realized the burning in her gut was easing up.

She'd just hurt her best friend, she realized—she'd gutted him and it broke her heart. But she couldn't keep that inside, either. Couldn't. She'd finally figured out what happened when poison lingered too long.

Law staggered as the door closed behind Hope.

I really don't think Joey ever planned on hitting me that first time. Cruelty isn't planned, Law. It just happens. And for some reason that I can't fathom, you decided it was better to be cruel to me.

He knew the value of words. Knew that sometimes they could be completely empty. And sometimes, without realizing it, they could totally rip a person's heart to shreds.

Squeezing his eyes closed, he muttered, "What in the hell did I do?"

He wanted to go to her. But he realized just then, he didn't have the right. At all.

Setting his jaw, he turned away from the door and started down the stairs. He wanted to be pissed off— hell, he *was* pissed off. But he wanted to be angry with Hope, and he couldn't be. Because she wasn't wrong. He wanted to be pissed off with Remy, but what in the hell had Remy done, other than be there for Hope?

Maybe he could try being pissed off at Nia. That was where he *needed* to be angry. He could try directing it at her . . . or maybe at himself. Hell, he'd fucked up as bad as she had, and she didn't owe Hope anything.

He, on the other hand, did. At the foot of the stairs, he stopped and sank down. His eyes were scratchy, gritty from the sleep he hadn't gotten the night before, but he couldn't, wouldn't be able to sleep.

Wearily, he rubbed his left hand over his eyes and then

lowered it, staring at the closed front door. His right arm was throbbing, had been ever since yesterday, but the last damn thing he felt like doing was going to see the doctor.

He wanted, *needed* to hang around here, on the off-chance that maybe Hope would come out and he could try to talk to her again . . .

I'm done talking about this.

Her voice echoed through his mind.

With a bitter curse, he shoved upright and grabbed his keys from the small table in the hallway. Shit, shit, shit. Yeah, *he* needed to see her, talk to her, try to get her to stop being so fucking pissed, try to get her past the hurt he saw in her eyes.

But that wasn't what *she* needed. Son of a bitch.

CHAPTER
SEVENTEEN

"JUST GO *TALK* TO HER."

Roz opened her mouth to argue with him, but Carter pressed his mouth to hers, cutting the argument off. "No. Don't give me this bullshit that it's not for the workplace and don't give me the other excuses either," he said after he lifted his head.

Staring down into her mutinous blue eyes, he said, "Go talk to her. And damn it, just stop being so stubborn and say you're sorry, for crying out loud."

"I ought to make you sleep on the couch for a month." She glared at him.

"If you don't feel better after you do this, fine. I'll sleep on the couch and I'll go down on you every night for the entire month, too."

Roz chuckled. "Well, that's enough to make me say I don't feel better even if I do." Sighing, she turned around, staring off in the direction of the kitchen. "Fine. I'll do it. I can't take not having one of my best friends talking to me anymore."

"There's my girl."

As she started off down the hall, Carter leaned against the door. Waiting. When she stopped and turned to face him, he said, "Stop thinking. Get it done."

Roz stuck her tongue out at him.

* * *

"How much longer are you going to ignore me?"

Lena sighed as she laid the knife down. "You know, Roz, it's never a good idea to do that to somebody who has a butcher knife in her hand. Especially if the somebody in question can't see."

She set the knife down, leaned against the counter. Shit, this was getting to be a headache and a half.

"Damn it, Lena, are you going to talk to me or not?"

"Sure." She grabbed a towel and turned around, facing Roz. "What do you want to talk about? I have to take Puck in to get groomed in a few days and he's not going to be happy with me. Ezra fucked my brains out last night, though, and that left *me* feeling pretty damn happy. How are you and Carter doing?"

"For fuck's sake, Lena, would you grow up!"

Lena bared her teeth in a mean smile. "Would you? You want us to be all buddy-buddy again, and I've already told you . . . it isn't happening again until—"

"I fucked up!" Roz shouted. "I get that. I fucked up and I've already tried calling Law, but he ain't answering the damn phone. I fucked up. I was wrong. I'm sorry—I wasn't a good friend to him, and now I see that I wasn't a good friend to you, either, because when I wasn't fair to him, I hurt you, too."

Lena pressed her lips together and braced her hands against the counter. She swallowed the knot in her throat. "You finally getting both those points, huh?"

"Yeah."

Tugging her glasses off, Lena rubbed her eyes. "He didn't deserve that shit, Roz. He's a good guy."

"I know. And you're right—I was way off, and I'm sorry."

"Okay." She took a deep breath and as she did, it felt like some aching, massive weight fell off her shoulders . . . and her heart. "Okay."

"So . . ." Roz murmured. And her voice was closer. Cautious. "Are we okay?"

"No," Lena said honestly. "But we will be, I think."

Roz touched her shoulder. Lena smiled and lifted an arm. Roz moved closer and pressed her shorter, curvy body up against Lena. "I miss you," Roz said.

"Yeah. I miss you, too."

"I miss Law. I miss all of us going out to breakfast. Carter is about to strangle me, too, because I'm so damn grumpy all the time, which is making *him* grumpy and he hardly even wants to be around. I'm chasing him out of his own damn house." She sniffled and squeezed Lena's waist. "Plus, I'm going through cookie withdrawal. I know I deserve it all, and that makes it even worse, because I can't even indulge in a good pity party."

Lena snorted. "You sound like you're doing just fine." She hugged Roz and then eased away. "Maybe I'll try to do some cookies next week."

As far as a peace offering, it was the most she was willing to do just then. She was already running behind and she hadn't had her lunch yet. She wasn't about to skip her meal just to make Roz her damn cookies.

Roz chuckled. "I won't say no, but if you don't want to, you don't have to. I'm consoling myself with some shortbread cookies I found at Target."

At her feet, Puck whined in his throat and she felt his tail wagging against her legs.

"Sorry, boy. You can't have any," Roz said.

"He's not excited about the cookies," Lena murmured.

Just then, there was a knock on the door.

"Hey."

"Law."

Even twenty minutes ago, the sound of his voice would have been enough to have her strained nerves shattering, but now, she made her way to him. "Hey, what are you doing out here?"

She slid an arm around his waist to hug him, but just that light touch was all it took to tell her something was wrong.

He stood rigid and unmoving as she squeezed his waist and when she eased back, her heart skipped a beat in trepidation. Too much weird shit going on—what in the hell was wrong now, she wondered.

"Are you okay?" she asked quietly.

"Yeah." He dropped a kiss on her brow. "Lousy day. Just needed somebody to hang with for a while. You eat yet?"

"Actually, no." She turned back to Roz. "I think maybe I'll go ahead and grab my lunch."

"Sure." Roz's voice was hesitant. "You okay, Law?"

"I'm fine."

"Ah . . . okay. Um, look, can I have a second?"

Law tensed. Lena reached up, laid a hand on his arm. "Sure."

She could hear the nerves in Roz's voice, the misery. And as she started to apologize, some of the tension in Law's body eased. Some. Not all.

"Anyway, I just wanted to say I'm sorry. I haven't been a very good friend to you, and I feel lousy about it," Roz said.

"Forget about it," Law responded, his voice brusque. "All the crazy shit we've got going on, none of us are acting normal, I don't think."

"Ahh. Well, okay, then. I've got orders to take care of, so I'm going to get."

Lena waited until the door swished shut behind her before she faced Law. "So . . . just how bad has your day been?"

He waited a beat and then asked, "Can we have lunch in the bar?"

* * *

"Hell, Law, if it was me, I might have been thumping you over the head," Lena muttered, disgusted. At the same time, she felt bad for him. She reached over and rubbed a hand down his back.

"Gee, thanks for cheering me up," he said sarcastically.

"Don't come to me looking to get cheered up," she said, shrugging. "I'm your friend, not your cheering section. But you apologized and that's the best thing you can do."

She scowled absently, twirling her straw back and forth between her fingers and wishing *she* could have a drink. But she still had too much of the workday left ahead and the rest of her staff would be in soon.

"You and Roz okay?" Law asked softly.

"We'll get there. We talked earlier."

"I figured. You know, you didn't have to get pissed at her on my account."

She leaned over, bumped her shoulder against his. "It wasn't on *your* account. She was wrong. Plain and simple. And it pissed me off. It made it worse when she kept trying to smooth it over like nothing happened, or just say trite crap like . . . *well, everybody else seems to think* . . . We're not lemmings, none of us. We can think on our own."

"So you got mad at her for being a lemming?"

"Oh, shut up." With a sigh, she checked the time. Her break was just about up. "I've got to get back." She brushed a kiss against his cheek and then grimaced. "You need to shave, pal. You're like a Brillo pad. And stop brooding about Hope. Just give her some space. It will be okay, though. She loves you too much to not forgive you."

"Thanks."

* * *

As Lena walked away, Law kept staring off into the distance.

Part of him knew she was right. That part of him was still edgy, anxious . . . *pissed*.

The giving Hope *room* part was the problem. He had a massive problem with patience and now he was supposed to wait and just let his friend work out the grief he'd heaped on her.

She had too much grief in her life already. . . . How could he have added to it like that? It was only the hundredth time he'd asked himself. He figured he'd do it another hundred times before he ended up putting it away.

Maybe after he'd put it away, he'd feel level enough to face Hope again.

Maybe.

"Bad?"

Hope pushed the keys into Remy's hand and gave him a strained smile. "Of course not. I didn't put a scratch on it."

He tossed the keys onto the desktop and said, "I'm not talking about the damn car." He reached up, cupped the back of her neck, and brought her against him.

"I know." She sighed and snuggled against him, resting her head against his shoulder. Once more, it amazed her at how *right* that felt, how natural. Like, maybe, just maybe this space had been made just for her. Absently, she lifted a hand and smoothed his shirt. "It was bad enough. He said he was sorry, for barging over to your place. And for earlier. All of it."

"Okay . . ." Remy stretched the word out.

Feeling a little foolish, she eased away from him and crossed her arms over her chest. "I can forget the deal with him barging over to your place. That's just Law.

He's got to get it in his head that he doesn't *always* have to protect me."

"That's not going to happen any time soon." Remy smirked and rubbed his jaw.

"I know. And I can forget that part." She winced and shot him a look. "I know maybe you might not feel the same . . ."

Remy sighed, leaned back against his desk. "Sweetheart, look, I'm not pissed off at him over last night. What he did last night was . . . well. Hell, it's typical Law. Hotheaded, impulsive . . . but he did have you in mind. You definitely hadn't had the best day and he *knew* that. If you'd been out with some guy just looking for an easy lay, well . . ." He ended with a shrug.

"Guys aren't going to put up with me just to get laid," she muttered, shaking her head. Not with all the issues she had. Running her hands through her hair, she linked them behind her neck. "But I'm glad you're not angry with him."

"Oh, I didn't say that." Remy's voice went hard and flat. His gaze was cold and wintry. "I'm plenty angry and it took more self-control than you can imagine not to deck him yesterday."

He pushed off the desk and came to her, cupped her cheek in his hand. "I've seen so many people say hurtful things to others, more than you can imagine, probably. And sometimes it really does get to me." Stroking his thumb over her lip, he gazed into her eyes as he murmured, "But I've never once felt that pissed off by somebody's *words* before, Hope. Never. I wanted to pound him into the ground for putting that pain in your eyes. So yeah, I'm angry. But this is between the two of you—you two are friends and I'm not going to come between that."

She wasn't sure, but Hope thought her heart might

have just melted. And for the second time that day, she was fighting tears. To hide it, she leaned forward and pressed her brow to his chest.

"It makes it worse not knowing why he did it," she muttered. "I just can't get it out of my head—*why* did he do that?"

"Did you ask?"

"Yeah." She closed her eyes, breathed in the scent of him. Man, she loved the way Remy smelled. Male . . . warm. Expensive. Idly, she noticed the same scent was on her, now. It was the soap he used. She'd discovered that in the shower when she lathered up with it. The smell was borderline intoxicating on him, not so much on her. Absently, she stroked her hands up and down his sides.

"Hope, you're making it very hard for me to have a conversation here."

"Hmmm?" Tipping her head back, she glanced at him through her lashes, saw that he had a look on his face that was rapidly growing familiar.

That lovely blue was heated, his lashes low over his eyes. And she found herself wanting to push up on her toes and tug his head down close enough to kiss him.

He groaned. "Damn it, are we talking or not?"

"We are talking," she said, but she was more interested in his mouth than his words.

Remy gripped her hips and pulled her close. Through their clothes, she could feel him and the feel of him had her shaking. Slowly, deliberately, he dragged her against him. Just once. But it was enough to set her nerve endings to sizzling and her mouth to watering.

Then he dipped his head and caught her lower lip between his teeth. "You're killing me. Are we talking or should I go lock the damn door?"

"Lock the door . . . ?" She blinked and then shot the

door a look. Blood rushed to her cheeks and then she backed out of his arms so fast, she almost fell.

"Guess that answers that." He snorted. With a pained look, he moved back behind his desk and sat down. "Maybe it will be safer for me back here."

"Ahh . . . sorry."

"I'm not." He slanted a grin at her. "Just looking at you can do that to me. It's just worse when you're standing so close. And I get the feeling you need to talk about the mess between you and Law."

Law . . .

That was enough to douse the fire dancing inside her veins. The energy drained out of her and she sank down on the couch tucked up against one wall. Burying her head in her hands, she said, "I just want to know why. And he can't give me an answer, because he doesn't know. He says he knows she won't be bothering us again and if he *says* that, I trust him. Law . . . well, he knows people, Remy. I can trust him on that."

Just the misery on her face was enough to set him off again.

But Remy knew she didn't want or need his fury, so he fell back on logic. Folding his hands across his belly, he waited until he knew his voice would be level before he said anything. "Hope, you know this doesn't have anything to *do* with whether or not Law thinks she's going to come back and hassle you two. It has to do with the fact that she never should have done it to begin with. She came there armed, and it terrified you. That alone needs to be dealt with."

"Hell, *I* understand that." She pulled one knee up against her chest and rested her chin on it, staring morosely off into the distance. "But it's not even about that for me."

Remy wanted it to be about that—very much. Fuck,

this was a mess. But he wasn't going to harp on that point . . . just yet.

"So what is it about?"

She looked at him and the haunted look in her eyes was like a bare-knuckled punch straight to his heart. "He can't even tell me why he was so willing to use our friendship for a woman he doesn't even know. He didn't even care about me, Remy. He's known me for thirty years, almost our entire lives. He saw her for five minutes. And he's willing to use me to protect her . . . and he can't even tell me why."

"Is that what he said? He can't tell you?"

Hope nodded, her gaze miserable.

Blowing out a sigh, he came out from behind the desk and settled on the couch next to her. He rested a hand on her back, stroked it from her neck down the curve of her narrow waist. "Then maybe he doesn't understand why either, and chances are, that's burning him up, too."

"That doesn't make any sense," she muttered. She got off the couch and started to pace, her quick, angry strides taking her back and forth across his office in dizzying circles.

As petite as she was, those legs of hers could really move when she wanted, he mused.

Under the faded cotton of her too-large T-shirt, her shoulders were hunched and rigid. Abruptly, she stopped in midstep and whirled around, glaring at him. "Damn it, just give me a *reason*, okay? It doesn't have to be *the* reason, but one thing that could explain why he did it. Maybe then I can let this go."

"One reason?" Remy cocked a brow. Uncoiling off the couch, he came over and stood in front of her. Idly, he combed his fingers through her hair, watched as the silken brown strands fell back into place. "You know,

I'm not really the kind of guy who is prone to violence. Not automatically. I usually think things are better solved a different way. I can remember the first time I saw you, though. How Prather had his hands on you, how you looked so scared . . . and even though he hadn't hurt you, I wanted to hit him. Just for scaring you. There isn't really any *sense* to that, I know. No logic. No reason. But I wanted to do it and I'd only seen *you* for a split second."

She lifted her gaze to his.

Slowly, he lowered his head, and staring into her eyes, he rubbed his mouth against hers. Without lifting his head, he murmured, "Then you took off running and all I wanted to do was follow. Not much sense in that, either, considering all you did was look at me for that split second and you wouldn't say two words to me."

Her breathing hitched. She reached up, curled one hand around his wrist.

"Sometimes a few minutes, a few seconds, even just one look can be all it takes," he said quietly, lifting his head and staring down at her. Resting a hand on her waist, he drew her close. "It doesn't excuse what he did, and I don't know if that's the reason. But it's one that makes sense in my mind. I can't think of any other reason why Law would suddenly decide to turn into an ass, at least where you're concerned."

Determined to see her smile, he added, "I think he's always been an ass, but at least with you, he tries not to show it . . ."

It worked, for just the barest second. But some of the misery faded from her eyes. Still scowling though, he noticed. Her brow furrowed as she smoothed her hands down his shoulders. "So you think maybe he's just, um, attracted to her?"

Remy grimaced. "Now you're asking for more than

I'm equipped to handle. You asked for a plausible reason and I gave you one. But yeah, maybe that's what it is. But *if* that's the case, I'd say it's more than attraction." Nuzzling her neck, he murmured, "After all, attraction isn't quite describing what I feel for you."

"Hmmm." She tipped her head back. "And just what does?"

"Oh, now that list could go on. And on . . ." He raked her soft flesh with his teeth and smiled as she shivered. "But if you really want me to go on, you really *should* lock that door."

And to his surprise, she pulled out of his arms, then went and did just that.

Remy grimaced as he glanced at the clock on the dashboard. He had way too much work to get done and there weren't enough hours left in the night to get do it.

"I made you run behind again," Hope said.

He shook his head. "No, you didn't. I'm the one who told you to lock the door." Then he grinned. "And you did it, too . . . I was a little surprised by that."

Hope grinned back at him, despite the blush on her cheeks. The smile faded as he came to a stop in front of Law's house.

"You okay?"

She nodded. "Yeah. I'm fine." Then she glanced at him. "I am, really. Something dawned on me, earlier. This isn't home to me, you know? I need a place of my own. Or at least someplace that doesn't just feel like . . ."

"Someplace where you're not a guest?"

"Yeah." She blew out a breath. "That's not Law's fault. He doesn't *treat* me like a guest. But this isn't home."

"Then find someplace that is." As soon as he said it, he wanted to yank it back. And because he wasn't about to see her leaving, he reached out and curled a hand around her neck, adding, "As long as you find it around here. Because if you try to find it elsewhere, I'll probably follow you."

"Really?"

"Yeah. Just found you . . . not losing you." He kissed her, sliding his tongue into her mouth and groaning roughly as she opened for him.

"I'm not too fond of the idea of losing you, either," she mumbled as she pulled away. She licked her lips, then made a soft little humming sound under her breath.

It drove him nuts.

"I might kind of look around, see what happens," she said, sighing. "I can't do anything fancy, but I can find something decent, I suppose. Law p . . . ah . . . well, I've fairly steady money coming in."

Law . . . He bit back a laugh and suddenly, he figured something out. That heavy-ass box she'd been fighting him over the day he'd come out here—it had been full of books, envelopes and stuff. *Law's* books.

She was working for the guy. Somehow.

Shit, no wonder she didn't feel at home here. Running his tongue along his teeth, he asked, "So . . . just where does that steady money come from? If you're looking for a place to stay, you'll need to list a job, you know."

Her eyes went wide, panicked.

"Ah . . ."

Remy cocked a brow. "I guess self-employed might work, if you had Law listing you as a contract employee or something—I don't know if writers do that sort of thing."

"What . . . you . . ." She snapped her mouth closed, staring at him.

Grinning at her, he shrugged. "Hey, I'm a lawyer. Between me and Nielson, we know everything about everybody. But don't worry. It's not like I plan on taking out an ad on it or anything."

"You know?"

"Yep." He rested a hand on her thigh and shrugged. "I just figured out what you were doing, though. You work for him. Assistant or whatever, I take it?"

"Yeah. Pretty much. He . . . well, Law's not exactly organized. I am. I handle all the stuff that he forgets, and the stuff that he doesn't have to do, so he can worry about what he needs to do—which is write. It works, better than I thought it would, actually."

"And he pays you."

She shot him a wide grin. "Oh, yeah." Her smile faded and she sighed. "Although I can't really put down 'author's assistant' on any application, can I?"

Remy shrugged. "Hell, self-employed will probably work. Besides, this is Ash. We're more likely to let things slide than some. And maybe I can help you find a place."

He wanted to offer his place, but that wasn't right, either, he realized.

As much as he'd love to have her there, she'd never *had* anything on her own. And the two years she'd spent after she'd left her husband, that didn't really count, because he suspected she'd spent every minute of that constantly moving around, fearing he might come looking for her.

Hope needed to settle, needed to see that she could stand on her own. By herself. She needed it.

"Maybe we can look around this weekend. There are some apartments and stuff in town," he said softly, stroking a thumb over her lip. "Although Law's going to lose it when you mention this to him. Especially with all the crazy stuff going on."

He reached down and brushed his fingers over the scars on her wrists. "Hell, *I* don't even like to think about it."

"And what if we never find who did it?" Hope shook her head. "I can't live in limbo."

"No." He looked back at the house, caught a glimpse of Reilly's shadow passing in front of a window. "You can't. And that's the argument you'll have to use with him. That . . . and the fact that you'll let Ezra help you pick out a security system. Would help if you picked a place in town. All the stuff has happened out here in the rural parts, so if you're in town, it might help."

He slid her a look. "What about a dog?"

"A dog?" A cautious look entered her eyes. "What about a dog?"

He chuckled. "We'll talk more later. I need to get home, and drown myself in work."

"Okay." She leaned over and kissed him.

"I need a few days to get caught up. But can I take you out Friday? Maybe you can stay the night and we can look around on Saturday?"

A smile curled her lips. "Yes. I think I'd like that."

When he finally saw Hope climbing out of the car, Law did *not* rush the front door.

That was his first instinct. But he didn't let it take over.

Instead, he sat in his chair, glaring at his computer and debating on whether he should take the pain medicine the doctor had prescribed him earlier. The office had worked him in before he'd gone by the Inn to talk to Lena. He hadn't damaged anything, but he sure as hell felt like something had been damaged. His arm *hurt*.

Of course, focusing on the arm made it easier to *not* think about Hope.

Space.

She needed space.

She needed Remy more than she needed him now.

And while Law was glad she had somebody in her life now, it left him feeling a little hollow inside.

Jealous as hell. Which only pissed him off more.

He listened to the door close, lock. Listened to her footsteps start across the hallway and he braced himself for her to walk right on by. But then she stopped. Slowly, he shifted his gaze to her. She stood there, her hands in her back pockets, her head cocked.

"Hey."

Leaning back in the chair, he said, "Hey."

They heard the car engine rev outside as Remy pulled away. Hope glanced toward the front of the house, as though she was tracking the car with her eyes, even though she couldn't see it.

When she looked back at him, there was a soft, happy little smile on her face. Law had seen a similar smile on Lena's face a lot lately. Hell. Hope was really falling for Remy.

He was happy for her. He thought. Yeah, he was happy for her. Remy had already more than proved he had feelings for her.

Sourly, he wondered if he'd be giving her away at her wedding in a few months. If he hadn't totally fucked up their friendship.

"I've got a question for you," Hope blurted out.

Law shifted his gaze back to her and lifted a brow.

"Is it because you're . . . ah . . . attracted to her? Is that why?"

A dull red flush started to creep up his neck. Briefly, he wondered if he could play dumb and get out of this. Hope looked miserably uncomfortable, but there was a steely glint in her eyes and he suspected getting out of it just wasn't going to happen.

Sighing, he shut his laptop and shifted it over to the table. As he did, he knocked over the bottle of pain medication and it went rolling off the table, hitting the floor and there, it decided to roll under his chair.

"Son of a bitch," he growled. Standing up, he pushed the chair back and knelt down, grabbed the bottle. As he stood up, he looked up at Hope, met her eyes.

"I don't *know* her," he said flatly. "I can't much say if I'm attracted or not."

She just stared at him.

Law fought with the bottle until he managed to get the stupid childproof cap off—one-handed made it very interesting. As he took two of the pills, he grabbed his cold coffee from the table and tossed it back.

The coffee hit his raw stomach and reminded him he hadn't eaten a damn thing. And he'd just taken a nice handful of codeine. Wonderful. Sighing, he rubbed the back of his neck and met Hope's eyes again. "I don't know her," he repeated. "But . . . well, before she jerked out the gun, there was definitely some part of me that was thinking I wanted to know her."

He grimaced. "Wanted to know her a lot. I don't think I've ever looked at a woman and felt it hit me that fast. Then . . ."

"Then she pulls a gun out on us." Hope looked away. Her narrow shoulders rose and fell on a sigh. "Okay."

Law stared at her.

"Okay?" he repeated.

She looked back at him. "I'm *not* saying I'm all cool about what happened. But I'm not going to let it stick between us either." Then she reached up and poked him in the chest, hard, her finger drilling into him. "But don't do that again."

"I won't." Shaking his head, he said quietly, "I promise."

"Okay, then." She leaned in and pressed her lips to his cheek. "I'm heading to my room. I want to finish up and get to bed early. I'm going into Lexington tomorrow."

"Why?"

She glanced down at her clothes, a grimace twisting her face. "Because I'm tired of Remy taking me out and him looking like a thousand bucks and I look like Raggedy Ann's ugly redheaded stepsister."

EIGHTEEN

She spent nearly three hundred dollars on clothes.

She felt almost giddy over it, too.

It should have seemed like a small thing—buying clothes. Okay, maybe not the *three hundred fricking dollars* part, but the buying clothes. It wasn't really such a big deal, or it shouldn't be.

It was, though. Especially for her. Hope hadn't let herself think about it much—if she had, she might have had a nervous breakdown. But as she left the TJ Maxx in Lexington, she thought about what she'd just done.

Other than the clothes she'd picked up from thrift stores over the past couple of years, and the shopping trip with Lena a month or so earlier, this was the first time she'd ever really done any shopping for herself.

On her own. It shouldn't be such a big deal. Just like the haircut shouldn't have been such a big deal.

But when she'd gone shopping while married to Joey, he'd always been there and *nothing* had been bought without his approval. He'd even helped her pick out her wedding dress. The clothes for the honeymoon. He picked out and bought all her damned underclothes.

Everything. Not this time.

She'd done it all by herself and she'd only bought the stuff *she* wanted . . . and a few things she thought that Remy might like. Jubilant, and in the mood for a celebration, after she stashed her clothes in the car, she treated herself to some ice cream before starting the drive home.

She was tempted to stay out longer, just to enjoy the feel of it . . . *without being afraid*. But if she was gone too long, Law would start calling, and even though she was still disgruntled with him, she didn't want to worry him.

With that mind of his, it didn't take much for him to start getting paranoid.

Even as that thought was circling through her mind, she glanced in her rearview mirror and caught sight of a light blue sedan, a few cars back.

Frowned. Because she'd seen one just like it on the drive in.

Light blue sedan.

She couldn't make out anybody through the windshield, at least not without wrecking. Focusing back on the road, she waited a minute and then looked again.

There it was. She crossed a few lanes of traffic. It crossed with her, hanging back, but staying there. Almost like the driver *wanted* to be seen . . .

"Get a grip," she muttered to herself.

It looked like . . . well, probably a million blue sedans in the world. But the sight of it sent a chill down her spine. Convulsively, her hand tightened around the ice cream cone and it crunched in her hand. Swearing, she dumped it in the open cup that held the dregs of her coffee. Then she shot her rearview mirror another glance.

Still there. Farther back.

But still there.

Her heart started to race and the euphoria she'd been feeling only moments earlier started to die.

Now it tasted like ashes on her tongue. Was the driver following her?

Or was it just all in her head?

And that was *not* a question somebody who had often doubted her sanity really wanted to ask . . . not at all.

Joe smiled as he trailed after Hope.

She'd made him—knew he was following her.

Oh, other than that one lane change she'd made, she hadn't shown much of a reaction, but his gut said she'd made him, and he believed in listening to his gut. He was tempted to close the distance between them. Tempted to drive alongside her, maybe even smile at her, wave.

See how she reacted.

But he didn't. When he let her see him, it was going to be when they had plenty of time alone. Not on a damn freeway.

Torn between disgust and amusement, he watched as Joe Carson hung on to his ex-wife's bumper. He suspected Hope had seen him—probably didn't know *who* was following her. But she knew somebody was. And the cop thought he was so damn smart.

Although, he had to admit, he did understand the appeal of the chase.

The chase, after all, was what led to his current mess . . . and his predicament.

He burned, ached for another chase. Needed it, hungered for it.

But he was going to have to hold off. Had to wait until there wasn't so much interest, so much focus. Besides, it wasn't like he didn't have a distraction.

Watching this fool chasing after Hope was actually very, *very* amusing.

* * *

It was Saturday.

In just over three hours, she was meeting Remy in town and they were looking at an apartment. The plans to spend the night at his place had fallen through—he'd been stuck dealing with things in his office for a lot later than he'd planned. But that was fine.

She'd spend tonight at his place instead. Even thinking about it made her smile.

But first, the apartment. It was in her price range—*just*—and she could just drive out to Law's for work. He wasn't going to like it, she suspected, but hey . . . he hadn't expected her to stay forever, right?

This was only supposed to be temporary. A fact she had to remind him of, repeatedly, the moment she told him her plans.

"You're *what*?" he demanded some thirty minutes later.

"Looking at an apartment," she repeated calmly. "This wasn't ever supposed to be long term, and you know it."

"Long term? Hell, it's barely been a couple of months." He looked dazed. Then he shook his head. "But . . . no. Look, Hope, I know we've got some problems here, but there's no reason to go leaving—"

She clapped her hand over his mouth. "Stop," she said flatly. "It's not about . . . that. It's about me. I need my own place, Law. I'm strangling here. And I need to prove to myself I can do this. That I can have a place, on my own, and not feel so terrified that I need to bolt. This is for *me*, and it doesn't have anything to do with you. At all. It's for me."

"How much of it has to do with Remy?" he asked sourly. His hazel eyes darkened as he studied her face.

And she noticed that he looked tired. Very tired.

"Not much," she replied. "It's about me, for me. It's

not about him. Or you. Or even Joe. Can you try to understand that?"

Law blew out a harsh sigh. Then he caught her hand, twined their fingers. "We went all this time and never had any trouble, you know. I never once hurt you. Why all of a sudden are we doing this?"

"Growing pains?" she offered with a smile. Maybe part of the problem was the fact they'd never once had any major bumps in their friendship—not between *them*. There had been external factors . . . like Joe. But nothing between them, not until recently. Maybe that was why she still had that faint resentment and for both of their sakes, she needed to let it go.

Pushing it aside, she eased close, wrapped an arm around his waist. His lean, rangy body felt harder, leaner. He hadn't been eating well or sleeping well lately and she wondered how much of that had to do with her. "Law, you've got to stop worrying about me so much. I'm going to be fine, I promise."

"You better be," he muttered, his voice gruff. He wrapped his good arm around her and squeezed. "Otherwise, I'll be pissed off."

That went okay, all in all, she decided as she pulled away from Law's house.

She was heading into town an hour early, but she couldn't just hang around Law's now. She felt too edgy. Restless.

She'd just walk around the square some, maybe hit the bookstore. She could use a book or two. Actually, that would be nice . . . she hadn't done much reading lately, and then she could go by the café—

A car came flying up behind her.

Blue. Dimly, her mind processed the fact that it was a blue sedan—light blue. Just like the car she'd seen following her on the interstate when she went to Lexington.

She was busy trying to control the car, and her fear, as the sedan shot into the other lane—bare inches separated them. She yelped, clutching the wheel, almost jerking it to the side.

She was driving too fast, though—right before she could do that, she made herself stop, pressing down on the brake, even as the car edged closer, closer. Shooting it a look from the corner of her eye, she saw a face.

A shock of pale, pale blond hair. A square ruddy face. Familiar—

Joe . . .

Her heart leaped into her throat and terror crowded her mind.

But then the car pulled ahead, and before she could so much as blink, it pulled in front of her and, with a squeal of the tires, sped away.

It was gone from sight long before her heart rate settled.

"Shit," she whispered.

Oh, shit.

Joe.

The look of terror on her face had been worth it. He didn't think she'd gotten that good a look at him. Not enough to be certain.

Just enough to suspect.

And if he knew anything about his mouse of a wife, she wouldn't dare call the cops. He knew how scared she was of them, after all.

Chuckling, he kept an eye on the rearview mirror, watching to see if the beat-up car she drove appeared in it. It didn't, though. Pulling off onto a side road in town, he parked so that he'd have a view of Main Street when she arrived. It was almost five minutes later.

He wished he could see her face.

Wished he could have been close enough to watch how she reacted.

Soon, he told himself.

Soon.

Her earlier excitement had faded and in the pit of her belly, there was a cold, hard lump. But she wasn't going to let that keep her from this afternoon.

She wasn't going to let it freeze her, wasn't going to let it control her.

And even though all she wanted to do was *run*, she wasn't going to let it chase her away, either.

Hope stood in the middle of the empty apartment and stared all around. Chewing nervously on her lower lip, she glanced over at the realtor and then back at the apartment. "It seems kind of . . . well, big for one person," she said quietly.

"Wait until you start trying to fit furniture in." Remy came up behind her and slid an arm over and around her upper body, easing her back against him. He pressed a kiss to her temple. "Trust me, it just looks this big because it's empty."

Relaxing against him, she tried to picture some furniture in the place and thought that maybe he was right. Maybe. A couch along that wall. A TV. She gulped and muttered, "Furniture. Hadn't even thought about that part."

The realtor beamed at her. "It's always so exciting, though, getting a new place."

Hope felt kind of nauseated. Exciting . . . getting a place of her own. A real place. Not crashing at a shelter or one of those damn long-term hotel type places, or sleeping in her car, renting a room over a garage. And not living with Law, or Joey . . . but her own place.

No, exciting wasn't the word she'd use. Terrifying.

Alone—

Abruptly, she found herself thinking of the car she'd seen earlier. Following her along the highway.

No. He hadn't been following her.

You've got to stop this, she told herself. Fear had dominated her life for too long. Way too long.

"I'll take it," she said, forcing herself to sound a lot more certain than she felt.

The realtor's beaming smile grew even wider. "Oh, wonderful . . ."

"You sure?" Remy murmured.

"Yes." She nodded. If she thought about this for too much longer, she was going to change her mind, and she couldn't do that—she needed to do this. Needed it.

Tipping her head back, she smiled at him. "I need my own place, Remy. I really think it's the best thing," she said, keeping her voice low.

Off in her own little world, the realtor was jabbering about the deposit—first month and last month's rent, the low monthly payments and how, isn't it just wonderful? Cable and utilities were included. "Of course, there will be a credit check . . ."

She couldn't help it—Hope tensed. Could she pass a credit check?

"Marta, we'll get to all of that," Remy interrupted, giving the realtor a smile. "Why don't you head on back to the office and start drawing up what needs to be done? We'll meet you there in a few minutes. I can lock up, if that's okay with you."

Marta chuckled. "Well, normally, I'd say no. But with you, Remy, not a problem."

Hope watched, focusing on the realtor with more concentration than she really needed. Marta actually *bustled.* It was a sight to see, really.

A few minutes later, they were alone and as Remy studied her face, Hope had to fight not to fidget.

She still hadn't settled from earlier. From seeing that damn car.

"What's wrong?" he asked softly.

"I don't know if I can pass a credit check." She forced a laugh and hoped he'd buy that line. "Plus, they'll want things like references."

But Remy didn't buy excuses, or lines, and she should have known better.

Lifting a brow at her, he suggested, "Try again."

"Look, I don't want to talk about it right now." Hope pushed a hand through her hair, and looked away, studying the little apartment and trying not to feel too disappointed. Even as nervous as she was about being on her own, some part of her was almost greedy for it. But stupid, stupid, stupid . . . she hadn't thought about things like credit checks, credit histories, references. Hell.

"Is it the idea of moving?"

She grimaced. "I said I didn't want to talk about it. And no. It's not that, at all. I *need* to get out on my own. It's not about getting away from Law. It's about being on my own, for a while at least . . . and not running while I'm at it. I have to prove to myself I can *stay* in one place, and not be afraid, you know?"

He cradled her cheek. "Then you can have it. Not having a credit history isn't the end of the world. As to references, you've got at least one solid one—and I'm not talking about me. You know Law will give you one." He stroked a thumb over her lip. "This isn't New York—we still take some things on faith around here, Hope. I can talk to Marta, and I'll co-sign the rental agreement for you, if you want—and that's *if* they insist it's needed," he murmured. "Or you can ask Law. He won't care. And the owner might not push the issue."

She grimaced. "It still feels like I'm leaning on others."

"It's not leaning. You're paying the bills. You'll be living here." Dipping his head, he rubbed his lips over hers. "But you may be surprised. It's not like you need that much of a credit history if you've got the money for the first month's rent, last month's rent, and all that jazz. Of course, if you're that concerned, then you wait awhile, build a bit of a history. Then try again."

"No." Hope scowled at him. "Waiting isn't an option."

"I thought you'd say that. Although I'm wondering why you're suddenly so anxious to get away. You're not still angry with him, are you?"

Angry.

Hope eased away from him and folded her arms over her chest, pacing over to stare out the window. From here, she could see the front windows of Remy's apartment. A plus in her opinion. He was close—real close.

Resting her brow against the sun-warmed glass, she said, "I don't know. I don't think so. I'm still . . . stunned, I guess you can say. Very stunned. But it's not just that. I just can't seem to breathe lately. At all. Law is constantly hovering and I can't handle it, and when I try to tell him, it's like he can't understand. He looks at me and just sees . . ."

Her voice trailed off and she sighed, shook her head. She didn't even know what she was trying to say.

"He failed you—that's what he remembers," Remy said quietly. "And every time he sees you, he remembers how he failed to help, and some part of him is driven to fix that, no matter what. He can't see past that."

"Law didn't fail me," she said quietly. "*I* failed me."

"That's bullshit. Neither of you failed. The person who failed you is that bastard who hurt you." Remy came up behind her and slid his arms around her waist, pulling her back against him. "I can understand why Law is beating himself up over it—I'd probably be doing the same. And I can understand why you want to beat yourself up. You keep looking back and wondering if you couldn't have gotten out sooner, if you could have kept him from hurting you if you'd done this, or that. But it's all bullshit, for both of you. The person who failed was your ex. Not you . . . and not Law."

"You make it sound so simple." Then she opened her eyes, staring out at the street, the festive Halloween decorations going up all along Main Street. Halloween. Almost time for Halloween.

The time for masks, and candy, and scares. She found herself thinking of that blue car . . . and the man she thought she'd seen. Had it been Joe?

Licking her lips, she said quietly, "I think I saw Joe earlier."

Remy stiffened. His hands curled around her shoulders.

She closed her eyes.

"What?"

"Joe. My ex-husband. I think I saw him."

"I know who he is," Remy snarled, his voice low and angry. "Where?"

"On the drive into town. A blue sedan," she said quietly. "The car came flying around me, came so close, I almost drove off the road to get out of the way—I can't be sure. I only saw his face for a second. But . . . it looked so much like him."

"Do you think it was him?"

Hope swallowed. The fear in her heart, clawing in her belly, all of it shouted, *Yes*. Turning her head, she met his gaze. "Yes."

Remy's eyes, dark and hard as blue diamonds, held hers. "Would he come here? After you?"

"Oh, yes. In a heartbeat." Unable to stop herself, she laughed, but it hurt her throat—it was like regurgitating jagged, harsh bits of glass.

"Yes, he would, if he got it in his mind that he wanted me back. He told me before that he wouldn't let me go. That's why I spent so much time running . . . I was afraid he would come after me. And I didn't want to be easily found."

"And you're sure it was him?"

A sound, strangely like a sob, caught in her throat. "Am I sure? Hell, I don't know." Shaking her head, she whispered again, "I don't know." She curled her hands into fists. "There's no reason for him to be here. None."

"You're wrong." Remy reached up and touched her cheek, stroked his finger along it and wondered if she knew just how wrong she was. He suspected none of them knew just how fucked up her ex-husband was, but he was definitely fucked up. In the worst possible way. And if he was in town looking for her . . . His gut knotted. His hands ached to pummel something. But he kept his voice quiet, soft, as he murmured, "You're wrong, Hope. To him, he's got every reason to be here—after all, you are here. You already made it clear he doesn't let go easily."

Hope swallowed. She closed her eyes and shook her head. "No."

"I'll ask again. Was it him?"

"You can ask me fifty times. A hundred times. The answer won't change. I just don't know, Remy." She sighed and leaned forward, resting her head against his chest.

The gesture made his heart ache. Reaching up, he curled his hand around her nape. He lowered his head and pressed a kiss to the top of her head, breathing in the scent of her hair.

"I only saw him for a minute. Just a minute. The hair was right . . . the shape of his face was right. It looked a lot like him. But I can't swear it was him." A shiver raced down her spine.

He wrapped an arm around her. The hand he'd laid on her neck, he stroked down her spine. She was cold, he realized. Chilled, although it wasn't cold in the room. Cuddling her closer, he whispered, "He won't touch you. He won't hurt you. I won't let him."

"If it was him . . ." Her voice faded away, then she shook her head.

"What?"

"Nothing," she said quietly.

He reached down and cupped her chin, angled her head back until she faced him. "Tell me, Hope."

Fear had darkened her eyes to nearly emerald. "Remy, if it was him, he's dangerous. Nobody else wanted to believe that. Just Law. But he's dangerous." She swallowed and then whispered, "I think he's crazy."

Abruptly, she laughed. "And that's a fucking laugh, isn't it? Coming from me. Pot . . . meet kettle."

"Hope, you're not crazy. You never were. I already know he's dangerous." He skimmed a hand through her hair. "Decent, nondangerous men don't have their wives admitted to a psych hospital for no fucking reason, but he did it and because he has a badge, because he lives in a town where people think his name, his word means something, they were able to keep you locked up. They violated your rights and took something they had no right to take, and he's the reason they did it. If he can do that to you, he can probably do it to others—I get that he's dangerous."

Hope grimaced. "That's not exactly what I'm talking about."

"I know." He stroked a hand down her cheek. "But I'm not a woman who's half his size . . . and I'm not one of the people he's bullied and intimidated for half of his life, either. Stop worrying about me."

Hope shook her head. "I can't." Staring up at him, she suddenly started to think, to wonder . . . what if it *had* been Joe? And he saw her with Remy? He'd gone ballistic just when she would talk to Law and he knew that her relationship with Law was nothing more than friendship. If he saw her with a guy who clearly wasn't a friend . . .

She started to shake. Her belly clenched and knotted. Her airway started to shrink down on her. Feeling that inevitable press of panic pushing down on her, she eased away from Remy. "I need air," she whispered. Turning away, she started to pace. She hated this—hated it. Hated how easy it was for that fear to sneak up on her, to take control, to drive everything, anything from her mind. Hated it . . .

She wanted to push it away, push it outside herself and not let it take control, but her imagination was running wild now and she could see it . . . what would happen if Joe discovered her relationship with Remy.

She could see it—Remy's lifeless body.

A sob trapped itself in her throat. She wanted to scream, but it was choking her.

What if it was him—

A hand touched her shoulder. She shrieked, spun around and found herself staring at Remy. Fine lines of tension fanned out from his eyes as he lowered his hand. "I'm sorry I scared you," he said quietly.

"It wasn't you," she whispered, her voice harsh, ragged. "It was him. Always him." Nausea churned inside her and she wiped the back of her hand over her mouth. "What if he hurts you? I couldn't stand it, Remy. I swear, it would kill me inside. Damn it, damn it, damn it."

She reached up, fisted her hands in her hair.

Maybe . . . she licked her lips. Maybe they should stop seeing each other. Until she knew.

She darted a look at Remy, saw that considering look in his eyes. But even as she opened her mouth to say it, he folded his arms over his chest and quietly said, "No."

"No, what?"

"No, we're not stopping seeing each other."

She jolted. Geez, was she really that easy to read?

He closed the distance between them and reached up, caught her chin. "You said something before, that you were tired of letting him control you. If you try to push me away over this, even temporarily, that's what you're doing. You're letting him have that control again."

"It's not about him controlling me," she whispered. "It's about keeping you safe."

Remy snorted. "First, I can take care of myself. Second . . ." He cupped her face in his hands, stroked his thumb over her lower lip. "And be honest here, Hope. Completely honest. Don't think about Joe, at all. Don't think about anything but you . . . and me. Do you want to stop seeing me?"

She stared into his dark blue eyes. She didn't need to think about that answer—it was already right there. She knew, knew it as well as she knew her own name, the shape of her face; she knew the answer. Quietly, trying not to let her voice shake, she said, "No, I don't want to stop seeing you. You . . ." She paused, licked her lips. "You, well, you matter to me. I don't want to give that up."

"Then don't." Remy dipped his head and rubbed his lips back and forth across hers. "It's as easy as that, baby. He can't control me, and he can only control you if you let him."

"And what if he tries to hurt you?" She rested her hands, curled her fingers into the soft, faded cotton of his polo shirt. Through it, she could feel the heat of his skin, the reassuring, steady warmth of his body. So strong. So solid. She pressed her heart against his chest as an ache settled in her heart. "What happens, then, Remy?"

"We deal with it. But you don't even know if it was him. And you're not giving me much credit here; I can handle myself, baby. I promise. Just don't go and disappear on me. Don't give him control. You worked too damned hard to take it away from him, anyway, right?"

"Yeah." She snuggled closer and wrapped her arms around his waist, clinging tight. If only she could just keep him here. Right here. Where she knew he was safe.

Nothing will happen, she told herself. And he was right . . . she didn't even know if it had been Joe. It could have been anybody. Anybody at all.

But deep inside her gut, she wasn't so sure. The body remembered things. Fear. Pain. And from the moment she'd seen the guy in the sedan, her body had been screaming a message: *RUN RUN RUN*.

She wouldn't want to run from a complete and total stranger. A complete and total stranger wouldn't paralyze her with fear.

But this one had. Or pretty damn close.

Swallowing, she turned her face into his shirt, breathed in the scent of him. As he brought up a hand to cradle her nape, she murmured, "You better stay safe. Or I'll make you regret it."

"Same goes," he muttered. "And I'll be fine, you'll be fine. Now stop worrying so much. . . ."

He watched as they left.

Then he glanced up at the apartment and smirked.

She'd seen him and she'd told the lawyer about it, too. Yeah. He could tell by the tight, unhappy look on the schmuck-lawyer's face.

Little bitch. Who did she think she was?

And that fuck, Jennings. Putting his hands all over Hope. It made Joe's head pound, made his blood boil.

He lingered in the café as they headed down the sidewalk, knowing it would be better if he kept well out of sight for a while. At least until he knew what the lawyer was going to do. Probably wouldn't do anything, pansy. But still. Joe wasn't going to get cocky and fuck up. He knew better.

Besides, he'd accomplished what he'd set out to accomplish after all. He'd made sure she saw him. Soon, it would be time to do more than that.

He was tempted, by God, he was tempted to just wring her fucking neck for what she'd done, dump her skinny ass. Maybe even leave her someplace where people might think the lawyer had done her.

But no. The more he thought about it, the more he realized what he needed to do. Take her home. Back to Clinton. Where she belonged. They'd deal with this divorce, he'd have his wife back, and she'd learn how badly she'd fucked up.

That was what he needed to do, and that was what he would do.

Soon. Staring through the window, he watched as Jennings lifted a hand, rested it low on Hope's spine.

The skirt she wore was too fucking short. Her hair was too fucking short. Jennings dipped his head and murmured to her and she looked up at him, smiled. And the sight of that smile hit Joe square in the chest. He slammed his cup down on the table. Hot coffee splattered all over his hand. Swearing, he bolted up from the chair just as the waitress came rushing to his side.

"Sir, are you okay?" she asked, her eyes wide.

Ignoring her, he dug a few singles from his pocket and flung them on the table.

She'd smiled at him.

Little bitch.

She'd fucking smiled at the pussy lawyer—she hadn't smiled at *him* like that in years. Oh, that little bitch. Wearing those slutty little clothes, cutting her hair . . . and flirting.

Yeah, she was going to pay.

But even as everything in him raged to go after them, he hung back.

Just watching.

And as they disappeared into a Realtor's office, he narrowed his eyes.

She was going to try to get that apartment, Joe realized. On her own?

She couldn't do shit on her own—he'd worked damn hard to make sure of that.

"Wait," he muttered to himself. "Just wait."

CHAPTER
NINETEEN

"THIS IS ALL I'VE GOT."

A week later, Hope stepped back from the bed and studied her meager possessions. She tried to ignore the nervous knots currently tangling in her gut.

She needed to do this. She wanted to do this. She had to do this . . . she'd already put the money down. And if she backed out, she'd feel like even more of a loser than she already did.

But damn it, this was hard.

"You sure you're ready for this?"

Glancing back over her shoulder, she met Law's gaze.

He was alone with her in her room. Remy was downstairs.

He had loaded her stuff into his car, all whopping five boxes and one suitcase. That was actually almost twice as much as she'd had when she came here a couple months earlier.

She knew why he was waiting down there, too. Giving them privacy.

Licking her lips, she turned around and rested her hips on the edge of the bed. "No," she answered honestly, meeting Law's hazel gaze. "I'm not sure. But I think I need to."

"Why now?" he asked quietly. His eyes were grim, and sad. The fight they'd had, it had driven a wedge between them, and although she wasn't angry with him, she suspected he was still pissed off at himself. That was a bigger wedge than anything else.

That, and the fact that both of them needed to figure out that she could take care of herself.

"Because if not now, then when?" She clasped her hands, putting them between her knees to keep from fidgeting. "If not now, Law, then when?"

"When things are a little more settled and I don't have to worry about somebody trying to hurt you?" he suggested.

He crouched in front of her, reaching up and closing his fingers around her wrists gently, angling them so he could study the healing scars.

They were no longer an angry, vivid red, but they'd always serve as a reminder of what somebody had tried to do.

"And if that person isn't caught?"

"What if it's Joe?" he returned, cocking a brow. He rubbed a thumb over the scars and shook his head. "I don't like this, sweetheart. I don't like it at all. It's too fucking strange, you seeing him on the highway and a few weeks ago, this happens."

"*This* was over a month ago," she said quietly. "And Joe wasn't around then."

"We don't know that." Law shook his head. "It's not like we can prove that."

"And we can't prove he was here, either." She sighed and rubbed her temples. "Law, if I sit around waiting to see what happens, then I'm putting my life on hold. I'm just now finding my life. I don't want to put it on hold anymore."

For a long, long moment, Law was quiet. Then finally, he nodded. "Okay." He stood and leaned, pressed his lips to hers gently. "But you're getting an alarm system. A killer one."

Hope grimaced. "Remy's already talking to Ezra about it. We've got somebody coming out on Monday. And he's . . ."

She blushed.

"Shit, Hope, if he's staying the weekend with you, surely you can say that without blushing," Law teased.

She narrowed her eyes. Ignoring him was probably the safest route, she figured. Deciding to do just that, she gamely continued on. "Anyway, on Monday, we've got somebody coming out to install the security system and Ezra said he'd come out for that."

"Good." Law grunted a little. "I'll pay for it."

"No."

"Yes." He gave her a grin. "You can consider it a housewarming gift."

"Law . . ."

"Come on, Hope." He shoved a hand through his hair. "Look at it like this—I know you, you're going to weigh the pros, the cons, and go with the baseline model because it's cheaper. I don't want baseline, but I know you'll have a harder time affording the bells and whistles . . ." He paused. "Unless you let me give you a raise."

Hope folded her arms and glared at him.

"Okay, then it's a housewarming gift." She didn't need to know he'd take care of the monthly cost—he'd just have a word with the technician. He'd get himself out here early on Monday and hang around until it was done. "Come on, Hope."

She sighed and rubbed her eyes. "Law . . ."

"Hope. I can afford it. And I'll sleep better. You probably will, too."

She looked away, but not before he saw that fear flash through her eyes.

Damn Joe Carson anyway. Why in the hell did he have to show up around here?

Night had fallen by the time Hope had her stuff neatly packed away.

Remy watched as she stretched her arms over her head and grimaced. "Man, that took forever."

Amused, he chuckled.

"What?" She aimed sleepy green eyes at him, a brow cocked.

"Baby, that was a piece of cake compared to my move." Then he skimmed a glance around the apartment and added, "But then again, I had more stuff than you did."

She made the Spartans look rather luxurious. Her living room had three pieces of furniture she'd bought over the past week, a couch, a coffee table and the small table that she'd bought to serve as a TV stand—when she bought a TV. Her bedroom had a bed and a dresser—that was it. Her dining room had a small, two-seater table that was probably going to be a desk. It already had the laptop Law had pushed into her hands just before they'd left.

She wished she could have found some pleasure in those shopping excursions, but this time, they'd just been a chore, another task she had to get out of the way.

"Yeah, I guess I don't have much stuff, do I?" Looking around, Hope wrinkled her nose. "I need curtains. And more than two pots and pans and four plates . . ." She sighed and flopped down on the couch.

"You can have a housewarming party." He sat down next to her. That wasn't close enough, though, so he pulled her into his lap, rested his hands on her slim thighs, pushed his hands under the hemline of the shorts she'd pulled on while they worked. "Make people buy you stuff you need."

"Ugh. No thanks. I don't do parties."

"Don't like them?"

She shook her head. "No. It's not that . . ." She bit her lip and glanced away. Then she sighed and looked back at him. "When I was married, Joe used to do parties. All the time. They were the catered kind and I never had to do more than organize them, but it was so nerve-wracking. Having people in there. And if I wasn't polite enough, or if people thought there was something wrong . . ." She paused, swallowed. "One time, there was a lady there. She was new in town. And she knew. I could tell. She knew what Joe did to me. She came up to me when I was coming out of the bathroom. She told me I shouldn't stay there, shouldn't stay with him. It was . . . well. It was kind of her. Trying to help. But Joe knew. Somehow. He hurt me bad that night."

Remy's heart ached as he watched her staring off into the distance, trying so hard not to cry, trying so hard not to let the strain show in her voice.

He wanted to say something—do something that would help. But nothing could. Or would. So he stayed silent and imagined what he'd do if he ever got his hands on Joe Carson.

Hope blew out a breath and said, "The next week, I found out that the woman's husband was being brought before the school board. He hadn't done anything wrong. I knew it then. And they both knew it. I saw her in the grocery store only once after that—it was right before they decided to move away. I told her I was sorry. She said she was, too. But she said she was sorry for me. Because she had a great guy, and she knew they'd be okay. She couldn't say the same for me. A month later was when I tried to kill myself."

Leaning forward, he buried his face against her neck. "Hope, if I ever meet that guy in person, I'm going to break him. Just so you're aware."

She gave a watery laugh. "Break him, huh?"

"Yeah. Into about a thousand pieces. That sounds right." He sat back and stared into her eyes. "So no party. And a party doesn't have to be a big thing, you know. Could just be Lena, Ezra, Law . . . me." He stroked his hands higher along her thighs. "They could bring you nice little housewarming gifts, and Lena can cook. She can cook like mad, too. It's not even about the gifts. Maybe you need to see you can do a party . . . your way. Not his way."

"Hmmm. That's sneaky, Remy." She leaned in, rubbed her lips against his. "Very sneaky. I don't know. I'll think about it."

"You do that. And after they leave, we could have our own party—the sleepover kind." He smiled against her mouth. "You like sleepovers, Hope?"

"Sleepovers?" She laughed. Her laugh turned to a sigh as he slipped his fingers higher, higher along her thigh, brushing the edge of her panties. "What kind of sleepover did you have in mind?"

"The kind where you run around in something skimpy and lacy and I peel it off you . . . then I fuck your brains out," he muttered. Catching her lower lip between his teeth, he bit lightly. "You don't have anything lacy on right now, but I could give you a demonstration . . . if you want."

"Why don't you? Since you're so keen on talking me into parties."

Remy eased her off his lap.

She stood, but when he went to reach for the waistband of her shorts, she glanced at the naked windows. "No curtains."

"Turn off the lights," he said quietly. "Nobody will be able to see in. Tomorrow, we'll head out and get the curtains."

She blushed, but did just that. She wasn't not having

him touch her the entire weekend—she should have
bought the damn curtains.

The lights clicked off, casting the room into shadows.
Remy's eyes adjusted just as she came back to stand in
front of him and he caught the waistband of her shorts,
stripped them off, but left the panties on. Maybe the
barrier would help him slow down a little. Tugging
her back down onto his lap, he stripped her shirt and
bra away. Immediately, he wished he'd thought about
curtains, because damn it, he wanted to see her. Even
though he'd seen her slender, sweet body before, it wasn't
enough. A hundred times, a thousand times wouldn't be
enough.

Trailing his fingers along the delicate line of her back,
he whispered, "I'm really getting addicted to you,
Hope." Tangling his fingers in her hair, he tugged her
head to the side and raked his teeth down the exposed
line of her neck.

Her breath hissed out of her. Her spine arched. Smiling against her soft skin, he flicked his tongue along her,
tasting salt and woman. "You like that?"

"Yeah," she whispered. "There's nothing you do that
I don't like."

"Nothing, huh?" Intoxicated by the taste of her, he
shifted around and spilled her back onto the couch, ma-
neuvering until he was half-kneeling, half-lying on the
couch with her, sprawled between her spread thighs.
"Let's see how you like this, then."

She gave a strangled groan when he pressed his mouth
to the silk-covered mound of her sex. He could feel her
heat through her panties, but she grabbed his hair, tried
to press her thighs together. "Remy . . ." she whimpered.

Shooting a glance at her, he pressed a kiss to the soft
flesh inside her leg. "Problem?"

"I haven't showered since this morning. I'm hot and
sweaty from all the moving . . ."

"Yeah. Me, too. We can shower later. After."

"But . . ."

"No buts," he muttered. Then he kissed her again. When he licked her through the silk, she moaned. Catching the fabric, he tugged it aside and licked her again. "Hot . . . fuck, yeah, you're hot."

Hope shuddered and fisted her hands in his hair again. But this time, she tugged him closer, gasping out his name.

He smiled against her and then proceeded to do to her what she'd been doing to him from the first time he'd laid eyes on her—driving him out of his fucking mind.

In moments, he had her twisting and groaning against him. When he pushed a finger inside her sheath, she cried out his name. He started to work her with both his mouth and his fingers and she came, so hard, and clenching down around him so tight, his cock jerked in jealous anticipation.

As she sagged against the couch, he sat back on his heels, reaching into his pocket. He'd planned ahead for this, thankfully. If he'd had to get up and walk away from her, even just to get a rubber, it might have crippled him. Severely.

He fought with his jeans, the damn rubber, and all of it took too long. By the time he was ready for her, he hurt with need, and he was hovering almost on the verge of climax himself just from looking at her. She reached for him and it was like she'd wrapped a fist around his heart with that simple gesture.

It hit him then.

He loved her.

He was fucking in love with this woman. Not just falling in love, but all the way in love with her, and he didn't ever want to let her go. Shaken, he reached for her. Drew her close.

Need. Lust.

It was a burning, twisting tangle inside him, and it almost faded as the ache in his heart rose to the front. Reaching up, he fisted a hand in her hair and tugged her head back. "Hope . . . I love you," he whispered against her lips.

Her soft, pretty mouth parted. Tears glimmered in the depths of her eyes.

". . . what?" she whispered.

"I love you." Lowering his head, he pressed his mouth to hers. "You don't need to say it back, although damn it, I hope you do, or can, one day. But I needed to tell you."

"Remy . . ."

"Shhhhh." He kissed her again. Soft. Slow. Teasing her mouth into opening for him. He felt something wet against his cheek. Skimming his mouth along her cheeks, he realized she was crying. He kissed the tears away, then returned to her mouth.

She shuddered under him, arched.

As she did, he felt the heat of her rubbing against his cock and he groaned. Shifting his weight to one arm, he reached down, wrapped one hand around himself, angled against her entrance. As he slid inside, her breath caught on a sigh. "Remy . . ."

"I love you," he muttered against her mouth.

Already, it was an ache in his chest, a burning, driving ache that would consume him.

She rocked up to meet him. Her hands streaked up under his shirt, bit into his flesh—tiny, sweet little pains. Her hips rose against his, the silken flesh of her sheath clenched around him. Hot, sweet . . .

Tearing his mouth away, he stared into glimmering green eyes.

"I love you," he muttered.

And she cried out his name as she came.

The sound of her cries, the feel of her climaxing

around him, under him, was enough to send him over the edge and he slammed into her, swearing as his own orgasm hit hard and fast.

When it was over, he lay, half on the floor, half on her, with his head on her belly. One of her arms curled around his shoulders and they both breathed raggedly, desperately.

Remy closed his eyes, a faint smile on his lips.

He loved her.

A few months ago, this was the last thing he'd seen coming.

And now, it was the only thing that seemed right. Seemed real.

She hadn't said it back . . . but she would, he suspected.

She would.

Hope came awake to the feel of his hands on her. His lips gliding down her shoulder. She wondered at the beauty of it, the pleasure. As he eased her onto her back, she sighed and opened her eyes, smiling up at him. His mouth took hers and she opened for him, twining her legs around his hips and shivering as the head of his cock nudged her. He pushed inside and she arched her back, tightened around him as he pushed deep, deeper. She clenched down around him and smiled as he shuddered.

A lean hand, strong, but so gentle, cupped her bottom, lifted her up. She rocked against him, staring up at him, lost in his dark blue eyes, lost in him. Lost in the way he made her feel. How could he make her feel this way? How could anybody make her feel this way?

His mouth brushed over hers, skimmed along her jawline to tease her earlobe, her neck. Shivers broke out along her skin and his name escaped her lips on a broken sigh.

It was so slow . . . so lazy and sweet, and the heat, the hunger built inside on a slow, gradual wave, breaking over her, breaking over both of them and leaving them shaking and wrapped in each other's arms.

As her breathing calmed, she realized she had both a goofy smile and tears drying on her face.

The things he made her feel . . .

Then he whispered against her neck, "I love you, Hope."

He loved her. This insanely perfect guy loved her. How was this possible? Turning her face into his neck, she held him tight. If ever there was a perfect moment in her life, she was pretty sure this was it. Clutching him close, she breathed in the scent of him and prayed this could just last, forever.

But it didn't. Perfect moments never did.

And just like perfect moments never could last long enough, it ended way too soon. Remy's phone rang, the musical tune blasting through the silence. He groaned against her neck, then swore.

"Shit." Rolling over onto his back, he reached down and groped around on the floor for his jeans, fishing the phone out of his pocket. "Jennings," he said. She tuned out the conversation, her mind still buzzed from sleep and sex. Then he laid a hand on her belly and her sleepy mind focused, heat burning through the fog in no time. Shivering, she rolled to her side and stared at him.

He gave her a smile, but there was a look in his eyes as he continued to listen to whoever was on the other end of the phone. That flat, focused look—his lawyer look, she realized. She recognized that look. It was hard not to, since there had been a few times when it had been directed at her.

Two minutes passed before he disconnected.

"I've got to go," he said quietly.

"I kind of figured." Stroking a hand down his arm,

she gave him a faint smile. "You got time to eat anything?"

"No. Need to shower. I've got extra clothes in my car so I'm good there—it's the weekend, so I'm not expected to be all suit and tie, but I don't have any time."

"Is everything okay?"

He curled his lip. "Yeah. Just a minor problem I need to deal with." He sat up and bent over her, bussing her lips with his. "Will you be around here all day?"

"Probably. Other than curtains." Aware of the blush creeping up over her cheeks, she shot the window a narrow look. "I can't run around this place without curtains up—just can't do it."

"If you can wait awhile, I might be able to go with you." He stroked his hand in absent circles over her belly and the heat of his hand, memories of the night they'd spent, had her aching to reach out and touch him. She curled her fingers into fists to keep from doing just that.

Focus, Hope. Just focus. Shifting her attention to the naked windows, she concentrated on them for about ten seconds and then looked back at Remy. "I can handle picking out curtains and rods on my own, I think," she said lightly. "I'm not helpless."

His fingers flexed. "It's not about you being helpless." His lids drooped low over his eyes, shielding them from her. "It's about him. I don't like him being around and us not knowing what he's up to, angel. I just don't like it."

Neither did she. But she'd be damned if she let Joe make her a prisoner again. "I can't just sit around waiting until I know what's going on with him," she said quietly. "I'm just going into Lexington—I'll find a Home Depot, something like that. I've already got the measurements and all."

A grim look tightened his face. "And if it was Joe following you on the road?"

Hope swallowed. Sitting up, she grabbed the sheet and wound it around her before she stood up. "If it was . . . it was." On her way to the bathroom, she stopped and looked back at him. "He used to lock me in my room, you know. After I got out of the institution. He'd figured out how much I hated being locked up. So that became his favorite form of torture. If I stay here, just because I think he might be out there . . . I'm just giving him the keys to lock me away again. And I'm not doing that."

Brooding, Remy scrubbed his hair and body with more force than necessary and hoped it would lessen some of the anger, the fear. Part of him wanted to tell her she was being foolish—reckless.

But how could he argue with her logic?

She didn't even know for sure it was Joe. Or so she claimed. He suspected she felt the same way he did.

It was Joe. He was here, looking to take his wife home, probably thinking he could intimidate her into doing whatever in the hell he wanted.

But what were they to do?

Hope couldn't stand being tucked away inside her apartment—he could see that clearly enough. And although she hadn't voiced it, he suspected she had finally realized she had a core of strength inside her, the strength that had gotten her through that hell.

Remy couldn't do anything that would take that away from her. She was trying so fucking hard to find herself again.

"And what if he does try to come after her?" he muttered. "What then?"

Shit. This was a mess.

What he wanted to do was keep her with him where

he knew she'd be safe, where he could watch over her and make sure nobody hurt her. But the entire damn reason she'd left Reilly's place was because she needed to prove to herself she could be on her own.

Fuck.

Remy already knew how he'd feel if somebody tried to tell him he needed to stay tucked away for his own safety. And despite the fact that Hope was a woman—*his* woman and he wanted to protect her more than he wanted his next breath—he also knew that if he did or said anything that would take away from the life she was finally building for herself, it would damage what they were building. Worse, it would damage *her*.

He couldn't do that to her.

No. This was best. She had to just keep living, keep building this life she was building . . . and he'd just keep watching her.

She didn't have to know that he was going to have somebody watching her, checking in on her from time to time. That wasn't really a bad thing to do, considering the circumstances . . . right?

After he climbed out of the shower, he left the water running while he made the call. It couldn't hurt. If Hope was wrong, then at least they'd know. But if she was right . . . then they would know . . . and she'd be safer for it.

TWENTY

NIELSON STARED DOWN THE STREET, EYEING THE blue sedan. He'd seen it before. Just once, from his window, the day Nia Hollister had come to his office, right before she'd left town that last day.

So far she hadn't been back, but he wasn't sure if that was a good or a bad thing. She was too hotheaded and that worried him. Of course, Nia Hollister didn't worry him anywhere near as much as what Remy Jennings had just told him.

Joe Carson. Hope Carson's ex-husband. There was a possibility he had almost run her off the road, that he had been following her on the interstate.

After the attack on Hope, Nielson had done some investigating about Joe Carson and he had to say, he wasn't too impressed with what he'd heard. Actually, he was downright pissed off. Nothing bothered him as much as a dirty cop.

Carson might not be on the take or anything like that, but a bastard who beat his wife, a bastard who had her locked away as he'd done . . . dirty didn't even describe him. The problem was Carson had quite a few people snowed. People who thought the guy shit daisies and could do no wrong.

Nielson's gut, though, said otherwise.

As did a few people who had been willing to talk, however abstractly. The words they said, and the words they didn't say, were enough to leave Nielson with a bad, bad taste in his mouth.

Carson didn't need to be in his town. That was all there was to it.

Nielson had enough shit going on around here—he didn't need this. Hope's safety could be in question. Plus . . . it was just a little too strange.

All these strange events started happening and there were too many connections to either Hope or Law or both. As much as Nielson didn't want to think it was at all tied to either of them, he'd been a fool to overlook a possible connection.

Joe Carson was a connection. To both of them.

Slumping down in the seat of his off-duty car, he kept the sedan in his line of sight, watching. Jennings had asked him to watch Hope, and that was exactly what he'd do.

Somebody was fucking with his town and he was tired of it. Was damned tired of wading through blood. The Hollister girl. Prather. What had happened to Hope and Reilly.

Enough was enough.

It was almost lunchtime when he finally saw Hope appear. Her dark hair gleamed under the fall sunshine, and Nielson waited until she'd pulled away, watched as the blue sedan did the same thing.

He, himself, waited an extra few minutes. Then he pulled away from the curb. This shit, it was going to stop, damn it.

She was alone. Finally. When Joe had seen Jennings leaving, he'd been all but ready to make his move then, but he knew better. Knew way too better. He couldn't make his move in town. Couldn't risk it, couldn't do it.

"Fucking cunt," he muttered, rage beating inside his head, an angry, roaring monster.

He'd watched them. The two of them, crawling all over each other.

His wife had fucked another man.

It made him sick, with fury, with disgust.

And something he couldn't even name, because not once had she lain there all still and passive like she had with Joe.

"Fucking *slut*," he snarled.

His hand itched, ached to pull his weapon, put a bullet in her head . . . badly, so badly he wanted to do that. But that wasn't how they'd end it. No. She was coming home, damn it. Home.

He wasn't giving up on his wife.

But he needed her out of town. Hell, even at Reilly's would be fine, now, because Joe would be just as satisfied if he plugged a bullet between Reilly's eyes. He'd enjoy doing that. Reilly was part of the problem, had always been part of the problem.

Hope wasn't heading to Reilly's, though. She was heading toward the interstate. No . . . that wasn't what he wanted. Not what he wanted at all. Run her off the road—that was what he needed to do. Run her off the road, get her into his car. Yeah.

But as he revved his engine to pull up next to her, he heard a louder, throaty purr.

Just then, a line of motorcycles appeared in his rearview mirror. And damn, what a line . . . it stretched on endlessly. Fuck.

That sedan was back there. Hope tried not to shake. Was tempted to turn around. Tempted more to stomp on the gas. But more than anything, she wanted to know if it was him. She had to.

The not knowing was worse than anything.

The not knowing was even worse than the fear.

An unknown fear was worse than a known fear and she was tired of it.

Her hands ached from clutching the steering wheel and she wanted to grab her cell phone, call Remy. Call Reilly. Call Ezra—somebody, anybody, so she wouldn't be alone on this stretch of road with her abusive ex-husband shadowing along behind her.

"*Maybe* shadowing you," she muttered.

She didn't even know and that was driving her nuts. She needed to know—*had* to know . . .

The sedan edged closer. Closer.

Sweat turned her hands slippery and she bit her lip.

Shit. Shit. *Shit*—what should she do?

It was even closer now and she had the sudden, sickening realization that he was going to do something, something bad. Run her off the road. What in the hell was he thinking?

Something roared in her ears, loud. So loud.

Engines. A lot of them.

Shooting another look at her rearview mirror, she saw the sunlight glinting off the chrome of a motorcycle. Then another. And another.

A fricking procession of them, one that stretched back farther than she could see. For some reason, it made her smile, soothed the ragged nerves in her gut.

The sedan backed off, allowing more and more distance to grow between them. A few minutes later, her heart rate slowed to something resembling normal and she kept shooting a glance at the bikers behind.

Whoever would have thought she'd be that happy to see a bunch of motorcycles?

Still, that uncertainty loomed in her mind.

Was it him? She had to know. Had to. Although, in her gut, she already did.

When she saw the sign up ahead for the little mom-and-pop gas station on the outskirts of town, Hope hit her turning signal like she was going to slow down, moving into the exit lane. But just as she was pulling off and the blue sedan was edging to go around her, she sped up and looked over.

The driver looked over at the same time and she found herself staring into Joe Carson's flat, emotionless eyes. It was him. Her gut knotted. Fear threatened to turn her bowels to water, darkening her mind. But she pushed it back. He smirked at her.

The sight of that smirk—that challenging *I-can-do-anything-and-you-know-it* smirk—flooded her with rage and fear. To her surprise, the rage edged in over the fear and she lifted a hand, flipped him off.

Without giving him another look, she pulled into the parking lot of the gas station, half-wondering if he'd follow her.

He didn't, though. Her knees wouldn't stop shaking. Still sitting there a good ten minutes later, she gripped the steering wheel and stared straight ahead, tried to convince herself she either needed to get out of the car, or pull out of the parking lot.

The bikers had pulled in behind her and through the crack in her window, she could hear them calling to each other, teasing and shouting. Just their presence grounded her, made her feel steadier.

Still, when somebody tapped on her window, her heart leaped into her throat and it scared her so bad, she screamed.

Pressing her hand to her mouth, she found herself staring at Sheriff Dwight Nielson.

He lifted a brow at her. Relief hit her, so hard and fast, it was almost dizzying.

"Oh, shit," she mumbled. Clumsily, she fumbled with the keys and pushed the button, rolling the window down. "Hi, Sheriff."

"Hope." He bent over, resting his arms on the car door. "Are you okay?"

"I'm fine," she lied. No, she wasn't. She was scared to death, she thought she might get sick and her gut was a clenched, nasty mess.

"You sure about that? You been sitting here for a few minutes, staring at the parking lot like it might bite you."

She shivered as she realized he'd been watching her. Who else . . . ? Who else had been watching her? Had he turned around? How long had he been here?

"I'm fine," she said again automatically. Then she stopped, shook her head. She couldn't lie about this—shouldn't lie. "Shit. No. I'm not fine. My ex-husband was just following me on the highway, Sheriff. And I don't know what to do about it."

For a long, long moment, he was quiet. Then he nodded. "Okay. You're sure it was him?"

"Yeah." She closed her eyes. "Yeah, I'm sure." All too sure this time.

"Okay, then. Well." He blew out a breath. "You want to see about filing a report? Some sort of restraining order?"

She laughed humorlessly. "It wouldn't do any good against him," she said quietly. "Nobody believes him capable of doing anything bad. They won't see the reason for one."

"You're wrong there," Nielson said quietly. "I believe he's capable, and I see a reason. But I can't make you do it and I can't do it for you. It has to be your call. Completely your call."

Something fierce, hot flooded her mind. Somebody

believed her . . . and not just Remy, although that was amazing, not just Law. Somebody believed her . . . *her*.

Somebody believed her over Joe. Somebody believed in her. Trusted her.

If she hadn't been so damn scared, she might have danced. But as it was, she managed a wan, tired smile and looked at him. "It's a piece of paper, Sheriff. You and I know how little those sometimes do. Unless he wants to pay attention to it, it won't keep him away from me."

From the depths of her memory, she heard Joe's voice, an ugly mockery of a promise, "*'Til death do us part, Hope . . . you're mine.*"

No, I'm not.

"Yes. It's a piece of paper," Nielson said, his voice soft and quiet. "We know sometimes they don't mean much. But this isn't his town, Hope." He leaned in closer, his voice hard and flat, his eyes serious. "It's mine. And I don't let abusive bastards run roughshod through my town. File the report. Let me do my job. Let me help."

He sounded so sincere. So serious. Licking her lips, she looked at him.

Then she stared back at the road, over the motorcycles that separated them. Those damn bikes. She had the weirdest feeling those bikes had spared her from something awful. Something horrible.

Closing her eyes, she nodded.

"Okay." She blew out a breath and said louder, "Okay."

She glanced down at the phone in the cup holder next to her, thought about calling Remy.

No. Later. She'd tell him later.

Remy stared at the slime-bucket who'd come in from Lexington to represent Pete Hamilton.

Thanks to this weasel, Pete was out of jail on parole,

but he wasn't overly pleased with not being able to see his kids.

And for the past two hours, instead of being with Hope the way he wanted to be, he was dealing with this shit. Well, actually, the first hour and a half had been a different matter, a true emergency. Then this had cropped up when Frank Isaacs waylaid him at the courthouse, and it was the last damn thing he wanted to mess with.

Wife-beaters never ranked very high with him, but right now, the kind of man who'd put his hands on a woman . . . well, Remy's patience was worn well past thin. If Hamilton had any sort of brains, if his lawyer had any understanding of Remy at all, they never would have bothered with this last-minute meeting.

And when Remy found out who in the hell had tipped them off about him being in the courthouse . . .

"No," he said for the second time.

"Now I don't see why you're not willing to talk about a deal," Isaacs said, a smarmy smile creasing his wide, pale face. He spread his hands and gave Remy his good ol' boy smile. "What we have here is a private issue between a husband and his wife. It should remain that way, don't you think?"

"Private issues between a husband and a wife cease being private when fists become involved and children see their mama being beaten in front of them," Remy said, flicking an invisible piece of lint off his shirt. "Now is this really why you insisted on meeting? It's the weekend, and this isn't exactly what I'd call an urgent matter."

Isaacs smoothed a hand down his silk tie. His suit was custom-made, Armani. Remy recognized the cut and he guessed he was supposed to be impressed, figured the bastard was thinking he was dealing with some small-time yokel.

"I'm anxious to help my clients at any and all hours.

And Mr. Hamilton is just so despondent about his daughter's birthday coming up." He glanced over at Pete.

As if on cue, Pete looked down. In a mournful voice, he said, "It's her thirteenth. That's a special birthday, you know. She's not going to be a little girl, anymore. Me and her mama, we'd wanted to make it special . . . I . . . look, I just want my family back."

"Really." Remy bit back a snort. "Special. Okay, so what sort of party were you planning?"

Pete shot a look at him. His lashes flickered. Rage danced in the murky depths of his eyes.

Remy cocked a brow. "So special and you can't even remember what sort of party y'all were planning? Slumber party . . . cookout . . . costume party. You tell me, I'll check with your wife, back up the story. You convince me how sincere you are."

Pete's mouth twitched, a mean snarl forming, but then he looked down. "Aw, now you know I've never been good at remembering that sort of thing, Jennings. It was always her mama that did the planning."

"But it was so special—her not being your little girl anymore. Damn, it must really matter to you." Shaking his head, he stood up. "Sorry. No deal. I plan on seeing you pay for the bruises you put on that woman, Hamilton. And for the scars you gave your daughter. Isaacs, next time you need to have this sort of conversation with me . . . call."

On his way out of the courthouse, he checked his phone.

No messages from Hope. No calls. He was tempted to call her.

But he needed to go to his office now and get some paperwork done, thanks to his unexpected trip to the courthouse. It wouldn't take long. An hour, maybe.

Since she'd gone into Lexington . . .

His hand tightened as thoughts of Joe rolled through his mind.

But Nielson had said he'd keep an eye on her. Personally.

Safe. She was safe. And he couldn't hover over her, could he? Couldn't, no matter how much he wanted to.

Deliberately, he shoved his phone into his pocket. He'd get his work done. Then he'd call her.

Hope pressed her lips together as she signed her name to the paperwork.

Her hand shook. She was doing this, damn it. It wasn't much—just a temporary restraining order and there was no telling if it would hold up—probably *wouldn't*, and she knew it, because all she had was her word against his that he'd been pretty much stalking her on the highway a couple of times.

But she'd done it. She'd stood up to him.

Adrenaline shuddered through her and her belly pitched and rolled, making her feel like she was about to puke. As she put the pen down, she curled her fingers into a fist to keep the sheriff from seeing how badly her hand shook.

"What now?" she asked quietly.

"Now I handle it." He gave her that same gentle, friendly smile. And although the smile was friendly, his eyes were pure steel. "You should go find Remy. Have him take you out for lunch or something."

She gave him a weak smile. Lunch. Even the thought of eating was enough to make her feel even more nauseated.

"He had something come up with one of his cases," she said absently, staring out. Her eyes landed on the blue sedan parked on the opposite side of the town square.

The sedan. Joe's car. Shit. He was out there again.

Shit.

Closing her eyes, she shoved her hands into her pockets and took a deep breath, tried to level out the fear before she spoke. "Sheriff . . . he's out there," she said quietly.

Joe sat in the café, chuckling to himself and feeling entirely too pleased.

As the sheriff came striding out of the courthouse, he straightened a little and watched.

It had cost him five hundred dollars to get the guy in the blue Chevy Malibu to come out to Ash, but it would be worth it. Assuming the guy didn't fuck it up. And if he did, well, Joe would cross that bridge when he came to it.

CHAPTER
TWENTY-ONE

"It wasn't him," Nielson said quietly. He sat down behind the desk, watching Hope's face carefully.

Hope swallowed, shook her head. "What . . . what do you mean?"

"It wasn't him. The guy out there is an amateur photographer, out here taking pictures of the area for a class he's taking at UK." Nielson glanced toward the window and then back at Hope. "He's about your age. Blond. Burly sort. It's possible you . . ."

"No." Hope stood up. "It's not possible. I know what my ex-husband looks like—the bastard tormented and abused me for years. I'm not going to get him confused with some total stranger."

Humiliation had her face flaming red, but she'd be damned if she backed down. Turning on her heel, she stormed out of his office, ignoring him as he called out to her.

She didn't need this shit. She'd thought he'd believed her—

Remy. Remy did.

She'd go and talk to him.

Even as she thought it, tears burned in her eyes, clogged her throat.

No. She needed to calm down first. She needed to calm down. Think. Cool down.

Because she couldn't stand the thought of anybody seeing her upset, she ducked into the bathroom, splashed water on her face, let the icy chill ease the burning of her flesh.

And still humiliation and anger crawled through her. She wasn't wrong.

She'd seen Joe. She knew she had.

Out on the highway. So maybe the car on the square was the wrong one. So what?

She'd just have to be careful. More careful.

Maybe she should wait until Remy could go into Lexington with her . . .

"No," she muttered, turning off the water with a snap of her wrists. Damn it, she'd been doing things on her own for *two years*. She wasn't going to let Joe turn her back into the sniveling, desperate coward she'd been, especially not now.

Not now . . .

Before she could change her mind, she left the bathroom.

She was going to Lexington, damn it. She was going to buy her damn curtains, her damn curtain rods, and if that bastard thought he could stop her, she'd beat him over the head with one of those damned curtain rods.

It felt good, being angry.

This time, there were no motorcycles.

He waited until they were on the long, three-mile expanse between Ash and I-64. And then Joe made his move.

Watching as Hope's car went flying off the side of the road, he smiled.

He glanced all around. Made certain nobody had seen as he pulled along beside it. Then he climbed out.

Nice job, he had to admit.

She was sitting behind the wheel, moaning, and pressing a hand to her head. She glanced at him, dazed.

One short-armed jab knocked her out and he hauled her limp body from the car. Another quick look around—so far, his luck held. He dumped her in the front seat, pulled off.

The whole thing had taken less than a minute and the damage to his rental was minimal. It was all about how you hit a car, after all. And how you hit a woman.

Absently, he reached over and laid a hand on her thigh.

They needed some private time, the two of them, before they headed back home. They had business they needed to settle.

She really did need to understand just how badly she'd fucked up.

Nielson's gut was crawling.

That blue Malibu had disappeared only a few seconds after he'd talked with the owner. And now Hope was gone.

It hadn't been Carson in the car. He couldn't really even say there was much of a similarity, other than the coloring.

Easy . . . too fucking easy. He could write it all off, and if she was the woman he was supposed to *believe* she was . . . ?

But she wasn't. The girl might be quiet, might have bent under all the shit life had dumped on her. But she hadn't broken.

Shit.

Nielson pinched the bridge of his nose as her voice echoed through his mind.

I know what my ex-husband looks like. Yes. He imagined she did. Frowning, he reached for the restraining order and stood up, heading outside.

He'd told Jennings he'd watch her. That's what he was going to do.

Nielson came on the accident scene only moments after it had happened.

Hope had left his office only five minutes before he had. He hadn't missed it by long. And the sight of her car was enough to have him swearing a blue streak.

He'd fucked up. Man, had he fucked up.

Crouching down, he studied the gravel. Another car had been here—pretty recently, he thought. He reached for his radio.

They had a big problem, he suspected.

A very big one.

And if he knew a damn thing about Remy Jennings, it was going to get even worse once the lawyer got wind of this.

Jennings was going to rain all sorts of shit down on him, but it was only what Nielson had deserved.

He'd fucked up. Closing his eyes, he muttered, "Please don't let that girl pay for it."

That was all he asked.

"What?" Remy growled.

"Missing," Nielson repeated as his men fanned out around him. He watched as the dogs sniffed the ground, but he didn't have the highest hopes.

She hadn't walked away from her wrecked car. She'd been taken. Her ex-husband had taken her. *Son of a bitch*.

He'd taken her and Nielson had given him the chance to get close. He'd fucked up and now Hope was out there paying for it.

"How exactly did that happen?" Remy snarled.

"If I knew that, I'd be that much closer to finding her," Nielson replied. "Now do you want me to find her or stay on the phone yapping with you?"

Remy hung up. But Nielson knew it wasn't over. The lawyer would be out here. It was just a matter of time. Fine by him.

The more people they had looking for her, the better. He already had an APB out on the sedan, not that he'd expected a whole lot to come of that, because, fuck, a blue sedan.

They were in Kentucky. This close to Lexington, Kentucky, there were quite a few *blue* sedans in these parts of the woods. It was a color that was popular with a number of locals thanks to the University of Kentucky. Plus, Carson was a cop—he'd known what to do, how to avoid getting caught.

But damn it, they had to try, and Nielson had to do everything he could. Because earlier, he hadn't done enough. At least he had the plates, although he couldn't be sure the plates wouldn't be changed.

With Carson being a cop, it made Nielson's job that much harder.

Fear gripped Remy as he tore out of his office. He was on the road as he made the call to Reilly. A split second passed before he also made the decision to call Ezra King. Not that he knew if it would do much good.

But the cop had a good head on his shoulders and right now, he wanted as much help as he could get.

What in the fuck had happened? And how had Nielson *let* it happen?

Remy just didn't know. And he couldn't blame Nielson either. He had to make sure he blamed himself, too, because he'd been worried about this.

Terrified about it, but he'd been trying to think about

what Hope needed, and he'd been trying to be understanding and supportive and *shit* . . .

"Please," he whispered. "Please, don't let anything happen to her."

Hope came awake, filled with a familiar and oh-so-unwelcome sensation. She hated, hated, hated it.

It hadn't been all that long since she'd felt this terror and she'd hoped she'd never have to feel it again. But even as it tried to overwhelm her mind, even as that darkness tried to pull her under and turn her into that desperate, whimpering, mindless *thing*, she pushed it back.

She might have to feel the fear—she couldn't control that—but she could control how she acted. She wasn't who she had been, damn it.

And Joe was about to find that out. Experimentally, she checked her body, wondering if she could move. She wasn't surprised to find that she could. Joe wouldn't have thought to tie her up. It wouldn't have occurred to him that she might try to run away from him.

Even though she'd finally gotten desperate enough to divorce him, that hadn't ever involved physically *running*.

He wouldn't be able to conceive of her openly, physically defying him. He was about to see it, though. She'd run. She'd fight. She'd kick, scream, bite, whatever she had to do to get away.

She could move well enough to do it, too, although she hurt. Her mind was one aching, muzzy mess and when she tried to figure out why, it only hurt more. She'd been driving. She remembered that. Driving. And then . . . shit. Joe had run her off the road. He had really lost his mind.

If she hadn't been so fucking terrified, she might have

laughed hysterically. Maybe Remy had been right to be so worried . . . she shouldn't have left home alone.

She lifted her lashes just a little, staring through them to look around. Where were they? A cabin—looked like a cabin. She didn't recognize it. She didn't know where they were. Didn't know where he'd taken her.

Swallowing, she shifted her gaze around, looking for him—and when she found him sitting at the foot of the bed, staring at her, she stiffened.

She barely managed to muffle her shriek, but she couldn't keep her body from reacting. And that told him . . . let him know she was awake. Wide awake.

Joe smiled and reached out, laid a hand on her ankle. "Hello, darling," he murmured.

"Don't touch me," she said, pulling away from him.

His face tightened. "You might want to watch telling me what to do." He stood up and came closer, sitting down on the side of the bed. "I'm already unhappy with you and you know it. You know what I do when I'm unhappy. Why make it any worse than it needs to be?"

Hope curled her lip at him.

He rested a hand on her belly, sighing. "I just don't care for that look on your face, baby. You've forgotten how things should be. I think I'll have to teach you everything all over again." He stood and turned away.

Hope took advantage of that to sit up, casting a quick glance around the cabin, peering through the window. Although she didn't recognize the cabin itself, she thought maybe the woods might be familiar. Was that crazy? Wishful thinking? Was it just her desperation that had her thinking maybe they were in or near the woods around Law's place? They stretched on for a while and she knew some people had hunting cabins out there.

"What are you doing here?" she asked as he turned back to her.

"I came for my wife," he said, giving her a vaguely puzzled smile like he couldn't quite comprehend why she was asking. As though she should already know the answer.

"I'm not your *wife*," she snarled, spitting the word out of her mouth. It made her sick to even think it. His wife—she'd never go back to that. Never.

Joe's eyes narrowed on her face. "Be careful what you say."

"I'm not your wife," she repeated. "Not according to the law, not according to me. We're divorced. End of story. It's over."

"'Til death do us part," he whispered. He came back to the bed, stroked a hand down her cheek. That light touch made her shudder.

When he fisted a hand in her hair, squeezing so tight it brought tears to her eyes, she almost cried out, but she bit it back. He'd made her cry *enough*, damn it.

Then he touched her again with his other hand. That same gentle touch. "'Til death do us part, Hope. It's not over. Because you're alive, and so am I."

Staring up at his face, she thought, *I'd be really happy to fix that problem.*

"We're going back to Clinton," he said, letting go of her hair and turning away again.

"The hell I am."

He turned around, backhanded her. Casually. Like he was flicking some lint from his sleeve. "Watch your mouth," he said mildly. "As I was saying, we're going back to Clinton."

Hope shoved off the bed, ignored the pain screaming in her cheek. Staring at him through the tears that burned in her eyes, she softly said, "I'll go back to Clinton only if you take me back dead, you bastard. There's no way in *hell* you can force me to leave here with you."

Joe stared at her. For a second, she saw something in

his eyes . . . she thought it might be surprise. "You'll have to write a letter to that pussy lawyer. I don't want to have to deal with him while we're picking up where we left off," Joe said, carrying on as if she hadn't spoken. "I've got paper here and I've already written down what I want you to say. You get to work and then we can have dinner and get some sleep."

Hope folded her arms over her chest.

"Write the letter."

Curling her lip at him, she said, "Go fuck yourself."

This time, when he came closer, she dodged away. She was small, couldn't fight against him, but she was fast. She managed to avoid the first hit. Even the second. But the third time he reached out, he caught the side of her head, and she went careening to the floor, screaming.

Blood filled her mouth and she almost choked on it as he hauled her up, closing a hand around her throat. Rage glinted in his eyes as he glared at her.

"You sit your ass down and write that fucking letter, bitch," he snarled.

She spat a mouthful of blood into his face.

It was his gut that led Nielson here. Just his gut, a hope, and a prayer.

He should wait for one of his deputies to get here, but they were spread thin as it was. They were already trying to cover too much ground and there just weren't enough of them.

Besides, this was likely nothing. He'd check it out, then join the others.

Brody had been out in this part of the woods when he'd seen the guy in the camo and mask.

A guy who'd been awfully close to Law's place.

Law. Maybe the weird shit had nothing to do with

Law. And everything to do with Hope. A fucked-up ex-husband . . . maybe. Nielson wasn't sure. But maybe.

Right now, worrying about the girl he'd let down, he was desperate enough to try anything.

Nielson heard the scream.

He took off at a run.

And although he didn't realize it, he wasn't the only one.

Joe squeezed, squeezed, squeezed . . . she was going to write that fucking letter, and she'd do it now, because he wanted that fucking pussy lawyer to know she was gone. Wanted him to know *why* she was gone, and who'd be between her legs now.

He even wanted Jennings to come after her, because then Joe was going to kill him. Cut him up like a Thanksgiving turkey. Slowly . . . so slowly.

The same way he envisioned choking the life out of Hope just then. Her spit and blood dripped off his face, but he didn't wipe it off. Her nails tore at his hands as he squeezed her throat.

As her eyes started to dim, he eased up. "You ready to write that damn letter, wife?"

"In . . . your . . . dreams," she rasped.

The door busted open. "Put her down, Carson."

He whirled around, jerked her body up as a shield. He stared at the sheriff. Shock, rage, they swamped his mind, made it hard to think.

What . . . how . . . no. Didn't matter. He'd been seen. That was all that mattered now. He'd been seen.

By another cop. Using her body to keep Nielson from seeing his actions, he drew his weapon.

"You put your gun down, I put her down," he said, stalling. Not that Nielson would believe him. That wasn't the point. But this was how the game was played, so that was how he'd play it.

"You want me to lower my weapon, then you give me a reason," Nielson said levelly. "Take your hands off her throat—"

Joe had his weapon in his hand. Ready. Smiling, he lifted it. "I'd much rather break her neck than let her go. Little slut. She giving it out to you, too? That why you so anxious to help her out? She's my fucking wife, Nielson."

"Ex-wife," Hope rasped, her voice a broken, hoarse ruin.

"Shut up, bitch." She drove her elbow back into his gut. It wasn't much of a hit. The shock of it, though—she'd hit him.

She'd fucking hit him. The shock of it was enough that his hold loosened, ever so slightly. And that gave her the slight chance she needed to tear away from him.

That was when Nielson fired.

Joe fired back, dodging to the side. Neither of them missed . . . completely. Joe felt Nielson's bullet tear through him even as he hurtled for Hope.

Fucking bitch. She'd fucking caused this. Fucking, fucking bitch . . .

Hope saw him reaching for her—saw the look in his eyes. She'd seen him angry before, but never like that. Never like that. She knew if he touched her now, she wouldn't live through it.

Not if he had anything to say about it. Backpedaling away from him as fast as she could, keeping him in her line of sight, she stared at his reddened, enraged face.

"Stupid bitch," he muttered. "All your fucking fault. All of it."

"Hope. Come over to me," Nielson said.

She could see him from the corner of her eye. Carefully, she made her way over to him, not taking her eyes off Joe. So it wasn't any trouble to see the gun he leveled at her.

Her heart slammed against her ribs.

He was an excellent shot—always had been. Loved to brag about the trophies he'd won as a teenager. He wouldn't miss. Not from here.

"You come to me, or I kill you," Joe said quietly.

"Hope, that boy over there, he doesn't want to die. And I can tell you, if he pulls that trigger, I'll take him down." Nielson's voice was friendly, polite—could have been discussing the weather. "He might want to hurt you, but he wants to live even more—I can tell just by looking at him. Don't go over there. Just keep on walking to me."

"Hope." Joe's eyes flashed. Full of fury.

She swallowed. And continued to back away. She'd made herself a promise, damn it. She'd keep it. She wasn't putting herself in his hands again. Not *ever*. If he shot her, then he shot her. She'd rather die than put herself in his hands again.

Remy.

Tears stung her eyes, but she blinked them back.

No matter what, she wasn't going to be sorry. She wasn't. She'd had some happiness with him. Some peace. It was more than she'd ever thought she'd have . . . the knowledge that a man could touch her and make her feel something besides fear. That a man, a *good* man could want her.

He squeezed the trigger—ever so slightly. She could see it.

Her heart slammed into her throat.

"Don't do it, Carson," Nielson warned. "You can walk away from this. All of us can. But you pull that trigger, you—"

It was deafening. Hope screamed.

Those seconds stretched out into eternity and she

waited—waited for the pain she knew was coming. Waited for the darkness.

And then, from the corner of her eye, she saw him. Nielson's body.

Slumped on the ground.

No . . .

Joe lunged for her, grabbed the back of her head and slammed it against the counter. "Little cunt," he rasped. "'Til death do us part, remember?"

Darkness exploded through her head. Just before she blacked out, she heard a crash. Bitter, desperate rage swamped her and she wanted to fight, wanted to scream.

No . . . it wasn't going to happen like this . . .

She'd promised herself . . .

CHAPTER
TWENTY-TWO

"'TIL DEATH DO US PART, REMEMBER?" JOE MUT-
tered, letting go of her head and watching as she fell to
the floor, her body limp.

He nudged her with a toe, watched as her eyes rolled
back into her head.

Good. Out. He'd have to deal with her, fast, and get
the hell out.

Shit. She hadn't written the fucking note—

Her prints on his gun. Needed to do that—

He heard footsteps.

He looked up and the visage of a masked face filled
his vision. For a few seconds, he thought he'd lost more
blood than he realized, and was hallucinating.

Staring at that masked face, he blinked. Then lifted
his gun and pointed. "Get the fuck out," he snarled.

Although all he could see was the man's flat eyes, he
had the weirdest feeling he'd amused him. When the
man lifted one big, mean-looking Desert Eagle, Joe almost pissed his pants.

One bullet from that—just one—and he was off his
feet, didn't matter where the man hit him.

"I don't think so," the man murmured. "Back away
from them."

Joe curled his lip. "Why don't you stick that up your ass?"

Instead, the man lowered the weapon. "How about I use it to blow your dick off?"

Joe backed away.

But the man didn't go to Hope. He edged around the spreading pool of blood surrounding the dead sheriff and when he lifted the sheriff's weapon in a gloved hand, Joe's gut turned to ice.

Still holding the Desert Eagle in his right hand, the man lifted the sheriff's service revolver in his left hand.

Joe didn't have time to blink before he aimed and pulled.

His left leg went out from under him as the fiery pain tore through him. Screaming, he hit the floor, hot blood gushing from him. Icy shock followed, only seconds later and for long, wasted seconds, he stared at the blood fountaining from his leg.

Too . . . much. Too much blood. For a few seconds, he couldn't think past the pain, and when he could, all he could think about was just how very much blood he was losing.

His tongue felt thick. Shock and adrenaline raced inside him, but they weren't helping.

Bad hit. Very, very bad.

Still gripping his gun, he lifted it, but his hands were slick with sweat, and he was already weak. The blood he'd lost earlier, and now . . . oh, fuck. This was bad. Very, very bad . . .

He eyed Carson for a few seconds, making sure the man wasn't going to be much of a threat. He didn't have much time. Not much at all, if he wanted to get clear of the cabin.

Joe Carson had been squatting here off and on for the

past few weeks, when he wasn't staying at a hotel over in Maysville.

He knew . . . because while Joe had been watching Hope, he had been watching Joe. And thanks to Carson's stupidity, he had a nice, neat little solution to his present problem.

As long as he was careful. But he had to get away. Fast. Before the people searching for Hope arrived. Before Hope awoke.

If she awoke—he didn't know what was wrong with her. She was hurt—alive, but hurt. She'd been on the floor when he'd arrived, and no telling what had happened. He couldn't linger, either, no matter how much he wanted to keep an eye on his little mouse. Hope lay sprawled on the other side of the room, blood slowly spreading in a dark pool from her head.

He paused by her and nudged her with his booted foot. When she didn't stir, he sighed. He really hoped she woke up.

Little mouse . . . she was his brave little mouse. Unlike some of his girls, he didn't want to watch her die. He wanted her to live. It was a weird little twist, one he hadn't seen coming.

Turning, he focused his attention on Joe Carson, who had finally emerged from his dazed shock enough to try and stanch the blood gushing from his thigh. The blood was dark, pumping from him hard and fast.

"It looks like it might have hit your femoral," the man said. Good. That had sort of been the plan. "If you don't stop it soon, you won't make it out of here alive."

"Fuck you," Joe panted. His eyes gleamed with madness and rage.

He smiled and came close enough to kick Joe's weapon out of reach. "Oh, you're the one who's fucked." Kneeling down in front of him, he said, "But I really should say thanks. You helped me out of a jam. I've been watching you, you know. Keeping an eye on you . . . and slipping in and out of here while you were gone."

Joe's lips peeled back from his teeth. His hands were slippery and wet, fighting to keep a tight grip on the belt he was using as a tourniquet. "Get . . . the . . . fuck . . . away."

In response, the man reached out and grabbed the belt, jerking on it, deliberately trying to pull it away from the other man, make him lose his desperate grip. He didn't really give a damn if he got it loose, but it was a lot of fun to watch the fear slip into the cop's eyes, to see him realize just how easily he could die.

And he *would* die.

"You really should have left her alone, you know," he said quietly. "Just walked away and left her alone. Stayed out of my town. You don't belong here."

Then he let go of the belt and stood up, watching as Joe all but sobbed as he tried to drag the belt tight once more. The blood flow was slowing down now. Slowing, and Joe was looking pale, almost glassy-eyed.

"You're bleeding to death, you know." He tugged a handkerchief out of his pocket, wiped the blood from his glove. Then, just to be safe, he pulled the glove off, turned it inside out and tucked it inside his pocket and drew out a clean one. As he snapped it into place, he peered at Joe and smiled. "You'll be dead in minutes, long before help arrives for Hope."

"Help me, for fuck's sake," Joe snarled.

He laughed. "Why would I do that? I came here to watch you die." He glanced at Hope's still body, then at the sheriff's. Both of them, almost lost because of this man. He had no sense of sport, really. He didn't like it at all.

But he'd be dead, soon enough.

"Who the fuck are you?"

With a smile, he reached up and pulled his mask up. "I might as well let you see."

Joe stared at him blankly and the man just sighed. "You really are a stupid fuck, aren't you? Been coming in and out of this town for the past few weeks and never once looked at anybody but her."

Letting his mask remain where it was, he went to the sheriff, eased him up off the ground. There was a small, almost neat hole in the center of Nielson's forehead. But the back half of his head was missing. "He was a decent man, you know. And he probably would have found out something about me sooner or later. So thank you."

"What are . . . you . . ." Joe's words came thicker, rougher.

"Oh, just some games of mine that got interrupted. I had to take a break from them because of some mistakes I made. But maybe I can pick them up again in a while." Then he patted around on the sheriff's body, searching for another gun. Ah, yes.

Ankle holster. How . . . clichéd. And convenient.

Still kneeling, he pointed it at Joe. Aimed. Watched as the man's eyes went wide.

Fired.

Joe slumped over backward. As the body hit the floor, he turned and put the gun into the sheriff's hand and squeezed again, one single shot that went into the wall. There—that should do it.

Carefully avoiding the blood on the floor, he moved closer and stared at the body.

Yes. Joseph Carson was dead. Now that all of that was dealt with, he put Joe's weapon back in his hand, pulled him to a half sitting position, fired off a few random shots. It wasn't perfect.

But there were no witnesses.

None . . . because Hope was still silent, motionless.

He paused long enough to tug his mask down and

then he moved to stand over her body. So very still. So very quiet.

He hoped she wasn't too hurt. Hoped she lived.

Would be a shame for her to die now. After all, her ex-husband was dead now . . . and he couldn't haunt her anymore.

She could find that peaceful, happy life of hers now. Before he left, he reached into the pocket of his jacket, tugged out a wallet and a pretty little gold watch.

It had belonged to his last girl. Jolene Hollister. Even had a *J H* engraved on the back. Jolene. The start of all this mess.

The start . . . and it seemed fitting to leave it here, where he had ended it. Inside the wallet was a picture of Jolene and her pretty cousin. He left the wallet and the watch tucked in with Joe's things, but the picture . . . that, he wanted found on Joe.

It took some doing to tuck it into Joe's pocket without stepping in the blood, but he managed. If it fell out, it could be assumed it had done so while Joe fought to stop the bleeding.

Everybody would think that he'd tried to get one last shot off. It would be muzzled and hazy, yes. But he'd done a better job staging *this* scene, he figured. Learned from his mistakes.

He slid back outside, losing himself in the deepening shadows. The shots had been heard.

Before he joined the rest of the search team, he used the wipes from his pack, made sure his hands were clean. Stowed his gun, the mask. There . . . none would be the wiser.

Just as he fell into step beside a couple of deputies, thunder rumbled through the skies overhead. He smiled.

Rain.

He loved a good thunderstorm.

* * *

"What are we doing out here?"

Remy half-tuned the person out. But another part of him wondered the same thing. The sheriff had sent search teams crawling off all over the county, but why here?

Zeke Mulroney—one of the volunteer firemen and Sergeant Keith Jennings's cousin, sighed and shoved a hand through his hair, glanced at his cousin. "You buzz the sheriff again? Ask him what we're searching for?"

Keith grunted. "We already know what." There was an odd look in his eyes as he said it, but he didn't elaborate other than to add, "We keep looking until we find her."

"Yeah, but not why *here*," Zeke mumbled. But he sighed, and the men studied the map. "I'll cover this spot. You with me, cuz?"

"Yeah. We can split up, cover a wide area once we get there. Remy?"

"I'll hit this one," Remy said, his voice strained and tight.

Behind him, Reilly and Ezra shared a look. "We're with Remy," Ezra said.

The rest of the men split up the area, going in groups of two or three, agreeing to meet back up in another few hours, keeping in contact through radio. Cell phones were useless out here.

Remy tried not to let a rush of hopeless anger swamp him. They were wasting *time* . . . he needed to be on a plane to Clinton, Oklahoma—so he'd be there waiting when that bastard arrived. He was trying to take her back home. That's what he needed to be doing . . .

But what if he was wrong?

The men split up, but not a one of them had gone more than fifteen yards when a shot tore through the silence. A few seconds later, there was another. Another . . . another.

The sound of gunfire in the rural area surrounding Ash wasn't unusual.

Hell, Remy knew how to fire a gun and once in a while, he could even be talked into going hunting with his brother . . . or back before his brother had gotten so lost in his grief.

The sound of a shot being fired hadn't ever turned his blood to ice before. Not until that cool night with the thunderheads piling up in the distance, turning the already dim woods into an endless, dank twilight. Taking off through the woods, ignoring Ezra, ignoring Reilly, ignoring the deputies who tried to reach out and grab him.

Nothing mattered. Nothing but Hope and in his gut, he knew . . . he *knew* . . . those shots weren't some guys out hunting, and he knew it wasn't some kids out being stupid.

Hope.

His gut was nothing but ice and knots, and he couldn't think, couldn't speak.

All he could do was hope . . . and pray.

Please God . . .

And he couldn't even manage anything more than that.

Just *Please God* . . .

He ran for what felt like forever.

After ever.

Forever—the moments were endless, but he had no idea how much time had passed before he came across the cabin. He didn't know who owned it.

Some of the forested areas around Ash were owned by the state and some were private property. He hadn't seen this cabin before, but it didn't matter. Hope was in there—in his gut, he knew it. That was all that counted.

He lunged for the door, but just before he reached it, hard, strong hands caught him, restrained him. "Stop it," Ezra growled in his ear. "Just stop—wait. Let the deputies do their fucking job and check—you go tearing in there, you can get her killed."

Remy struggled, trying to tear away from Ezra, even though, logically, he knew the guy was right.

Hope was in there . . . Hope—*fuck*.

"Just give them a few minutes," Ezra said. "Just wait."

"Could you?" Remy snarled. "If it was Lena? Could you?"

"Yeah. I'd hate it and I'd need somebody to do the same damn thing I'm doing, probably, but if I knew it was the only thing that might save her life? Yeah. Now just wait . . ."

If the run to the cabin had seemed to take forever, if the entire day had dragged on endlessly, it was nothing like those long, eternal seconds it took for the deputies to move to peer through the windows, their feet almost soundless even though the ground was littered with damp leaves and broken twigs.

Tense, silent moments ticked away.

"Oh, fuck . . ." Keith muttered.

As he lunged for the door, Remy's heart stopped beating.

For those few moments, his entire world went dark. Then, with a sudden jerk, he tore away from Ezra.

No.

Fucking hell, *no*.

He'd just found her, damn it. Just got her and . . . *no*.

He shouldered past the deputies, not giving a fuck that they'd tried to stop him, not caring about anything but getting inside that damn cabin . . .

She was there.

Lying in a crumpled heap on the floor.

Pale.

Blood spread out from her head in a dark, dark pool. Déjà vu rippled through him and for a moment, he thought for sure he'd see blood seeping from her wrists.

Not caring about the blood, or anything else, he ran to her and just as he knelt by her side, she groaned, and the thick, black fringe of her lashes fluttered.

Once more, his heart started to beat.

Oh, shit.

"Hope."

She sighed. Without even opening her eyes, a faint smile curled her lips. "Remy . . ." Then she looked up at him. "You came for me."

Gently, he slid his arms under her, pulling her against him. "Damn straight. God, baby, are you okay?"

Her fingers curled into his shirt. "Am now. I . . . he wanted me to write you a letter. Say I was leaving. Leaving *you*. Wouldn't do it. He couldn't make me do it, Remy. Couldn't make me . . ."

"Shhh." He stroked his free hand over her, searching for injuries. The arm he had under her neck felt sticky from the blood and as he gently probed her skull, he felt the edges of a jagged, open wound. Long and shallow. "You hit your head again, baby. You need to quit doing that."

"Okay. He couldn't make me write the letter. Wouldn't do it. Not leaving. I'm not leaving you. Not ever . . ."

Those words reached inside his heart, wrapped a fist around it.

Pressing a kiss to her brow, he murmured, "I hope to hell you remember that. I plan on holding you to it."

Then he closed his eyes. *Thank God.*

All around him, he heard voices buzzing, radios crackling, and he knew Reilly was kneeling just a few feet away and he needed to let the guy see Hope for a second.

But not just yet. A few more seconds.

Just a few more seconds so he could really start to believe he hadn't lost her right after he'd just found her.

CHAPTER
TWENTY-THREE

LONG AFTER REMY AND REILLY HAD CLIMBED INTO the ambulance with Hope, Ezra remained at the cabin. He stood at Keith Jennings's side, along with the deputy sheriff, a quiet man by the name of Steven Mabry. Together, the three of them stared down at Nielson's body, and Ezra tried to wrap his brain around what he was seeing.

The guy was dead.

"Why was he out here alone?" Ezra asked.

"We were meeting up. He didn't think this was going to be worth the time it would take to get another deputy out there. I guess he didn't want to pull anybody away from the rest of the search area. I lost radio contact with him about twenty minutes before we heard the shots," Keith said, keeping his voice quiet. "He told me he was following a hunch, to come out here. Looks like he was right."

"Guess he was right." Mabry sighed and shook his head. "I don't believe this."

The sheriff had indeed been right—it had cost him his life . . . and probably saved Hope's life. "Who owns this cabin?"

Jennings sighed, reached up and rubbed the back of

his neck. "Shit. If I'm remembering right, it belongs to Deb Sparks's kids. Their daddy bought it and left it to them when he died. She always hated the place. The guys use it some, not a whole lot."

Ezra glanced around, eyed the neatly made bed, the obvious lack of dust. "Somebody's been out here fairly recently. And often."

"Yeah." Mabry knelt by Carson's corpse and eyed him. "I'm thinking maybe he was squatting out here. If he's been wanting to keep an eye on his ex-wife, but not be seen . . . well, here's a good place for it."

Ezra blew out a breath, thinking about the night Brody Jennings had seen somebody in the woods near Reilly's place. "How close you think we are to Reilly's?"

"Oh, it would take awhile to drive. But cutting through the woods? Maybe a forty-five-minute hike. Even less if you're in good shape and know the way."

"Mabry?"

Ezra glanced up as one of the other deputies called over from across the room.

"Yeah?"

"You need to come see this."

Mabry grimaced as he stood. "Shit. I'm not the fucking sheriff."

Ezra looked at the still body near his feet. No. The sheriff was dead. He and Jennings watched as Mabry made his way over to the other deputies. "He doesn't want to be the sheriff, but he's stuck with it now," Ezra said, keeping his voice low.

"Yeah." Keith glanced down at Nielson. "Damn it."

A voice muttered in the back of his brain, but he shoved it aside. Ezra couldn't think about that right now. He tried to push all the pieces into line, tried to make them fit—but they weren't lining up. At least, they weren't lining up the way he wanted them to.

"Well, shit."

There was enough heat and shock in Mabry's words to cut through Ezra's musings and he turned, made his way over there, taking care with his leg. It hurt like a bitch after trampling around through the woods all day. He wanted a beer, a bed, and Lena something awful.

There was something in his pocket that he'd planned on giving her earlier, and now those plans . . . well. Hell. He'd had all sorts of plans. Roses. Champagne, even.

Then this happened.

He came to a stop by the bed and stared down, eyeing what the younger deputy held in his gloved hands—a picture. Bloodied and wrinkled. He held it gingerly, by one corner.

"Wonder who this is," the deputy muttered.

"Can I see that?" Keith said, holding out a gloved hand. As the other deputy turned it over, Ezra moved around to study the picture. There were two women—a striking woman of mixed race—he didn't know her. But the other woman . . . yeah. He knew who she was. He'd never forget her face. Ever.

Swallowing, he said, "That's Jolene Hollister, I think. Jennings?"

Keith sighed. "Yeah. Yeah, I'm pretty sure it is."

"There's a wallet over here, Mabry," one of the other deputies called out.

Ezra met Jennings's gaze and after the picture was bagged, they moved across the cabin to the deputy sheriff's side. Tucked inside Joe's things, the little pink leather wallet stood out like a red thumb.

Mabry was gingerly going through it. "It's got Jolene Hollister's license in it."

Jolene Hollister.

Jolene—the woman who bore a striking similarity to Ezra's girlfriend.

Turning, Ezra stared at Joe Carson. His heart thudded inside his chest and blood roared in his ears. Too neat, he thought. This wasn't his case, hell, he was barely even a cop anymore. But none of this fit.

He stripped off his gloves and stood there, staring at Carson's lifeless body. Then he slid a hand into his pocket, stroked the nubby velvet of the box there.

Ezra's world didn't start to realign until he saw her, standing on the porch, waiting for him. She was pale, her fingers buried in Puck's fur, and she looked like she hadn't slept at all.

She hadn't ever looked more beautiful to him.

As he mounted the steps, she started toward him. He met her before she'd taken even three steps. Catching her in his arms, he buried his face against her neck, clutching her tight.

"Are you okay?" Her hand stroked up and down his back.

"I am now," Ezra muttered. He wasn't okay—not yet.

But he would be. Slowly, he breathed her in, then eased his grip, knowing he had to be crushing her. She rested a hand on his chest, just above his heart, as she slid the other one, cupped his cheek. "Law called. Told me he was at the hospital with Hope—that she's okay. And . . ."

She bit her lip, catching the shuddering sob of a breath before it could escape.

"Nielson's dead," he said softly. "Son of a bitch shot him. But the sheriff probably saved Hope's life."

Hearing the growl of an engine, he looked up, watched as Carter Jennings parked his sedan and climbed out, weariness written all over his face. He started toward the Inn, giving Ezra a tight, strained smile.

"Hey," Carter said, his voice heavy and rough.

Moments later, the door opened and Roz launched herself at her husband, wrapping her arms around his neck.

Ezra had brought Lena out here before going on the hunt for Hope, but now all he wanted was to get her out of here, back to her place—*their* place. So he could ask her the most important question of his life. Screw roses and champagne. He'd been reminded, again, just how fucking fragile things in life were. He wasn't letting this chance slip by him.

Pushing his hand through Lena's gleaming, dark red hair, he kissed her brow and murmured, "You ready to go home?"

Roz said, "Oh, you two don't need to leave. Stay for the night. It's late. And it's been one hell of a day . . ."

"No." Lena softened it with a smile but shook her head. "I need my bed, Roz. My bed, some wine . . ."

"Okay. Just . . . well. I'll see you soon. Call you. To-morrow, maybe. Or I guess later today," she muttered. Then she sighed, leaning against her husband. "I can't believe Dwight's gone. That son of a bitch."

In a blur, Ezra said good-bye, watched as Lena rounded up Puck and got him settled. He barely remembered the drive home, barely remembered following her to the house.

He couldn't focus on anything, but her.

And the ring. And the question.

She'd barely gotten Puck's leash off before it tore out of him. He couldn't wait—couldn't.

Pulling the ring out of his pocket, he came up behind her. Slid one arm around her waist. "Lena . . ."

She leaned back against him, a sigh slipping out of her. "It's been one hell of a day, huh? And we were sup-posed to have some sort of fancy date tonight, weren't we?"

"Fuck the date," he muttered. He stroked his fingers down her left arm, caught her hand and lifted it. The somewhat practiced proposal was lost to him—he'd had the words, he knew he had. But now, they were lost.

Slipping the ring onto her finger, he whispered gruffly, "Marry me, Lena?"

A sob caught in her throat. "Wuh . . . what?"

He turned her around, his hands resting on her slender hips. "Marry me. That's what the fancy date was for . . . I had this nice little evening planned, was going to wine you, dine you, maybe try to get you a little tipsy before I fucked your brains out. Then I was going to ask you to marry me. Everything exploded, though, with Hope and that Carson bastard . . . and I know I shouldn't be doing this right now, I should wait, do it over, do it right, but I was thinking about how close Remy came to losing Hope, and it made me sick inside, thinking about what if it had been you and damn it, I'm screwing this up—"

Her mouth came against his, soft, cool and firm. "Ezra. Shut up."

He shut up as her fingers curled over the back of his neck. The noise in his brain abated a little and when she pulled back, her lovely, ice-blue eyes resting on his face, he muttered, "Shit. I can do better than this. Just . . ."

"I don't need better. It's already perfect." Tears gleamed in those lovely eyes and she lifted her hands, cupped his face. "I've got you, what more do I need? I love you . . . and hell, yes, I'll marry you."

"We'd like to keep her overnight."

Panic shot through her.

Hope clutched Remy's hand and tried not to let the doctor, or him, see it, though.

But no . . . no hospitals.

No . . .

Even though her head was aching, and even though it felt like it was stuffed full of cotton, she didn't think she could handle being in there. Couldn't. All she'd done was hit her damn head—she didn't need to be hospitalized for a bump on her skull.

Remy rested a hand on the back of her neck, warm, comforting. He'd been at her side from the time she'd opened her eyes, and she knew he'd stay right there. When the deputies had tried to slip in earlier and talk to her, he'd told them in a brusque voice, "It can wait a few hours. Got it?"

And now here he was running interference for her. Again. She loved him for it . . . even though she knew she couldn't let him keep doing it.

"If it's just a concussion, why does she need to be kept overnight?" he asked.

The doctor gave him a polite smile, but focused his attention on Hope. "You live alone, Ms. Carson. You've got a concussion. The wound to your head is small and has stopped bleeding but we do need to monitor you. Might I add—this is the second concussion in a relatively short period of time. You can't be alone for the next twenty-four hours."

"She—"

Hope reached over and touched the back of his hand. He closed his mouth, then smiled and leaned in, nuzzled her hair. "You can stay with me . . . you know that."

"Yeah. I know that." Then she focused on the doctor. "I won't be alone. I'll go stay with Remy for a few days." *Maybe the rest of my life . . .* It just might take that long to get over the fear still crowding her mind. Geez, between the fear and the residual panic and shock, it was a wonder there was any *room* for pain.

The doctor glanced at Remy, then cocked a brow. "She'll have to be woken up. Regularly. You won't get much sleep."

Remy grimaced. "I won't get much anyway, because if she doesn't come home with me, I'm staying here. I'm not leaving her."

Hope snuggled closer. His arms tightened around her.

The fear, the panic receded. Even the pain fell to a tolerable ache.

Now that she didn't have to worry about staying here, and now that she had figured out what she was doing with herself, she was going to let Remy worry about the rest of it.

While she leaned against him and just enjoyed being alive . . .

Three hours later, after a hot shower to clean away the blood from her body, she was settled on Remy's couch, wrapped in a cocoon of blankets she didn't really need, but she didn't have the heart to push them away after he'd done so much to get her comfortable.

When he came back with *another* pillow, she reached out and caught his hand. "Remy . . . stop. Sit. I'm fine."

A look darkened his eyes. His face tightened. Then . . . it cleared and he smiled. "Sure. I'll sit."

"Yeah. You do that and tell me what that look was for."

"What look?"

Hope narrowed her eyes. "Remy . . . I'm not going to break. Stop acting like I am. Stop hovering and just sit down and talk to me."

He gave another tight, strained smile, went to sit—then he surged back up.

"Shit. You want me to fucking relax. Sit down and talk . . . like I almost didn't lose you today, all because I didn't listen to my gut. Damn it," he snarled. Pacing the living room, his blue eyes almost black with fury, he looked everywhere but at her. "I knew something was seriously fucked up with him, but I didn't listen to my instincts, and look what happened. Damn *it*."

Hope eased the blankets away, watching as he continued to pace, barely even aware of her. He was too caught up in the storm of emotion, too lost in it.

She stood, bracing a hand on the arm of the couch as she waited to make sure her head wasn't going to start spinning around. It wasn't going to help either of them if she ended up flat on her face, she didn't think. Once she was pretty sure she was steady, she started toward him.

She hadn't taken more than two steps when he stopped.

He took a deep breath, shoved his hands through his hair. "You need to be off your feet, Hope. Shit, I'm sorry. You don't need this."

"I don't think either of us need this—hell, what person needs this kind of crazy going on?" she asked softly and she kept going, right until she was close enough to slip her arms around his waist. She rested her head against his chest. "You can't blame yourself, Remy. Hell, if *anybody* should have known better, it would be me, and I never thought he was so far gone that he'd run me off the road in broad daylight. Or grab me in broad daylight. Never thought he was that far gone."

Remy sighed. "It's worse than you realize, I think." He paused and then added, "Nielson's dead, Hope. Joe killed him."

Shock reached up and wrapped an icy, brutal fist around her throat, even as grief punched her in her battered heart. "What . . . ? No." She shook her head, pushing away from him as she lifted her hands, pressing them to her face. The pain in her head became a raging, tormenting beast as she tried to think through the fog of memories.

Nielson—yeah. She remembered him showing up. Remembered Joe pointing his gun at her . . . firing. But he hadn't hit her.

A moan rattled out of her chest and she whispered, "Oh, no."

He'd killed him. Joe had killed Nielson. Guilt reached up and grabbed her. "Shit. This is my fault . . ."

Remy sighed and came up behind her, wrapping her in his arms. "No. No, it's not. If you don't want me blaming myself for what happened to you, you can't go blaming yourself for what happened to Nielson. He knew what he was doing, what the risks were—and he chose to go there without backup. For whatever reasons."

"But if I'd stayed home—if I had—"

Pressing a kiss to her temple, Remy stared out the window. "He was crazy enough to kill a fellow cop, Hope. It was just a matter of time." Then he sighed. "Just a matter of time before he would have tried something else. But it's over now. You're safe. He's gone."

Over, he thought. In a lot of ways. Ezra had called while Hope was having a CT done, told him what they'd found in the cabin. He wasn't entirely sure he was buying it . . . but if Joe had thought planting a dead woman's body on Reilly's property would scare Hope into running, making her that much easier to grab . . .

It made sense. Made a lot of sense.

Of course, Carson hadn't taken into account that Hope was a lot stronger than he'd ever realized. Hadn't taken into account how much she'd trusted Law.

The forensics team was already turning up his prints all over the place.

Maybe it was over. Maybe.

What mattered to him, though, was that Hope was safe.

The only person who would have wanted to torment her was her fucking ex. And he was on a slab, next to the cop who had died protecting her. Irony there—Remy hated one of them with a passion, and the other, he owed a debt he could never repay.

Blowing out a breath, he tightened his arms around

Hope and buried his face in her neck. "Man, I was so scared I was going to lose you. I just found you. Can't handle losing you," he whispered.

She sniffled. "Me, too." She tipped her head back, peering up at him. "I was thinking about you. When . . . well . . ." She swallowed. "I was thinking about you. And I was thinking about us. And I wasn't sorry. You made me happy . . . and I wanted to tell you that."

"Hope . . ." He reached up, laid his hand on her cheek.

A wobbly smile curled her lips and she shrugged. "I can't rush into anything. I just can't. But you matter to me. So much. And . . . well . . . um. I think, no. Shit. I love you, Remy. Maybe that's one thing I would have been sorry about—if he had killed me and I died before I had the chance to tell you."

For the second time that day, the strength just drained out of him. Sagging to his knees in front of her, he pressed his face to her belly and wrapped his arms around her. "Hope . . ."

Her hand combed through his hair. "Remy?"

"Just gimme a minute," he muttered and to his utter disgust, he realized he had tears stinging his eyes. Almost lost her. "Can't think about that—you dying. Then you go and throw both of them in there together. Damn it, Hope. I love you. You . . . I can't lose you. You mean too much. You're everything."

She sank down to her knees in front of him, curled her arms around his neck. "You didn't lose me. I'm right here. Right here." She rubbed her lips over his. "I love you."

Stroking a hand up her back, he tried to convince himself of that. She was here. Right here. Need tore through him, but he throttled it down. Beat it back. Not right now. She was battered, suffering from a concussion, shaken, in shock.

Not right now.

Slowly, he came to his feet and pulled her into his arms, cradling her slight weight against his chest.

"We're not doing this ever again," he muttered. "Nothing like this. Ever."

"That sounds like a good plan." She turned her face against his neck. "I'm tired, Remy."

"Then get some sleep." He sank down on the couch, cradling her. "I'm right here. I'll wake you in a few hours, baby."

It didn't take her long to drift to sleep, evidence of the wear and strain the day had put on her.

He continued to hold her, though. Needed that connection, desperately.

As the night wore on, he stared out the window.

Joe was dead. So was his friend, Nielson. Hope was here with him . . . safe.

She was safe . . . and that was what mattered the most. The rest of it, he'd come to grips with. For now, he had what he needed.

It was over. *Over*, he told himself. Joe was gone and it was over.

But part of him didn't believe that.

Author's Note

Some creative license was taken with this trilogy. Carrington County is a fictional county set in Kentucky, roughly an hour away from Lexington.

While I spoke with several lawyers and law-enforcement professionals while writing the stories, I realize certain aspects are still not going to be completely true to life. I hope it doesn't take away from your enjoyment of them.

Acknowledgments

This is yet another book that couldn't have been written without a lot of help.

This time, the help came from a few particular people . . .

Thank God for letting me live this dream . . .

Namely, a crazy chick by the name of Lime who likes shoes and wine.

As well as my friends Beth Kery and Julie James, who helped me more than they'll probably know while we sat in the restaurant one night in Columbus, Ohio.

Hammering out the details for this story proved to be a lot more complicated than I thought.

*Read on for an exciting preview
of Shiloh Walker's next thrilling romantic
suspense novel*

IF YOU KNOW HER

JOLENE HAD BEEN DEAD FOR SIX MONTHS.

Six long months.

Nia Hollister lay on her bed, staring up at the ceiling as she tried to will herself to sleep, but sleep wasn't coming. It wasn't getting any easier. *Nothing* was easier. Sleeping. Living. Moving on with her life.

But how was she supposed to get on with her life, when her cousin, her best friend, her only family was gone? Murdered . . . dead and buried, brutalized by some monster for reasons that Nia couldn't even fathom.

Even after six long months, she still felt like she had a hole in her chest the size of the entire state of Virginia.

The fact that the man who'd killed Joely was dead made no difference, not to her. It changed nothing. It helped nothing, eased none of her pain. Not even watching as they'd lowered his worthless corpse into the ground had helped.

That should help, right?

He was dead—the man who had killed her cousin was dead. That should give her closure, right?

Closure—

Shit.

Did people really think having *closure* helped?

It sure as hell wasn't helping her. Knowing who did it . . . how did that help?

Exhausted, sick at heart, and still as miserable now as she had been the day she'd found out the truth, Nia sat up in her bed and rummaged around on her bedside table until she found a mangled pack of cigarettes.

She'd stopped smoking three years ago. She'd started again five and a half months ago. She kept telling herself she'd stop, and she knew she needed to, but she just couldn't work up the energy to care.

Right now, she couldn't quite give a fuck if she was polluting her lungs—what did it matter? Right now, she was having a hard time finding anything that mattered.

Sighing, she lit a cigarette and climbed out of bed, moved to stare out the window. It was dark and quiet. She was far enough outside the city that the lights from town were muted and she could see the stars.

There had been a time when she had loved nights like this.

Now she hated them, hated the quiet, hated the peace. It seemed like that was when she heard it the loudest. Heard *her*. It was just her imagination, but it seemed so real.

Joely's screaming . . . God, how she must have screamed. Had she begged? Had she pleaded?

"Shit."

Heedless of the smoking cigarette in her hands, she pressed the heels of her hands against her eyes, as though that might keep her from hearing the screams, might keep her from thinking about her cousin.

Her best friend.

The woman who'd been murdered by some sick-ass bastard who was now rotting away under six feet of dirt. She should take comfort in that, Nia reckoned.

But she couldn't. Didn't. It just felt too . . . unfinished.

Blowing out a breath, she lowered her hands and eyed the cigarette. "Going to catch my damn hair on fire," she muttered. Putting it between her lips, she inhaled. As the smoke filled her lungs, she tipped her head back and stared up at the darkened ceiling.

Yeah, it felt damned unfinished.

But Joe Carson had been found with Joely's watch on him, and her clothing and other evidence had been found at the cabin where he'd been squatting.

What were they supposed to do?

In some sick, convoluted way, it even made sense, once somebody had explained things to her.

Hope Carson had left her abusive ex-husband and spent two years on the move, because she feared he might come after her. Finally, she'd decided she was going to settle in with her friend Law Reilly. The ex must have been watching her pretty damn close. Timing-wise . . . no. Nia didn't quite buy the timing bit, because her cousin had been grabbed *before* Hope had arrived in Ash, Kentucky, but the cops had shrugged it off.

There wasn't any secret that she was friends with Reilly. Reilly had confirmed she had been making plans to come stay with him. They'd speculated that Carson had just made a lucky guess, or suggested maybe he'd had some inside knowledge—their suggestions hadn't meant shit to her.

So, Hope arrives in Ash and her ex-husband waits until she sort of settles in, and then he kills Nia's cousin. Leaves her body right where Hope can all but trip over it. Trying to scare Hope into running . . . just trying to scare her? Warn her? *This will be you if you don't toe the line?*

"It's all so fucked up," she whispered. "Damn it, Joely, what am I supposed to do? Why can't I let go?"

But there wasn't any answer.

Leaning her brow against the chilled glass, Nia smoked her cigarette and suffered the miserable silence alone.

Her name had been Mara Burns.

She'd been his first—a man didn't forget his first. His first fuck. His first love. His first wife.

His first kill.

He'd had different firsts . . . Mara had been his first kill, and she'd been . . . sweet.

It hadn't been planned.

At all. It had been back in college and she had been a hot, sweet little bitch, but the first few times he'd tried to ask her out, she hadn't given him the time of day.

That changed his senior year—and she'd been the one to ask *him* out. As a ploy to make a boyfriend jealous, mostly, and he had known. They'd gone out, fucked in his car . . . and she whispered for him to hit her. To choke her.

He hadn't. But he'd imagined it.

When he took her home, she'd mocked him, but he'd been so caught up in those images, he had barely noticed. That night, he'd dreamed about it. Choking her. Hitting her.

Thoughts of it consumed him.

Weeks passed, turned into months, they rarely spoke, but he saw her, and each time, it made those fantasies burn hotter. Brighter.

One night she'd been walking home from her job. He'd seen her . . . because he'd been watching. Watching . . . and dreaming. He had offered her a ride. Because it was starting to rain, or maybe because she wanted to taunt him some more, she'd accepted. But then he hadn't taken her home and she had put her bitch-face on. He'd backhanded her.

Instead of getting pissed, or scared . . . she'd been turned on.

They went back to the quiet, secluded little area out-side of Lexington where they'd fucked that first night, and they went at each other like animals. They started out in the back of the car, moved to the trunk, and eventually ended up on the ground.

He'd hit her, and she would come. He'd squeeze her neck until she almost blacked out, and she'd come harder. For hours.

But then, toward the end of the night, as he was driving into her, chasing another climax, his fingers digging into her silken neck, he'd squeezed, and squeezed, and squeezed . . . he'd let go, watched as she sucked in a ragged breath of air right as he climaxed so hard it had almost hurt, and he'd thought about how he hadn't wanted to let go.

Then, when she was smiling at him, he'd closed his hands around her neck.

For reasons he couldn't understand then, he'd started choking her again. And that time, he hadn't stopped. Not when her heels beat on the ground, not when she had torn at his hands with her nails, real fear beginning to flicker in her eyes. Not even when her bowels and bladder had released.

His mind had remained cool, detached throughout all of it, even as his heart had raced at the thrill.

His first kill.

Yes . . . Mara had been one of the most beautiful firsts of his life. A man didn't forget his first. He'd worried for years somebody would discover her, discover what happened to Mara, and somehow link her back to him.

But in the end, she wasn't the one who was coming to haunt him.

Hers wasn't the face he dreamed of at night now.

And she wasn't the reason he had been forced to put a stop to his games for a while.

Because he couldn't indulge in those games, he was all but burning, all but dying to feel that thrill again, the pleasure he found only when he took a life. She wasn't the reason he felt like a ticking time bomb, one that burned hotter, brighter, every damn day.

No, that honor belonged to one Jolene Hollister and one Lena Riddle. Jolene had almost gotten away from him, had screamed bloody murder . . . and Lena had heard her screaming, had called the cops, had stirred up too much attention.

Six months. It had been six months.

He knew how to wait.

Sometimes he felt like a lump of coal under extreme pressure, like he'd emerge a diamond—after a bit of polishing and cutting down.

Other times, he just felt like he was going to explode and right now was one of those times. Six fucking months.

It was worse being in here in this crush of people.

A wedding was a big deal in a small town like Ash, though, and Lena and Ezra hadn't spared any expense. The Inn was full to bursting. The reception had been going strong for more than an hour and he had no doubt it would keep going for another hour at least.

He couldn't even make a quiet escape, though. It would be too easily noticed.

So he waited, chatted, and danced.

He danced with the bride, he danced with the bridesmaids, he danced with the flower girl, he danced with the married women whose husbands wouldn't dance, and he danced with the tittering, blushing girls who were still learning how to flirt.

He danced with so many women . . . so many.

Tall, short, lean, lush.

Short hair that barely brushed their jawline, long hair that fell to their hips. Hair upswept to leave their shoul-

ders bare. Jewelry sparkled and glowed against toned
and tanned flesh.

Over by the bar, he spotted Roslyn Jennings talking
with the bride, her curves poured into a dark green dress
that clung so lovingly. Gold glinted at her neck, ears,
and wrists.

On the dance floor, he saw Hope Carson, dancing
with her beau Remy Jennings, wearing a dress just like
Roslyn's, the same deep, deep green. But where Roslyn
looked like a witch, Hope looked like some fey, wood-
land nymph. Sweet and innocent and lovely. She wore
little jewelry, but there were flowers in her short, shiny
hair.

Then there was the bride, her deep red locks glowing
against the white of her dress, pearls at her neck, gold
on her fingers.

All the women . . .

Hunger pulsed inside him, driving him mad, making
him greedy and desperate.

Desperate—but not too desperate.

Not so desperate he'd get foolish again. Not here. Not
now.

At present, he had a girl—just barely out of college—
wrapped around him, and it pissed him off. Perhaps it
turned him on a little as she pressed her breasts against
his arm, smiling up at him and trying to act like she was
so much older than she really was. But she was just a
child. Besides, he also had a lady nearby who would
notice before much longer and although she would understand, he didn't want her upset.

Especially not by an obnoxious little bitch like this.

As she swayed a little too close, he dipped his head
and murmured, "Estella . . ."

"Star. I'm going by Star now. Estella is so *old*," she
said, giving her lower lip what she probably thought
was a seductive stroke of tongue.

"Estella Price," he repeated. "I don't know why you keep rubbing against me like that. I've known you since you were in diapers. I'm pretty sure I probably even changed one or two."

He hadn't. But it had the desired effect. She turned almost as red as the lipstick she'd slicked on her mouth and jerked away from him. Suppressing a chuckle, he lost himself in the crowd and headed toward the cash bar. He needed a drink, and he wanted to see if he couldn't work his way out of here yet.

If he didn't get out of here soon—

This wasn't where he wanted to be . . . wasn't where he *needed* to be. Except the whole damn town was here.

There were places a guy wanted to be in life—in bed with a long, lean woman wrapped around him? That topped the list, as far as Law Reilly was concerned.

Although he wouldn't mind a cabin in the mountains, just him and his laptop. He'd be fine with swapping out the laptop for a long, lean woman.

Or even a shack on a beach, just him and his laptop. Again, the swap-out—his laptop for a long, lean woman? That would work. And some beer on hand.

The place he didn't want to be, though?

A wedding in small-town Kentucky.

Namely, Ash, Kentucky, where he'd been living for the past ten years. Long enough that he could call the place home, long enough that most of the people knew him by face, by name . . . and by bank account, even if most of them didn't entirely know where the money came from.

They just knew he wasn't hurting for cash and at a wedding with a lot of single women, and that was always dangerous. Even if he'd been in his sixties, balding, and carrying a spare tire, it would be dangerous.

But Law was thirty-four, still had a full head of hair,

and while he might not see himself as the cover model for any magazine, he didn't have a spare tire, either.

Yeah, this was a dangerous place to be, and he was in a lousy mood, anyway. His mood got darker and uglier each time one of the single women would come up and flirt, attempt to make some sly remark about his single status.

He could handle this—get through the reception. He just had to have a game plan, and be cautious.

Things had been going fairly well, too, for about the first hour.

At a wedding, a guy didn't want to make eye contact, didn't want to stand around looking like he might be anything resembling lonely. None of that stuff, because sometimes, the single women got ideas in their heads.

If he wanted to make it out of there sane, and without making himself look like an ass at his best friend's wedding, he had to exercise caution.

Law Reilly's plan—hanging out with friends until he could politely slip away—had been going just fine. Sometimes, caution could serve a man well.

And sometimes, so could throwing caution to the wind.

Law Reilly was tempted to throw caution to the wind and just get the hell out of the inn, especially after Mackenzie Cartwright came simpering up to him, pressing her breasts against his arm, angling herself so he could see clear down to her belly button if he wanted.

He looked—hell, why not? She put herself there on display.

But she also was in the mood to dance . . . and maybe leave early . . . weddings always made her . . . She'd actually trailed off with a suggestive giggle as she slid her hand down, resting it on his hip.

Shit.

"Part of the wedding party, kid," he said, tacking the

kid on just to annoy her. She was twenty-three, definitely too young for him, although hardly a *kid*. "I think I'm supposed to hang around awhile."

Then he put some serious floor space between them and wondered how long he needed to hang around. He didn't want to be there. Didn't want to watch as Lena Riddle snuggled up against Ezra King for what had to be their fiftieth damn kiss. But she wasn't Lena Riddle now. She was Lena King.

And he wasn't jealous—exactly. Well, he was.

He was damn jealous, but not because he wanted to be the one she was pressing her pretty mouth against. There had been a time when that was exactly what he wanted.

But he wasn't the one for Lena.

Lena was happy with the guy, happier than Law had ever seen her. He couldn't begrudge her that happiness, even if once upon a time he'd imagined himself in Ezra's place.

There was an ache in his heart, though. Yearning wisps of envy that had him wishing he was anywhere but here. Okay, anywhere but here, or anywhere with Mackenzie.

Home, alone, sounded good.

Weddings weren't exactly his favorite way to pass the time, but this was one of his best friends . . . and even though once upon a time he'd desperately loved her, seeing her happy was important to him.

With just about anybody else, he could have just ignored the invite.

Except he was the one who had given away the bride. Hard to ignore the invite when that was the case. Sighing, he tipped his beer back and counted down the minutes until he could make a polite escape.

For Lena, he could be polite.

"You look about as happy to be here as you'd be at your own funeral," a soft, quiet voice said.

Glancing down, he made himself smile.

Hope Carson stood barely five foot six, even in the three-inch heels she'd worn with her maid of honor dress. She was slender . . . and she was the only other person in the entire world with the power to get him into a monkey suit.

Her dress was as green as her eyes and gleamed against her pale skin. She'd always had that delicate beauty, but tonight, he had to admit, she looked amazing.

And every guy that looked at her longer than two seconds probably felt the lingering stare of her boyfriend, the county DA, Remy Jennings.

Well, every guy but Law. Law was nothing more than a brother to Hope, like she was nothing more than a sister to him, a fact that Remy was more than well aware of. So when Hope leaned against him and hugged him, Law wasn't overly concerned when Remy's eyes lingered on them. Hell, he enjoyed needling the guy anyway.

That was what had him leaning down and brushing his mouth over Hope's. Pissing the DA off was a favorite pastime of his. Had been for a while. Passing a hand over Hope's hair, careful not to dislodge the delicate spray of flowers placed over her right ear, he said, "You look amazing, sweetheart."

"Thanks." She smoothed a hand over one narrow hip and sent a look over her shoulder, smiling in Lena's direction. "It looks like her day went well, right?"

"Hell, she's married. That was the goal, right?"

Hope rolled her eyes. "You're such a guy. Yes, she's married . . . and that's the goal. Sort of. But getting there, how they do it, the memories . . . it matters."

"Whatever." Law took another drink of his beer, shooting Remy another look. He was talking to one of his cousins, Carter Jennings—Roz's husband.

Hank Jennings was also there with some woman Law couldn't immediately place. Hank was the mayor, and in Law's opinion, a class A asshole. Although he'd gotten a little better over the past few months.

The Jennings clan—the whole damn county was lousy with them. Three cousins served on the town council. The vice principal of the high school was also a Jennings. Several of the county cops were Jennings by blood, a few were Jennings through marriage, and at least one person on the minuscule city police department.

A quarter of the people in Ash were related to the Jennings clan in some way, shape, or form. Hope would probably be one of them before another year was out, Law had no doubt about it.

"Speaking of goals . . . you thinking you might make a run for that goal with Remy any time soon?"

Hope blushed and hunched her shoulders. "I . . . I don't know."

"You haven't talked about it?"

Her blush deepened.

Law laughed. "That's a yes." And knowing her as well as he did, he suspected she was terrified and excited. Dipping his head, he kissed her again, this time, pressing his lips to her brow. "Go for it, kid. You know you're not going to find another guy who'll love you the way he does. And you're never going to love anybody as much as you love him."

She sighed. "No. You're right. I just . . ."

Something dark and ugly moved through her eyes, memories that would take a lot longer than a few months to fade.

"He's gone, kid. Dead and gone."

"I know. It's just . . ." She didn't have to say.

Law knew her as well as she knew herself sometimes. Hope and Law had gone to high school together, back in Clinton, Oklahoma, a small town that was pretty much dominated by one family, kind of like the Jenningses seemed to dominate Ash, Kentucky. At least in size.

But the Carson family wasn't a kind dictator.

Hope had married the golden boy, Joseph Carson, not too long after they'd graduated. His control over her had been subtle at first. *Dress how I want you to dress. Act how I want you to act. Wear your hair the way I want.*

And when she didn't, that's when the real abuse started.

Years passed and it got to the point to where Hope felt the only escape was through killing herself. She'd tried . . . and failed. Her ex-husband had been a cop and he'd abused his badge and his family's name, managed to get her locked away in a mental institution.

When she got out, the abuse had gotten so much worse.

It wasn't until Law finally managed to get back in touch with her after a few years of sketchy communication that he realized just how bad things had been. He no longer gave a damn about any so-called power the Carson family might have had, and at that point, he'd been more than capable of causing his own brand of trouble.

He'd gone looking for Hope, and he would never forgive himself for not doing it sooner. Once he realized how bad things were, Law had been ready to kill Joe.

Although Hope had never confirmed it, he suspected that was what had given her the courage to leave. Not fear for herself, but fear for what it would do to Law's life.

Why in the *hell* hadn't he gone back sooner? Why hadn't he known? She'd gone through hell, and if he'd listened to his gut, he could have done . . . something. Anything.

Like killed the bastard. Killed the bastard, and saved Hope all that heartache. Damn the consequences.

A storm of memories burned in the back of his mind,

memories he struggled to hold at bay. Fuck that bastard
to hell and back—

"Law."

A soft, cool hand touched his cheek and he looked
down, met Hope's sad eyes.

"It's not on us, right?"

He just stared at her.

"You keep telling me, I can't blame myself for what he
did. I can't blame myself for Nielson being dead, and I
can't blame myself for how he killed that girl."

Nielson—the cop who'd died saving Hope when Carson came after her.

And Joely.

That girl . . . the memory of the woman who'd lost
her life was imprinted on his mind forever—a wound
he'd carry for always. *That girl.* Swallowing, he looked
away. His voice was gruff as he said, "Her name was
Jolene. Joely Hollister."

"Joely." Hope looked away. "I know. I know her
name. But you keep telling me I'm not to blame. How
can I believe that, though, when I look at you and see
just how much you blame yourself?"

Swearing, he shoved a hand through his hair. The
dark, overlong golden-brown hair fell right back into
his face. Closing his eyes, he shook his head and said,
"It's not the same, Hope. Damn it, I *knew* something
was wrong, and I didn't listen to my gut. I didn't *do*
anything . . ."

"Neither did I," she said flatly. "All the times he left
bruises on me, I didn't just *know.* I had proof, physical
proof. I could have left, I could have come to you—even
a phone call would have been enough. But I stayed. I can
try to move past my guilt, but it's going to be damn hard
to do it, if I see my best friend wallowing in his."

He narrowed his eyes at her. "That's pretty damn manipulative."

"Yeah. It is." She cocked a brow at him. "But if it works . . ."

Then she shrugged and pushed up onto her toes, pressed a kiss to his cheek. "Stop brooding. Go talk to people. Ethan's here . . . that deputy from the sheriff's office. You two hang out some. Go talk to him. Have fun. You look like you're facing an IRS audit or something."

Law grimaced. Shit. He'd rather face that. He had an accountant he paid to handle that shit.

But he couldn't pay somebody to handle this for him.